Dylan Thomas
A Farm, Two Mansions
and a Bungalow

Dylan Thomas
A Farm, Two Mansions and a Bungalow

David N. Thomas

seren

seren is the book imprint of
Poetry Wales Press Ltd
Wyndham Street, Bridgend, CF31 1EF, Wales

© David Thomas, 2000
Foreword © Paul Ferris, 2000
Cover photograph, 'Dylan Thomas in Iran', and that of the 1950
Eisteddfod Chair © BP Amoco plc

Drawing of Majoda and the map of the Aeron Valley © Jacky Piqué

Photographs 1999 © Bruce Cardwell

ISBN 1-85411-275-9

A CIP record for this title is available from
the British Library

*The publisher works with the financial assistance of the
Arts Council of Wales*

Printed in Plantin by WBC Book Manufacturers, Bridgend

Dedicated to the last of the Pontarddulais Paraffin Gang
– Doug, Nancy and Margaret –
and in memory of Kathleen Thomas

NO GHOSTS AT GELLI

There are no ghosts at Gelli,
only a peaceful past
shading the permeable present.

Trees long felled add their silence
to the deepchested vespers
of the remaining beeches.

Monks have left behind
the prayer of their domesticity
and a garden wall.

An arched casement still looks out
from high in the sycamore trunk, though
no tawny owl sits there.

No seat now under the looped boughs
where a poet lapped still-warm milk
holding his mug in both hands.

Kitchen, cowshed, neat rows of tools.
What change in human need
can make a barrier of three hundred years?

No grief so haunting
but could find rest here, waking
to the daylight fact of happiness.

Stevie Krayer

Contents

Photographs and Illustrations

Foreword

Not many new books about Dylan Thomas break fresh ground. This is one of the exceptions, and if it has a modest remit – Thomas's relationship with Cardiganshire in general and the little town of Newquay in particular – the quality of the material that the author has uncovered will make Thomas's biographers, and certainly makes me, aware of things they wish they hadn't missed.

What the book achieves is a vivid portrait of a distant country, the far west of Wales as it was fifty or sixty years ago, where Dylan and his wife lived from time to time during the Second World War. David Thomas makes a passionate and well-documented case for Newquay and its cast of characters as the template for *Under Milk Wood*; teeth will be ground in Laugharne. Even the original 'Milk Wood' is discovered, would you believe, lurking along the valley of the River Aeron in farms with milky names. And poems written around the end of the war, in what turned out to be Dylan Thomas's last sustained burst of energy – and some other poems as well – are seen as linked to places and events in Cardiganshire. There is plenty of scope for argument in all this; David Thomas's achievement is to ensure that it will be better informed than it was.

Perhaps inevitably, the book is tempted to connect itself with other branches of the Dylan story. The murder of an elderly Laugharne woman in January 1953, a crime of which a local deaf-mute, 'Booda', was suspected but acquitted, is added to the events which, says David Thomas, helped create a 'psychological vulnerability' that affected the poet towards the end of his life.

On thinner ice, the book examines the story that when Dylan Thomas was commissioned by the Anglo-Iranian Oil Company to write a film about Persia, where they sent him in 1951, he was or already had been recruited by British Intelligence. When this yarn appeared in print in 1998 I said I thought it barmy, and I still do. David Thomas is sceptical but has at least found out everything available about the murky sub-world of oil company, Foreign Office and spymasters. He tells us to be open-minded and wait till the files are released. I am not holding my breath.

But whether it is dealing with espionage, louche characters in Newquay, T.S. Eliot visiting Ciliau Aeron or the famous case of Dylan and the man with the Sten gun, this is a work of authority; not to mention charm.

Paul Ferris

Chronology

This is not a standard chronology of the life and works of Dylan Thomas. It is more a chronology of the events that are discussed, or referred to, in this book.

1888   Margaret Maria Phillips born in Cardiganshire

1912   Evelyn Phillips born

1913   Caitlin Macnamara born

1914   Dylan Thomas (DT) born

1916   Vera Phillips born

1930   Geoffrey Faber buys Tyglyn Aeron, Ciliau Aeron, Cardiganshire

1933   T.S. Eliot's first visit to Tyglyn Aeron

1934   DT travels to Aberystwyth, Cardiganshire, to see Caradoc Evans

1936   Alastair Graham buys Plas y Wern, Newquay

1937
April(?) DT makes a second visit to Caradoc Evans
July   He marries Caitlin Macnamara

1938
April   DT and Caitlin return to Bishopston, Swansea, to live with his parents
May   They move to Laugharne, first in Gosport Street then at Sea View. They stay for six months
Sept.   T.S. Eliot travels from Tyglyn Aeron to visit DT at Laugharne
(?)   Howard de Walden leases Plas Llanina, Newquay, and DT visits with Augustus John

1939

January   Llewelyn Thomas is born

Feb.   Vera Phillips appears in *Land of My Fathers* at the
          Empire, Swansea

March   DT and Caitlin move back to Laugharne until December

1940   Vera Phillips meets William Killick

1941

Feb.   DT and Caitlin stay in Plas Gelli, Talsarn, for the first
          time

April   DT's friend, literary columnist Roger Roughton, kills
          himself

1942-43 DT and Caitlin at Gelli again; also at Talgarreg and
          Lampeter. Plus visits to Newquay and Plas Llanina

1943

March   Aeronwy Thomas is born

August   Vera Phillips and William Killick marry

Sept.   DT in Newquay

Oct.   William Killick leaves for Greece

1944

March   Poet Alun Lewis dies in India

May   Rachel Killick is born

Sept.   DT, Caitlin and Aeronwy move to Majoda bungalow,
          Newquay

Oct.   DT fails to turn up as best man at Vernon Watkins'
          wedding
          Newquay resident Tim Thomas kills himself

Dec.   *Quite Early One Morning* is finished

1945

Jan.-Feb. DT and Caitlin ill with gastric flu

January   Caradoc Evans dies

March   The shooting at Majoda
          David Lloyd George dies

June   William Killick tried for attempted murder and acquitted

July   DT and Caitlin leave Majoda and go to Blaen Cwm,
          Llangain

Aug.	Atom bombs dropped on Japan
Dec.	DT and Caitlin move to Holywell Ford, Oxford

1946
Feb.	*Deaths and Entrances* is published

1947
January	DT elected to the National Liberal Club
April	DT, Caitlin and the children go to Italy until August
	DT's friend, poet and feminist Anna Wickham, hangs herself
Sept.	He moves to South Leigh, Oxfordshire

1948
January	Information Research Department set up within the Foreign Office
Feb.	Communist coup in Czechoslovakia
June	Berlin blockade

1949
March	DT goes to Prague
	Elected to the Savage Club
April	Margaret Phillips dies of cancer, aged 61
May	DT and Caitlin move to the Boat House at Laugharne

1950
January	George Orwell dies
Feb.	DT goes to America
June	North Korea invades the South
Sept.	Caitlin learns of DT's friendship with Pearl Kazin
Nov.	Trade agreement concluded between Iran and the Soviet Union

1951
January	DT goes to Iran for six weeks
Feb.	Iran leader General Razamara assassinated
April	DT and Caitlin consider leaving Laugharne
May	Mossadeq takes power in Iran
June	Guy Burgess defects to the Soviet Union
August	MI6 officers Monty Woodhouse and Robin Zaehner arrive in Iran

Two of DT's acquaintances, including painter Ralph Banbury, kill themselves
Bardic poet Dewi Emrys dies

1952

January   DT goes to America
??   The film *Persian Story* is released by Greenpark
July   DT appears before an Income Tax tribunal, and is visited by National Insurance Inspectors who threaten to sue
          He travels to Bangor to give two lectures
August   Welsh poet James Kitchener Davies dies of cancer, aged 50
Nov.   DT visits Aberystwyth to read poems at the Arts Society
          Collected Poems published
          America explodes hydrogen bomb
Dec.   DT's father dies

1953

January   Elizabeth Thomas is murdered in Laugharne
          Marged Stepney-Howard dies from an overdose of drugs and drink
          Caitlin has an abortion
          The Laugharne sub-postmaster is imprisoned for fraud
          Derek Bentley is hanged
          Floods devastate the English east coast and Holland
          The Irish ferry sinks
          Critics pan DT's performance in Sitwell's *The Shadow of Cain*
Feb.   DT learns that the Welsh poet Idris Davies is dying
March   George Roberts (Booda) is tried for the murder of Elizabeth Thomas and acquitted
          Another crisis over Llewelyn's school fees
          Stalin dies
          Queen Mary dies
          Four women are found strangled in 10, Rillington Place
April   DT's sister, Nancy, dies of cancer in India, aged 46
          Idris Davies dies of cancer, aged 48
          DT goes to America
          Time magazine publishes a personal attack on DT
May   First presentation of *Under Milk Wood*

June	Julius and Ethel Rosenberg are executed in America for spying for the Soviet Union
July	DT hears of the death of a friend called Helen
	John Christie is hanged for the Rillington Place murders
	Hillaire Belloc dies of extensive burns to the body
August	MI6 and the CIA topple the Mossadeq government
	Soviet Union explodes hydrogen bomb
	DT notes the death of Norman Cameron earlier in the year, aged 48
Sept.	Krushchev takes over in the Soviet Union
	Aeronwy goes away to boarding school for the first time
	The poisoner Louisa Merrifield is hanged
	Britain announces atom bomb tests in Australia
October	Two of DT's closest friends, Bill and Helen McAlpine, leave to work in Tokyo
	Kathleen Ferrier dies of cancer, aged 41
	The Duke of Bedford kills himself
	Britain explodes an atom bomb at Woomera
	British troops sent to British Guyana and a state of emergency is declared
	Israeli Army kills fifty-five Arabs in Jordan
	Mossadeq's court-martial begins in Iran
	Vice Premier Nasser of Egypt warns of war with Britain
	DT goes to America on October 19th
	Liz Reitell ends the relationship with DT
	Caitlin sends a letter to say the marriage is finished but
Nov.	DT dies in New York before reading it.

1. Llareggub by Roy Morgan, 1954 (Paris House – top picture – was a shop in Newquay).

Introduction

This book is about Dylan Thomas. It came slowly spawning through a series of chance events involving unsolicited mail, an overgrown walled garden, and in typical Llareggub fashion, two parrots and a monkey.

One morning, the postman delivered a new brochure from our local hotel, the Tyglyn Aeron, situated just above the village of Ciliau Aeron in West Wales. I flipped through the pages and was astonished to find a photograph of T.S. Eliot asleep in the drawing room of Tyglyn Aeron in the 1930s, long before the mansion became a hotel. A round of conversations in the village shop yielded the information that Tyglyn Aeron had been bought in 1930 by the publisher Geoffrey Faber. According to Faber's personal diary, their first night in Tyglyn was August 20th. Within days he had ordered *Welsh Made Easy*. By the end of the year, he was taking tea with the clergy, shooting rabbits with a local farmer and chairing a meeting on "Some patterns of nutrition in agricultural districts".

2. Tyglyn Aeron in the 1930s

Tyglyn Aeron had been built in 1825 by Thomas Winwood, an ironmaster's son from Bristol. Faber carried out a number of improvements, including a swimming pool, tennis court and the installation of home-made electricity and a piped water supply to the house. He also had a weather station built. It consisted of wet and dry thermometers in a wooden cage, a glass ball that recorded the hours of sunshine and a rainfall gauge whose daily readings were sent to the British Rainfall Society. The whole lot was surrounded by railings, partly because Faber was worried that a local witch might steal the ball.

The Visitors' Book[1] shows that Eliot had stayed at Tyglyn Aeron for ten days or so every summer between 1933 and 1941. He would accompany the Fabers and their small children to the sandy beaches around Newquay, particularly Cei Bach. He cut a distinctive figure in his plus fours. Every so often, Eliot helped in entertaining to tea Miss Davis from the neighbouring estate of Ty Glyn Mansion. This was owned by a Major Davis, a shy and reclusive bachelor. Miss Davis was his sister, and she had come from London to look after him. She missed the city greatly and she found consolation in Eliot's visits and conversation, and the occasional tea with him at the Lampeter Lawn Tennis Club.

3. T.S. Eliot at Tyglyn Aeron

Geoffrey Faber sold Tyglyn Aeron in 1941 and that was the last the village saw of Eliot. The house was sold and bought, and sold again becoming a country club and then a hotel.

Major and Miss Davis continued to live in modest circumstances in Ty Glyn Mansion. They had brought in a young local man called Gwilym Jones, and over the next thirty years he worked hard in transforming the estate, particularly the two-acre walled garden. On his retirement, the garden fell into disrepair and became totally overgrown. In the early 1990s, it was given by Mrs Betty Davis to the local community. I became part of the committee that put in a successful bid to the National Lottery to restore the garden. A neighbour told me that Gwilym Jones was still alive and living near the coast. I managed to track him down, and we interviewed him about the design and planting of the garden. Quite by chance, Gwilym mentioned Geoffrey Faber. I was so intrigued that I came back and did another interview in which Gwilym told me about Faber's relations with the villagers in Ciliau Aeron, as well as a little about Eliot.

There was a point in this interview (see Appendix 1) when Gwilym compared Eliot to Dylan Thomas, describing how much more sociable Dylan had been with local people in Talsarn. The village of Talsarn was just a few miles upstream from Tyglyn Aeron and I wondered whether the two poets had ever encountered each other on the river bank. I also had to admit to Gwilym that I hadn't realised that Dylan had stayed in Talsarn. In Plas Gelli, Gwilym had replied, and he told me how to get in touch with Amanda Williams, who had lived in Gelli whilst Dylan and Caitlin were there. By now, I was losing interest in Eliot, both as a person and a poet, and thinking more about Dylan Thomas' connections with the Aeron Valley and Cardiganshire.

Another piece of luck strengthened my interest in Thomas rather than Eliot. I went to a fund-raising meeting about the long-term future of the Ty Glyn walled garden. There I met Jacqui Lyne and, over the tea and biscuits that preceded the discussion, I mentioned that two escaped parrots had settled in the garden. Her late husband, she replied, would have known what to do about them. He had been a vet in Aberaeron. One of his many claims to fame was that he had known Dylan Thomas. This encounter brought me information about Dylan's friendships with Thomas Herbert the vet and with Newquay resident, Alastair Graham, who had been Evelyn Waugh's lover. This in turn led me to diaries about the sex life of Newquay in the 1940s, and on to gay occult parties, Dennis Wheatley, Guy Burgess, Tom Driberg and the head of counter-subversion in MI5, but also to Cardiganshire friends of Dylan, such as the bard Dewi Emrys, whose fame did not extend very far outside Wales. I even received a letter from John le Carré.

Then I heard about the lady with the monkey. She was one of the few remaining real 'characters' in the area. She hadn't known Dylan, she said, but she knew a few people who had. This led to what researchers call 'blue nose syndrome', an occupational injury that occurs when too many doors are slammed in your face. Newquay, I soon discovered, was uptight about Dylan

Through this happy combination of events came this book. It is essentially about the time that Dylan Thomas spent in Cardiganshire (today called Ceredigion), and the influence of its places and people upon him.

Cardiganshire is a beautiful but demanding land. Its farming economy has often seen difficult times, producing a culture of hard work and thrift. It has been a county of small shopkeepers, with a strong tradition in the woollen and drapery trades. In the 1920s and 1930s, many Cardis took their families to London and opened dairies and corner stores. It is also a county that has been dependent on fishing, and the recruitment of its men to the merchant marine. Its people, raised largely in the disciplines of the non-conformist chapels, have a reputation for learning and self-improvement. The county is host to the National Library of Wales, and to the university colleges of Lampeter and Aberystwyth. There's hardly a page of *The Oxford Companion to the Literature of Wales* that doesn't contain at least one entry for a Cardiganshire man or woman.

My interest has been Dylan's associations with the Aeron Valley and Newquay. But as the first chapter makes clear, it's hard to understand Dylan the Cardi without knowing about his friendship with Swansea neighbour, Margaret Phillips and her family. Margaret was born in Cardiganshire, not far from the Aeron Valley. The valley, and Plas Gelli in particular, helped to shape some of Dylan's work, and some of its farms gave rise to the name 'Milk Wood'.

Margaret Phillips had invited Dylan and Caitlin to Plas Gelli. It was her daughter, Vera, who helped them move to Majoda bungalow in Newquay in 1944. This was to be one of Dylan's most productive periods. It came to an abrupt end in March 1945 when Vera's husband William Killick, an SOE (Special Operations

Executive) commando home on leave, fired his machine gun through the kitchen window of the bungalow.

Whilst this book mainly covers the period from the 1930s to 1945, it also looks at events in the early 1950s, such as Dylan's 'spy' trip to Iran. This curious affair also has a Cardiganshire aspect, including links to Goronwy Rees and Alastair Graham.

I hope through the following chapters to show that we must re-assess the influence of Cardiganshire on *Under Milk Wood*, and on other work, taking account of the time that Dylan spent in the county, not just at Newquay and Talsarn, but in the other villages and their pubs that he visited in the company of local friends. Cyril Connolly alone has recognised the importance of Cardiganshire. Talking of the period before 1946, he writes that Dylan

> was able to undergo a slow acclimatisation to the toxins of liter-
> ary life without damage to his imaginative energy; his metaphors
> remained in a state of grace. Marriage and the coast of
> Cardiganshire preserved him....[2]

Indeed, it seems that the people and places of Cardiganshire became stronger elements of Dylan's life just as he was open to new sources of inspiration in the period following the sale of his notebooks in 1941. But Dylan didn't simply stay in Cardiganshire; he actively explored the county on foot and by car. We know that he had his eyes and ears wide open: one of the themes that runs through the Colin Edwards interviews[3] with people who knew Dylan at this time was that he was vigorously, but unobtrusively, in pursuit of new material:

> He was just interested in people, any character at all, and listened
> to them, and busy with his notes at all times....
> > (Jack Patrick, Newquay)

> He was always on the probe, he enjoyed company of a different
> kind all the time...as if he was trying to get knowledge...
> > (Edward Evans, Lampeter)

> Dylan was quite apart from politics, he was tremendously inter-
> ested in people, not movements. He loved people and their stu-
> pid characteristics...he loved to find out things about people that
> made them different..."
> > (Evelyn Milton, Gelli, Talsarn)

> He liked to talk to ordinary people, and he sought them out. That
> was one of his great successes in life.
>
> (Mrs Warfield-Darling, Newquay)

The trouble is that biographers don't often have the time, or the
local connections, to talk with the 'ordinary people' to be found in
the everyday lives of the good and the great. This is particularly
unfortunate in Dylan's case, for he much preferred the company of
locals, and did some of his best writing amongst them. As far as
Dylan is concerned, it is almost too late to rectify the situation, since
many of those who knew him in Newquay and the Aeron Valley are
dead.

1. The Farm

The names of the people described in this opening chapter may mean little even to Dylan aficionados, but they played an important part in Dylan's life and in some of the events that shaped it. They appear in many of the chapters of this book. They may well have been overlooked in the past because they are women (and Dylan's biographers have been men) and because they helped Dylan in the 'traditional', easy-to-take-for-granted, backroom roles of carer, provider and companion. They did not have the renown of a Sitwell or Hansford Johnson, or the money and connections of a Margaret Taylor or a Stepney-Howard. They were the wife and two daughters of an insurance agent from Swansea.

The Bryn-y-Mor Girls

Dylan's time in Cardiganshire was rooted in his friendship, since early childhood, with the Phillips family of 12, Bryn-y-Mor Crescent, Swansea, particularly Margaret Maria and her daughters, Vera and Sarah Evelyn. The Phillipses were directly responsible for bringing Dylan both to Gelli, Talsarn, and Majoda, Newquay, and his experience of these places was partly mediated through Margaret Phillips' own Cardi roots and identity.

Margaret Maria was born in Cardiganshire in 1888, probably in the village of Llanarth, just outside Newquay. Her mother was called Maggie but we do not know her last name. Margaret Maria's father was a William Jones, from a farm called Ffôs Helyg near Synod Inn, Newquay (see Appendix 4). Maggie refused to marry William Jones. Her reasons are not known but there are two stories in the Phillips family: the man's love making had been violent; and his approach to bringing up children too strict. Nevertheless, close contact was maintained with the family at Ffôs Helyg, particularly between the children. We know from family letters and conversations that there were at least two 'Ffôsyrhelig boys', and two older girls, who became known as aunts. These were:

Ellen and Marie – who eventually ran the inevitable Dairy shop in Croydon...Auntie Ellen...had rather lank [...] yellow hair – but Auntie Marie her sister had a halo of sparkling, electric silver all round her head – I did envy her..."[4]

Maggie left Margaret Maria to be looked after by her family, and went off on her own to the coal mines to work. At about the age of eleven, Margaret Maria was brought to the Rhondda when her mother married William Morgans, whose name she took and gave to her daughter. He was probably her second husband and was

a gentle and thoughtful man who could read and helped Margaret Maria to satisfy her thirst for literature, and from original....ideas – 'Rights of Man' etc.[5]

The move to the Rhondda proved challenging for the young Margaret Maria: she

found it very difficult on leaving Cardigan – all Welsh – get used to everything in English – and all fences, gates etc in metal – everything in the country was made of wood![6]

School was particularly difficult as she spoke only Welsh. Not surprisingly, Margaret Maria failed her exams, but excelled in arithmetic and soon started work in the Refuge Insurance Company. Here, she met Thomas Dilwyn Phillips and they were married in 1909. Like Margaret, he was Welsh-speaking and had been born in Llanstephan, Carmarthenshire, just across the Tâf estuary from Laugharne. He eventually became a Divisional Inspector in the insurance company. Besides Vera and Evelyn, there were two older sons: Evan, who became a scientist in the BBC, and Billy, a stained glass maker in a business part-owned by Stuart Thomas, Dylan's Swansea solicitor. Billy was an accomplished but reluctant painter; two of his pictures were in the Swansea Art Society exhibition in 1949 at the Glynn Vivian Art Gallery:

Nothing shows more diversity than the still life pictures. Two by W.W. Phillips... said to be the only pictures he has ever painted, and [one] took three years, are what one expects colour photography to attain some day. They are miracles of photographic realism.[7]

4. The Phillips family: Billy, Margaret Maria, Vera and Evan, with Dilwyn and Evelyn behind.

Margaret Maria Phillips was an out-going, generous and sociable person. She was, like her mother, independently-minded and cared little for the middle-class pretensions of the Swansea Uplands. She was on good terms with Dylan's mother, Florence, who was equally sociable, and they were two of the original Kardomah Girls:

> She [Florence] was very fond of meeting her friends in the Kardomah in Swansea at that time and you could see her almost every Saturday with a little crowd of her friends...she was very entertaining...always delightful...[8]

Margaret Maria loved the company of young people, and had a real soft spot for Dylan. Most weekends she held open house for the Kardomah Boys, and in the summer they also came to the Phillips' hut at Langland Bay. One of the group, Charles Fisher, has talked about

> ...Vera Phillips and Evelyn Phillips who painted and danced...and whose home and family meant so much to us all, for we spent a great deal of time there, eating tiger cheese. Dylan, too, came

29

often to Vera Phillips' house. They were beautiful and talented girls....they anticipated by twenty years many of the things being done today [1960s] in self-expression, in liveliness, behaviour and in their friendship with most people in Swansea who were trying to do anything in that period.[9]

Margaret continued to stay in contact with Dylan, visiting him, for instance, when he and Caitlin were at Laugharne in 1938, and making him welcome at Gelli, which she had rented from the early days of the war.[10]

Evelyn Phillips

Evelyn's first memory of Dylan is of a camping expedition at Mewslade Bay on the Gower, in their early teens. She recalls hearing Dylan from the other side of the sand dunes:

> I heard this beautiful voice, coming from a skinny little chap, he really was terribly thin, and he had just this mass of hair and these great gooseberry eyes.

One of the architects of Dylan's voice was another Bryn-y-Mor Girl. This was Gwen James, who lived at number 23 with her sister Hetty. Gwen was Dylan's elocution teacher. Later, Evelyn took over and ran Gwen James' elocution school in Llanelli.

Evelyn was not slow in asking to be introduced to the owner of the "beautiful voice", and soon Dylan sought her opinion about a poem he had just written:

> We both lay on our stomachs in the grass, I can remember the feeling of it more than the sight of it...it was quite different to 'school poetry'.... He gave me the impression even then that this is what he wanted to do in life.... He wasn't going to do anything else.... The great thing about Dylan was that coming from a Welsh, very respectable background...that he was still prepared to live the kind of life that he wanted to live himself. He wasn't going to be influenced by outside people, and this is a trait to be admired...so many of us are bamboozled and dragooned into doing things which are not really in our nature...how many of us Welsh people are square pegs in round holes because we've got this bug of respectability?[11]

5. Evelyn Phillips, Lady President of the Students' Union

There is another account of this meeting with Dylan in which Evelyn, or Tich as she was mostly called, remembers being "slightly shocked" by the "innuendos and little rhymes he produced, seemingly out of his head...". She gives two examples, including Dylan's limerick:

> There was once a boy of Algiers
> Who said to his harem, "My dears,
> You may think it odd of me,
> But I've given up sodomy."
> And all of them answered "Loud Cheers."

Dylan could, said Evelyn, have been reciting Keats, as he rolled out the words of the limerick with a mock serious expression on his face:

> We didn't smirk, or pretend we didn't understand. We just laughed. He was so young, so innocent looking, so naughty – like a baby satyr.... So, at 15, when I first came across him all the potentials of the famous-to-be man were there – the rich enthralling voice, the poetry, the bawdiness... I like to remember him as he was then.[12]

31

6. Evelyn at the Little Theatre, late 1930s

Evelyn was very active, as was Dylan, in the Swansea Little Theatre, and later appeared as an American tourist in the film of *Under Milk Wood* shot in Fishguard. She went to the university in Swansea and the London Royal Academy of Music, and then took up a teaching career. Both Colin Edwards and Paul Ferris have noted that in Dylan's notebook of 1933 'The force that through the green fuse' was dedicated to 'EP'. They suggest this was Evelyn, though she herself was sceptical about it. At the time, she was Lady President of the Students' Union at Swansea. She was living at home, and still very much friends with Dylan.

Evelyn's boyfriend and future husband, Jeff Milton, was in the fruit importing business. He was also a member of the Little Theatre, and got on reasonably well with the Kardomah boys (who called him 'Grapefruit'). He once organised a disastrous party for Dylan to meet his golfing friends. Dylan terrified a young woman by standing close to her and staring at her continually. Jeff managed to get him outside:

> I quietly locked the door but within a few seconds the door was in and the lock was broken. Dylan looked at me with a rather contemptuous and triumphant look....[13]

Vera Phillips

Vera was born in Swansea on January 30th, 1916. Margaret Phillips and Florence Thomas would push Vera and Dylan to the park and the shops in their respective prams. The two children often played together and they both attended Mrs Hole's school in Mirador Crescent where another pupil, Joan Hardy (née Bailey), described Dylan as "a pale, thin little boy with an incredible halo of blonde curls" (1995). Vera told Paul Ferris how she once came across Dylan in the lane behind the school:

> He was shouting, 'Look, I can write God Save the King,' and peeing all over the wall.... All the other little boys were trying to do it, too. (1997, p48)

Some of Dylan's biographers, FitzGibbon for example, have tended to be rather disparaging about Mrs Hole's school. Ferris' treatment is more balanced, and is best read in conjunction with Hardy's account in the *New Welsh Review*. Hardy has also drawn attention to the way in which the school played a part in developing Dylan's love of words:

> Mrs Hole really taught us to appreciate 'words'....it was being taught at Mrs Hole's school that led me to really enjoy reading, reciting, acting and writing a little. 'Words' were always important. I remember 6-7 year olds, the 7 to 8s and the 9-10s being given 'A-H', 'I-P' and 'Q-Z', and being told by Mrs Hole to write down one or two words starting with their letters in each group. And Dylan, who was the second group 'I-P', said he wanted 'Q-Z' because the words were more interesting. I think he was allowed to do it after doing his own group... I realise that [Mrs Hole] taught us the beauty of words. I recall her saying, 'Even ugly is beautiful because as you say it, your mouth curls up into a smile.' I'm sure she gave Dylan and all of us a wonderful start.[14]

Vera and Dylan went their separate ways to grammar school but remained teenage friends, meeting almost every day in the shelter in Cwmdonkin Park. Vera, like Dylan, was considered a little delicate, and the Park was used by their parents for recuperation:

> Dylan's mother was convinced he was very delicate and 'chesty'. After a few days away from school, she would wrap him up in a

big woollen scarf crossed over in the front and pinned at the back and tell him to go and sit in the Park. I seemed to have mysterious attacks of tonsillitis, and when better I, too, would be sent off to the Park to sit in the sun. I suppose I was about 12, and Dylan a year or so older – both of us hopelessly mollycoddled!! Still, it was very enjoyable and Dylan had a fine fund of stories even then and was amazingly good at line drawings – all very abstract and fascinating. I thought..the line drawings were something really strange. I kept one for years – 'Mannikens on the Water' it was called.[15]

Vera's interest in art developed at grammar school. She became friends with Fred Janes and became involved with the Swansea School of Art. She went to London in 1934-35 to study interior design at Chelsea Polytechnic in Manresa Road. She lived at 4, Cathcart Road, where she organised Sunday tea parties for 'lonely people', an act that was wholly in keeping with her generous nature. Vera was, said Evelyn, a great organiser of people, but a little inclined to be bossy, even dogmatic in her opinions. Dylan was being very unfair when he told Vernon Watkins that Vera was lazy. Writing from Majoda on November 15th, 1944, he said:

> ...I didn't tell you that Vera Phillips, now Killick, for she married a man called Killick but who, for years, we thought was called Waistcoat, is living in the next bungalow to us on this ratty cliff. She lives alone except for her baby daughter who is five months old and, during all that time, has screamed only twice. Vera says it is because of character. We say it is because of laziness. Vera lives on cocoa, and reads books about the technique of third-century brass work, and gets up only once a day to boil the cat an egg, which it detests.

Caitlin was far closer to the truth when she described Vera as "very emancipated...in with the Chelsea bunch" (1986, p88). She certainly caused eyebrows to raise when she returned to Swansea during the Polytechnic vacations: she worked in a factory and scandalised the other women on the factory floor by not wearing stockings. As for appearance, Vera was

> tall for Wales, as Dylan says, and she had long silvery-blonde hair which she sometimes wore long, and sometimes wore in a bun in the back. She was willowy...she had quite plump legs but the

7. Vera, 1935

general effect was willowy.... She was the sort of person people wanted to paint... (Evelyn Milton)[16]

While at college, Vera worked as a waitress in a cafe called The Chelsea Pensioner, which was part-owned by a friend called Elizabeth, a former dancer who was married to a Maltese artist, Paul Taylor. Vera also became involved in acting. She, too, had been a member of the Little Theatre in Swansea, and had joined the Principality Players, a professional group of touring actors under the direction of Thomas Taig. She appeared in Jack Jones' *Land of My Fathers* on February 20th 1939 at the Empire, Swansea, and thereafter in venues across South Wales, ending up in the Winter Gardens, Brighton in April. Vera was also the Stage Manager; the Music Director was Tom Warner, another friend of Dylan's[17]. Also in the cast was Desmond Llewelyn, who went on to play 'Q' in the James Bond films. Vera was, he told me, "a very attractive woman – unfortunately, I was married at that time. I gave her lifts everywhere in the MG". When the war started, Vera signed up to entertain the troops, appeared in a number of films as an extra, and stole the show as a walk-on in a production of *Othello*. Her stage name was Maria Ffoshelig, the name of the farm outside Newquay.

35

The friendship between Dylan, Caitlin and Vera developed in London, but there were also meetings between the Thomases and the Phillipses in Swansea. Evelyn has described a party she went to, probably in 1940, held above a laundry in the Mumbles. Vera and Dylan entertained the guests by singing improvised opera, and Dylan and Caitlin put on a show of ballet-burlesque. Caitlin got very drunk. Dylan wanted to sober her up before returning to his parent's home in Bishopston. He put his finger on the back of her tongue to make her sick and was bitten for his pains: "She bites the hand that makes her sick," he complained.

8. Vera, with her portrait by Kenneth Hancock

Vera met her future husband, William Killick, in *The Antelope* pub, Sloane Square, in 1940 when Killick was between army postings. Vera was with Caitlin and Dylan, and they got into conversation with William. He took a fancy to Vera, and at the end of the evening he offered to get a taxi to take them all home. When the taxi arrived at the destination, Dylan, Vera and Caitlin got out and disappeared, leaving William alone in the taxi. He returned the next night to *The Antelope*, and found Vera there. "My sister," said Evelyn, "seems to have been quite a drinking companion. She wasn't a tremendous drinker herself, but she liked, as an art student, to go around with people who did drink and talk."

Certainly, Vera enjoyed herself with Caitlin and Dylan: she told Paul Ferris that

> I had more fun with Dylan, and with Catty too, than with any-
> body else, before or since. He was such a selfish little bastard, it
> was surprising to find him married to someone it was so easy to
> get on with. (1993, p93)

Vera and Caitlin became close friends during the war years. One strand in their relationship was that Caitlin's brother, John Macnamara, was, like William Killick, a commando in the Royal Engineers, though he was not in the SOE. It is likely that they fought together on the first experimental commando raids on the French coast. Some information on Macnamara's role is provided in Nicolette Devas' book, as well as a brief account of Dylan's drinking and fighting sprees with him (1966).

William Killick was away for much of the war serving in the SOE though, as we shall see in the next chapter, he sometimes came home on leave to Gelli. He married Vera on August 14th, 1943. The ceremony took place in the Chelsea Register Office, opposite the *Six Bells*. Dylan was the best man and the marriage certificate was wit- nessed by Caitlin. (The other witness was Ann McDonnell, William's sister, and the Registrar was Mr Algernon Whiting.) Dylan had given Caitlin money to buy a new winter coat, but she spent most of it buying a hat, with a huge kingfisher on it, for Vera to bor- row for the wedding – it cost seven guineas from Peter Jones. Perhaps Caitlin should have spent the money on herself and Dylan: they turned up looking so ill-kempt that Vera sent them away to find better clothes and the ceremony was held up whilst they did so.[18] At the time of the wedding, Vera was living at 84, Old Church Street, a few minutes walk from Manresa Road where Caitlin and Dylan had taken a flat.

The Bryn-y-Mor Girls, including mother Margaret, constituted between them an almost unbroken line of friendship and support (moral, emotional, financial, practical) that began in Dylan's child- hood and lasted until 1945. William Killick was part of this: it is clear from Paul Ferris' notes of his interview with the Killicks in 1975 that

William had been financially supporting Dylan and Caitlin from the early 1940s:

> I used to finance them. I quite liked the fellow, he was a fair drinker.

Margaret Taylor (wife of historian A.J.P. Taylor) bankrolled Dylan after 1945 when he was a rising star, but it was Vera and William who helped keep him going during the war, long before he was famous. Vera was a very generous person, just like her mother. Perhaps the later lack of recognition for the Killicks was a matter of class. History preserves the good deeds of the wife of a famous Oxford don, but not those of a subaltern engineer.

9. The Phillips family, 1940: Dilwyn, Margaret Maria, Vera, Evelyn, Billy and Evan

Vera's friendship with Caitlin, and the support she offered during the difficult moments of the Thomas' marriage, is another important aspect of the help given by the Bryn-y-Mor Girls. This friendship lasted, as we shall see later, until well into the 1950s. It was a particularly important element of the Thomas' relationship at Majoda. Not just help with baby-sitting, but companionship during the long winter months when Dylan was writing so much, or away in London on film business. Olive Jones, another friend of Caitlin's, has remarked that

> He used to disappear for days on end, and nobody saw him, and that's when he did his writing...we wouldn't see him for a week sometimes.

Dylan's productivity at Majoda was due in no small part to Vera's support for Caitlin. "Their friendship," said Vera's daughter Rachel, "was strong and that of like open mindedness."

2. Two Mansions

In this chapter, I write about Dylan's time at Plas Llanina, Newquay, and Plas Gelli, Talsarn. They are at the centre of Dylan's adult experience of Cardiganshire, but I want to start by looking at the way in which the county may have impinged on the younger Dylan. It's not unreasonable to suppose that Dylan's emotional association with Cardiganshire began with his great uncle, Gwilym Marles. He was a distinguished Unitarian minister, poet and radical leader in the county, and his influence was at its strongest in the area between Llandysul and the Aeron Valley – see Edwards, 1999.

We noted in the last chapter that Margaret Phillips had been born and brought up in Cardiganshire, before moving away as a young girl. The circumstances of her birth and early upbringing were not kept secret by the Phillipses. Margaret loved her Cardi roots and relations; Evelyn, when teased about being careful with money, used to retort that she was a true Cardi. The "Ffosyrheligs" became such an established part of the family culture that the young Vera was more than happy to use them for her stage name.

Margaret assiduously maintained her contact with the Newquay area. Family holidays in the 1920s were often taken there or with one of the relations in the surrounding countryside such as her sister Ellen, who lived in Maen-y-Groes, just a mile outside Newquay, or her aunt Ellen who ran the post office in Cross Inn ("I loved staying with Auntie Ellen...", Vera once wrote to her niece, Jane Gibson). Margaret also regularly visited her relatives (on the occasion of a birthday, for instance), usually taking her daughters with her. There is no evidence that the young Dylan accompanied Vera on one of these trips to Newquay but, knowing how generous Margaret Phillips was, it is possible that he did. Dylan's mother, Florence, would certainly have agreed to Dylan going, for what better place could there be than the Cardiganshire coast for a chesty child to recuperate?

Margaret Phillips was a Cardi on both sides. It was a badge that Vera was proud to wear, and Dylan would have known all about it. He would have heard accounts of the numerous visits that the family paid to Cardiganshire, as well as colourful stories about the

"Ffosyrheligs". He may also have encountered the "Ffosyrheligs" in the Phillips' house. Vera has described how the Newquay relations turned up at Bryn-y-Mor Crescent:

> ...don't forget Swansea was quite a 'lower hautemonde' seaside resort, so they kept pouring in, and also the local hospital was the surgery [place?] for South Wales, so always there were relations being chopped up or being healed in some form or another – I used just to watch the visitors that [poured?] about 'Maggie's house' all gabbling away in Welsh of which I understood not a word![19]

Dylan may have drawn on the 'Ffosyrhelig' history when, at the age of twenty-two, he wrote 'It is the sinners' dust-tongued bell'. The last stanza of the poem goes

> I mean by time the cast and curfew rascal of our marriage,
> At nightbreak born in the fat side, from an animal bed
> In a holy room in a wave;
> And all love's sinners in sweet cloth kneel to a hyleg image,
> Nutmeg, civet and sea-parsley serve the plagued groom and
>   bride
> Who have brought forth the urchin grief.

There are three elements in the poem: a church, a birth and the sea. It is possible that the last stanza refers to the circumstances of Margaret Phillips' birth in Llanarth not far from the sea. It is of interest that Dylan used the word "hyleg", which the *Oxford English Dictionary* tells us a "ruling planet of a nativity." It is remarkably similar to "helyg", as in Ffôs Helyg, the usual spelling of the farm's name. In his letter to Desmond Hawkins of August 14th 1939, Dylan writes

> It's a freak word, I suppose, but one or two every now & then don't hurt: I think they help. It was what I wanted & I happened to know the word well. I dessay I could explain this selfishness at intolerable length, but I want you to have this scribble right away.

It's possible that Dylan knew the word well, not because he was interested in astrology, but because of its similarity to "helyg". We should note, too, that Dylan's teenage poem 'Greek Play in a Garden' was inspired by a performance of *Electra* in the garden of the home of Mrs Bertie Perkins, Derwen Fawr, Swansea. The house was called Rhyd-y-Helig.[20]

The young Dylan had certainly travelled in West Wales. He visited Hendre Farm, St Dogmaels, on the Pembroke-Cardiganshire border, in the summer of 1930 aged sixteen and still at school. He wrote a poem, 'To Bonnie', which was put in the autograph album of Bonnie James.[21] In 1936, Dylan travelled with Fred Janes to Fishguard, where Augustus John and Caitlin were visiting the Eisteddfod.

SAILORS' SAFETY, DINAS CROSS. Beautifully situated, Apartments or Board. Near Sea, Fishguard, and Goodwick Bay. Safe Bathing and Boating. Parties catered for. Wines and Spirits, best quality. SALT'S duration Ale and Stout   Terms very moderate.

Perhaps it was on this trip that Dylan first heard about the Sailors Safety inn at Pwllgwaelod, Dinas Cross, just north of Fishguard. The inn was run by Arthur B. Duigenan and his wife Jim, who had bought it in the 1920s. Duigenan was a colourful character, with an interest in poetry and literature, which he would read aloud, wearing a monocle, to his friends. The inn was very popular and widely known. Dillwyn Miles told me that

> I was instrumental in making the Sailors Safety known to people like Cynan, J.C. Griffith Jones and Hannen Swaffer during the 1936 Eisteddfod, but I do not think that Augustus was there then. I saw him on the Eisteddfod field and he appears to have returned to Carmarthen: going on to Dinas would have been out of his way. Sailors Safety was well known in those days: people came from some distance, even from Swansea, for the duck and

green peas or lobster dinners, for which the inn was famed. Dylan might have come there at any time, either from Swansea or New Quay, either before or after the war.[22]

Much later, Dylan took John Malcolm Brinnin and Bill Read to the Sailors Safety in the summer of 1951. Brinnin complained that "the magnificent lobster dinner" promised by Dylan did not materialise.[23] This is surprising; whilst Duigenan had left in May 1949, his successor, Mrs Monté Manson, had maintained the inn's reputation. She was a fine cook, and a calm person ready for any eventuality, not at all like the "flustered proprietress" described by Brinnin.

Another occasion for a trip to West Wales arose when John Davenport visited Laugharne in the summer of 1938. Dylan arranged an outing to Pembrokeshire. They drove to St. David's and went out to the cliffs where Dylan read his birthday poem, 'Twenty-four years'.[24] In 1940, Dylan and Davenport wrote *The Death of the King's Canary*, one scene in which is set off the Cardiganshire coast.

Dylan's first known trip to Cardiganshire was in October 1934, when he was twenty years old. He went with Glyn Jones to visit Caradoc Evans in Aberystwyth, and stayed the weekend there. It was through Evans' writing (for example, *My People: Stories of the Peasantry of West Wales*) that the young Dylan acquired other, more negative images of Cardi land, especially of the men of the cloth (drapers and tailors as well as ministers) who Evans despised and Dylan ridiculed. Dylan drew on some of Evans' portrayals of Cardiganshire people in 'Where Tawe Flows' written in 1939.

Dylan paid a second visit to Evans – an account has been given by Evans' stepson, Nicholas Sandys.[25] He does not provide the date but Harris (1988) suggests it was probably in 1937 – and we do know that Dylan was in nearby Machynlleth that April.[26] Evans, of course, knew a good deal about Cardiganshire. He had spent his childhood in the county but also knew it well from his association with a touring repertory company called Rogues and Vagabonds, set up to launch the career of his step-son. The company put on one-night shows in Aberystwyth, Aberporth, Lampeter, Newquay and Aberaeron. Sandys claims in his article that on this second visit, Evans encouraged Dylan to write a play, and that Dylan was inspired by Evans' play, *Taffy*, to produce *Under Milk Wood*.

The influence of Cardiganshire would also have come through other friends associated with the county. These included the poet

11. Arthur Duigenan (centre, rear) and his wife Jim with a cockatoo on her shoulder.

Dewi Emrys, and the writer A.E. Richards, who had been born in Borth, and was also a friend of Caradoc Evans. Richards, who had known Dylan since the late 1930s, is another who has claimed that he gave Dylan the idea for *Under Milk Wood* (Matthews, 1994).

As early as 1938, Dylan was corresponding with T.S. Eliot who, wrote Dylan, was staying in a place some thirty miles from Laugharne.[27] In fact, Eliot was at Geoffrey Faber's country mansion in Ciliau Aeron, and journeyed from there to Laugharne for afternoon tea with Dylan and Caitlin. The Visitors' Book at Tyglyn Aeron confirms that Eliot stayed there with the Fabers between August 26th and September 3rd. Within a year, Dylan made the return journey to Cardiganshire, not to Faber's mansion, but to that of Lord Howard de Walden on the outskirts of Newquay.

1. *Llanina*

'hoofed with seaweed, did a jig on the Llanina sands'
(Dylan Thomas, 1949)

Plas Llanina was one of de Walden's many homes. He was an extremely wealthy man, owning large tracts of London, including much of Marylebone and St. John's Wood. He was well known in his time as a reforming landlord and had sued John Lewis, the founder of the store of that name, who had suggested he was not. After the court case, which he won, he gave all his tenants leases of 999 years so that they virtually became independent.

De Walden was famous, too, as a patron of the arts and for his concern, in particular, with the culture of Wales, with which he deeply identified. *The Dictionary of National Biography* notes that "his concern with Cymric affairs was strong, he bred the native ponies, learned Welsh and fostered the study of that language." De Walden was instrumental in setting up the Welsh National Theatre at Llangollen. In the 1920s, he was patron of the Portmadoc Players, of

12. Plas Llanina, 1940s, with Lady Howard de Walden

which Dylan's friend, the author Richard Hughes, had been a
founder-member. Using the family name of Scott-Ellis, de Walden
wrote small-scale operas, the most famous being *Dylan, Son of the
Wave*. With music by Holbrooke, and conducted by Thomas
Beecham, it opened in Drury Lane in 1914, the year in which Dylan
Thomas was born.

Poet amongst the Apples

Plas Llanina is only a few hundred yards down the road from
Majoda. Its core was built in the seventeenth century, with additions
built on until the nineteenth century. It has been usual to describe
Llanina as an unspoilt example of a small-scale gentry house of the
period, not often found in Cardiganshire. Its main feature was the
virtual absence of reception rooms: it was built with a panelled din-
ing room that ran the entire length of the house. The mansion used
to be part of a thriving village, most of which has fallen into the sea
as a result of coastal erosion.

When we assess Llanina's influence on Dylan's poetry, we must
take into account that Llanina was, like Gelli, a holy place. The pre-
sent church is the third to have been built there, and the first was an
abbey. It is named after Ina, a relative of St. David, the patron saint
of Wales. Llanina is a 'holy cluster': the family chapel, the graveyard
and church are but a few yards from the front door of the mansion.
Cistercian monks planted the ancient mulberry that still survives in
the walled garden. Perhaps they were from the community at Gelli,
coming to Llanina to set their fish traps.

Dylan may have heard about Llanina and its lost village on one of
his trips to Newquay in the 1930s, or from Augustus John or
Newquay-born Dewi Emrys. Dylan may have been told the Llanina
ghost stories by Margaret Phillips or one of her daughters. But he
first met Howard de Walden at Llanina in the late 1930s:

> I believe my father met Dylan Thomas through Augustus John,
> whom he had known for many, many years, and that this meet-
> ing with Dylan Thomas took place at or near Llanina in the mid-
> dle 1930s but I cannot place it accurately. It is my recollection
> that it was before 1938, but I do not know when my father
> bought Llanina – probably the meeting took place then or there-
> abouts.[28]

Howard de Walden is not shown on the chain of title of Llanina, which suggests that he took out a long lease on the property. This is confirmed by V.B. Keen, the Property Manager at Chirk Castle, which had been de Walden's principal residence: "I understand Howard de Walden leased Plas Llanina from the late 1930s."[29]

Dylan's visit to Llanina may have been in 1937, when he made his second trip to Aberystwyth to see Caradoc Evans. Or he might have come in 1938 when he was living in Bishopston and Laugharne. Augustus John was in Laugharne in the spring of 1939 when he came down for the christening of Llewelyn, Caitlin and Dylan's first born child. John, who shared a studio in Chelsea with de Walden, often came to Llanina in the war years and Rosemary Seymour, another daughter of de Walden, remembers that he "came to stay and I can clearly visualise him asleep on the stony beach, cap over his eyes, hands clasped over his ample paunch, snoring!"[30] John was allowed to use the family chapel as a make-shift studio.

Contact with de Walden continued through the war. John Davenport approached de Walden in September 1940 to seek support for Dylan and Caitlin. De Walden sent a cheque for £50, and Dylan responded with a letter in December asking for help with accommodation.

Little is known about Dylan's various stays at Plas Llanina. One account is given by Margherita, Howard de Walden's wife:

> One time, when we were at Llanina and I had finished washing and ironing and (how domesticated we had become!) sewing on his buttons, I said I would just go over to the Apple House and collect a few for lunch. "No, no," said Tommy. "You can't go to the Apple House, there is a young man living there!" I was intrigued because the place was so uninhabitable with a hole even in the roof. It appeared that Augustus John, who sometimes passed our way, had talked of a brilliant young poet who was looking for somewhere to sleep and work, and suggested our Apple House! And so the now famous Dylan Thomas took up residence there for a while. I fancy Tommy did more for him than that but I do not know....(1965, p263)

Margherita de Walden does not date this incident though it would have been before her departure for Canada in 1940 or after her return in November 1943. Rosemary Seymour remembers Dylan at Llanina in 1943. Tatiana Mallinson, de Walden's grand-daughter, told me that Dylan was there "off and on throughout the war." She says that Dylan wrote in the Apple House but did not live in it. We may never be sure of the dates, but the Apple House, an early nineteenth century summer house at the bottom of Llanina's walled garden, should now take its rightful place on the long list of sheds, caravans and summer houses that Dylan used for his writing.

We should note, too, that Dylan also wrote in a small, stone building (now roofless) near the cliff edge, and today just visible from the beach below. This was probably a watch-house put there in the previous century by the Customs and Excise.[31]

To date, Llanina has been overlooked by Dylan's critics. Only John Ackerman has noted its influence on the development of *Under Milk Wood*, pointing out that it opens, not with the graveyard dead, but with the voices "of the long drowned". Llanina, Cei Bach and Newquay were shipbuilding communities: some 200 vessels were built there in the nineteenth century, though over half were lost or wrecked, a good many in the treacherous waters of Cardigan Bay. Passmore (1992) has counted over 150 deaths in local graveyards of

13. The Apple House, Plas Llanina

men who died at sea or in foreign ports between 1850 and 1914. The long drowned sailors of *Under Milk Wood* also relate directly to one of the local legends of Llanina, a story of a sailor who haunts the sea shore, wearing an old-fashioned midshipman's outfit – a three-quarter length coat and a soft peaked cap.

'Ballad of the Long-legged Bait' was Dylan's first use of the ballad, and the idea for this form may have originated in the early contacts with de Walden, who loved the Border Ballads. De Walden and Dylan were on good terms and had got on well together "because they both knew and liked Border Ballads, and they used to stride over the hills declaiming them."[32]

Dylan appears to draw upon Llanina in the 'Ballad of the Long-legged Bait', written in early 1941. It is the old village of Llanina, together with its graveyard, church and fields that had been washed out to sea, that Dylan seems to refer to in stanzas 22, 46, 51 and 53. Stanza 37 shows, too, that Dylan was aware of the story of the woman's severed hand that haunted the house. One of the Longcrofts who had lived in Llanina was an officer in the Royal Navy. The story goes that on returning home from many years at sea, he learnt that his wife was entertaining her lover. Blind with anger, he waylaid them in the walled garden and killed the man. His wife fled to the house. As she tried to bar the door to him, he brought out his cutlass and cut off her hand. Since then, the house has been haunted by a woman's white hand, severed and bleeding at the wrist.

An account of these and other ghosts at Llanina can be found in the *Cambrian News*, August 17th, 1973. No doubt these were amongst the ghost stories that Dylan narrated at the house in New York of Santha Rama Rau, a few days before his death.

The lost village exercised a powerful influence over visitors to Llanina. Rosemary Seymour recalls that

> My husband and I spent a part of our honeymoon in Llanina in 1946, which was lovely. It was a really magical place and he loved it as well as I did.
>
> One evening, he was looking out of our bedroom window across the Bay. He asked if there was a church with a choir and bells ringing.[33]

★★★

Kathleen Davies was the cook and housekeeper at Llanina. She is said to have burnt a good deal of material relating to Dylan. She strongly disapproved of him because, they say locally, Dylan had made one, if not several, passes at her. Her husband, Birsha, was the general handyman, as well as the chauffeur. He was willing to do anything, but not always with success. Howard de Walden came down just after the war and was shocked to see how much damage the sea had done to the cliffs upon which Plas Llanina stood. It was estimated that the cliff was disappearing at the rate of a foot a year. He instructed Birsha to build some sea defences, suggesting this should be done in the traditional way with wooden breakwaters. Birsha was adamant that concrete should be used. For the whole of the spring and summer he and Wilfred, his son, moved enormous boulders along the beach to the bottom of the cliff, and finally encased them all in two feet of concrete.

When the first storm of the winter came, de Walden and his family walked across to the cliff edge with Birsha to see how well the concrete held back the sea. Tatiana Mallinson remembers a huge wave coming in and smashing against the concrete defences. When the sea retreated, it took the concrete with it. Birsha stood weeping on the cliff edge, and Mrs Mallinson remembers him shaking his fist at the sea,

14. Lord and Lady Howard de Walden

50

and shouting: "Davy Jones, I'll be even with you yet." They walked back to the house, leaving Birsha alone on the cliff. They found him later in one of the farm buildings. He had swallowed a bottle of aspirins. He was rushed to hospital and recovered.[34] Six large remnants of the concrete can still be seen on the beach, about a hundred yards along from the footpath that leads down from Plas Llanina.

★ ★ ★

After Howard de Walden's death in 1946, his daughter Elizabeth lived in Plas Llanina with her daughters. In the early 1950s, the estate was bought by Col. J.J. and Mrs Betty Davis. Curiously, both Col. and Mrs Davis are linked to the circles round Dylan. Like William Killick, the late J.J. Davis had been in the Royal Engineers, engaged in 'hush-hush, diplomatic work' (as he once described it to his wife) in Greece and Egypt in 1942-43, though not in the SOE. It is possible that he and Killick would have come into contact with each other. Betty Davis never met or knew Dylan when she lived at Llanina. But her mother, writer I.G. Bartholomew, was a good friend of Edith Sitwell and, like her, a member of the Sesame Club. Betty Davis recalls her mother's stories of how enthusiastically Sitwell championed Dylan, both as a man and a poet.

Unwittingly, the Davis's sold Plas Llanina to a Midlands leisure company in the 1960s, and moved to Ty Glyn Mansion, Ciliau Aeron. The company wanted to turn Plas Llanina into a casino and the fields along the cliff into a caravan park. The caravans duly arrived but the casino proposal fell through. The house was left to the mercy of the elements, which had none, and vandals and builders stripped out its fine features. By the late 1980s it was a pile of rubble but in the last ten years it has been completely rebuilt by a retired international banker.

2. Gelli

> What bard that Aeron sees can fail
> To sing the charms of Aeron's vale? (Anon)

One morning, Dylan took himself in hand and masturbated over Talsarn bridge, or so he wrote to his London friend, the art critic Tommy Earp, in August 1942. The river was the Aeron, which rises

15. Plas Gelli, today

in the north of the county, and falls southwards across the bare hills to Talsarn. Here it turns west, curving and curling through fields of thick grass and fat cows to the sea at Aberaeron. This is mansion country: in the six fertile, frequently-flooded miles between Talsarn and the coast there are no fewer than eight country houses, nine if you include Monachty that looks down on the Aeron from afar, as if its founders couldn't trust themselves to be too close to the sewin-drenched waters. In recent years, the fortunes of these grand houses have been mixed. Some are still in private hands, but of the other houses one is a hotel, another the offices of a cheese factory and the last on the river, Nash's wonder at Llanerchaeron, is owned by the National Trust.

There have been few attempts to explore Dylan's time at Plas Gelli. This is partly because Dylan said so little about it himself, and partly because it's hard to tell how much time he, rather than Caitlin, spent there between 1941 and 1943. In some ways, this matter of time is irrelevant: Gelli was a significant element of Dylan's Cardiganshire experience, and one of his friends, Thomas Herbert the vet, has described how Dylan saw the Aeron Valley "as the most precious place in the world." Dylan certainly found Gelli a congenial spot in which to work, and to recover from the excesses of London. In the same August letter to Tommy Earp, he wrote:

> I have been here for over a week with Caitlin, with milk and mild and cheese and eggs, and I feel fit as a fiddle only bigger; I watch the sun from a cool room and know that there are trees being trees outside and that I do not have to admire them; the coun-try's the one place you haven't got to go out in, thank Pan.

Gelli was owned by the Revd Felix Davies, who lived in the vic-arage in Llanddewi Brefi, but it had been rented out since the early 1900s to Thomas and Mary Davies, who farmed the 75 acres. They lived in what was called the 'farm part'; this was the original Jacobean farmhouse, built in the 1680s on the site of an old abbey. In the late eighteenth century, a small, four-room cross wing was added to the farmhouse. This was the 'posh part' rented by Margaret Phillips in which Dylan, Caitlin and the Killicks stayed. (Further details on Gelli and the living arrangements are contained in Appendix 1 in the two interviews with Amanda Williams, the grand-daughter of Thomas and Mary Davies who lived with them on the farm.)

Gelli is an interesting and somewhat complex building. There are excellent notes and photographs on the house in the archive of the Royal Commission on the Ancient and Historical Monuments for Wales. It is usual locally to say that John Nash was the architect of the cross-wing addition but Richard Suggett of the Royal

16. Plas Gelli from within the circle of trees, 1940. Dylan's front bedroom window is on the right-hand side

17. The entrance lodge at Gelli

Commission has rejected this possibility. Gelli is a Grade II listed building because it is one of the best surviving smaller gentry houses in Ceredigion. The octagonal thatched lodge at the head of the drive is also listed, "as a very rare example of a picturesque entrance lodge of the type associated with John Nash". One of the last people to live in the lodge in the 1930s was Liza Botel, so-called because the shape of the lodge was similar to an ink bottle. Like Llanina, Gelli has a walled garden.

It is hard to exaggerate the beauty and peacefulness of Gelli, or the way in which the house is completely engulfed by huge trees. There would have been even more trees when Dylan stayed there. In the 1970's, many mature beeches were felled along the driveway and in front of the house. The stumps were so large they could be removed only by dynamite. And it was the trees at Gelli that seemed to have made the strongest impact on Dylan; in the same letter to Earp he wrote that

> O the summer grew suddenly lovely as the woodland rose in a phalanx
> And the painted privates I thought were bushes moved in their Nash parades.

Seeking Asylum

It's not clear exactly when Margaret Phillips took her family to West Wales. Jeff Milton told Colin Edwards that it was sometime in 1939; this seems to be confirmed by a photograph of Gelli dated 1940 in the possession of the Killick family. Gelli was chosen because it was close to the country of Margaret's childhood, and her various relatives around Newquay. Dylan probably visited Gelli early on in the war, but his first known visit was in 1941. He and Caitlin were living with his parents at Bishopston at the beginning of that year, though they managed to escape for the weekend of February 10th to John Davenport's house.[35] Their next move was to Gelli. FitzGibbon tells us that Dylan and Caitlin went there after the bombing of Swansea in the Three Nights Blitz of February 19th-21st. Dylan was back in Bishopston by March 2nd, writing on that day to H.J.C. Marshall, mentioning that he had been away.

Caitlin and Dylan were back and forth to Gelli until they went to Laugharne in May. The visits became more frequent after Evelyn became pregnant (she had married Jeff Milton in November 1941) and moved out, thus creating more space in the house. Over the next two years, Dylan came down from London to Gelli whenever he

18. The Jacobean 'farm part' of Gelli. The back window of Dylan's bedroom can be seen in the cross-wing

could: "We had a lovely time there, Catty and I," Vera Killick told Paul Ferris. "Dylan used to appear now and again." Theodora FitzGibbon, in whose flat Dylan often stayed in London, has suggested more frequent visits: "Once more, Dylan made the endless journeys back and forth to London." (1982, p.104). It is worth noting that Dylan's visits were frequent and/or long enough for him to have stayed both in Lampeter and Talgarreg – see below.

Vera and Caitlin – who also stayed together at Laugharne – would spend their time at Gelli reading, walking and riding. They also danced together around the house, and Evelyn Milton remembers them having a large collection of records. Caitlin started writing at Gelli, but Dylan, reports Evelyn, didn't approve of this and discouraged Caitlin, on the basis that he was the writer in the family.

Dylan wrote few letters in 1942, and there are just two from Gelli, both in August. One of these was to Ruth Wynn Owen, and it hints at Gelli as a place of refuge, a retreat from the real world:

> I shall go back from Wales on Tuesday. Will you wire me? I think that is best: everything that comes here is unopened except

bottles.... The cocks are crowing in the middle of the afternoon, and the sun is frying.[36]

Evelyn Milton also remembers Dylan at Gelli in 1942 with a film-crew, though she cannot recall the name of the film being shot. It was probably *Wales: Green Mountain, Black Mountain*, a film made for the British Council but released, after several months delay, by the Ministry of Information in March 1943 in both English and Welsh.

1942 was a difficult year for both William Killick and Dylan, and it was then that they probably saw most of each other at Gelli. Killick had returned from Africa in March, and was hospitalised for many months as a result of being trapped under a boat. He spent much time convalescing at Gelli. In November, he was posted to a parachute battalion for training but broke his leg on one of his first jumps. Dylan was having a mixed year, too. He had sold his notebooks to the London dealer Bertram Rota and was now in need of new inspiration for his poems. Norman Cameron had published a poem, 'The Dirty Little Accuser', attacking Dylan for his dirty habits and stealing,

19. The back window of Dylan's bedroom at Gelli where he sometimes worked

sponging ways. Both Dylan and Killick found consolation at Gelli.

The visits to Gelli in 1943 are equally difficult to establish, though Vera was spending more time in London, often with Caitlin. They used to go pubbing together in the West End, and Ferris describes one such outing (1977, p.186). Dylan's letter of Spring 1943 from London indicates the growing friendship between the two women:

> Last night I called on pudding Vera who has been in bed for over a week with apathy and illusions and who said she'd written to you about Gelli. She did not know you were in Laugharne, & when I told her she said could she spend a week or a bit in Laugharne with you before going on with you to Gelli for a week or a bit? And I said I'd tell you, I knew nothing about it.

Another letter was soon on its way: "I think I can get Vera a little part in this film: a tiny part as a pudding-faced blonde sloth but I shan't tell her that." By this time, Vera was preparing for her wedding, and there would have been contact with Dylan and Caitlin in London leading up to the marriage to William Killick in August 1943.

In 1944, Dylan and Caitlin spent April, May and June in Sussex and then near Beaconsfield before moving to Blaen Cwm in late July. It is not clear what contacts there were with Vera and Gelli but some there would have been around the time of the birth of Vera's baby, Rachel, in May, and in setting up the rental of Majoda.

A Gentleman and his Molly

Talsarn is about half-way between Aberaeron and Lampeter, and it was not a remote village, as some books on Dylan have suggested. It's only a few minutes from the A482, which connects with the A40, the London-Carmarthen trunk road, at Llanwrda. Talsarn also had its own railway stop, Talsarn Halt, which linked it with Lampeter and Carmarthen and thus with Swansea and London. This rail connection was one reason the Phillipses chose Gelli. Dylan could have also taken the direct rail service from Swansea to Llanwrda, from which the journey to Gelli by taxi was only forty minutes.

Talsarn is an ancient settlement. Translated, it means 'end of the road', a reference to the Roman road known as Sarn Helen which crosses the countryside near the village. (Helen was a Welsh princess and wife of Maximus, who had designs on being the Emperor of the western Roman Empire.) In Dylan's time, Talsarn was only a tiny village with a handful of houses, the Red Lion pub, a garage, blacksmith, post office and shop. Further up the road towards Gelli was St. Hilary's church and a small country school next to the remains of Trefilan Castle. The Register of Electors for 1939 shows 125 people in Talsarn and its outlying farms and hamlets; only twenty-six of these were in the village itself. A description of the village as it was in the 1940s can be found in my interviews with local man Jenkin Emrys Davies in Appendix 1

Dylan, Caitlin, Vera and William made an impact on the village, partly because Caitlin was Irish and Vera and William were seen as "English people from London...Big bugs." Their appearance also drew them to the attention of Jenkin Emrys Davies:

> Mrs Killick was a lovely blonde, very attractive girl. Oh, Mrs Killick was very, very attractive. Mr Killick, he had fair hair, with a longish face, rather lanky...[37]

The locals were amused to see how Dylan and Killick pushed a pram full of beer home to Gelli every day. They were both noisy after a few drinks, and Killick could become loud and argumentative, even aggressive, understandable in a soldier who was on wartime leave from active service as an elite commando.

When he wasn't writing or drinking, Dylan spent his time walking in the Aeron Valley and talking with the locals. He took an interest in the farm animals at Gelli, as Amanda Williams describes in her first interview. Dylan was also interested in gardening and plants. Dai Isaac Morgan, whose father looked after the garden at Gelli, told me that

> They enjoyed themselves with him, just men from the village. I think he spoke a lot about gardening.... Dylan used to come into the garden to watch my father work, and he knew all about plants and things, so he must have been gardening himself. He knew all the plants.[38]

Perhaps Dai Isaac's comments help to explain why Dylan appeared to be familiar with L.I.F. Brimble's book on British trees, and Reginald Arkell's gardening verse.[39]

Lyn Ebenezer's article in the *Cambrian News* (1967) describes

20. & 21. The Red Lion, Talsarn and The Vale of Aeron, Felinfach

how Dylan enjoyed talking with the local shopkeeper and other tradespeople in the village, gathering information as he was to do later in Newquay:

> While waiting for the [Red Lion] to open he'd spend the time of day sitting on a wooden box by the counter of the local shop chatting to the shopkeeper about everything but literature. He still remembers him as a very ordinary and likeable young man, well spoken with the eternal cigarette drooping limply from his cherubic lips.

Dylan is remembered with more affection at Talsarn than he is at Newquay. Both in the village and the Red Lion, he was regarded as 'a gentleman', though none knew of his growing reputation as a poet. Miss Evans, sister of the landlord of the Red Lion, treated him with great respect:

> Miss Evans thought he was a real gent, a gentlemen to be looked up to. He was very well dressed, you know. Every afternoon, Miss Evans called him from the bar 'You ready, sir?' She used to bring the tray with the tea into the parlour, just for him, and he used to accept it, cakes, and best china, lovely jugs, and he was only on his own, he used to drink his tea in there and he used to come back and have some more beer.[40]

Still, there was worry about newly-born Aeronwy: Dylan used to bring a rope from Gelli and tie her pram to the spot where the horses were tethered. There were also raised eyebrows about Caitlin and Vera:

> The women were all disgusted with Caitlin and Mrs Killick being in the pub. All the women in Talsarn had one eye out of the door watching them going in the Red Lion. That's how it was in them days.[41]

Dylan and Caitlin also used to walk from Talsarn to Felinfach to the Vale of Aeron pub, as Delme Vaughan recalls:

> The only memory I have of Dylan is that he used to walk down from Gelli, cut across from Llanllyr to Glanwern and down to my father's pub.... He was very friendly with my father, Thomas Vaughan, being that my father was a good conversationalist and

had very good English as well.... My father used to have two papers every day and he knew current events pretty well. A good many people came for his conversation. Even when the English people filtered down to this part of the country, once they called with the old man, they'd be there very regularly. He was a born publican, and quite a good scholar. I think he was the attraction for Dylan to come down from Talsarn, it's quite a walk, a good three miles. Caitlin and he were down here very often.[42]

Further information about Dylan at Gelli can be found in the interviews in Appendix 1. Ebenezer's article in the *Cambrian News* also contains extracts from interviews with Talsarn residents, and describes the ordinariness of Dylan's days in the village, and Caitlin's horse-riding adventures. "The people of Talsarn," writes Ebenezer,

don't remember anything of a drunken genius and his vivacious Irish wife but they do remember a young man called Dylan and his beautiful wife known as Molly living up the road at Gelli: 'A lovely couple they were.'

Excursions from Gelli

There were a number of occasions when Dylan and Caitlin, or just Dylan on his own, choose not to stay at Gelli. He once lived in Talgarreg, a small village some five miles inland from Newquay. Thomas Herbert[43] met him there in the Glanyrafon Arms in 1942 (see the interview with Jacqui Lyne, Appendix 1). It's not clear why Dylan was in Talgarreg or how long he stayed. It could be that Gelli was feeling a little crowded, with Killick home recuperating from his illness. Perhaps it was a search for family roots: Gwilym Marles' chapel at Bwlch y Fadfa is a mile and a half from Talgarreg, and his grave at Llwyn Rhydowen just a few miles more. And Ffôs Helyg farm was only two miles away.

It's possible that Dylan was attracted to Talgarreg by the poet Dewi Emrys, who lived in a small cottage opposite the Glanyrafon Arms. Born in Majorca Cottage, Newquay, Emrys won the Crown in the 1926 National Eisteddfod, and the Chair four times. He also wrote in English, and had spent some years in London as a preacher, journalist, bohemian and tramp before settling in Talgarreg in 1940 at the age of 59. He was a cosmopolitan man, and had known writers like Chesterton. He was also a drinking man, carrying beer across the road from the pub in a white enamel jug, cursing "Llaeth, llaeth, llaeth" ("Milk, milk, milk") as the frothy head spilled on the road. He was, according to the *Oxford Companion to the Literature of Wales*, a colourful personality. "He wasn't a drunk," says Eluned Phillips, his biographer, "he liked people and pubs." This, of course, is a description that has often been applied to Dylan. Indeed, Phillips describes Dewi Emrys as "the all-Welsh prototype of Anglo-Welsh Dylan Thomas" (in Macdonald, 1976, p.99).

Eluned Phillips confirms that Dewi Emrys and Dylan knew each other from their London days, and that she met with both of them there.[44] She says that Dylan and Caitlin were not likely to have stayed with Dewi Emrys because they were not such good friends. There is no indication as to where they were staying in Talgarreg.

FitzGibbon (p.253) tells us that Dylan sometimes took a room in the Castle Hotel, Lampeter, when he was unable to find peace and quiet at Gelli. In the Colin Edwards tapes, the landlord of the Castle, Edward Evans, confirms that Dylan often stayed and ate there, working hard to finish film scripts. Dylan drank in the public bar... "he wasn't very fond of the satins and silks." Evans remembers that Dylan "was very Welshy in his normal conversation." He showed no interest in religion or politics but "if he felt someone was having a wrong deal, he was an aggressor to the administrators." Dylan enjoyed singing Welsh hymns with the boys from the rugby team, and spent much time walking in the grounds of Lampeter theological college, whose architecture he admired. Evans recalls that Dylan was liked around Lampeter and that

> I never saw him overdoing it in company..he stuck to beer very severely...although he had one little thing that he taught me. He'd have a gin and tonic in the morning and he'd call it an eye opener, and I've always stuck to it.

Evans sometimes met Dylan in London "and we used to go places where we'd meet Welsh singers, and nothing pleased him more than to join in an afternoon's singing.... He'd love hymns, it was amazing the knowledge he had of Welsh hymns...". 'Dafydd y Carreg Wen' was Dylan's favourite.

The Gelli Poems

I believe there are three poems that were about Gelli or set there: 'In Country Sleep', 'Love in the Asylum' and 'A Winter's Tale'. I shall also explain in the next section how Gelli inspired the title *Under Milk Wood*. It is hard to say what other poems were worked on at Gelli. The best approach is to examine *Deaths and Entrances*. If we exclude poems written before February 1941 and those written at Newquay from September 1944 onwards, then we have only a handful of poems to consider, and most of these can be dated to places other than Gelli:

The hunchback in the park	revised Laugharne in July 1941
On the Marriage of a Virgin	revised January-June 1941
Ceremony after a Fire Raid	written at Bosham 1944
Among those Killed	written in Bradford 1941
Lie still, sleep becalmed	written at Bosham 1944
Ballad of the Long-legged Bait	written at Bishopston January -April 1941
Vision and Prayer	finished by August 1944
Holy Spring	finished by November 1944
Poem in October	finished by August 1944

We know from the notes at the end of *Collected Poems* that the last three poems were developed at various times through the war and it is likely therefore that they would have been worked on at Gelli, and elsewhere of course. 'On the Marriage of a Virgin' and 'Ballad of the Long-Legged Bait' probably received attention at Gelli, too.

Finally, for the sake of the record, we should note the 'war poem' about Gelli contained in Dylan's letter to Tommy Earp of August 30th 1942. The fighting language of the poem is due not just to the war but also to the presence of William Killick at Gelli, and to the name of the house a few hundred yards north of the mansion – Foxholes. Quite close was another called Eden. There is a reference in the poem to the training of commandos; no doubt Dylan would have learnt something of this from Killick. The last part of the poem seems to poke fun at the fieldwork techniques used by under-cover soldiers.

Love in the Asylum

Dylan sometimes wrote about the supernatural, and one of these poems is 'Love in the Asylum'. Dylan's letter to M.J. Tambimuttu of February 19th 1941 indicates that the poem had been started but was unfinished. It was sent to Tambimuttu for publication at the end of the April 1941, so it is clear that Dylan would have worked on it whilst he was staying at Gelli after the Swansea blitz and before going to Laugharne. 'Love in the Asylum' is a poem that has attracted no comment from Dylan's biographers, and little interpretation from his critics. This is probably because few people knew about Dylan's time at Gelli, and biographers such as FitzGibbon have even described Gelli as a very small and crowded cottage.

'Love in the Asylum' could have little meaning unless the reader knew about the ghost at Gelli (see the second interview with Amanda Williams, Appendix 1) and the evacuees who had come there from Liverpool. It is a moot point whether the not-right-in-the-head stranger was a reference to the ghost or the evacuee teacher who had come with the schoolchildren. If the latter, then Dylan's bawdy line about riding "the imagined oceans of the male wards" was not a reference to hospitals but to the hot-loined schoolboys put in the teacher's charge. However, it seems more likely that the reference is to the woman ghost at Gelli, who shared Dylan's room, as he describes in the first stanza. It was in the small window of Dylan's bedroom that Amanda Williams' grandfather used to see the ghost as he walked across the farmyard.

The word 'asylum' is a double entendre; it is meant to refer to Gelli as a house inhabited by a mad ghost, but also as a house that was a place of safety for Caitlin and Dylan i.e. the house was 'heaven-proof', as Dylan put it in the second stanza, keeping them safe from the bombs that were raining down from the heavens, and thus proof from death (the ascent to heaven). The poem is a direct response to the bombing of Swansea, from which Dylan escaped to Gelli, but it is also a general comment on "the madness of war's air raids and blackouts" (Davies, 1997a).

In Country Sleep

This poem was written mostly in Italy between April and July 1947.

I suggest that Dylan drew on his memories of Gelli in writing the poem, which some believe is addressed to Aeronwy. It is set in a damp and misty vale, and I am sure this is the Vale of Aeron. The poem evokes the lush Welsh countryside that Dylan missed so much in the oppressive heat and dryness of Tuscany. The reference to buttermilk in stanza twelve recalls the days when Dylan sat writing in the yard at Gelli whilst Amanda Williams' grandmother milked the cows.

The first stanza of the poem refers to a house at the heart of a wood. This points to Gelli. In the fourteenth stanza, the house is described as 'haloed'. Gelli was owned in the 1940s by a local vicar, and was built on the site of an abbey. The footpath that runs from east to west between Gelli and the Aeron is called 'The Monks' Trod'. Gelli has a powerful spiritual atmosphere. It is what the early Celtic Christians called a 'thin place', where one feels close to God and the divine. The trees at Gelli are an outdoor cathedral, (a dome of leaves, as Dylan describes it, in the fourth stanza of the poem) with the white mansion a little altar within. 'In Country Sleep' is a poem of sacred places, of nunneries (the neighbouring mansion of Llanllyr stands on the site of a nunnery), prayers and chants, bells, saints and angels, three Marys, gospels and miracles, the sanctum sanctorum, a saint's cell, a priest's house. The poem begins with a reference to a woman riding across the countryside which is exactly what Caitlin did at Gelli. It's also a poem of trees and woods, full of shady and mysterious places, set in a mist-filled vale of ferns and dew, Bethel rooks cawing above the farmyard and acrobatic squirrels in the grove beyond. And the humble thatched house in the seventh stanza is the Lodge that stands at the entrance to the main driveway.

The poem take us back nostalgically to the Gelli-green, tree-full, dragon-less days before the Killick shooting, before the alphabetical bomb, before the coming of all these thieves and more. Gelli was a place of sanctuary, Dylan's "greenwood keep", as he calls it in the poem.

A Winter's Tale

This poem was sent to Vernon Watkins on March 28th, 1945. It had been written at Majoda during a long winter which culminated in what the *Cambrian News* called "the coldest spell within memory", so cold in fact that many rivers froze[45]. It is clear from the first three stanzas that the countryside of "floating fields" and a farmhouse cupped in the folds of a vale is the flood plain of the Vale of Aeron. The Vale was, and still is, prone to flooding each year, sometimes to disastrous effect, as described in my interviews with Jenkin Emrys Davies. The folded nature of the country around Gelli can best be appreciated by taking the footpath ('The Monks' Trod') from Talsarn. Climb up past Wern Fach cottage, with Gelli just a few hundred yards to your right, until you emerge on a high meadow. Here you can immediately see why Dylan talked of "the cup of the vales" and "a fold/Of fields".

The views of the farmyard described in the fifth and seventh stanzas are exactly those Dylan would have seen from his little, back bedroom window at Gelli. The spit and the black pot and the bread in the sixth stanza refer, as Amanda Williams describes in her second interview, to the Ty Pair, the old servants' quarters containing an open fire, a cauldron, a bread oven and a wicker chimney, which are still there. The "home of prayers" in the eighth stanza recalls the "haloed house" of 'In Country Sleep', and is another reference both to the time when there was an abbey on the site of Gelli, and to its ownership in the 1940s by a local vicar.

The stream in the thirteenth stanza is the Nant y Fergi which Dylan could see and hear from his front bedroom window. Why does he describe the stream as baying? Because a 'bergi' was a breed of dog with very short legs, once used for turning spits. Nant y Fergi means Bergi Creek, or the creek of the short-legged dog. The reference in the seventh stanza to statues on the stables confirms that Dylan was thinking of Gelli. The second interview with Amanda Williams reveals that there had once been a statue at the Gelli stables.

Another clue for the literary detective is the position of 'A Winter's Tale' in the collection *Deaths and Entrances*. It is the second of five poems that Dylan placed next to each other and which deal, in different ways, with the themes of war, love and marriage. It is a confusing poem and Dylan admitted it was not a coherent piece, despite having taken months to write. It is possible that Dylan was working at Majoda on drafts of the poem when the news came to Vera in December 1944 that Killick was safe and would soon be on his way home. Perhaps this news changed the development of the poem.

The Gelli Notebook

William and Vera Killick's daughter, Rachel Willans, has a notebook which was given to her by her mother. The notebook came from Gelli. The first page is a preliminary list of poems for *Deaths and Entrances*, and the second contains the first twenty-three lines of 'Unluckily for a Death' with which Dylan had intended to start the collection. Both pages are written in Dylan's own handwriting. The rest of the notebook is filled with a play written by the eight-year old Rachel.

The list for *Deaths and Entrances* was probably written in the autumn of 1941 or early 1942 since the last poem – 'My Twenty Seventh Year' – refers to Dylan's birthday in October 1941. This poem was published as 'Poem in October' in *Deaths and Entrances*, with the first line "It was my thirtieth year to heaven". It is reasonable to suppose that this poem was sufficiently well developed in late 1941 for Dylan to consider it for inclusion in *Deaths and Entrances*. It was not written, therefore, at Blaen Cwm in 1944, as Ferris tentatively suggests.[46] This birthday poem is, as Dylan observed in his letter to Vernon Watkins of August 26th 1944, a Laugharne poem, probably originating in Dylan's time there in the Spring of 1941.

The holograph of the first lines of 'Unluckily for a Death' is

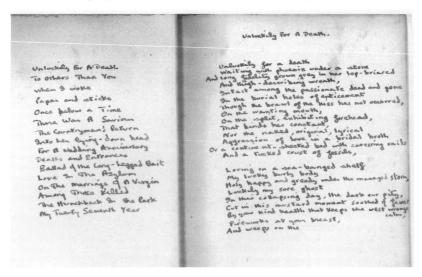

22. Dylan's Gelli Notebook

exactly as the poem was published in *Life and Letters Today*, October 1939 as 'Poem (To Caitlin)'. The interesting thing about this holograph is why Dylan stopped so abruptly in the middle of the twenty-third line when writing it out.

Dylan was unhappy with 'Unluckily for a Death' as soon it was written but it was not revised until he was at Blaen Cwm in September 1945. I shall suggest in Chapter 4 that the revision partly reflects his experience of the Majoda shooting but it is also worth noting that there are clues in the poem that Dylan was actively thinking about it whilst he was at Gelli in 1942 and 1943. In particular, it contains a number of the religious references that we find in the two other Gelli poems, 'In Country Sleep' and 'A Winter's Tale', namely, saints, cloister, choir, nunnery, breviary, and prayers, all of which were absent from the 1939 version. The repetition of 'shades' also evokes arboreal Gelli.

The Milky Valley

The town of Llareggub lies under, or below, Milk Wood. Brinnin has claimed that Dylan first suggested the title in September 1952, after complaints that Americans would not take to Llareggub Hill, or see

23. The milking wood, Ciliau Aeron, the 1970s

the joke. On the other hand, Dylan says in his letter to Prys-Jones of November 21st 1952, that the play has "No title yet, only an unprintable one." – Llareggub. But by March 18th 1953, it was referred to in a letter to Brinnin as *Under Milk Wood*, and performed for the first time at the Poetry Centre, New York, in May.

There have been surprisingly few attempts to explain the name, and those who have tried emphasis the need to understand Dylan's love of word play. Ferris refers to "one ingenious critic" who mooted a connection with milkwood trees, which secrete latex (1977, p288n). Cardwell has suggested a link with the hamlet of Nant y Caws (Cheese Brook) through which Dylan would have travelled many times on his way to Blaen Cwm.[47] There may also be an association with Selwood Place (salt wood or white wood), the London address of Dylan's friend, Mary Keene. Llwyn Gwyn (white grove or wood) was the name of the farm near Blaen Cwm where some of Dylan's relatives lived. And Caradoc Evans' home at New Cross was only a few miles from the hamlet of Wenallt (white wood or hill).

In this section, I want to suggest two origins of the name, and they are not in the least mutually exclusive. First, the 'cows and trees' theory. This was put forward by John Ackerman in *Welsh Dylan*. He speculates that the name has something to do with the cows kept for "generations past" on the wooded slopes of Sir John's Hill, Laugharne. This sounds reasonable but much more can be made of it within the context of Newquay. Jack Patrick of the Black Lion kept a herd of milking cows in the fields ("Cae Black Lion") on the wooded hill above Newquay, and ran a dairy from the hotel. The cows were driven down through the streets for milking at the stables (now an amusement arcade) next to the Black Lion. Thus Newquay lay below, or under, the milky, wooded slopes of Cae Black Lion. The contiguity of woods, cows and the Black Lion is caught in Roy Morgan's 1954 painting of Llareggub, which shows the gable-end of a pub and, just as it was at Newquay, cows in a stable next to it.[48] The painting is reproduced on page 20

But I believe that the name Milk Wood mostly derives from Dylan's time at Gelli, which means "grove", and is one of the many Welsh words that can refer to a wood. I have already described how the woodland around Gelli and its farm buildings does indeed rise like a phalanx: huge beech trees, interspersed with oaks and red-woods, surround the house, so much so that Gelli is virtually invisible except from high ground.

24. Under the redwood, where Dylan wrote.

25. The redwood and the house at Gelli.

Amanda Williams relates in her interviews (Appendix 1) how Dylan used to write sitting on a stool in the farmyard. She also describes his great liking for the fresh milk that her grandmother

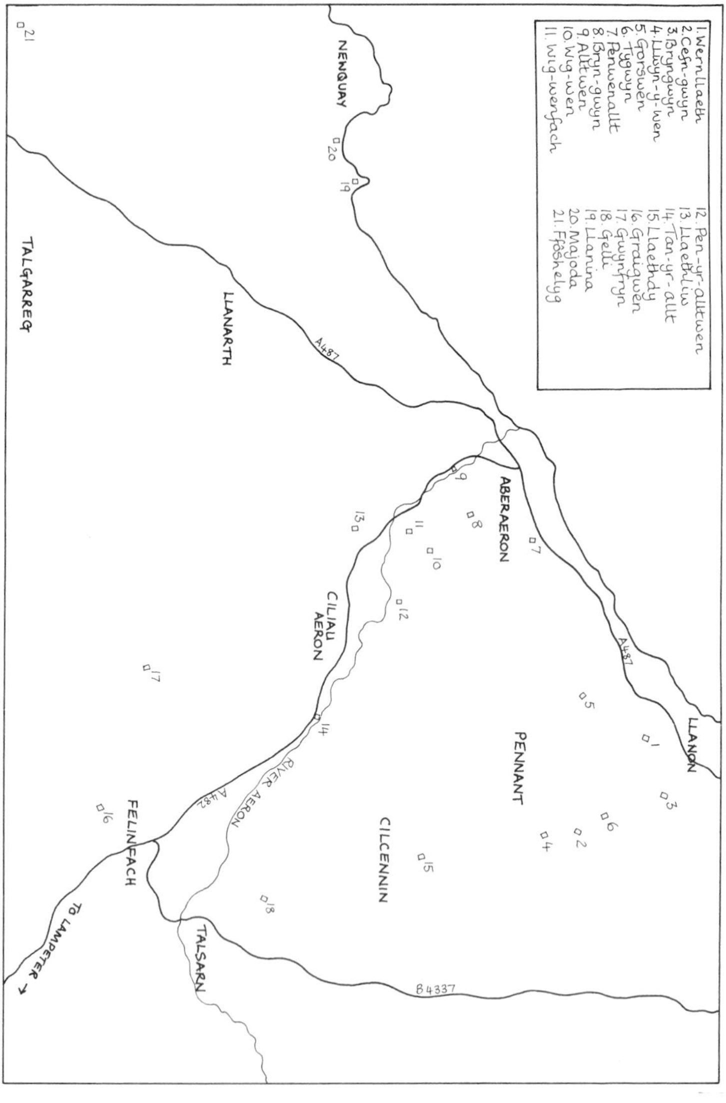

26. Newquay and the Aeron Valley

brought him, and how he used to talk with her whilst she was milk-
ing the cows. The stool on which Dylan sat was under a Canadian
redwood that is at least three times as high as the mansion, and only
a few yards from its door. The tree, with its branches hanging down
like a ballerina's outstretched arms sweeping the stage, was closely
circled by eight (now seven) beeches, forming a huge, wood-framed,
leaf-skinned, sky-touching wigwam in which Dylan sat. It was here
on his stool, under the wood, that Dylan enjoyed his daily tumblers
of frothy milk. And Dylan himself gives us the significant clue: in the
verses of Rev. Eli Jenkins' morning service, the tiny dingle of Milk
Wood is compared with the other, much larger and better-known
Gelli – Golden Grove (Gelli Aur), near Llandeilo.

Yet it was the whole of the lower Aeron Valley and its surround-
ing hills, not just Gelli, that provided the inspiration for the name
Milk Wood. To explore this, we need to know the many words in
Welsh for a wood (wern, gwig or wig, gelli, llwyn, allt, coed, for
example) and just as many for a hill (allt, rhiw, bryn, cefn). Note,
too, that the Welsh for white can appear as gwyn or wen. Thus *Under
Milk Wood* is usually translated into Welsh as Dan y Wenallt (alter-
natively expressed as Dan yr Alltwen), that is, Under the White
Wood or White Hill.

The area in and around the Aeron Valley from the sea to Talsarn
abounds with houses and farms that take their name from white
woods and hills. It would be hard to find such a concentration in any
other part of Wales. Wernllaeth Farm is of particular significance
because it means Milk Alder-Grove Farm but translates more natu-
rally as Milk Wood Farm. It is a few miles from Gelli at Pennant.[49]
Around Wernllaeth Farm, we find Cefn-gwyn Farm, Bryngwyn Farm
and Llwyn-y-wen Farm. This milky, wooded constellation is further
strengthened by Gorswen Farm (white bog) and Tygwyn (white
house).

Starting at Aberaeron and following the river Aeron inland, we
find farms called Penwenallt (top of the white wood/hill), Bryn-gwyn,
Alltwen, Wig-wen, Wig-wen Fach, Pen-yr-alltwen and Llaethliw
(Milk Aspect).[50] All these are within a mile or so of each other and
form a distinctive white woody cluster. And then, a little further up-
river, we find Tan-yr-Allt Farm (Under the Wood Farm – a variant
of 'Dan yr Allt').[51] Directly above Tan-yr-Allt in the village of
Cilcennin we find Llaethdy Farm (Milk House or Dairy Farm). We
should note, too, that Tan-yr-Allt Farm is less than two miles from

27. Wernllaeth

28. Llaethliw

29. Llaethdy

30. Tan-yr-Allt

the Vale of Aeron pub where Dylan used to drink. Quite close in the hills behind the pub, there's Graigwen Farm (white rock) and Gwynfryn Farm (white hill).

All this might have passed Dylan by, had it not been for his friendship with Thomas Herbert, the vet in nearby Aberaeron. As a local man and a family historian, he knew these farms and houses well. He was bilingual, and took as much interest in word play, and the origin and meaning of words, as did Dylan. According to Jacqui Lyne, Herbert was particularly interested in local place names. This was confirmed by Ron Matthews, former history master at Aberaeron School, who told me:

> I was walking past Tommy Herbert's house, he was outside painting the railings. I asked him about the place up north where the eisteddfod was being held, just trying to catch him out. We got talking about Dylan and Tommy mentioned how he was always explaining various place names to Dylan.

It's appropriate to acknowledge Herbert's role, and perhaps that of Margaret Phillips, in helping Dylan understand the significance of the short stretch of bosky valley between Aberaeron and Talsarn that inspired the name Milk Wood and thus the title *Under Milk Wood*. Not just milky Gelli, nor the farms named after white hills and woods, but especially the farms called Milk Wood, Milk Aspect, Milk House and Under the Wood.

Thomas Herbert lived close to Milk Wood – his house in Belle Vue Terrace, Aberaeron, was just a few doors away from one called Wenallt. And Herbert, who enjoyed a long friendship with the bardic poet Gwenallt, may even have reminded Dylan that Dylan himself had lived under Milk Wood – Alltwen is a small village outside Swansea, not a milk splash away from Cwmdonkin Drive. Later at Newquay, the milky white images of the Aeron Valley would have been reinforced by the names around Majoda: Traethgwyn, Morfa Gwyn, Maesgwyn and Brongwyn.

We must remember, too, that Dylan loved the Aeron Valley, as Tommy Herbert noted in his interview in *Y Cymro*: "Dylan had lived for a period in Talsarn, and he always wanted me to take him up through the Aeron Valley, one of his favourite areas."[52] Herbert makes the same point more forcefully in his essay:

He spoke of the Aeron Valley as the most precious place in the world, and we decided to go to Llangeitho some sunny afternoon before long. Going for a walk from Talsarn to Llangeitho at that time was magical. That was the era before they widened and straightened the road. There were cottages and smallholdings at the side of the road, and you'd see people gossiping together; sometimes a hamlet or collection of dwellings, like Llundain Fach, every house with flowers round the door and windows. Dylan had walked it a number of times and made friends with the talented people who lived along it, like Jac Pentrefelin and Griff Sychpant.[53]

The Aeron was a river of plenty; not only was it bursting with salmon and sea trout, but the very word 'aeron' means fruits, berries and grain. It is the river of the autumn harvest. The stream of fertility and fecundity that flows through *Under Milk Wood* welled up in the Vale of Aeron. It was here, on the banks of the fruitful river, under white woods and milky farms, that baby Aeronwy was conceived, and much, much else besides.

Indeed, the milky farms were so productive that on May 10th 1951, some eighteen months before Dylan's trip from Laugharne to Aberystwyth, the Milk Marketing Board opened a processing and distribution depot at Green Grove,[54] a wooded mansion just up the road from the Vale of Aeron pub at Felinfach, and not two miles across the river Aeron from Plas Gelli. Green Grove had become Milk Wood.

A Majoda Poem

(untitled)

Dear Tommy, please, from far, sciatic Kingsley
Borrow my eyes. The darkening sea flings Lee
And Perrins on the cockled tablecloth
Of mud and sand. And, like a sable moth,
A cloud against the glassy sun flutters his
Wings. It would be better if the shutter is
Shut. Sinister dark over Cardigan
Bay. No-good is abroad. I unhardy can
Hardly bear the din of No-good wracked dry on
The pebbles. It is time for the Black Lion
But there is only Buckley's unfrisky
Mild. Turned again, Worthington. Never whisky.
I sit at the open window, observing
The salty scene and my Playered gob curving
Down to the wild, umbrella'd, and french-lettered
Beach, hearing rise slimy from the Welsh lechered
Caves the cries of the parchs and their flocks. I
Hear their laughter sly as gonococci...
There slinks a snoop in black. I'm thinking it
Is Mr Jones the Cake, that winking-bit,
That hymning gooseberry, that Bethel-worm
At whose ball-prying even death'll squirm
And button up. He minces among knickers,
That prince of pimps, that doyen of dung-lickers.
Over a rump on the clerical-grey seashore,
See how he stumbles. Hallelujah hee-haw!,
His head's in a nest where no bird lays her egg.
He cuts himself on an elder's razor leg.
Sniff, here is sin! Now must he grapple, rise:
He snuggles deep among the chapel thighs,
And when the moist collection plate is passed
Puts in his penny, generous at last.

Part of a letter/poem sent by Dylan Thomas to Tommy Earp
from Majoda, September 1944, *Collected Letters*.

3. The Bungalow

...home was not built in a day.
Dylan to Princess Caetani, September 1951

Dylan and Caitlin lived in Majoda from September 1944 to July 1945. Dylan did some of his best work there, and his output in the autumn and winter of 1944 was prodigious. It has become common to think of Dylan and Newquay only in relation to these nine months. Dylan's association with the town goes much further back, and I've suggested in Chapter 1 that he may even have visited the area as a child with Margaret Phillips. Moreover, Dylan had a first cousin in Newquay, Theodosia Legg, who had moved there from Swansea in 1929. Her son, George, remembers stories that Dylan visited the Leggs "on the scrounge" and that this was "almost certainly" in the middle-to-late 1930s.[55] This might have been at the time of Dylan's visits to Caradoc Evans in Aberystwyth in 1934 and 1937. One of Dylan's first references to the chapel 'Bethels' appears in his letter of October 1934 to Pamela Hansford Johnson describing his encounter with Evans. 'Bethel' is a common name for chapels in Wales, but it is also the name of the chapel that dominates the upper part of, and the entry to, Newquay.

It is difficult to trace Dylan's movements during the war years, not least because he seems to have put less effort into his correspondence, as Ferris has noted:

> Thomas's movements, never easy to follow, become baffling in wartime. He wrote fewer letters than before, and shuttled between Wales and London, seeking work and dodging bombs. (1985, p.468n).

There are only thirty-four letters in 1941, seventeen in total for 1942 and 1943 and thirty in 1944, compared with one hundred and seventeen in 1939. We have, therefore, to rely much more on individual 'sightings' and reports of Dylan and Caitlin if we want to establish where they visited and lived.

It is more than likely Dylan called at Newquay when he visited

79

Llanina in 1938/39. Jacqui Lyne recalls her husband Thomas Herbert describing a drinking session with Dylan in the Black Lion in 1942. Dylan was also likely to have been in Newquay that year for the filming of *Wales: Green Mountain, Black Mountain* (the film ends with a reference to Cardigan Bay and the film crew were at Gelli with him, as we noted in the previous chapter). Wendy Flenard remembers Caitlin in Newquay at that time:

> Wendy recalls Caitlin in NQ possibly '41, but definitely summer '42, pushing a pram in front of Cliffside, adjacent park, and going into the Cambrian Drapery then owned by NQ old timer 'J.P.' (Davies). Wendy went into the WRNS Feb. '43, and did not come back to NQ until after the end of the war. By then Dylan and Caitlin would have come and gone.[56]

Jacqui Lyne has confirmed that Dylan was in and around Newquay and Llanina when Augustus John was doing his portrait of Rosemary Seymour. Mrs Seymour has said that this was in 1943.[57] Certainly Dylan knew the town (and the Cross Inn a few miles outside) well enough by 1943 to write about "the secret life of Newquay" in his "side-splitting and scandalous" pub poem.[58] There were certainly other visits to Newquay in 1942 and 1943 but we will probably never find out about them.

We know, too, that Dylan met Newquay people in London so that he would have been kept up to date on the town between his visits. It has been suggested that

> Dylan would have, in conversation with his Newquay friends, been well informed on the goings-on that had occurred well before his arrival in the village [in 1944].[59]

This continuity with the people and events of Newquay, both through his own pre-1944 visits and the stories told to him by Newquay people in London, is important in understanding the town's influence on *Under Milk Wood*.

The Cardi Boys

Majoda was on the outskirts of Newquay, about a mile out of the town. This did not prevent Dylan and Caitlin playing an active part in many aspects of the town's social life. They quickly acquired a

31. Jack Patrick and Betty Evans, 1930s

range of friends and drinking companions, both locals and those escaping the bombing of London and other cities. Here I introduce some of these people; with one or two exceptions, their friends were men.

The person who is key to understanding Dylan's contacts in Newquay is Jack Patrick Evans. He was usually known as Jack Patrick and he was the landlord of the Black Lion (he had previously been a clothing buyer in London in the 1930s).[60] He and his wife Betty kept a very hospitable pub, often with scarce attention to licensing hours, and with a great willingness to provide food for Dylan and his group into the early hours of the morning. Jack Patrick was fifteen years older than Dylan and the two of them were close friends, but Jack was always reluctant in later years to talk about their time together. Dylan refers to the Black Lion in a number of letters, but the most extended description is in his August 1946 letter to Margaret Taylor, in which he writes:

TO J. P. WITH THE COMPLIMENTS OF
THE "TRE-DARE" BOYS.

32. Jack Patrick Evans,
early 1950s

One day, how odd and good it would be to spend together, in this timeless, drizzled, argufying place, some very unOxford days. I wish New Quay had had more sun for you, though Jack Pat loves it as it is for then he has his guests all trapped and cosy in his godly grot. Time has stopped, says the Black Lion clock, and Eternity has begun.

Dylan also asks in this letter "Did Pat bring his horse in the bar?" Jack Pat was very keen on fox hunting and frequently rode to hounds, often coming back inebriated. On one occasion, he rode his horse into the bar of the Black Lion, causing so much damage that the repairs took several days. He was, nevertheless, an accomplished horseman; when in London, he had earned extra money by teaching the children of the aristocracy to ride in Hyde Park.

Jack Patrick was an avid reader, and had a special arrangement

33. Dora Pengraig and her brother, John Oswald Jones, early 1920s

with the library to take out ten books a week. His niece, Ann Brodie, told me that his bedroom

> ...was floor to ceiling with books and I remember piles of books always by the side of his bed... he had a brilliant mind and a great spirit... the people that came to the Black Lion in those days were wonderful. Clever, educated, fascinating people... Jack Patrick Evans was one of the most fascinating of those characters."

Many painters were attracted to Cardiganshire, including John Piper, Grant Murray and, occasionally, Ceri Richards. Murray was the inspirational Principal of the Swansea School of Art. He regularly came to Newquay and the Black Lion, and his paintings can still be found in some of the houses of the town. On one occasion, Jack

Patrick held onto Murray's ankles as he leaned out of the window of the Pier Hotel to paint the harbour. Jack Pat was often absent or *hors de combat*, so the day-to-day business of running the hotel lay largely in the hands of Dora Pengraig. She got on well with Dylan and Caitlin. Besides looking after Aeronwy, she sometimes had to put Dylan to bed, usually in Room 13 in the Lion. Dora also helped them to find supplies of food, often bringing potatoes and eggs from her brother John Oswald Jones, who had a neighbouring farm to Ffôs Helyg.

The circle of friends that were brought together in the Black Lion included Thomas Herbert, Alastair Graham, Captain John Davies, Captain Tom Polly, Dewi Evans (Ianthe), Griff Jenkins Senior and Thomas Jones (Butcher OK). Augustus John was also an important person in Dylan's Newquay life, not least because he walked the Thomas' dog and often looked after Aeronwy – he was spotted early one morning leaving Plas y Wern pushing a pram: "There'd obviously been a heavy session and Caitlin and Dylan were out for the count so Augustus John had to baby-sit for them."[61]

Thomas Herbert first met Dylan in 1942 in Talgarreg but only

34. Thomas Herbert

really got to know him well in 1944-45. Herbert had qualified at the Royal Veterinary College in London and his practice was just along the coast from Newquay in Aberaeron. He had a passion for words and language, and a great love of literature and local history. He became an accomplished raconteur and writer, producing one book written in Welsh about his experiences as a vet. He is still remembered with affection in the town, for his charitable work, his service as a councillor and his frequent broadcasts and lectures.

Alastair Graham was the person who dealt effectively with William Killick on the night of the infamous shooting. Graham was from Border landed gentry. He was the nephew of the Duchess of Montrose and, on his mother's side, related to General Robert E. Lee. Born in 1904 and educated at Wellington, Graham went to Brasenose College, Oxford, where he was Evelyn Waugh's lover and closest friend. He appears in *A Little Learning*, the first and only volume of Waugh's autobiography, as 'Hamish Lennox'. Waugh has confirmed that Graham contributed to the character of Sebastian Flyte in *Brideshead Revisited*.

35. Alastair Graham (centre) with Tom Rees (right) and friend

36. Plas y Wern, 1936

Graham joined the diplomatic service in 1926 and left in 1933, after a gay sex scandal involving the second Viscount Tredegar, poet, painter and patron of the arts in Wales. Graham, who knew both Augustus John[62] and Howard de Walden, lived in Plas y Wern, a large mansion on the outskirts of Newquay, which he had bought in 1936 after returning from Tangiers. He had come to Newquay and found Plas y Wern whilst staying in Portmeirion with Clough Williams-Ellis. Even before Graham's arrival, the Wern "long had as strong a lure for the literary stranger as for the wandering antiquary... with its thick walls and massive chimneys, bell-shaped roofs and imposingly carved entrance door."[63] Henry Tudor is reputed to have slept there on his way to the Battle of Bosworth.

Graham was an extremely private man, both at Newquay and before. "I was good friends with Alastair for years," Michael Williams told me, "but I knew virtually nothing about him." Graham managed to evade the close attentions of Waugh's biographers and prying journalists, and only Fallowell (1990) has succeeded in uncovering some detail, but not a good deal, about Graham's life after Waugh. Little has ever emerged about his forty-six years in Newquay.

Graham led an active social life at the Wern, including house parties for visitors from London and elsewhere. We shall see in Chapter

6 that these included people from the intelligence services. There were visits, too, from Graham's friends in literary circles, the aristocracy (including his former lover, Lord Tredegar) and, according to Tommy Herbert, from Edward VIII. Other friends included David Bowes-Lyon, Anthony Lygon and Compton Mackenzie, who often visited the Wern, and shared Graham's passion for Greece, where he, Mackenzie, had been in counter-intelligence during the 1914-1919 war. When the Stone of Scone was taken in 1951 from Westminster Abbey, the authorities thought Mackenzie was responsible. Graham was subject to questioning by both the police and MI5, who thought the Stone had been hidden at the Wern.[64]

Graham's interests at Newquay were varied: books and literature, cooking, cheese making, entertaining, sailing, playing the oboe, painting, embroidery, interior decoration, decorative knots and braiding, and making deck shoes out of sail cloth and rope.[65] He published a pamphlet called *20 Different Ways of Cooking New Quay Mackerel*. He took a part in promoting the well-being of Newquay, using his political connections to further its interests e.g. he was instrumental in preventing the closure of the lifeboat station just after the war. He was liked and respected, and was generous to Newquay residents, often bringing them cakes and tarts he had cooked himself. He also gave away his 'treasures': Eleanor Lister and her husband were presented with, but refused, a silver belt, too heavy to hold in one hand. But Graham was also very self-centred, with exacting standards both for himself and others. He had an "an evil temper", and on one occasion stuck a fork through the hand of local resident Capper Jenkins.

Dylan, Herbert and Graham were drinking and reading companions, though Graham's views on Dylan could often be very uncharitable. They were occasionally joined by Clough Williams-Ellis. Thomas Herbert has related in two television interviews in the late 1980s that the bardic poet Dewi Emrys of Talgarreg was also part of the group that oscillated between the Black Lion and Plas y Wern.[66]

Captain John Davies was retired from the army. He had left his wife in middle age and lived in the hotels and pubs of Newquay. By day, he painted scenes of Newquay life and sold them for a small living. By night, he was active in the pubs and a party-goer at Plas y Wern. Davies was also a friend of Thomas Herbert the vet, and Herbert notes the Captain's friendship with Dylan on a letter he received from Gwen Davies.[67]

Tom Polly was Captain Thomas Davies who lived in Gomer House, opposite the Black Lion. He started work as an apprentice in a chemist's shop in Swansea but ran away to sea and eventually became a master mariner. He had retired in the late 1930s and his favourite pastime, besides being in the Black Lion, was to stand outside his house watching the 'monkey parade' move up and down the hill, and keeping an eye on the activity in the harbour below. In the summer, he and his wife took in visiting holidaymakers. His expression for opening time at the Black Lion ("codi'r latch", meaning "lift the latch") became part of the Newquay vocabulary. For some of the war, he was a censor based in Fishguard, reading the letters going to and from Ireland.

Dewi Evans was, amongst other things, Dylan's volunteer driver, often giving him a lift home from the pub. He was an ex-merchant marine officer, and ran a little electrical and radio shop in Aberaeron, opposite the Town Hall. He was also known locally as Dewi Ianthe, after the house in which he lived, though Dylan tended to call him Dewi Battery. A tall, cheerful man, he was practically-minded and,

37. Dewi Ianthe in his Royal Observer Corps uniform

as far as we know, had little interest in books and poetry, though he did play the mandolin, as well as the mouth organ and piano.

Griff Jenkins Senior came from an old Newquay family and lived in Arfon View, Francis Street. He had joined the RAF in 1930 and reached the rank of Flight Lieutenant, but was redeployed in the early part of the war to the Air Transport Auxiliary because of a recurrence of TB. He first met Dylan in London in the early 1940s. Griff also became friends with Augustus John at that time. He was, too, on good terms with some of John's friends, especially Trelawney Dayrell Reed, with whom Griff Senior stayed at his Dorset farm during the war. This was a strange friendship, for Dayrell Reed hated planes. Indeed, he was once tried (and acquitted) for attempted murder after shooting at, and hitting, a low-flying aircraft with his shotgun. Griff was also a very good friend of Alastair Graham – they bought a boat together named the *Osprey*. One indication of the strength of their friendship was that Graham, who hated leaving Newquay, flew to Davos with Griff's girlfriend, Josephine Macdonald, to visit Griff in a sanatorium there before his death in 1947.

38. Tom Rees and Griff Jenkins Senior at the Wern, 1944

39. Griff Jenkins, Alastair Graham and   40.Trelawney Dayrell Reed, early 1940s
Josephine MacDonald, Davos, 1947

Griff and Dylan were drinking companions both in London and Newquay but they also had one other thing in common: dancers. Josephine Macdonald had worked in the 1930s for C.B. Cochran Productions. Dylan had a fifteen year friendship with dancer and actress Elizabeth Ruby, who had come to London from Glasgow in 1937, and had small parts in Jack Buchanan films. She told Colin Edwards that she and Dylan had "a romance but not an affair". Dylan, she said, had

> rescued me from this sophisticated set of film people when I made an awful faux pas thinking a lesbian was an omelette... Dylan overheard this and felt sorry for me and took me under his wing, which really meant that he introduced me to Bohemia.[68]

Thomas Jones the butcher was known as Thomas OK or Butcher OK because OK was his every second or third word. He was also known as 'Covered Wagon', after his horse-drawn, canvas-covered butcher's cart. Thomas OK lived in Bwlchcefn, just above the cross roads at Cnwc-y-Lili and a few minutes walk from Majoda. Thomas

41. Elizabeth Ruby   42. Thomas Jones, Butcher OK

OK was one of Dylan's "greatest friends and companions...they used to walk in very often in the evenings together... most evenings" (Olive Jones).

Dylan's circle also included other local people such as Gwyn James the fireman also known as Gwyn Dobbin; Tom Evans (King Kong) who used to bring his gramophone to the Black Lion; Tom Rees the shoe traveller who lived in High Terrace just along from the Black Lion; and Meurig Lewis, a lobster and mackerel fisherman and always known locally as Meurig Fisherman. Meurig was also friendly with Rex Harrison when the actor was in Newquay in 1954, filming *The Constant Husband* with Kay Kendall and Margaret Leighton.[69]

Tom Rees was an important networker and bringer-together of Newquay people. Described as "plump with an entertaining personality", he taught the latest dances to Newquay's young women. On regatta days

> he would dress in drag, swishing and swaying along the pier to the delight of the spectators. Then he would perform on the Greasy Pole, erected at horizontal to the sea at the end of the pier. Well, you can imagine the rest! (Anon.)

Rees had the added attraction that he brewed his own beer in an old smithy next to his house, where he and his friends would gather for after-hours socialising. Foremost amongst Rees' friends were Alastair Graham and Dr Griff Thomas, father of 'Neville the Spy' (see Chapter 6) and Marjorie, with whom Graham collaborated to decorate the bar of the Penwig Hotel in the 1950s. The hotel was owned by George and Miriam Green, who were active members of the swinging set invited to Graham's parties at the Wern.

Dewi Rees was Tom's brother. He looked after the *Osprey* for Alastair Graham and Griff Jenkins, doing the routine maintenance, moving the boat in and out of moorings and checking the lobster pots. Dylan and Augustus John sometimes came to eat these lobsters at lunches at Griff Senior's home. On one occasion, the young Griff was amazed to see John devour two whole lobsters. Unlike his brother Tom, Dewi was a quiet, reserved man who liked gathering with other former sailors in Glanmor Rees' cobbler's shop on Stryd Bethel.

There were also Dylan's friends mentioned in his letter to Margaret Taylor of August 1946: Dai Fred, who bottled ships, was David Frederick Davies, mate on the *Alpha*, a boat owned by the Lancashire and Western Sea Fisheries Board; Evan Joshua was Evan Joshua James, a Swansea man who had settled in Newquay and become manager of Neuadd Quarry; Taffy Jones ("He's not very nice") was Ira Jones, a famous First World War fighter pilot; Norman was Norman Evans, known as Norman London House after his sister's grocery shop in which he worked when he wasn't brawling. Norman was

> ...New Quay's noisiest and least successful fighter; every summer he starts a fight, & every summer some tiny little ape-man knocks him yards over the harbour-wall or bang through the chemist's window.

Jack the Post was Jack Lloyd the postman, who had once been in business in London, and whose wife, alleged Dylan, already had two husbands:

> ...he once married a pretty widow in London & everything was fine, he said, except that wherever they went they were followed by men in bowler hats. After the honeymoon, Mrs Jack was arrested for double bigamy. And all the husbands appeared in the court and gave evidence as to her good character.[70]

43. Meurig Fisherman, 1954

44. Norman London House, 1940

45. Dewi Rees, 1938

46. Dai Fred and his brother Luke Shaylor

We shall see in Chapter 7 how Dylan drew upon three of the people mentioned in the Margaret Taylor letter for material for *Under Milk Wood*.

Other writers have already commented on Dylan's preference for the company of 'ordinary' local people, and this was certainly the case in Newquay. We saw earlier that he was active in making notes about them. But there seem to be three interesting characteristics of many, but not all, of the Newquay locals with whom Dylan was friendly. First, they were Welsh speaking. Second, they were 'cosmopolitans' in the sense that they had experienced the world outside Newquay. For example, they may have lived in London for a period, or travelled the world or, perhaps, just Wales and England. Third, they were often 'gatekeepers' to the community around them i.e. the nature of their work (publican, postman, butcher, grocer) brought them into contact with the goings-on of Newquay, and Dylan could make use of their stories as much as he used his own observations.

In short, Dylan's time in Newquay, which started long before his Majoda residence in 1944, was his first prolonged immersion in the ordinary, everyday affairs of the tradespeople of a small Welsh town, and it formed the bedrock from which the *petite bourgeoisie* of Llareggub was developed.

Moving to Majoda

The chance of a house in Newquay arose quite quickly in August 1944. There was no mention of it in Dylan's letter of July 27th to Vernon Watkins – indeed, in that letter Dylan was still thinking of Laugharne. But in his letter of August 26th, Newquay had become a distinct possibility. On September 4th, Dylan, Caitlin, and baby Aeronwy arrived at Majoda. They were accompanied by a black labrador (not Mably, who was a collie mongrel), which Thomas Herbert soon had cause to treat for mange. Dylan's first letter from Majoda was a poem to Tommy Earp with the following description:

> It's a long way from London, as the fly bombs,
> And nothing of Donald's guile can lug me
> Away from this Wales where I sit in my combs
> As safe and snug as a bugger in Rugby.
> We've got a new house and it's called Majoda.
> Majoda, Cards, on the Welsh-speaking sea.

And we'll stay in this wood-and-asbestos pagoda
Till the blackout's raised on London and on me.

Like much of his life before, Dylan's arrival in Newquay was bound up with the Bryn-y-Mor Girls. Margaret Phillips was, of course, living a few miles inland at Gelli. Her eldest daughter, Evelyn Milton, was living in Newquay at Traethina. And her other daughter Vera had moved from Gelli to Ffynnonfeddyg,[71] a wooden bungalow a hundred yards down the road from Majoda, sometime after the birth of her daughter Rachel in May 1944. We know that Vera and Evelyn were definitely living in Newquay in October 1944 because they completed an electoral registration form, as did Dylan and Caitlin, and appeared in the 1945 Register of Electors.

How might Vera and/or Evelyn have helped Dylan find Majoda? Its owner was Dr Albert Evans of Lampeter who was the family doctor at Gelli, and his brother John owned Ffynnonfeddyg. If the two sisters helped in this way, it is yet another example of the Phillips'/Killicks' support for Dylan and Caitlin in the period before Margaret Taylor became their patron.

There also seems to have been a helping hand from Griff Jenkins Senior, whom Dylan had asked about accommodation. Griff contacted his sister Margaret, who in turn spoke to a school friend called

47. Dr Albert Evans, owner of Majoda, with his father, Capt. John Evans

95

Nansi Evans of Lampeter, daughter of the John Evans who owned Ffynnonfeddyg. They did not want, or were unable, to rent Ffynnonfeddyg to Dylan, perhaps because it was already rented to Vera Killick. Margaret was told that Majoda was free and a family friend, D.E. Phillips, manager of Lloyds Bank, approached Dr Albert Evans, the owner.[72]

Dylan's arrival in Newquay was low-key. Jack Patrick described it thus:

> He came here a very shy man. He was too shy to introduce himself so what he did was to leave a copy of a magazine in every pub, a magazine which contained a story about him and with a photograph of him. I think that the magazine was *Lilliput*.[73]

The pattern continued and Jack Patrick told Colin Edwards:

> We enjoyed his company with little thought that we had a world celebrity in our midst... we just treated him as one of ourselves... he never gave an inkling of his connections with world-famous people of letters that he knew intimately..."

The modesty or shyness extended to his writing. According to Olive Jones, Dylan would never read his own work in public, neither would he discuss it. Dylan often used the typewriter in her house and Olive once looked at what he had been writing:

> I said to him one day 'Well, Dylan, honestly, I've had a peep at those slips and I don't understand a word.' He said 'Oh, neither do I Olive, don't worry, I don't understand them myself...' [the slips] were little bits of poetry about six inches long.

There was, however, nothing low-key about Dylan's engagement with the drinking and social life of Newquay. Within days of Dylan and Caitlin arriving, Augustus John was worn out and wrote a note to Alastair Graham:

> It's a pity to leave; the day has been beautiful. I have done nothing but explore a little the fairy wood below with the goats. An expedition yesterday with Caitlin was not a success. I'm still a little exhausted by the strain of life at The Black Lion and my task at Aberayron....[74]

Apart from his poem to Earp sent on September 21st, Dylan makes few references to the life of the town, whose population at that time was just under a thousand. His letter to Donald Taylor of October 26th 1944 refers to the Nautical School. This taught seamanship, and the students had been evacuated from London.[75] Writing to Vernon Watkins on November 28th, Dylan mentions two deaths in the town: Mrs Prosser dying in agony; and the suicide of a coastguard. This was Tim Thomas, the barber in Stryd Bethel, a local councillor and an auxiliary coastguard, who was drowned in the bay on October 11th. His body was washed ashore some weeks later, and could be identified only by his wristwatch. Locals said he had tied himself to his canoe, and capsized it, but the Coroner found no evidence of suicide.[76] It is likely that this incident had some effect on Dylan; his letter to Marguerite Caetani in September 1953 describes being handcuffed and blindfolded, and thrown in a sack to the bottom of the "mantrapping" sea. Tim Thomas' fate may also be reflected in the drowned and fish-nibbled sailors that open *Under Milk Wood*.

Life in the Bungalow

Dylan mostly referred to Majoda as a bungalow, though once or twice he was less complimentary – "a shack at the edge of the cliff where my children hop like fleas in a box" was one description that he gave.[77] It had been made with a timber frame, onto which thin asbestos sheets were fixed to provide the external and internal walls. A three-foot band of shiplap timber ran around the base of the bungalow from the ground up to the bottom of the windows. The pitched roof was covered in polygonal asbestos slates. There was a small kitchen and scullery at the back, leading through to the living room, which contained a red-brick, coal fireplace. A door and window opened out from the living room onto a tiny veranda that faced the sea. On either side of the living room were two bedrooms, also with windows facing the sea. Majoda was not spacious – only some eight yards square – and in style and appearance, it looked like a small, 1930s cricket pavilion.

The bungalow had been named after Dr Albert Evans' children, Marjorie, John and David, and Dylan often joked that he would rename it Catllewdylaer. The rent was £1 a week, with calor gas for light, cooking and heating by paraffin stoves and water from a tap on

48. An impression of Majoda

the road – Caitlin called it "cheaply primitive." It was sparsely fur-nished, and it was also cold and draughty; Dylan and Caitlin were there with Aeronwy through one of the coldest winters on record. Locals who visited them found the bungalow was sordid and ill-cared for, though 'bohemian' was often a word used to talk about it. Olive Jones told Colin Edwards:

> It was all very rough and ready, dirty dishes piled up everywhere, a sink full of them. She [Caitlin] washed a couple of cups, and we had a cup of beer each. Then we went into see old Dylan who was lying in bed writing by candlelight, with no sheets on the bed, no pillow slips, just a couple of blankets thrown over him... they sat on the floor most of the time, on cushions... it was all very higgledy-piggledy... the children seemed to thrive on it.

Griff Jenkins Junior told Edwards that Dylan more or less ignored the children: "Caitlin was the typical, overworked housewife, over stewing pots and pans with bawling brats at her feet – that was the kind of atmosphere it was."

Majoda sat on the cliff top overlooking Cardigan Bay, quite close to the mansion and church at Llanina. "It's in a really wonderful bit of the bay," wrote Dylan to Vernon Watkins, "with a beach of its own. Terrific."[78] The cliff-top land between Majoda and Newquay

49. Traethgwyn, the beach below Majoda, late 1940s

was open countryside at this time, small fields with tight hedgerows packed with song birds. Sheep and cattle grazed here, not static caravans. Local people remember how the fields were full of skylarks, rising and falling and rising again, as if they were trying to squint over the horizon to see the sights of Dublin. To Dylan, the cliff-tops were ridden with mice and rabbits, which Caitlin trapped, though on one occasion Vera's cat was caught and killed.

Caitlin has described how lonely she was for much of the time at Majoda. There was little to do over the cold winter months, though she did go swimming when the sea warmed up: "Right below us was the roaring ocean. I used to have a marvellous time down there in the waves...." (1986, p.89).

Vera was close at hand for friendship and support, and Evelyn Milton has described how they worked out a baby-sitting system for the evenings: Dylan would take Caitlin out whilst Vera looked after the babies, and then he would take Vera out for a night or two whilst Caitlin stayed at home. No doubt it was this arrangement that fuelled the gossip that Dylan and Vera were intimate, and stimulated the speculation that the shooting occurred because of a *ménage à trois*.

When Dylan and Caitlin did go out, it seems that they often went their own ways. Mrs Warfield-Darling told Colin Edwards:

I don't think they were *very* happy together, but there were times

99

when they were most affectionate. I think she rather bored him. She used to take the two children down to the Black Lion and put them to bed there. She used to leave Dylan there and go around on her own rounds. She used to say to Dora the girl there 'Have you got an empty room? Pop these two into bed, will you?' They were charming little children. Then she'd go off, nobody knew where she went... and come back for the children between eleven and twelve.

In fact, Caitlin used mostly to go to the Dolau, her favourite pub. But she'd also walk up to the Penrhiwllan at the top of the town. She once stole Dai Fred's bike, crashed into a wall and had to have seven stitches in her head. 'Serve her right,' said Dylan. The Penrhiwllan was very popular since it offered both a taxi service and access to black-market goods. It was a spartan and cramped pub and most of the customers sat out the back in a tin shed fitted with old bus seats.

As we read Dylan's letters from Majoda we are left with the impression that he found it a noisy place. In February, he wrote sarcastically to Vernon Watkins about the peace of the countryside and references to noise litter his Majoda letters: the baying sea, the din of pebbles, shrieking rabbits, screaming mice, rooks in the trees, Dan Jones' wheezy cough, howling Augustus John, the rattle of a sten gun, the crunch of gravel, the noise of children playing on the beach, and the students from the Nautical School practising on their bugles.

One of the drawbacks of the bungalow was the lack of privacy for Dylan to write – "I work among cries and clatters like a venomous beaver in a parrot house." He wrote to Donald Taylor complaining that

> this little bungalow is no place to work in when there's a bawling child there... the rooms are tiny, the walls bumpaper-thin, & a friend arrived with another baby with a voice like Caruso's.[79]

Olive Jones has described how Caitlin and Aeronwy – "a sturdy two-year old with the determination of a dictator and the strength of Hercules"[80] – were sent into Newquay on extended 'shopping' trips. Dylan also worked at the Black Lion: Jack Patrick told Colin Edwards that Dylan "seemed to do his best writing among us local people, he was always with a pad on his knee during convivial hours, busy making notes on any local characters who came in...". Olive Jones has described how Dylan "did quite a lot of typing in our house because

50. Newquay from Majoda today

he used my husband's typewriter." This must have been when her husband, Ira Jones, was away in London on RAF business, because he and Dylan were not on good terms.

Dylan also took a room in a "nearby house".[81] This may have just been a reference to the Apple House at Plas Llanina, but it seems unlikely that Dylan would have described it in this way. There were only three other possible houses 'nearby': first, Traethgwyn House, a few hundred yards along the cliff top from Majoda. This was owned by John Beynon (Evans). Second, Traethina, further along the cliff, where Evelyn Milton was living. Each of these houses had a fine view of Newquay and the bay, and would have provided both the vantage point and the inspiration for the germinating *Under Milk Wood* and other writing assignments. Third, Parc-y-Pant, five minutes walk up the road, going inland, at Cnwc-y-Lili. Two aunts of Jack Patrick lived in Parc-y-Pant so it's as possible that this was the house.

Dylan's first few months at Majoda were happy ones. "Newquay," wrote Caitlin, "was just exactly his kind of background, with the ocean in front of him as it later was in Laugharne, and a pub where he felt at home in the evenings." (1986, p.92). It was, however, less convenient than Laugharne. There was no train service, and the bus journey from Carmarthen to Newquay was slow and tedious. The return fare, Dylan wrote in one of his letters, was five shillings. Communication with the outside world was through letter, telegram and telephone. Dylan often relied on telegrams, not least because phones were not at that time common in the countryside. Caradoc Evans had other reasons for preferring the telegram, or the 'wire' as it was often called:

> Welsh is too gutteral to be a language for the telephone and wireless.... Their voices are sing-song and have no idea of the English language.... A Welshman prefers to spend a shilling on a telegram rather than twopence on a phone call because the 'phone conversation would probably cost him half a crown in the end owing to unintelligible voices.[82]

Certainly, Dylan used a public telephone box to talk with friends and work contacts in London, and sometimes the phone in the bar at the Black Lion. The bar could be very noisy and on at least one occasion discussions with Donald Taylor at Gryphon Films went awry:

> I feel very badly about it that our conversation some evenings ago should have disturbed you... I can only say that I'd just come out of a gastric chamber, had had a few hurried drinks to see if I were still alive, and then spoke to you, not in a quiet box as I usually do when I ring up, but against a background of maudlin sea-captains and shrewd, if stunned, travellers in petrol. One ear was hearing you and the other ear was busy shutting out the buzzing of those Cardy drones.... Let me know if you wish me to ring you again soon; & this time I shall choose the privacy of a public booth not the propinquity of a public bar.[83]

The letters from this period suggest he missed having visitors: there are a number of heart-felt pleas to Tommy Earp and Vernon Watkins to stay but, as far as can be gleaned from the letters, they did not come. People who did visit included Donald Taylor, Fanya Fisher, John Eldridge, Mary Keene, Augustus John and Daniel Jones. Dylan's mother also came from Blaen Cwm to look after the children whilst Dylan and Caitlin were at William Killick's trial. The Colin Edwards tapes tell us that Ebie and Ivy Williams from Laugharne were also visitors.

Still, Dylan was content: he wrote to Vernon Watkins declaring "I am quite happy and am looking forward to a gross, obscene and extremely painful middle-age." Moreover, his itching feet which he had complained about in his July letter to Watkins from Blaen Cwm ("I have to take my shoes off many times a day and rub my soles with my socks") appeared to be better, cured no doubt by the salt air, Buckley's bitter and the daily walks to the Black Lion. Dylan's contentment showed in his output. Between September 1944 and March 28th 1945, he wrote 'The conversation of prayers', 'A Refusal to Mourn the Death, by Fire, of a Child in London', 'This side of the truth', and 'A Winter's Tale'. He also revised or finished 'Lie still, sleep becalmed', 'Holy Spring' and 'Vision and Prayer'. In addition, he completed *Quite Early One Morning* and made a start on *Twenty Years A-Growing*. It is likely that much of this work was completed before December 1944 – *Quite Early One Morning* certainly was, and so were the revisions and 'A Winter's Tale'.

Dylan even invented a bicycle that could be carried in the pocket! He was the precursor of Moulton and all those others who thirty years later designed bikes that you could fold up and carry on the train or in the boot of your car. See his letter to Vernon Watkins of November 28th 1944. His idea, in the same letter, for a machine for draining ditches of witches has yet to find an enlightened commercial backer.

Other interests also developed at this time, including the meaning of local Welsh place names and a half-hearted enquiry about learning Welsh – he asked Myra Evans to teach him.[84] She was a writer and a competent artist and she did a portrait of Dylan in Ffynnonfeddyg. She would have been an important person in building Dylan's understanding of Newquay: she had from the early 1900s been collecting notes, and doing portraits, of the town's characters, which she published in 1961.

Dylan's time in Welsh-speaking Newquay seems to have crystallised his feelings about the language. There were several discussions about Welsh with Thomas Herbert, which are conveyed in the interview in *Y Cymro*, and in Herbert's essay on Dylan in the Jacqui Lyne papers. Herbert noted that "Dylan deplored the fact that he couldn't speak Welsh" and that he "loved hearing Welsh being spoken... I was surprised at his knowledge of early Welsh poetry, but he had also spent time in the company of contemporary Welsh writers." In one discussion, Herbert asked Dylan why he didn't learn the language. Dylan replied: "It's too late, Tom." Herbert reflected:

I had the feeling, from the way he said it, that it was not a ques-

Dylan Thomas: A Farm, Two Mansions and a Bungalow

tion of his inability, but the fact that he was totally possessed by his craft and that there was no room for anything else in his remarkable world.

On another occasion in the Black Lion, writes Herbert, Dylan said

the most significant thing about his failure to learn the language. With the two of us drinking out of two half-gallon jugs, full of bitterness he said "My father was a working-class man who became a teacher. So Welsh wasn't good enough for Dylan bach."

The wonderfully productive year at Majoda to which so many critics refer could, in fact, have been a mere four or five months.

51. *He wanted me to teach him Welsh!* "This drawing is the property of Mr Tom Evans – a drawing by his mother, Mrs Myra Evans, the author of a number of books. Mrs Evans drew it in Ffynnonfeddyg, the home of Dylan's neighbour, and she wrote on the book that the poet asked her to teach him Welsh." – *Y Cymro*, 7/11/1978

January and February 1945 were bedevilled by gastric flu in the family: "...my wife has influenza and I am trying to combine the duties of housekeeper and children-minder along with my own work..."[85] Caradoc Evans had died in January though this is not likely to have touched Dylan very much. He had certainly kept in touch with Evans, 'bumping into' him in Aberystwyth in 1944.[86] Some locals also remember Dylan visiting New Cross, Evans' new home in the hills outside Aberystwyth.[87]

There is a suggestion in Dylan's letter in early February to Earp that he was wanting to move to another house. By the end of the month, the shine had rubbed off Majoda, and a letter to Vernon Watkins tells of the horrors of everyday life and of making physical and social contact with people. Dylan was in decline, and the shooting in March pushed him further down the slope. He wrote nothing of consequence until September. This was not just because of the shooting, but also the demands of Killick's trial and mounting money worries, as Dylan confirms in his letter to Donald Taylor of April 1945, complaining that it was impossible to live on eight pounds a week, which was sufficient only for rent, food, oil and coal, leaving nothing to "buy a pair of trousers though my bum is bare to the sun." Thomas Herbert also noted the strain on Caitlin:

> Looking at the little family, I could feel how much of an effort it was for Caitlin to keep things going while Dylan was spending whatever he made through his great talent on ale and horseraces, even though he had small children to bring up.[88]

By the end of June, Dylan was back in "worse-then-Belsen London", missing the "Cardy dark, by the sea", complaining about the *News of the World* report of the Killick trial but reassuring Caitlin that "I think, by the way, that our court expenses will be sent to me at Majoda. If they are, you'll be okay."[89]

Come July, they were back in Blaen Cwm living with Dylan's parents, and thinking of America. Dylan wrote to Oscar Williams, his unofficial literary agent in America:

> We would all come together because I do not want to return to this country for a long time...The rain has stopped, thank Jesus. Have the Socialists-in-power-now stopped it? An income tax form flops through the window, the letter box is choked with dockleaves. Let's get out, let's get out.[90]

The Poet and the Locals

Dylan's time in Newquay was spent gossiping with the locals, writing poems, broadcasts and scripts, and socialising in the pubs in the evening. His favourites were, of course, the Black Lion and the Commercial, but he also went sometimes to the Dolau and the Penrhiwllan. It was in the Penrhiwllan that Thomas Herbert captured Dylan's alliterative exchange with Augustus John:

> I remember them mocking each other one night. "You know what you are, don't you?" said Augustus. "You're nothing but a pot-bellied purveyor of pornographic poetry." "And you," Dylan said, "are a bigoted begetter of bastards."[91]

Dylan and Caitlin stirred up strong feelings amongst Newquay locals. Even today, there is ambivalence towards Dylan, as well as a good deal of hostility. "Counting him as a man," said one elderly resident, "he was rubbish. Counting him as a poet he was brilliant." Attitudes to Dylan were based not just on his unpaid bills but also on his drinking and sponging. People were puzzled about how he earned his living; and 'refugees' from the war who might be viewed, however unfairly, as 'draft dodgers' could be coolly received in a town that had seen twenty-nine of its men killed and others held prisoner in German and Japanese POW camps. Worse still, strangers were always suspect because they might be 'spies' from the Ministry of Food, putting Newquay's flourishing black market and creative ration allocations at risk. The town was very sensitive about this: one tradesman had been fined £100 for selling the fire station's petrol allocation. Willie Lewis, a magistrates clerk, had been charged with slaughtering his own pig; his bench found him not guilty but he was eventually brought to book and forced to resign.

None of this should lead you to conclude that Newquay was an insular, inward-looking community. Far from it. Newquay was more "worldly" than many of its counterparts, not least because of its sailors who had travelled the world, and its connections to London through the dairy trade. The town's residents rubbed shoulders easily with the South Wales visitors during the summer months. Newquay had taken evacuees from London and Liverpool, as well as adult escapees from the Blitz. The town had also welcomed many Belgian refugees during the 1914-1919 war. Some of its men had volunteered for the Spanish Civil War.

Nevertheless, the bohemian lifestyle of the Majoda crowd attracted criticism, as well as Dylan's personal habits: "He was filthy," said one informant. "Stank to high heaven and *she* dressed like a gypsy." Being like a gypsy meant, for example, that Caitlin wore odd earrings because she was always losing one of a pair. It meant wearing gaudy and not matching colours: "Caitlin used to dress in just any old thing that she had... a scarlet jersey and a blue skirt and a bit of blue round her neck...." (Mrs Warfield-Darling). But Gina Potter (née Davies) of Rock Street, and niece of Dai Fred of the *Alpha*, remembers Caitlin being fussy about her evening wear, and credits her with introducing the New Look to Newquay some way before its time.

Then there's the question of how baby Aeronwy was looked after. People are still concerned when they remember that she was sometimes left in the cold outside the Black Lion, and had to be taken in and fed by the families in Gomer Crescent opposite. There are stories, too, about Aeronwy sleeping in the cellar of the Black Lion, or in Jack Patrick's bed in Room 3:

> Several times when I went to bed in the early hours I would see a mop of golden curly hair on the pillow. Caitlin would have put

52. The Black Lion, hotel part, date unknown

her there to sleep without me knowing anything about it.[92]

Vera Killick and Caitlin also took turns to baby-sit, and Dylan sometimes asked the teenage relatives of his friends to look after Aeronwy. Gina Potter remembers doing this, and being paid a pound by Dylan, making her the only person in Newquay, she suggested to me, to get any money out of him.

Whilst feelings ran strong in Newquay, you'll also find many kind words about Dylan that balance the critical comments:

> He was a brilliant poet and a charming man... he wasn't a womaniser or a lecher... (Mrs Warfield-Darling).

> He was always very charming, kind... a gentle personality, unassuming... he kept so quiet, we didn't realise he was becoming so famous... I never saw him boisterous... I was horrified [by the Brinnin book]...I hadn't seen that side of Dylan at all, I never saw Dylan any the worse for drink and I never saw him drink anything but beer. (Olive Jones)

No doubt the ambivalence and ill-feeling in Newquay was due partly to the fact that, in *Under Milk Wood*, Dylan captured the eccentric and sexual goings-on of the town. He held a mirror up to Newquay and people saw themselves in it:

> We'd love him here if he hadn't written *Under Milk Wood*. It was too close to the bone, we recognised each other. We were only a small community, and we're getting smaller, the old locals that is, and the feelings about Dylan still run deep.

One for the Road

Whenever he was staying in Cardiganshire, there was always a reason or opportunity for Dylan to travel. His letters from Majoda tell us that he was at the farmers' fair in Cardigan, and travelling to collect his mother from Blaen Cwm. He met Gwyn Jones in Carmarthen and Aberystwyth. Donald Evans of Talgarreg recalls being told about Dylan visiting Newcastle Emlyn and hitch-hiking back in a lorry to Newquay. Jack Patrick tells of the time that he and Dylan went to the fair at New Inn, and they were forced to walk back the ten miles to Newquay in a freezing snow storm.[93] Thomas Herbert reminisces about walking with Dylan along the Aeron Valley from Talsarn to Llangeitho (see Chapter 2). In short, Dylan was immersing himself in the heartland of Cardiganshire, absorbing its atmosphere, meeting the local characters and hearing the stories of the countryside, always, of course, with a notebook at hand.

Dylan would often accompany Thomas Herbert when he was doing his rounds, taking the opportunity to stop off at various pubs on the way. David Birch, who worked with Thomas Herbert in his veterinary practice, told me that Dylan and Herbert were frequent visitors to the Ship Inn, Llangrannog. This small, seaside village just south of Newquay was part of Herbert's practice: "not so many cows," says Birch, "but lots of old ladies with cats." It was, and is, a pretty village in a beautiful setting but part of the attraction may have been blacksmith and poet Dafydd Jones (Isfoel), who wrote witty, and sometimes bawdy, poetry. Herbert knew Isfoel, but we cannot be sure that he knew him in the 1940s.[94]

Other favourite stopping places for Herbert and Dylan were The Ship at Pennant, and the Three Horseshoes at Llangeitho. Dylan was also a frequent visitor to Aberaeron, where both Herbert and Dewi Ianthe lived, as well as other drinking companions such as Wyn Lloyd the stone mason, and once a member of the local drama group. Herbert has described a futile search for Dylan through the town:

> I saw Dylan sitting with a half-gallon jug of beer in front of him on the little table. He got up, pulled up another stool and invited me to sit down. 'Glad to see you, Tom,' he said; he had called at my house that morning but I was out. 'Your mother asked me to wait, as she was expecting you home in a little while, but Dewi Ianthe was in a hurry.' – his great friend and volunteer chauffeur. It wasn't that Dewi was in a hurry – Dylan's thirst was the spur that prevented him waiting. I was home soon after and went from one pub to the next in Aberaeron, always getting the same message: 'Dylan Thomas has just left.'[95]

Herbert and Dylan used to go the Central Hotel and the Commercial Inn (now called the White Swan) in Llanon, a small coastal village between Aberaeron and Aberystwyth. Herbert went often to Llanon to see his fiancée, Tessa Dean.[96] Tessa was the daughter of Lady Mercy Greville and Basil Dean, the film producer. Lady Mercy lived in Cwm Peris, a remote valley behind Llanon, with her aptly-named third husband Captain Marter. Thomas Herbert's papers confirm that Lady Mercy was an old friend of Alastair Graham, and frequently present at his parties. Their own gatherings in Cwm Peris were as bacchanalian as some of Graham's.

The landlord of the Commercial Inn was a colourful character called Dai Hughes, who also ran the Llanon Steam Bakery. He was always known as Hughes the Bread and it's possible that this is where Dylan got the name 'Dai Bread' that he used in *Under Milk Wood*. Hughes was also prominent in the local amateur dramatic society that toured Cardiganshire. The landlord of the Central Hotel, Evan Davies, was also the kind of local character with whom Dylan got on well. He had been in the dairy business in London before coming to Llanon to the Central. His main pleasure in life was betting on the horses, an interest that was shared by Dylan. In 1944, Evan moved to a house in the village, and passed on the hotel to two Londoners, an Ernest Mann and a Mr Marks.[97] They were both Jewish and thought to be gay, which, no doubt, endeared them to Dylan, though they were looked upon with great suspicion by the locals, not least because they wore suits with no pockets. A drink or two with Mann and Marks, who were on very good terms with the Williams brothers of Wernllaeth Farm (Milk Wood Farm), may have been sufficient to remind Dylan of Bert Trick's poem which concluded:

> You are MAN
> As Christ and Marx
> Were men;
> Crucified on the Cross
> Of man's blind ignorance.
>   (quoted in Thompson, 1965, p.300).

After Majoda

Did Dylan return to Newquay after July 1945? This is an important question for those who wish to understand the influence of the town on *Under Milk Wood*. If he did return, then its people and places remained fresh in his memory in the period that led up to the drafting of the play.

There would have been many opportunities for Dylan to come to Newquay. For example, he may have visited in the summerof 1946 on his journey to and from Ireland (the port of Fishguard is only 45 minutes away) or whilst he was at Blaen Cwm with his parents. His letter to Margaret Taylor of August 29th 1946 suggests a continuing familiarity with Newquay (the references in the first paragraph are in the present tense) after his departure from Majoda.

Thomas Herbert wrote in his essay on Dylan that he did not see him ever again after the shooting incident. Cadwell Davies, one of the brothers who ran the Newquay taxi service that Dylan used, says categorically that Dylan, who ran up a large (unpaid) bill with the firm during the Killick trial in Lampeter, did not return after the war. Yet Margaret Jones of Llanon remembers seeing Dylan in Newquay: "he was definitely there after the war."[98] Catherine Davies remembers being told by her mother that she had served Dylan and Caitlin in the Dolau. Her parents, Bill and Maudie Bennett, were in the services during the war, and were not demobbed until late 1945. They then ran the Penrhiwllan for two years, opening the Dolau for business in 1948.[99]

Whether Dylan returned or not, the memories of Newquay, and of the Aeron Valley, remained powerful, as he himself confirmed in his 1949 broadcast, *Living in Wales*. Walford Davies has summed it up thus:

> It is of course natural to think that he would have been tempted back to a place he so greatly relished, vivid memories of which helped form, along with those of Laugharne, his mental picture of Llareggub in *Under Milk Wood*.... But I don't personally know of any evidence that he *did* go back. They say, don't they, that you *shouldn't* go back. Perhaps he did so only in his poet's memory.[100]

We certainly know that Dylan did go back to Cardiganshire, if not to Newquay. He travelled to Aberystwyth to give a poetry reading on the evening of November 12th 1952, and stayed overnight with Professor Gwyn Jones at his house in Bryn-y-Môr Road. As Dylan did not drive, he would have taken a taxi (he often used them, even for long distances) or caught the train.[101] In either case, his route would have taken him from Carmarthen to Lampeter. By taxi, he would have then proceeded to Aberystwyth either via Talsarn and Llanrhystyd or Aberaeron, giving him plenty of opportunity to visit former watering holes, even Newquay. The route by train would have taken him from Lampeter, skirting round the Aeron Valley, to Tregaron, Ystradmeurig and then past Wenallt (Milk Wood) to

Llanilar (with a view across the river to New Cross where Caradoc Evans had lived) and onto the coast. Whether by train or taxi, the journey would have been very evocative and a powerful stimulus to the 'poet's memory', reminding him of Cardiganshire precisely at the moment that he was working on *Under Milk Wood*.

53. & 54, The Black Lion today (the pub part) and The Commercial, taken in the 1960s.

55. & 56. The Penrhiwllan and The Dolau

4. The Shooting

Baby Aeronwy stole the show at Vera and William Killick's wedding on August 14th 1943, gurgling and crying during the ceremony, and being over-indulged in the reception held in The Chelsea Pensioner. As was common in wartime, the honeymoon was brief. William borrowed a motor-bike and he and Vera spent a couple of days touring the Welsh border country. He then flew to Cairo for further training in demolitions for his work in Greece. He was to be a member of the Allied Military Mission, an SOE operation to assist Greek partisans in their fight against the occupying German forces.

Aeronwy's presence clearly blessed the marriage with fertility; Vera and William were to have five daughters, the first of whom, Rachel, was born in May 1944. Vera continued to work on the stage in the early months of the pregnancy, but then returned to Gelli and Swansea for Rachel's birth, soon moving to Newquay.

Meanwhile, after several unsuccessful attempts to infiltrate by parachute, William Killick's 22-strong party flew into Greece on October 21st 1943 in a Dakota, and landed on the airstrip at Neurada, Thessaly. The beginning of the mission was not very auspicious: the plane was bogged down for almost two days, and managed to take off only minutes before the Germans arrived. According to Killick, the atmosphere in the party "was not particularly healthy", as one of its members was a partisan leader who had been blacklisted by other partisans, "and no-one at the station seemed very well informed as to what was what."

Killick's personal equipment was much like that of all SOE troops in Greece: a revolver, Sten gun and ammunition, knife, compass, torch, flares, a map made to look like a silk scarf, field-dressings and a belt of sovereigns which were to save Killick's skin. He also had a mess tin, water bottle, hard rations, Benzedrine pills, a poison pill and two RAF badges so that he could, if caught, pass as shot down aircrew.

Killick's group marched for several days through the mountains to report to Monty Woodhouse, second in command of the Greek operation, at his HQ in Pertouli. Two days later, they were marching again, and eventually holed up at a remote village, only to find that the Germans were advancing on it. The village was soon surrounded. The partisans ran off but Killick took part in a fierce shoot-out on the hillsides. He managed to escape at night but had "to pay seven sovereigns and one pair of boots to bribe the hire of three mules." He reached Mavrillo, and with mounting frustration waited 15 days for instructions. Whilst there, he experienced other aspects of Cairo's incompetence:

> During this time I occupied myself in fixing charging engines. Both Major Harker and Power had been off the air owing to being unable to charge their batteries for several days. Their operators knew nothing about charging engines.... Suggest all operators in the field should have mechanical training as many stations were at times off the air through complete lack of elementary mechanical knowledge.[102]

Killick was also becoming disillusioned with the partisans "who were not in the least bit cooperative as regards sabotage against the Hun." A decision had been taken to de-rail a train carrying British POWs. Killick and his team had laid the charges, and lay waiting for the partisans to signal from the hill-tops that the train was approaching:

> We, the demolition party, were to do nothing until signalled. We waited 36 hours. Many trains passed by day and night and no signals were given... we later learned that two POW trains passed through whilst we were on the line but no signals were given.

Killick spent Christmas Day, 1943, on the top of a mountain that he called Kaimaxillar, and stayed there three weeks in snow and freezing temperatures. One of the party died of exposure, and many others suffered from frostbite. Eventually, they managed to walk back to Paikon where they had been told to expect a drop of arms and food. Killick and the partisans stood for twenty five nights in deep snow waiting for the drop. The plane did not come. This was another experience of the unreliability of SOE in Cairo.

May Day brought another huge German drive on the village in which Killick and his small party were positioned. The large part of the partisan force fled the village but Killick, now working largely on his own initiative, stayed behind with a Corporal Chapman ("an ex-POW and a most excellent man") and twelve sapper partisans. They mined the paths leading to the village: "One was a great success, killing 18 Huns and wounding six. The nearby trees were full of bits of clothing for months...." Killick and Chapman were now in an area where some 6,000 German troops were stationed. Killick decided to blow up the main railway line. Local villagers persuaded him not to, for fear of reprisals, not least from the Security Battalion troops, "brought there by the Hun. They were terrorising the villagers and were behaving in a more bestial manner than the Hun himself." In typical style, Killick decided to attack the HQ of the Security Battalion, situated in a local school. Plans were drawn up and Chapman and Killick entered the village at night. There they were met by partisans and extravagantly wined and dined, and eventually persuaded not to carry out the attack, much to Killick's anger and frustration.

It was now late spring. They had been working on their own behind enemy lines for over a month. Between May and September 1944, Killick and Chapman worked with partisans to carry out attacks on dams, mines, bridges and railway lines. In between times, he and Chapman would go off to find road bridges to demolish. On one such occasion he came close to capture:

> We put on local shepherds clothes and went down. The bridge was 900 yards long, but very narrow. We were inspecting the road-bearers at about the centre of the bridge when a Hun convoy of trucks appeared. We had no time to leave the bridge. We stood up and let the trucks pass. In spite of the fact that we were wearing army boots which no shepherd ever had, and are both fair, the Huns did not give us a second glance, although we could have touched them as they passed in their trucks. Anyway, the recce was successful and two months later we did blow the bridge.

On October 22, Killick, Chapman and 400 partisans took on over 2,000 Germans at a village near Kilkis. The battle started at 4am and continued to nightfall, with both sides eventually 'retiring', as Killick put it. He described the battle as a shambles:

> Both sides wore the same varieties of uniform. I myself was shot at twice by the partisans. I blazed away with a Sten at a fellow wearing a German helmet but luckily I did not hit him as he was a partisan.

As if this was not enough, Killick was out the next day capturing "a stray German truck" and taking it intact. On October 30th, he rejoined the Allied Mission. The day after, he heard that some trains were still running "so I returned with two mule loads of explosives to the target area." He chanced upon 30 tons of explosives which he defused, as well as discovering an explosive charge amongst 80 cases of 3 inch mortar bombs which, he says modestly, "I removed."

On November 12th 1944, Killick rejoined his Mission once again, carried out various routine tasks, was flown to Cairo, and returned to the UK in February 1945 for re-deployment to another operation. Of his time in the SOE, his personnel file notes that "he was a very tough and aggressive officer, who volunteered for extremely hazardous and demanding missions and had an excellent operational record." Whilst in Greece he worked "in the most difficult and dangerous area of that country at high altitude in the mountains and in extreme conditions in winter... he served with distinction... and carried out sabotage work and the training and command of partisans in an exemplary manner."

Killick had been away for almost eighteen months, fighting continuously behind German lines. His return was a very emotional time. He had been on an extremely dangerous mission, and there must have been great doubts as to whether he would come home safely. And, of course, he had never seen baby Rachel, though Cairo had been able to inform him by wireless of her birth.

But there were soon rows with Vera over money, and the relationship between Killick and Dylan became strained. Within days of his return, Killick was summoned to the office of his bank manager who complained that Vera had run up an overdraft. Killick was furious: whilst he had been working in great peril behind enemy lines, his army pay was being used by his wife to subsidise Dylan's drinking and bohemian lifestyle. Vera, on the other hand, saw this as sharing, not sponging, though there was

> one dreadful occasion, I admit, when Dylan went too far. I heard a noise outside. I looked out and saw Dylan staggering back along the cliff. Next day, I asked Caitlin about it. She said Dylan had wanted some onions and thought there'd be some in my shed. I didn't have any onions. Dylan had taken the daffodil bulbs and eaten them up.[103]

On March 6th, the day of the Majoda shooting, Vera took the baby to visit her mother in Gelli. Relations between Killick and Vera were so strained that he may not have appreciated a visit to her family: not only was Vera's mother at Gelli, but so too were her sister, Evelyn, and her mother's 'adopted child', Annie Mitford-Slade, on a visit from Ilfracombe. Killick spun a coin about whether or not he should accompany Vera on the visit. He went into Newquay to find a pram, perhaps for Rachel or for pushing the beers home to Ffynnonfeddyg as he had done at Gelli. At lunch time he started a pub crawl, drinking rum.

Dylan had certainly been too busy to pay much attention to William Killick on his return. He was behind on his writing assignments, and Gryphon Films were particularly worried with his lack of progress on a film script. To speed him along, Gryphon had sent two people down from London, Fanya Fisher and John Eldridge. They worked solidly in the Black Lion, as Jack Patrick has described:

> We had to start in the middle of the day with strong coffee...there was a secretary and scriptwriters, and they stood over him and he just finished off his script in just three-quarters of an hour, dictating to them. I understood the film was half-made and the artists were on the stage in London...one of the secretaries was a Russian lady and she seemed to get Dylan moving on his dictation.[104]

On the day of the shooting, Dylan took Fisher and Eldridge home to Majoda for tea. Then, at about 6.30 p.m., they left for Newquay. They called in a few pubs and at 8.30 arrived at the Commercial. It was a small, unprepossessing pub but it was one of Dylan's favourites in Newquay. It served Buckley's beer, and the landlord, Sammy Evans, was very tolerant of his behaviour. Dylan especially liked the back room of the Commercial. It had the atmosphere of a small, private salon, rather than saloon, in which he could hold forth, and, as he described in his August 1946 letter to Margaret Taylor, he liked the large, coloured prints of Louis Wain cats on one of the walls.

William Killick was in already in the Commercial. Dylan took Eldridge and Fisher past Killick without greeting him or making introductions, and sat at a table away from the bar. Killick was not invited to join them and he probably felt that Dylan did not consider him good enough to be introduced to the film people from London.

At that moment, Killick realised he had been exploited and that he was no longer of any use, either for money or friendship:

> They cut me quite dead, I haven't a clue why. I thought they didn't want to see the goose that had been laying the golden egg. I'll put the wind up these buggers, I thought, make them think the war's really come.[105]

Dylan and Fanya Fisher had started talking about the war. She was Jewish from a Russian family background, and seems to have been active in or around the Communist Party. She has often been described as a kind, motherly woman but she was clearly quite forthright in expressing her political opinions. William Killick approached their table, and remonstrated with them about their views on the war. Comments were exchanged about Russia and something was said about Jews, to which Fisher replied: "You cad." This was a mild rebuke in the circumstances, not least because the horror of Belsen and the other extermination camps was becoming public knowledge.

Killick moved away, and Dylan took the group to the Black Lion. Dylan ordered a bottle of cider, which was an unusual drink for him, and "talked morosely to retired sailors in dusty corners, provoking nobody, so I thought." Then Killick came into the bar. He sat down and had another, more amicable, conversation with Fisher but still persisted with his challenge that she "didn't know what it was like 'out there' ". Come closing time at 10 p.m., Dylan and Fisher went to the passage leading out of the hotel. Killick was also on his way out. He squeezed past Fisher, words were exchanged, and he slapped her. She hit back and scratched his face badly. Dylan started fighting with Killick. They traded punches for a few minutes and Alastair Graham separated them. Eventually, Killick was thrown out of the bar.

Fisher and Eldridge went to their rooms upstairs. According to Graham's account in *Y Cymro* and his testimony to the court at Killick's trial, he drove Dylan home to Majoda. There were, said Graham, a number of people already in the bungalow. We can be sure that these included Caitlin, Mary Keene, Dewi Ianthe and Griff Jenkins Senior. (Newquay man Islwyn Roberts, a farm worker and later a postman, may also have been present but I have not been able to confirm this). Caitlin had stayed at Majoda that night with Keene, who was down on a visit from London with her baby, by now fast asleep in the bedroom with Aeronwy. Dylan stood with his back to the fire, with most of the party sitting around him on the floor: the scarcity of chairs in the bungalow was to save their lives.

Killick had come slowly home from the Black Lion, pushing the pram which was full of the rations he had bought during the day. Vera was staying overnight at Gelli with her mother so Ffynnonfeddyg was in darkness. Killick lit the oil lamp in the sitting room and searched for his weapons: he was determined to give Dylan and his cronies a taste of the war. Armed with a machine gun and hand grenade, he walked down the road to Majoda, crunched across the gravel drive, stood outside the kitchen and let off several rounds from the gun through the window. The bullets went straight through the asbestos walls into the sitting room. Some went into the beams of the ceiling, and others travelled through into the children's bedroom, "missing us by inches and Aeronwy by feet." What happened next is best told in Dylan's own words, taken from the trial reports:

> We all dropped to the floor.... There was another burst of firing... bullets came into the house... I was frightened. Then the front door was burst open and Captain Killick appeared. He had a machine gun in one hand and a grenade in the other. He was wearing coloured glasses and there were scratches on his face.
>
> I think we told him not to be a fool and told him there were two young babies in the house. He then fired a burst into the ceiling of the bungalow. Capt. Killick said we were 'a lot of egotists.' He seemed to quieten and laid down the gun.

At this point, Dewi Ianthe rushed from the bungalow but in the darkness of the drive he fell over a woodpile and badly damaged his nose. He found a phone, probably at Llanina, and called the police, as well as Dr James Ty-nant. Caitlin was also on her feet. She pleaded with Killick to stop shooting, and he muttered something about having been beaten up in the pub. Caitlin replied that there was no-one in the bungalow who had a quarrel with him. Dylan suggested that Killick should go home but he refused to do so without his machine gun. He raised the grenade in the air and threatened: "If you don't give me my gun I will throw the grenade and we will all go up together." "What," asked the judge at Killick's trial, "did you do?" "I gave him his gun," replied Dylan.

Alastair Graham came across and started talking to Killick, in Greek, about the war, and the state of Greek politics. This seemed to calm Killick down and he said: "I've been stupid. I've had too

57. William Killick, niece Jane, Rachel and Vera outside Ffynnonfeddyg, Easter 1945

much drink." Graham took him out and walked him up the road to his cottage. He persuaded Killick to show him where the guns and ammunition were stored, placed them under a cushion on a sofa, and sat on them until the police arrived. William Killick was taken away to the police station in Newquay.[106]

Back at the bungalow, things had almost returned to normal. Caitlin and Mary Keene were comforting the crying babies, Dr James was repairing Dewi's nose, and Griff Jenkins Senior was running down to the beach to make good his departure before the police came. Dylan, no doubt, was searching for another bottle of Buckley's. Perhaps he recalled his premonition of the shooting: only a few months before, in November 1944, he had written two letters to Vernon Watkins, one about traps and steel jaws and screaming rabbits, and the other promising he would visit Watkins if Gwen promised to bury her sten gun in the garden.

The Trial

In the weeks after the shooting, relations between the Thomases and the Killicks were tense but gradually improved. Alastair Graham was an important influence and he was particularly concerned with helping William Killick through a very difficult time. Graham was, said Charlotte Bacon, "extremely supportive...warm, caring and completely non-judgemental. Just what Father needed."[107] Graham also tried to use his influence to ensure that Killick was not charged; it is understandable that he was concerned as much for himself as for Killick. A trial had the potential to endanger the privacy he had carefully preserved since leaving the diplomatic service. He had no wish for the scandal with Evan Tredegar to be raked over, nor his connections to SOE and the Foreign Office revealed. His attempts were unsuccessful: William Killick was charged with attempted murder, and with three counts of intent: to endanger life, to inflict serious bodily harm and to cause serious damage to property. He was given bail of £50 in his own cognisance, on condition that he reported to the police station every evening. This was soon modified to once every three days, and dropped entirely at a hearing at the end of March.

In the run up to the trial, Caitlin and Dylan decided to tone down their evidence, and agreed to say nothing about Griff Jenkins' presence on the night of the shooting because of his position in the RAF. He did not, however, escape without reprimand. Griff Jenkins Junior told me that the day after the shooting "my martinet grandmother sure gave him hell – she was bloody furious."

Killick's superiors in the SOE were optimistic about the outcome of the trial: "I understand that, on the evidence which the prosecutors intend to bring on the charge formed, there is a reasonable chance of this officer's acquittal."[108] Indeed, SOE had approached the Director of Public Prosecutions to bring the trial date forward "as Capt. Killick is required for urgent operational duties." One of the witnesses for the defence, Lt. Col. David Talbot Rice of the SOE, was a close friend of Alastair Graham, who was to appear for the prosecution. Talbot Rice phoned Graham before the start of the trial and may even have stayed with him at Plas y Wern.[109]

But there would still have been some unease in SOE about the outcome of the trial. Killick had the reputation of being headstrong; he had already been charged with an offence whilst in training at Ismailia in 1943, prior to going to Greece. There had been some concern, too, that his time in Macedonia had eroded his discipline: a memo written four days after Killick's return from Greece suggested that Killick was "possibly a little spoilt by the free life in the field." Killick's temper was well known, and there would have been a worry that he would be presented in court as someone who usually acted first and then thought after, if at all. In his SOE training report of August 1943 was a note that he was often inattentive at lectures and added:

> Being not particularly studious, the more detailed parts of theory have not held any great interest for him.... His written work left much to be desired.... In spite of this [he] is an extremely reliable man in practical demolition work.

Of course, Killick's training had been partly directed to harnessing his natural aggression to good purpose: the same report noted that his "...previous experience, coupled with an aggressive attitude and a good turn of speed, have resulted in his becoming a first-class shot with Pistol, T.S.M.G. and Sten." The report also noted Killick's "enthusiasm" and his "outstanding" ability as a natural leader. These were excellent characteristics in a soldier but there may have been worries that a skilful prosecutor could present them in a more sinister light.

Captain William Killick came to court at Lampeter Assizes on June 21st 1945, before Mr Justice Singleton, and a jury of five men and two women. The judge had opened the Assizes with a service at St. Peter's Church, and lunch with the High Sheriff at Lampeter College. He then proceeded to the court with "a posse of policemen" and a contingent of men from the 5th Battalion of the Manchester Regiment.

Mr Justice Singleton had a reputation for tough sentencing, and he dealt swiftly with the cases that were on the list before Killick: three men were imprisoned for offences against teenage girls, and a cinema manager was dispatched to jail for taking money from the till. The court room filled up when the Killick case was called. The trial, said the *News of the World*, had "aroused intense local interest", as had the preliminary hearings and committal.

The case against Killick seemed a strong one. When he had been charged, Killick had said: "I am responsible and am prepared to make good the damage." His defence could not suggest that Killick had acted impulsively in the heat of an argument: a good forty minutes had elapsed between the incident in the hotel and his arrival at

Majoda. Neither could they argue that the shooting had been a momentary matter: PC Williams of Newquay gave evidence that he had recovered fourteen empty bullet cases on the gravel outside, and five from within the bungalow. There was also the small matter of the weapons that the police had found in his home after the shooting: two sten guns, a revolver, a grenade and 100 rounds of 9mm bullets.

Yet defence and prosecution witnesses alike were doing their best to help. Caitlin and Dylan played down the incident in their evidence, as they had promised to do. Dylan even lied to the court, saying he had known Killick for only two years. He also testified that Killick wasn't drunk at the time of the shooting. Fanya Fisher said that she had not provoked Killick by calling him a cad. All these testimonies helped to pave the way for the shooting to be attributed solely to the battle fatigue of a courageous and patriotic soldier. Lt. Col. Talbot Rice confirmed that Killick was an expert marksman, implying that, had he really been intent on murder, he could not have possibly failed.

However, Mr Justice Singleton was to prove more tenacious. He was extremely concerned with Killick's ungentlemanly behaviour in the Black Lion. Why had he slapped Miss Fisher? he asked. She told me to get out, replied Killick, adding that he had only slapped her gently.

> "Is that any reason why a man of your build and rank should smack a girl in the face?"
> "No, sir."

Why was Killick in possession of a machine gun when he was on leave? His counsel could only suggest that because Killick had been in Greece "and as the only way he could receive orders was by wireless, possibly he did not know of the regulation." But Mr Justice Singleton knew Killick had been in the army since 1939.

Why had he gone to Majoda late at night?

> "I decided to use antiseptic on the scratches [caused by Fanya Fisher] and went to the bungalow to ask Mr Thomas for some."

Why had he worn dark glasses?

> "I wear contact lenses, as my normal sight is very poor, and at

the hotel one of my eyes was bruised. I put on the dark glasses
to ease my eye."

The jury did not need to be reminded that it had been a dark night,
and a blackout was in force.

Why had he taken the machine gun to Majoda?

I thought it would be amusing and a practical joke to frighten
them.

Why had he fired into the kitchen?

By a light in the living-room I could see that there was no-one in
my line of fire. So I fired at a partition, thinking the bullets would
not penetrate it. I did not know it was of thin asbestos.

Why had he fired the gun into the ceiling of the living room?

I was afraid if the men rushed me it would go off, so I cleared it.

"Wouldn't it have been easier to go out, back to your own place?"
asked Mr Justice Singleton. "Didn't that occur to you?"

"No, sir. I realise now that I behaved in a stupid way, but I had
no intention of killing anyone," replied Killick. "I had had too much
to drink, and I do regret what I did that night. The whole affair was
a bluff."

"Do you call it a bluff to shoot bullets into a living room?" asked
Mr Justice Singleton.

Matters got worse for Killick when his defence called a Major
Kendell of the War Office, who had been instructed to attend. Mr
Justice Singleton took a dim view of this: "If the War Office send an
officer down to assist the solicitors for the defence, I don't know
where we are coming to."

Major Kendell explained that he had been sent to examine the
bungalow. This infuriated Mr Justice Singleton: "Is it suggested that
the police are not fit to provide the necessary information? I think it
is a waste of public money, and a waste of this officer's time. I think
it is worthy of an inquiry."

At this point, Killick seemed doomed, and he must have believed
that his fate was sealed when Mr Justice Singleton described the
"case as serious and important as many people would be leaving the

Service with a comprehensive knowledge of firearms. Above all," he declared ominously, "an officer should set an example to others."

But then Mr Justice Singleton, who himself had been an officer in the Royal Field Artillery,[110] completely surprised the court. He turned to the jury and told them that he considered there was no evidence to justify any verdict of guilty of attempt to murder, and the same view could be taken of the lesser charges. William Killick was warmly greeted outside the courtroom by Vera and Margaret Phillips, and a large group of well-wishers:

> Officer and civilian friends congratulated a captain in the Royal Engineers renowned as a guerrilla and sabotage expert in Greece after he stepped from the dock at Lampeter Assizes... Killick's pretty young blond wife, and Wing-Commander Ira Jones, DSO, DFC, MC, MM, famous flying ace of the last war, and a close friend, were among the first to greet him. (*News of the World*, 24/6/1945).

The Killicks went off to celebrate, doing a round of Lampeter pubs and eventually ending up at Gelli where Margaret Phillips had organised a party. Dylan and his group went to the Castle Hotel to drink. Caitlin went home on her own, presumably to relieve Dylan's mother of the baby-sitting. "She seemed perfectly calm," remembers Douglas Ward of Cei Bach, who told me he had given Caitlin a lift back to Majoda, "which was strange because they were so volatile usually, not stable, always quarrelling."

Dylan seemed upset at the reception that Killick received, and the prominence given to it by the *News of the World*.[111] But Alastair Graham told *Y Cymro* that "We were all glad, including Dylan, when the Captain was cleared by the jury. He was a gentleman....". There had been a good deal of popular support in Newquay and Lampeter for William Killick, reflected in the unfounded boast of Edward Evans, landlord of the Castle Hotel, to Colin Edwards:

> Evans told me how he persuaded the woman jurors to let Killick off on attempted murder charge...while jurors were going to the ladies room at his inn.[112]

The support for Killick was matched by some antagonism towards Dylan. Killick was seen as a war hero whereas Dylan was viewed, however unfairly, as someone who had wheedled his way out of war service.[113] Such was the strength of local feeling, that there is a story that the police officer who charged Killick was subsequently demoted, though this seems unlikely. The other factor in Killick's local support was that his mother-in-law, Margaret Phillips, had been born a Cardi, with several relatives in and around Newquay; Killick was on Ffôs Helyg territory.

William Killick also looked every inch the daring, romantic war hero, and no doubt this influenced local opinion. He was tall, fair and handsome, "like a Greek God", said one of his nieces, and always immaculately dressed. Dylan, on the other hand, was short, dark and podgy with poor dress sense: "I remember him in a fisherman's jersey with a gaily knotted tie...round his neck, with long flowing ends to it."[114] There is another partial description of Dylan at the time provided by poet Idris Davies who was living near Llandysul:

> He looked very well, rather stout, and he was sober... he told me that Dent's are bringing out his next book of poems shortly – as gloomy as buggery, he said they were. I had heard of the New Quay case, but I didn't mention it to him. (Glyn Jones, 1981).

A few weeks after the trial, Dylan and Caitlin went back to Blaen Cwm because Dr Evans wanted Majoda for the summer. Killick left the SOE and was sent to a Royal Engineers depot. This was not, however, a 'punishment' for the shooting incident. Whilst awaiting his trial, SOE assumed that Killick would still be an important member of future missions. So strong was this assumption that Killick was sent in early May to Gumley Hall, Market Harborough, for training. That he left the SOE was mainly due to the fact that the Commandant at Gumley Hall did not consider Killick ready for action.[115] It appears that the shooting incident, and the anxiety about his trial, had undermined Killick's concentration, commitment and performance. He himself was, perhaps, a victim of the shooting at Majoda.

The Killicks moved back to Gelli and then went to Suffolk in 1947. William started work as a consulting engineer. Vera became a full-time mother with five children to look after. Later, she found time to join a local drama group, and went to art classes in the evenings. She also began writing short stories.

Majoda was eventually sold, re-built and extended. All that remains today from Dylan's time are the bottom few courses of bricks of the outside lavatory, and the wooden garage in which

58. Dylan at Blaen Cwm during World War II, probably
1944-45, with Alun Thomas

Caitlin kept her rat poisons and rabbit traps. Ffynnonfeddyg, where
the Killicks had lived, was also re-built and 'improved'; it now looks
more like a Spanish villa than a Welsh cottage. The fields between
Majoda and Newquay are today a permanent caravan site, and the
only skylark to be heard is the one that chugs out of Newquay har-
bour taking tourists along the coast to see the smugglers' caves.

The shooting marked the end of Vera's friendship with Dylan.
She did not see him ever again after William's trial in 1945, nor did
they correspond. She did, however, keep in touch with Caitlin. They
wrote to each once or twice a year until the late 1950s. Vera was very
interested in how Aeronwy, Llewelyn and Colm were getting on.
Vera's correspondence before and during the war with Caitlin and
Dylan was destroyed in a fire in the furniture van taking her and
William's possessions from Gelli to Suffolk. Evelyn Milton also kept

in touch with Dylan and Caitlin: her daughter Jane, then about four or five, remembers being at a party in Swansea after the war with Aeronwy.

The Whys and Wherefores

Silence and exaggeration often go hand in hand. All those present on the night of the shooting have said very little about it, even preferring to describe it as 'the evening' or 'the episode.' Even today, people in Newquay are reluctant to talk about what happened. Dylan himself said virtually nothing about the shooting, either in his letters or in public. Alastair Graham gave nothing away until 1978, and then only tit-bits in a Welsh-language newspaper where the story was likely to stay buried. Likewise, all of Dylan's biographers have passed the incident by, often not naming the Killicks, let alone discussing cause and motivation. This has partly been in deference to Killick's own wishes on the matter.[116] When Vernon Watkins approached him about the publication of Dylan's letters, Killick asked for deletion of the references to the 'attempted murder':

> ...I do not wish to try to explain to you the ramifications of this wretched affair, of which you can have no knowledge, and which are best forgotten.... Dylan Thomas's name and reputation as a poet has greatly increased since his death, and I have no doubt but that your publication will be widely read. Some persons of inquisitive or morbid tendencies might be interested in who this attempted murderer was.... I have five daughters. They know nothing of this affair. I do not wish someone, someday, to say to anyone of them, "Oh, wasn't your father the man who attempted to murder the poet Dylan Thomas!" Or words to that effect.... You see, I did not attempt to murder him.[117]

Rumours, half-truths and exaggeration have flourished in the absence of detail and explanation. The most persistent falsehood about the shooting is that William Killick had returned from the war to find that Vera was part of a *ménage à trois* with Dylan and Caitlin. There is no evidence for this, and Caitlin has strenuously denied it. So, too, did Vera:

> I had remarked to Vera that, in spite of everything, in her books Caitlin Thomas was determined to say nothing pleasant about

Vera or William. I leave the last word to your mother, as she would have liked: 'Caitlin always thought I had an affair with Dylan but' wagging her finger, 'I never did, boyo, I never did. I knew him too well.'[118]

Neither is it true that Killick had started shooting because he found an orgy in progress at Majoda that night. The court record is very clear about the timing of the incident: Dylan left the Black Lion at 10.00, and drove with Alastair Graham to Majoda. Killick started shooting at around 10.40; there was barely time to put the kettle on, let alone take any clothes off. And Majoda was simply not the place for an orgy! Its rooms were tiny, and it was discouragingly ill-cared for and very cold.

A gloss on the orgy story is that 'the London people' were filming it. A super-gloss is that Dylan and Fanya Fisher were lovers, and the miscegenation shocked William Killick. And if everybody was present who locals say were there, then poor Majoda would have collapsed under the strain. It's worth repeating that Vera was at Gelli. Augustus John was not there. Neither was Thomas Herbert or Jack Patrick. Fisher and Eldridge, say the trial reports, were tucked up in their bedrooms in the Black Lion. Both at the trial and in a letter to Vernon Watkins,[119] Dylan confirms that only Caitlin and three friends were present in Majoda; the three were Alastair Graham and Dewi Ianthe (both mentioned in the trial reports) and Mary Keene. Of course, nothing was said about Griff Jenkins Senior. Caitlin has written (1986, p.91) that she was in the Black Lion with Keene when the incident started. This is not the case. Graham's account in *Y Cymro* makes it clear that he took only Dylan home from the pub, and that there was a group already at Majoda. Dylan explained both to the court and Vernon Watkins that he had returned to Majoda and told Caitlin about what had happened in the Black Lion. Mary Keene had also told the court that she and Caitlin had been at Majoda all evening.

So why did the shooting happen? Killick was drunk, to be sure, and angry with Dylan's sponging and his refusal to acknowledge him in the Commercial earlier in the evening. We know, too, from the interviews with Amanda Williams and Jenkin Emrys Davies that Killick had a strong temper; his SOE reports also tell us about his aggression which was used to good effect in the war.

Relations between Killick and Vera had become strained over money matters; the incident in the pub with Fanya Fisher seems to have triggered a massive release of emotion. This, indeed, was Killick's own explanation: "There was trouble between me and my wife and I just blew my top."[120] After the high-adrenaline activities of Greece, Killick would also have found it hard to adjust to life in Newquay, as well as to the roles of husband and father. He found, too, that he had little in common with Dylan and his friends. Vera observed in her interview with Paul Ferris that "All the word play, joking and arseing about wasn't really my husband's scene." Killick was a man of action with a distinguished war record; he would have been completely out of tune with people like Dylan who had idled through the war making films and propaganda throw-aways. Whilst Dylan was writing 'A Winter's Tale', Killick was freezing in the Greek mountains, ambushing German patrols single-handedly, surviving on berries and snails, and writing a more spartan and olympian counterpart to *Quite Early One Morning*.

The tension and anger that erupted that night at Majoda could as easily have been primed by demob anxiety. Although Killick had gained experience during the war and in South Africa, he had no specific occupational training. He had returned a hero but his future was very uncertain, and there was a young baby to provide for. It's also been suggested that Killick was suffering from battle fatigue; we do know that for the next twenty years he would have dreams and nightmares about his experiences in Greece.[121]

It is sometimes said that Killick, whose own brother had been a pacifist through the war, had also been upset by the anti-war views held by Dylan and others in the arty-farty Newquay circles. Killick could have spent the war in safety and comfort in South Africa, and made a small fortune. But he had returned immediately to Britain once war had been declared, and enlisted. Within three months, he was fighting in France. Apart from the enforced period of rest in hospital, he had been in active service, or training for it, for the whole of the war. This must have imposed a great physical and emotional strain, not least because he served in the most demanding and dangerous of units, the SOE. It's hardly surprising that his temper snapped in the Black Lion: Dylan may have peed 'God Save the King' on a wall but Killick had seen it done in British blood.

It is possible that Killick's emotions went much deeper. It would not be surprising if he had come back from Greece angry and frustrated by the lack of commitment of the partisans he had been sent to train, and by the ineptitude of his superiors in Egypt. He had arrived in Cairo for his training just as the annual purge of SOE staff was taking place: the Head of Mission and the Chief of Staff were changed each year in the autumn. This led to disorder and often chaos, that was compounded by the rivalry and plotting that went on between SOE and SIS (Secret Intelligence Service). Killick had experienced for himself how hopeless SOE in Cairo were but some of his colleagues were to fare much worse: Nigel West has noted that the lack of logistical support from Cairo for men in the field was "chronic" (1992). He has given a number of examples, including the commando who had radioed "First frost today, no clothing, no money, no food. Help. Help." SOE in Cairo sent him his tennis trousers and silk pyjamas.

Killick's bitterness towards Cairo could have been exacerbated by his experience of the social divisions in the British army: a sapper officer wasn't quite the same thing as a gentleman officer. Perhaps this was why he felt that the value of his work in Greece had gone unrecognised, and that men who had showed far less courage and initiative had been decorated, whereas he had not been. It may also have rankled that at the Welcome Concert held by the Newquay Welcome Committee in the February of his return, he was not amongst the servicemen who were each presented with a cheque for three guineas.

Dylan's failure to bring Killick into the group at the Commercial may have triggered deep-seated feelings about the rejection that he had experienced at the hands of both the partisans and the so-called 'gentlemen officers'. His cry "You're nothing but a lot of egotists" could have been as much about the smug self-importance of the fighting regiments and the prima donna leaders of the partisans as it was about Dylan and his party. The social divisions and slights continued well after the war: when Monty Woodhouse, Killick's senior commander in the field, wrote his autobiography and included an account of SOE activities in Greece, he advised the reader that "Temporary war-time ranks of officers and NCOs are omitted." (1982).

After Shocks

Assessing the effect of the Majoda shooting cannot be a 'scientific' matter; we can only look at various clues in Dylan's letters and poems, make some deductions which may include both intuition and guesswork, and then come to a reasonable and cautious view of the effect of the incident. We can certainly assume with safety that the shooting's impact was not negligible or trivial. Caitlin has written that Dylan was "distressed" by the incident, and FitzGibbon that it "upset Dylan greatly." A 'normal' person might recover from such an event within a matter of weeks or months. But Dylan was not normal. His psyche seems to have been weak and insecure. He had what you might call a "swaddling syndrome". He needed to be looked after, cuddled and petted, fed his cakes and sweets and warm milk, wrapped up in voluminous jumpers, and buttressed with hot water bottles. He was at his most comfortable in little houses and rooms. He could only write well in small spaces, like his sheds and the caravan at Delancey Street.

Dylan was most at ease with family and close friends, and was fearful of the intrusion of strangers or of meeting them. The fragile state of his mind is clearly evident in his letter of February 26th 1945 to Vernon Watkins, written only a few days before the shooting incident. Dylan describes how the ordinary events of daily life are beginning to terrify him, that he is almost too afraid to wake up in the morning, to walk up the street, to greet people, to make phone calls. In the same letter, he raises again "that old fear of death."

Today we are more likely to realise that someone like Dylan may need help in dealing with such a frightening and disturbing incident as the Majoda shooting. Dylan, of course, had no such help available to him, and indeed may not have realised he was in need of it. Certainly, his one experience with a psychiatrist in the year following the shooting ended in farce and bad feeling. As Tremlett has noted, Dylan was not able or willing to share his inner world with anyone. It is perplexing that so much attention has been given to physiological explanations of Dylan's demise and death, and so little to psychological ones, though Ferris and Gittins have pursued the matter well. I am not competent to explore this point much further but hope that these observations will lead to fresh enquiries about the disintegrating state of Dylan's internal world that certainly began with the blitz, was exacerbated by the Majoda shooting and was fatally concluded with the murder of Miss Elizabeth Thomas in Laugharne in 1953. I shall deal with this murder, a traumatic event close to Dylan's own death, in Chapter 5.

Looking for Clues

Was the shooting a profound psychological trauma for Dylan, and one which exerted a major influence on his subsequent poetry? Did the shooting bring about a serious undermining of Dylan's physical and mental well-being that was to contribute cumulatively to his final illness and death in New York?

The shooting certainly had a short-term effect on Dylan. The most obvious indicator is that for three weeks after the event, Dylan, who had been a vigorous and prolific letter writer since his teenage days, seems to have been unable to write to anyone. When he finally picked up his pen on March 28th 1945, he wrote four letters. The first was to Donald Taylor, his employer at Gryphon Films. He described himself as limp and exhausted, but hopeful of being fit, and able to work again on his writing. In the second letter to Vernon Watkins, he describes the shooting and he writes about how frightened he is, and jokes uneasily about sleeping under the bed. The third, brief letter is to Gwyn Jones, editor of *The Welsh Review*, and is concerned largely with the deaths of poet Alun Lewis and writer Caradoc Evans. Dylan must surely have brooded that Wales could so easily have lost, not just two of its finest writers, but three, and all within the space of a year. The fourth letter is to Oscar Williams. Here, only three weeks after the shooting, Dylan seriously raises the possibility of going to America. His letter writing then peters out: he managed only six letters between the time of Killick's committal on April 5th and his assize trial on June 21st.[122]

The failure to write letters is, of course, only suggestive. It may be that he did write in the days after the shooting but the letters have not survived. We can find other gaps in the correspondence in other years that do not seem to be associated with trauma. On the other hand, we can find at least two other examples where presumed trauma is followed by an apparent cessation of correspondence. The first is after the death of Dylan's father in 1952, and the second after the murder of Elizabeth Thomas in Laugharne in 1953.

The content of the post-shooting letters is also illuminating: in April and May, Dylan confided in Vernon that he was depressed and worried. The shooting, he says in another uneasy joke, has nearly put him off drinking. In a letter of May 21st to an unknown woman, Dylan writes vividly of his terror of the past, of the knock on the door, of the crunch of footsteps on the gravel outside the bungalow. There are references to Belsen, guns and drowning. Most tellingly, he writes sarcastically about the serenity of nature, with an extended nine-line description of the noise around him. Dylan's sensitivity to noise may say more about his mental state after the shooting incident than the actual level of noise around Majoda, which even today is remarkably peaceful.

We should note, too, how the shooting seems to precede the fracture in Dylan's friendship with Vernon Watkins. He virtually stopped writing letters to Watkins after the shooting. Dylan had written 55 letters to him between April 1936 and February 1945; after the shooting on March 6th to his death in 1953, Dylan wrote only 12 letters to Watkins, most of which were brief and inconsequential notes.

Perhaps the most significant indicator of the way in which the shooting had incapacitated Dylan is his failure to deal with the proofs of *Deaths and Entrances*. These arrived from Dent on May 30th. Dylan knew full well the importance of this book, both for his reputation and his finances. Yet he did not attend to the proofs until September. A little, but not all, of this delay may have been caused by Dylan's wish to complete poems such as 'Fern Hill'.

James Davies is one of the very few who have tried to draw attention to the effect of the shooting on Dylan. He suggests that Dylan's cool behaviour during the incident can be seen as bravery, but it

> could also suggest that he had lost self-concern. That loss may well have been linked to the shattering of such beliefs as he might have had that New Quay was the long-sought sanctuary. The realities of debt – which had destroyed life in pre-war Laugharne – had not been avoided; now even the realities of war had penetrated that quiet place. Certainly a darker, more despairing note enters his letters during the rest of 1945. (1998, p.69).

In July 1945, Dylan moved from Majoda to Blaen Cwm, and for the next month or so he had a miserable time commuting back and forth to London, still unable to write, except to work on film scripts which he needed to do for the money. It was in July, only a few weeks after Killick's trial was over, that Dylan wrote in desperation to Oscar Williams again asking him to find a way to help him leave Wales for good. Would Dylan have died if he had not gone to America, and would he have been so obsessed with escaping from Wales had it not been for the shooting at Majoda?

There was a vast improvement in late August and September. Dylan started to work again, returning the proofs of *Deaths and Entrances*, writing 'Fern Hill' and 'In my craft or sullen art', and completely revising 'Unluckily for a death'. But within six months, he had collapsed and was taken to St. Stephen's Hospital suffering from alcoholic gastritis, nervous hypertension and nervous exhaustion.

As for the long-term effects, it does not seem reasonable to assume a direct or simple link between the Majoda incident and the events and poems of the early 1950s. But the shooting may have created a platform of psychological vulnerability which varied from better to worse over the next eight years. Its consequence was that Dylan was less able to deal with the pressure of everyday events so that, for example, receiving a huge income tax demand would throw him back into the abyss. Outside events such as the war in Korea and the threat of atomic warfare, as well as daily intrusions such as the explosions on the Pendine range, would have had a similar affect. Perhaps these outside events would not have so affected Dylan mentally, and thus shaped his later poetry, if the Majoda shooting had not already created a basis of psychological crisis.

Dylan became a wanderer after the shooting, unable to find peace or safety in any particular place. He moved more times than in any previous period. Even when he managed to settle, as with the Taylors in Oxford, he was travelling to London every day, and going off for periods to Ireland, Cardiff, Bristol and other places. He was always on the move. Some of this nomadism would be prompted by quite ordinary events, which most of us could take in our stride, like receiving his bill for back income tax in 1948. That day, the vultures roosted on the roof of Dylan's house in South Leigh, as FitzGibbon put it, and Dylan was soon off.

Paul Ferris has been the only commentator to hint at a relationship between the Majoda shooting and Dylan's subsequent decline. Ferris noted that Liz Reitell found Dylan in his New York hotel room only days before his death

> drinking whisky and raving about war, blood and mutilation. He implied that he had taken part in wartime combat himself, that his family had been in danger, that Turkey or the Middle East had been involved.

This may have been Dylan's disturbed mind processing the Majoda incident, where William Killick's experience in Greece had become Turkey, and Dylan's fight in the Black Lion with Killick had become Dylan's own 'wartime combat'. Ferris concluded

It seems likely that the Commando captain, bursting into the bungalow at New Quay with his machine-gun, was in [Dylan's] mind.

The Post-Shooting Poems

What effects, if any, did the shooting have on Dylan's writing, particularly his poems? We can explore this question in two ways. Do we find the shooting reflected in, or 'responsible for', particular poems? Second, can we identify a thematic development in Dylan's work that came after the shooting? In both cases, I shall make suggestions that the reader can follow up with his or her own examination of the eleven poems in question. These are 'In my craft or sullen art', 'Fern Hill', 'In Country Sleep', 'Over Sir John's hill', 'Poem on his Birthday', 'Do not go gentle into that good night', 'Lament', 'In the White Giant's Thigh', 'In Country Heaven', 'Elegy', 'Prologue' and the revision of 'Unluckily for a Death'.

Both Caitlin Thomas and Paul Ferris have suggested that 'Fern Hill' was conceived in the aftermath of the Majoda shooting incident. Ferris has written that 'Fern Hill' is

> a doomed poem: the poet will wake to death.... It is tempting to see the machine-gun shooting at Majoda as an incident, both ludicrous and ugly, that drove Thomas back into himself, to levels of memory that produced the poem. (1977, p.201)

It is also a nostalgic poem, a poem without grown-ups, a poem about "lost childhoods that ended a phase of his life" as Ferris put it. To be precise, it was the Bryn-y-Mor phase that had come to an end: Dylan's friendship with Vera that had started in childhood was now over, together with the food, beer, money and housing that the Bryn-y-Mor Girls, and William Killick, had provided.

'Unluckily for a Death' is another poem that seems to have been influenced by the shooting. It was written in 1939 as 'Poem (To Caitlin)' and published in the October issue of *Life and Letters Today*. The poem was radically revised in Blaen Cwm in September 1945. Whereas 'Poem (To Caitlin)' had been a love and marriage poem, the new version was about death. Its words and imagery are about dying, mortality, the funeral pyre, the holocaust and the grave. 'Poem', on the other hand, tells us of love, light and happiness. Of course, 'Unluckily for a Death' reflects events in the external world such as the fighting in Europe, the 'discovery' of the death camps and the atom bombing of Japan in August 1945. But we should still be open to the possibility that the poem was also influenced by the events of March 6th when the war came bursting into the living room at Majoda in the form of William Killick and his machine gun.

'In my craft or sullen art' was also written after the Majoda shooting, and was sent to Dent on September 18th with the proofs of *Deaths and Entrances*. Dylan tells us in the poem that writing poetry is a selfless art, not done for bread or ambition, or "the strut and trade of charms", nor for the great and the good or the "towering dead." Dylan Thomas, he says, writes selflessly for lovers "Who pay no praise or wages/Nor heed my craft or art." This notion of the dedicated, altruistic poet may be Dylan's response, perhaps unconscious, to the accusation that William Killick had shouted across the room on the night of the Majoda shooting: "You're nothing but a lot of egotists".

Perhaps Dylan saw Killick's taunt and the shooting itself as symbols that the rich, arty-farty days of the thirties were over, that the new utilitarian post-war order would leave no room for the poet, except in the hearts of lovers or in serving the interests of the state, as Dylan himself was doing, making propaganda films for the Ministry of Information. Dylan knew about socialist realism, and of how artists and poets had been harnessed to the state both in Russia and Germany. He had written to Tommy Earp the previous September that peace would bring the cultural police, the verse inspectors, the form troops. Was this the moment that he began to fantasise that America was the only place left for the selfless artist? Was 'In my craft or sullen art' Dylan's American prospectus?

There is a large increase in the number and variety of predators in the post-shooting poems (see Appendix 2). The image of the predator also changes. The harmless stuffed fox in the pre-shooting 'After the funeral', for example, has become in 'In Country Sleep' a fox kneeling in blood. The predatory nature of a number of birds is also significantly developed in the post-shooting poems, and this is especially true of the hawk. Nowhere is this more clear than in 'Over Sir John's hill'. The increase in predators may be indicative of how Dylan saw the world around him after the trauma of the Majoda incident, and supportive of the view that the shooting played a part in his physical and mental decline.

Not surprisingly, there seems to be a persistent theme in the post-shooting poems of being trapped, of encirclement, of the threat of physical intrusion and psychological impingement. The clearest expression of this is to be found in 'Fern Hill', 'In Country Sleep' and in 'In the White Giant's Thigh', though these were pre-figured by the concern with invasion in 'Deaths and Entrances'. Appendix 2 also shows an increase in the number of birds in the post-shooting poems. Compared with *Deaths and Entrances*, the number of references to birds doubled; and compared with *25 Poems*, they increased five times. To the extent that birds are symbols of freedom, light, and hope, they may represent in the post-shooting poems Dylan's feelings about the need to start a new life. These poems, indicate the strength of Dylan's wish to escape, to find freedom, to flee the traps, to avoid the predators. In this context, Randolph Fullylove's comments to Colin Edwards are of interest:

> I remember an occasion we went to a little pub between Laugharne and St. Clears, and it was an oil-lit, little public house. And they'd got these boxes of stuffed birds around the little bar. And Dylan called for a pint as usual... and just as he was about to start this pint drinking, he spotted this one bird in a cage, in this box, stuffed, and simply flung this pint mug at this box – smashed the glass to smithereens. Well, I expected a rough house, I expected the landlord to come and get the police... but nothing happened, apart from the landlord apologising to Mr Thomas. He [Dylan] said 'Don't you ever let me see you keep a bird like that up there again.' That was a heron...I remember going into another house in St. Clears, where they'd got a china model of a heron dipping into a sort of ashtray.... He destroyed that himself by smashing it on to the fireplace.

John Ackerman, in his excellent *Dylan Thomas: A Companion*, traces the development of Dylan's pastoral, pantheistic poetry through his late poems to its apotheosis in *Under Milk Wood*. Ackerman suggests that the pastoralism of Dylan's poetry started with his move to Laugharne in 1949. It's possible, however, that Dylan's "absorption with nature" may have begun earlier, and been triggered by the machine gun shooting at Majoda. The eleven poems written in the years after the shooting contain 132 references to animals, birds, fishes and other creatures, compared with the substantially lower number of references in the four collections of poems prepared before the shooting. Figures are provided in Table 1 in

Appendix 2. Almost three-quarters of the increase is accounted for by the poems written after the move to Laugharne but the process had begun beforehand and is evident in 'Fern Hill' and 'In Country Sleep'.

The increase in pastoral imagery is also present in Dylan's letters written in the aftermath of the shooting, particularly in the letter to an 'unknown woman' of May 21st 1945, and in that to Oscar Williams of July 30th. The number of references to animals etc. in these handful of letters far exceeds the number found in all the letters written in the twelve months previous to March 1945.

It seems that William Killick, and his machine gun, were the unwitting architects of a major change in Dylan's poetry and writing. Poetic genius, like political leadership, is not immune to the influence of 'events'.

5. The Murder

I have suggested in the previous chapter that the Majoda shooting played a part in creating a 'platform of psychological vulnerability' which varied in its severity over the next few years of Dylan's life. The early 1950s were years of particular crisis; not only were Dylan's personal affairs deteriorating, but events in the outside world would have seemed calamitous, not least because Britain exploded its first atom bomb, following on the previous explosions of hydrogen bombs by America and the Soviet Union. By contrast, the early days in Newquay must have appeared paradisical. If *Under Milk Wood* hints at a paradise lost, or one to be regained, then perhaps Newquay, and maybe Gelli, were not far from Dylan's mind, blocking out the grim events that blighted the last years of his life.

Ferris has described the way in which Dylan's crisis was particularly severe in 1952 and 1953. Dylan felt "harassed and trapped", writes Ferris. He quotes John Davenport, who thought that Dylan was in "a great state of terror", and Aneirin Talfan Davies, that Dylan was in a "bewildered haze" (1977, pp281-286). It's also reasonable to suppose that part of Dylan's crisis in 1953 was his own heightened awareness of death, and of the brutality that can accompany it. Within the space of a few months, he had seen his father and sister die, his child aborted, his neighbour murdered and his new patron die from an overdose. The story is best told chronologically so the full impact of events on Dylan can be completely understood:

> November 6th, 1952: Dylan writes to Princess Caetani in deep despair. The Muse is dead, he says, he is completely unable to write, and *Under Milk Wood* remains unfinished. A voice tells him that he will soon be dead.
> November 22nd: The income tax inspectors and local tradesmen are bearing down on him. He writes to Stephen Spender; he confesses to his spendthrift ways and warns that he is at the edge and end of things.
> December 16th: His father dies. As with the trauma of the Majoda shooting, the flow of letters from Dylan dries up. He

writes only a handful of brief notes, all to family friends about his
father's death, until on December 29th, he manages to write to
Dent about the body-snatchers, Burke and Hare. He learns his
sister also has cancer. He seems to recover and writes five letters
on January 5th and 6th. But on...

January 10th. 1953. A Laugharne villager, Miss Elizabeth
Thomas, is battered and stabbed to death. There are no letters
from Dylan for almost a month.

January 22nd. His good friend Marged Stepney-Howard, who
had promised to be his patron, dies.

January 28th(?). Caitlin has another late and bloody abortion.

Such were the winter beginnings of Dylan's autumn death. But
another kind of death was happening, the death of identity, love and
hope: Dylan was in great depression about the decline in his creative
powers and output, and here, too, he may have brooded on the con-
trast with his productivity at Newquay. He was also anxious about
his waning sexual potency. His debtors were threatening action, and
he was faced with the prospect of homelessness once more, as
Margaret Taylor was no longer prepared to finance the Boat House.
The marriage with Caitlin was dead and buried. He learnt of her one-
night stands with the village boyos, kicking her in the face when he
intercepted one of their letters. In short, it was Laugharne that was
as good as dead at the beginning of 1953, and all it meant and stood
for. Perhaps there was no more portentous sign of this for the debt-
ridden, cheque-bouncing Dylan than the imprisonment for fraud of
the Laugharne sub-postmaster, John Eric Jones, on January 13th.
Dylan wrote gloomily to poet Idris Davies in mid-February:

> We... will be moving from Laugharne fairly soon. We're losing
> our love for the place, which is just as well for we're losing the
> house we live in too. I don't know where we are going – to peo-
> ple with no money in a split, warring, witch-hunting passported
> world the possibilities are small....[123]

As this extract from the letter shows, events in the outside world
were also pressing in on Dylan. January had been an especially diffi-
cult month: the bloody war with the Mau Mau in Kenya's Aberdare
Mountains had intensified; the Soviet Union and its eastern bloc
allies began to harass and expel Jews; the campaign against Mossadeq
in Iran started to take effect; the row with Egypt over the Suez Canal

59. Dylan's sister, Nancy, shortly before her death.

was beginning to simmer; the Cold War grew colder with disputes over Berlin and the shooting down of American bomber planes; and fighting broke out again in Korea.

As if all this were not enough for one month, January ended with the hanging of Derek Bentley, and with hundreds drowning as huge seas swept across the east coast of England. The ferry to Ireland sank off the Ulster coast and storms killed over a thousand people in Holland. The heavy rain was replaced in early February by extensive blizzards throughout Britain, leading to more loss of life. Perhaps the only consolation for Dylan in all this was that sweets came off rationing at midnight on February 4/5th.

Death continued to haunt Dylan through the rest of 1953: his sister died in April, followed by the poets Idris Davies and Norman Cameron, and a friend called Helen. The effects on Dylan of early deaths brought about by cancer may have been compounded by events in the outside world, such as the slaying in March of over two hundred loyal Kikuyu by the Mau Mau. In June, the Rosenbergs were executed in America for spying, an event that upset Dylan.[124] It was followed in July by the hanging of John Christie for the Rillington Place murders. August was particularly grim: hundreds were killed in earthquakes in Greece, and in the bloody overthrow of the Mossadeq regime in Iran. Nineteen people were killed on British roads on the weekend of August 24th. Apartheid was extended to public services and buildings in South Africa, and the whole of Europe was badly affected by a general strike in France.

Even escaping from all this to America might have seemed perilous to Dylan: there had been air crashes happening regularly throughout 1953, but August was especially bad with thirteen civil and military planes crashing between August 1st. and September 3rd. Four days before Dylan was due to fly, a Belgian airliner crashed killing all on board, including Sir George Franckenstein. The same day two RAF planes came down, one in Cardigan Bay. No wonder Dylan gave the thumbs-down sign as he left Victoria Air Terminal for the airport on October 19th.

There was, too, the continued threat of nuclear warfare. Dylan had been greatly concerned about the possible catastrophe that had faced the world since the bombing of Japan in 1945. His last year was one in which the deaths of family and friends may have seemed to presage not only his own but the imminent destruction of the whole world. President Truman had warned in January 1953 that

> From now on, man moves into a new era of destructive power capable of creating explosions of a new order of magnitude, dwarfing the mushroom clouds of Hiroshima and Nagasaki.

The effect on Dylan of the imbrication of local tragedies and global events was caught by Griffith Williams, who was in a pub with Dylan near Laugharne. A fisherman had described the awful circumstances of the death of a relative. Dylan

> ...walked aghast to the window and stood in silence for a long while. Then he said: 'Well, that's terrible. I hope that never happens to me, but I know what my end will be – I shall die from the effects of an atomic bomb.'[125]

It is reasonable to assume that Dylan was affected by these major political and social events in the outside world, though we cannot say how greatly they impacted upon him, or even how much he knew about them through, say, the *Western Mail*, the wireless or talk in the pubs in Laugharne.[126] None of these deaths and other events may have been important on their own but we need to be aware of their possible cumulative effect, over a period of just a few months, on the declining Dylan. After all, he was obsessed with death and murder, and had reacted in his war poems with pain and outrage to the bombing of British cities.

Dylan made his first escape in April, spending two months in America. On his return, there were fearsome rows with Caitlin. He also had to cope with the 'death' of his reputation (*Time* magazine's savage personal attack on him had appeared in April), and with the prospect of the departure to the British Council in Tokyo of Bill and Helen McAlpine, who were probably his closest, and most faithful, friends. The Thomas family was also in the throes of change: not just the rapid deterioration of the marriage, but ten-year old Aeronwy was going away to boarding school for the first time.

By September, the surface of Dylan's sanity had started to splinter, as his unsent letter to Princess Caetani clearly shows. He was desperate, trapped and engulfed, making his final escape from Laugharne on October 9th. In the ten days that Dylan spent in London, waiting to fly to New York, he must have thought that the world was moving closer towards disaster: Britain exploded an atom bomb on the Woomera Range and suspended the constitution in Guyana, sacking the Prime Minister, Dr Cheddi Jagan; Yugoslavian troops were poised to invade Trieste; and the Israeli army killed fifty-five Arabs in a raid in Jordan.

Of all the events in 1953 that are part of the process of Dylan's decline and death, the murder of Elizabeth Thomas is the one we know least about. She is not mentioned by any of Dylan's biographers. No-one seems to have noticed that the man arrested and tried for her murder was well-known to Dylan and Caitlin and was daily in and out of the Boat House. The front pages of the *Carmarthen Journal* in January, February and March 1953 tell all: the murder may have been as significant as the Majoda shooting in Dylan's psychological disintegration and death.

★ ★ ★

Elizabeth Thomas of 3, Clifton Street, Laugharne, was born in 1875 in the county of Carmarthen. She spent fifty years of her life in service. She was, said Mrs Brayshay of The Glen, her last employer, "a quiet, unassuming person, a hard and conscientious worker with an amiable disposition." She was well-known in the village, an active member of the Women's Institute, cleaner of St. Martin's Church and dutiful washer of the choir surplices. In the late afternoon of

January 10th 1953, she left her white-fronted cottage and went to the parish church to watch a wedding. By the time she left for home, it was already dark and cold, and the village was filling with fog funnelling in from the sea. At about 5.30 p.m., she stopped at the shop opposite her cottage, J.F. Phillips, grocer and confectioner. She bought some mint humbugs and a Mars bar, and then went into the back room to chat with Mrs Phillips, who was preparing boiled eggs for the family tea. She was soon on her way, saying she would have eggs herself.

She left the shop to cross the road to her home. Mr Phillips noticed that George Roberts, nicknamed locally as Booda (presumably a corruption of Buddha), was hanging around outside. Mr Phillips waved at him but said nothing because Booda was deaf and dumb. Several other villagers passed at the same time and also saw and greeted Booda. It was quite usual for Booda to be hanging around the village when he wasn't working the ferry across the estuary or doing odd jobs.

At six o'clock, Ron Jones was passing 3, Clifton Street and heard screams coming from the cottage, and then noises that he described as whimpers and moans. He ran to the garage where off-duty police sergeant T.J. Morgan of St. Clears happened to be buying petrol. They rushed to the cottage, together with the garage owner, Mr Jacques de Schoolmeister. Sergeant Morgan looked in through the key hole and saw a person inside. He rattled the handle and banged on the door, and all three saw the light go off in the cottage. Sergeant Morgan then broke in through the top half of the small ground floor window, and found Miss Thomas on the floor in the passage. Her assailant had gone. The sergeant noted that the glass of the oil lamp was still warm. Ron Jones bent over the dying Miss Thomas, and she whispered the name of her attacker to him.

Miss Thomas died the next day in hospital. The South Wales pathologist, the aptly-named Dr. Freezer, later told the court that Miss Thomas had multiple head injuries caused by a heavy object, namely, a piece of wood that she used to block draughts at her back door. The murderer had fractured the right side of Miss Thomas' skull, splitting the roof of the right eye socket, and breaking the skull above into fragments. Her right eye had been blackened, and her cheek and forehead bruised. Her right forearm had been broken, presumably whilst defending herself. There were seven stab wounds to her chest and back.

Nothing had been taken from the house but some £200 was found under Miss Thomas' mattress. It was assumed that her assailant had meant to rob her but had been disturbed before he was able to search the house.

Such was the impact of the murder that the Chief Constable, who had attended the scene of the crime himself on the evening of January 10th, was also at the funeral five days later, as was a good part of Laugharne. There were over 150 people present, including the Portreeve, councillors and magistrates. Three priests officiated at the funeral. The murder of this quiet and unassuming servant had, said the *Carmarthen Journal*, stirred the people of Laugharne to their depths.

Scotland Yard detectives were called in to help the local police. More than thirty officers were drafted in from all over Carmarthenshire. The village was turned upside down. All the men

60. Booda carrying Dylan across the estuary at Laugharne, 1940

amongst Laugharne's 960 inhabitants were interviewed, and every house visited. Many of the men had fingerprints taken, and casts made of their wellington boots. A few days later, Booda was taken to the police station and interviewed. This would have been no easy task since he had not only been deaf and dumb since birth but had never learnt sign language. He stayed there several days, was released and then a few days later arrested and, with the help of the Llanelly Deaf and Dumb Institute, interviewed and charged with murder. He was granted legal aid.

After the inquest and three remand hearings, Booda was sent for trial at the ancient village court of St. Clears, one of the smallest in Britain. He appeared before the magistrates on February 24th, represented by his solicitor, Mr Myer Cohen of Cardiff. Up until then he had been held in Swansea prison, where the authorities had tried unsuccessfully to teach him the rudiments of sign language. But attempts by the magistrates to get Booda to understand the evidence being presented proved ineffective. "It is simply useless trying to put the evidence to him," said the interpreter. There were lengthy adjournments, and Booda was allowed to warm himself by a large coal fire in the court room. On his committal, he made vigorous attempts to explain he had no idea what was happening to him.

The account of the committal appeared in the *Carmarthen Journal* on February 27th, and also in the British press as a whole. The case created enormous publicity because of the legal complexities: how could a man be fairly tried if he did not understand the charge or the evidence presented against him, and was unable to communicate with his defence counsel? Next to the *Journal* account was a story about a conference that had taken place that week on how to improve the well-being of "deaf and dumb people" in West Wales.

Booda was sent for trial to the Glamorgan Assizes at Cardiff, and appeared before Mr Justice Devlin on March 24th. He was represented by Edmund Davies, QC. It seemed that the whole of Laugharne had travelled to Cardiff. Some villagers were to be called by the prosecution, but most were there to show support for Booda or to speak on his behalf. But the trial ended almost as soon as it had begun. After discussions with the prosecuting and defence counsels, the judge ordered Booda's acquittal. The evidence to be offered by the prosecution, he said, "was very slender indeed. So slender, that it is hardly worth considering and it seems to me that the position of the prosecution is a rather doubtful one."

There had been no blood on Booda's clothes even though the passage in the cottage had been awash in it. There was no other kind of forensic evidence, either. Booda's confession had been elicited by a Superintendent Spooner of New Scotland Yard who knew no sign language, and neither, of course, did Booda. The so-called confession included a drawing by Booda of a row of cottages on a piece of paper. He had pointed to one of them, and then wiped his eyes as if he were crying. That Booda was hanging about the vicinity was an irrelevancy, said the Judge; so were many other people that dark and foggy night, and the police had failed to deal with evidence of identification that was based on a person wearing a light coat and soft cap.

There were two other matters critically wrong with the prosecution's case. The murderer had extinguished the light when Sergeant Morgan had banged on the cottage door. The murderer was obviously someone with sound hearing, not a deaf mute. Furthermore, Ron Jones had previously testified that when Miss Thomas whispered her attacker's name "it was not Booda. It was something like Harry."

Accordingly, the jury found Booda not guilty as directed by the judge. Mr Justice Devlin explained to the court that Booda was not being acquitted on a technicality and added "It may be that it will have to be considered elsewhere if civil rights have been infringed." So Booda was free but he didn't know it. He had been unable to hear the jury's verdict. He looked round the court room in desperation, scanning the faces of the villagers, until his solicitor gave him the thumbs-up sign, and applause broke out in the court.

But events moved in quite an unexpected direction. Eight months later on Friday, November 13th. 1953, the front page of the *Carmarthen Journal* was dominated by three stories.

On the left side of the page, it reported the disappearance of Mr and Mrs John Harries of Llanginning, near St. Clears.

On the right side of the page was an account of the death in America of Dylan Thomas, "a flamboyant, eloquent Bohemian, with a voice of striking resonance, one of the few writers of modern times to build an international reputation solely on poetry."

Squashed between these two major items was a smaller report on the trial and acquittal of George Roberts. It announced that Mr Sidney Silverman MP would on November 19th put questions to the Home Secretary about the circumstances in which two Scotland Yard detectives had obtained an eight page written and signed confession from someone who had been deaf and dumb since birth and who had never learnt sign language.

A week later, the paper reported that the bodies of Mr and Mrs John Harries had been found and that their nephew, Ronald Harries, aged 25, had been arrested and charged with murder. Harries lived at Ashwell Farm, Pendine, only four miles from Laugharne. There were striking similarities between the Harries murders and that of Elizabeth Thomas a few months earlier. Evidence revolved again around a coat and cap; Ronald Harries had killed his uncle and aunt for financial gain; and, as Dr Freezer was again to testify, both Mr and Mrs Harries had received multiple head injuries with a heavy object.

Booda had been rightly acquitted in March 1953: the name of Miss Thomas' murderer, said Ron Jones who had listened to her last words as she lay dying, "was something like Harry."

Ronald Harries was found guilty of murdering his aunt and uncle at their farm near Laugharne and was sentenced to death on March 16th 1954. He was the last person to be hanged at Swansea prison.

Survival by Denial

It is not easy to be certain of Dylan's reactions to the murder of Elizabeth Thomas. He was aware of it, and was one of those interviewed by the *News of the World* (29.3.1953) in its five stories on the case. It is unlikely that he saw the murder as unimportant in his own life or that of the village. It was a monstrous and brutal murder that paralysed the village and county with fear.

It is the effect on Dylan's letter-writing that may point to the extent of his trauma. He wrote no letters for almost a month after the murder, as had happened after the Majoda shooting and after his father's death. When he did start writing again on February 6th 1953, it was as if nothing out of the ordinary had happened in Laugharne. He apologises to his correspondents, saying he had been up in London and ill with the flu. This is not a convincing explanation: illness and trips to London had never previously stanched the flow of letters, as his output in November 1952 shows. He makes no mention of, or allusion, to the murder until June 22nd., when he jokes uneasily to Oscar Williams about the killer wandering around with an axe dangling from his belt.

Why did Dylan write nothing about the incarceration of Booda in

Swansea prison, the numerous remand hearings, the committal hearing at St Clears, the trial at Glamorgan Assizes and the grotesque travesty of obtaining a confession from a deaf mute? It was not as if Booda was a stranger to Dylan. He'd known him for many years – it is Booda who is seen in Rupert Shephard's 1940 photograph carrying Dylan piggy-back across the estuary. Booda lived in the Ferry House which was almost directly underneath the Boat House. He was in the Boat House every day, running errands to the shops, playing with the children and 'gossiping' with Dolly Long, Caitlin's daily help, who was one of the few villagers who had learnt to understand his language of grunts, grimaces and hand signs.[127]

How could someone like Dylan, with such a passion for murders and detective stories, and an abhorrence of blood, be so silent? Dylan wrote nothing about being interviewed by the police, as he would have been, or of the finger printing in the village, the thirty policemen and numerous newspaper reporters who flooded the village, and crowded Brown's Hotel. He says nothing about Caitlin's fears about being left alone in the Boat House, or the worry they would have felt for Dylan's mother living alone in Pelican, not many doors away from the scene of the murder. The tension and anxiety in the town would have been particularly acute from March onwards after Booda's acquittal: the murderer was still at large. Even by September, the atmosphere in the town was grave enough for John Malcolm Brinnin to note that Laugharne was still in the grip of fear (1988, p.227).

I can only speculate that the murder of Miss Thomas had posed such a threat to Dylan's own psychological and emotional stability that his survival mechanism was to blank it out completely, to pretend that nothing had happened, that Laugharne was still the wonderful place that he needed it to be. His letters show that he was successful in repressing the murder in the short term but by the middle of October, in New York, it seems to have caught up with him, perhaps helping to fire the madness that burst like a lanced boil over Liz Reitell. On October 27th, the day of his thirty-ninth birthday, he broke down and wept, and talked about his 'agony'. He confided in Reitell that he thought he was going mad, that there was something wrong with his mind, that perhaps an analyst might be able to help. Thirteen days later he was dead.

On November 27th, 1953 the *Carmarthen Journal* carried a report of Dylan's funeral. There were many literary celebrities and friends present, and much brawling and drinking in the town. Booda had dug the grave, some say in the shape of a banana on his first attempt because, he had indicated, it was Dylan's favourite fruit. At the house, Booda sat by the open coffin, taking on the role, as Daniel Jones has described, of "master of ceremonies" as people came to view Dylan's body. As each person looked at Dylan's powdered, rouged and lip-sticked face, Booda would indicate by signs what he expected of them. When the due respects had been paid, he would usher them from the room, announcing without speaking that the show was over, the curtain had fallen, the stage was empty.

6. The Spying

"I'm glad the Spy Service didn't take you..."
Dylan to Charles Fisher, December 1939

If the Majoda shooting and the murder of Elizabeth Thomas were the most dramatic events in Dylan Thomas' colourful life, then perhaps one of the most curious was his extended trip to Iran (Persia) in January 1951. He went there, with director Ralph 'Bunny' Keene, to make a film for Greenpark Productions, which had been commissioned by the Anglo-Iranian Oil Company (later BP), whose extensive interests were being threatened by political unrest in Iran, and by proposals to nationalise the company's assets. The AIOC was under attack for the extent of its profits, its domination of the Iranian economy, its autonomous rule in those parts of Iran where the oil fields lay ("a state within a state"), and the low wages and poor housing of many of its Iranian workers.

Desert Shivers

Dylan first mentioned going to Iran in a letter to Benjamin Arbeid on December 7th 1950 – "some kind of technicolor documentary, though God knows what it will turn into". His visit has aroused curiosity because no-one is quite sure why he went, exposing himself to the privations of the desert, the dreary round of ex-pat parties and Keene's hypochondria:

> The long Bunny is still in bed, groaning: he has a 'little chill', he says, has a huge fire in his room, two hot water bottles, an array all over his bedside table of syrups, pills, syringes, laxatives, chlorodyne, liniments and compresses; he uses a thermometer every hour.[128]

Dylan's letters capture his experiences in Iran and describe how shocked he was at the poverty in the country, and with the attitudes of the "horrible" oilmen and government people that he interviewed, and the "Scotch engineers running down the Persian wops". Dylan

61. Dylan in Iran, 1951

was most affected by a visit to a hospital in Tehran:

> In the children's wards, I saw rows and rows of tiny little Persian
> children suffering from starvation: their eyes were enormous, see-
> ing everything & nothing, their bellies bloated, their matchstick
> arms hung round with blue, wrinkled flesh.... After that, I had

155

lunch with a man worth £30,000,000, from the rents of peasants all over Iran, & from a thousand crooked deals. A charming, and cultivated, man.[129]

Thomas Alban Leyshon, one of Dylan's Swansea friends, met him immediately after his return from Iran. Leyshon told Colin Edwards that Dylan had been

horrified at the condition under which the Persian people were living.... He came back writhing with indignation, but this, of course, only lasted until he was indignant about something else, or delighted about something else.

None of those interviewed in Tehran by Colin Edwards in the 1960s recalls Ralph Keene, though their memories of Dylan are strong and affectionate. He was always the focus of attention in any gathering, and so it proved to be in Iran. Mr A.H.S. Shaffari told Edwards that "Dylan Thomas was the man... the rest were in the background... they were a sort of shadow." Mrs Olive Suratgar, too, had eyes only for Dylan, as is evident from her description of the effect on her of Dylan reading his poetry at the British Council in Tehran:

He read so beautifully that I was shivering with delight. I had that delightful sensation up one's spine, when a reading is so beauti-ful... that one shivers with joy. I remember moving about in my chair because of that, and also losing a valuable earring... I had wriggled so much in my ecstasy. It was a memorable experience.

It is not clear whether the British Council in London or Tehran arranged the reading – there might have been help from Dylan's friend Bill McAlpine who had been appointed to the British Council in London in July 1950.[130] There had been parties, if not readings, at the British Council during Dylan's visit to Italy in 1947 and both he and Vernon Watkins had been invited by the Council to give read-ings in Paris in 1948 (though Dylan's was cancelled). The reading in Tehran was certainly 'official' for the British Council Representative's annual report for the year noted that "Mr Dylan Thomas, who was in Persia to write a film script, gave a reading of modern English verse."[131] It had been well attended – Mrs Suratgar remembers over a hundred people present, with a good deal of vodka being drunk beforehand. Dylan's reading included 'Fern Hill' and "the one about his father" – probably 'Do not go gentle into that good night'.

Contact with the British Council at least gave Dylan a respite from Keene ("the long drip") and the oilmen, and provided him with the semblance of decent company and drink. He may also have found some comfort amongst the large numbers of Welsh people who worked for the AIOC. The St. David's Society was very active in Abadan, and organised eisteddfodau and other social and cultural events. It had presented the Bardic Chair to the National Eisteddfod at Caerphilly in 1950. The Chair had been made "by a 73 year old Persian craftsman in the joiner's Department of the Main Company Workshops in Abadan, [and] was despatched on the B.T.C. tanker *British Fame*."[132] It was won by Gwilym Tilsley for his poem on the coal miners of South Wales, making an apt poetic fusion of fossil fuels.

On the whole, however, Dylan was miserable: Caitlin had been told about his friendship with Pearl Kazin[133] and refused to answer his letters; he suffered greatly from gout on the trip; complained about the absence of nightlife and the cost of drinks; and mis-calculated on the weather. He was continually upset by the poverty around him:

> Now all the weather's changed. In Tehran, it was brisk, sunny spring. A wonderful climate. Here, 24 hours nearer the Gulf, I'm sitting dead still panting & sweating. What it's like in the summer, Christ knows. In Tehran, they said: It will be cold down here. I brought a tweed suit & a duffle, & the temperature's nearly a 100. There are great palm trees in the garden, & buzzards overhead. At every station of this 24-hour journey... children rushed up to the train from the mud-hut villages: three quarter naked, filthy, hungry, and, mostly, beautiful with smiles & great burning eyes & wild matted hair: begging for the smallest coins, pieces of bread, a sweet, anything. I gave the first lot my lunch, & and woof! it went in a second.[134]

It would be understandable, but wrong, to think that Dylan might be exaggerating a little in his descriptions of life in Iran. The British Government was equally concerned that the substantial oil revenues had not been used to undertake "extensive economic development". A letter from the British Ambassador in Tehran to the Foreign

AM

Betrol Gwell

Rhan o gynllun yr A.I.O.C. i brif ymlediad cynnyrch eu coethfeydd ym Mhrydain Fawr ydyw helaethiad Coethfa Llandarcy yn Ne Cymru.

Tu ol i nod-masnach B.P. y mae holl adnoddau
CWMNI OLEW ANGLO-IRANIAN CYF.
un o brif gynhyrchwyr creigolew y byd. Pan ddychwel
'mathau' fe waranta hynny ansawdd y B.P. Petrol.

62. From the programme for the 1950 National Eisteddfod

63. The 1950 Bardic Chair being made in Abadan

Minister, Anthony Eden, made it perfectly clear that the standard of living of the people was "deploringly low".[135] The Foreign Office worked closely with the AIOC to protect British interests but it was also critical of the AIOC's "out-moded attitudes...[its] 19th century line." Likewise, the American State Department thought that the AIOC had not passed "the state of Victorian imperialism." (quoted in Bamberg, 1994, p410).[136]

So why did Dylan go to Iran? For many years, the watering holes in London and Cardiff frequented by retired BBC hands have buzzed with rumour that Dylan had gone to Iran to spy for MI6.[137] Dylan, they say, was asked to gather information that would help MI6 and the CIA deal more effectively with the threats to British oil interests from the popular National Front leader, Muhammad Mossadeq. Perhaps it would be unwise to be too dismissive of such bar stool theorising. After all, the BBC, particularly the Persian Service, often worked hand in glove with MI6 and the AIOC to further the company's, and British, interests in Iran – see below.

This aspect of Dylan's visit needs further investigation or we shall have to wait to 2001 when official papers become available under the fifty-year rule. Even so, the records may say nothing if the visit had only been an unofficial shopping trip for MI6. I have set out what I know below, and indicated at the end of the book the source materials that I have used. Dylan certainly had extensive connections with people in and around the intelligence services, including links that involve old Cardiganshire contacts such as William Killick, Alastair Graham and Goronwy Rees. Not to mention Aberystwyth's favourite CIA agent, Evan Yardley, who has written a book about his exploits (1988).

We must also look for clues in Dylan's own life. Perhaps the most significant is Dylan's breakdown on October 26th, 1953, in the Algonquin Hotel, New York, in which he raved about his involvement in war in the Middle East (see Ferris, 1977, p.301). We saw in Chapter 4 that Ferris has linked this breakdown to the Majoda shooting. Might it also have had something to do with Dylan's Iran trip and the complicity he might have felt in the bloody events that had taken place in Tehran only a few months before, when, on August 19th, the CIA and MI6 toppled the Mossadeq government and installed General Fazlollah Zahedi in its place?

Callard's Canard

The speculation about Dylan and MI6 gained some measure of respectability by appearing in *The Guardian* (and other newspapers) on the last day of 1998. Dylan Thomas the "iconic Bohemian", announced the paper, "was a secret propagandist for British intelligence in the tradition of eminent literary figures, including Daniel Defoe and Christopher Marlowe...". *The Guardian*'s story was based on a short article by David Callard (1998) that had appeared in the *New Welsh Review*.

Paul Ferris' response to the story was to describe the whole idea as "barmy." This is hardly surprising since Callard's article was mostly conjecture. It was based on the views of one unnamed "elderly man in a whisky-nasty mood" whom Callard had not even met, and whose opinion was conveyed to Callard in 1980 by a "megalomaniac... minor English beat poet" who had encountered the elderly man at a drinks party in the "late Fifties or early Sixties." Callard lists no interviews or primary research (for instance, at the BP or Foreign Office archives) that he may have undertaken for his article. The only books he cites are Ferris' biography of Dylan and *Collected Letters*.

Callard's argument partly rested on his view that Dylan was an ideal choice to allay Iranian suspicions of westerners because Dylan was the most famous living British poet, and known to have leftist sympathies. This is unfounded: Dylan Thomas was unknown in Iran, as is confirmed in Colin Edwards' interview with Olive Suratgar, resident in Iran since 1936 and a lecturer in the English Department at Tehran University. Dylan barely made it onto her syllabus at that time, and he certainly hadn't been translated into Persian (Farsi).

Both Callard and *The Guardian* article seem to suggest that there is something sinister in the fact that Paul Ferris was told in the mid-1970s that 'The BP file has disappeared'. But Ferris' informant, Ronald Tritton, had retired from BP in March 1967, several years before Ferris contacted him. Callard admits himself that multinational corporations do not keep every file. The policy at BP has been to retain 'higher level' files, for example those dealing with management, finance or strategy. A file about making a film would have been considered 'administrative' and unlikely to have been kept. With sometimes as many as 112,000 files to be reviewed in a year by only one or two staff, a low-level (i.e. administrative) file containing the occasional reference to Dylan could have been overlooked. (Of the other fifteen films that Greenpark made for the AIOC/BP, only three have files in the BP Amoco Archive today[138]). The only reference to Dylan's trip that can be found in the Archive is a brief mention in the company magazine NAFT of June 1951 which reports that Dylan had been in Iran to study places of historical interest.[139] There is no mention of his part in the making of a film.

Callard carefully refers only to the "British intelligence services," since the elderly informant seems not to have been very specific. Was it MI6 or MI5 that was involved? Or the covert Information Research Department in the Foreign Office which extensively used writers and film makers? Or perhaps it was the more overt Information Policy Department whose role was to spread 'positive' propaganda about 'the British way of life'? And why Persia? The elderly informant had not mentioned a country. Persia was Callard's doing, as he makes clear in his article, and the choice seems very arbitrary. Is it not as likely that Dylan was working for intelligence when he went to Italy in 1947? After all, the British and American governments were worried about the growing communist influence in the country after 1945, and Dylan would have been ideally placed to acquire information from the Florentine intelligentsia and Elba iron-workers, whose company he preferred. "Elba is a wonderful island," wrote Dylan in August 1947. "Rio Marina is a communist town: communism in Italy is natural, national, indigenous, independent." No wonder that the CIA felt impelled covertly to help the Christian Democrats to defeat the communists in the 1948 Italian elections.

Then again, perhaps Dylan was recruited when he went to Prague in 1949, and asked to take soundings amongst the intellectuals there after the Communist coup in 1948. If we are chasing intelligence hares, why exclude the Italian and Czech visits?

It is as likely, too, that Dylan could have been recruited after the defection of Burgess and Maclean to the Soviet Union in June 1951. Dylan was on good terms with Burgess, and with people in his entourage such as Goronwy Rees. The defection threw the intelligence services into great panic, and they may have been anxious to recruit someone from outside the contaminated Oxbridge circles to provide information on the British intelligentsia around Burgess.

Callard's article also failed to deal with the question of *why* the intelligence services should want to send Dylan to Iran to gather information. What was in it for them? MI6 and the CIA already had expert agents in Iran who had also recruited a number of Iranians and others to act with them, including Shapur Reporter, Queen Soraya's English teacher. If MI6 wanted to add to the information being gathered by their agents, they had available the large number of British people working in Iran, including the universities and British Council. Why send a naive, indiscreet, drunken poet?

Callard notes that Dylan made little use of the Iranian material, apparently contributing only five minutes to a radio programme called *Persian Oil* that was broadcast in April 1951. Callard then makes a good deal of Ferris' statement that a proposal for a "more elaborate" radio programme did not go ahead because, according to a BBC producer, "the Anglo Iranian Company have some kind of hold over what Dylan might say." (1977, p.258n). Callard dismisses the idea that the AIOC could have any hold whatsoever over Dylan, and boldly asserts, without a fragment of evidence, that the pressure not to do a more elaborate programme came from "British Intelligence".

Callard has unwittingly been led astray here by Ferris, who unfortunately gives the reader the impression that the proposal for "a more elaborate, Third Programme, script about Persia" came *after* the broadcast of *Persian Oil* on April 17th. This is not the case. Maurice Brown of the BBC had suggested to Douglas Cleverdon in early 1951 that "Dylan might do a programme about Persia which he was then visiting." Cleverdon replied on March 13th:

> I don't think Third will commission any more scripts from him until he has finished the two or three which have already been commissioned for some time. Moreover, I imagine that Persia is a rather tricky subject as regards policy; and I understand that the Anglo Iranian Company have some kind of hold over what Dylan might say.[140]

As this quotation makes clear, the "AIOC's hold" was not the only, or even the most important, consideration; it just seemed so because Ferris reproduced only the last part of Cleverdon's note. And since Brown had written to Cleverdon whilst Dylan was in Iran, it is clear that the "AIOC's hold" was nothing more than its prior claim on the material which Dylan had been sent to Iran to collect. Cleverdon also had other reasons to keep new commissions away from Dylan. His letters to Dylan in the BBC archive indicate that his major concern from October 1950 onwards was to get Dylan to finish the script that was to become *Under Milk Wood*:

> I long to see the rest of it. By all that you hold most holy in Wales, do try and finish it.

If Cleverdon's aim was to keep Dylan focused on Llareggub, he was unsuccessful. Both Ferris and Callard have overlooked the fact that a more elaborate programme was indeed commissioned. At some point in 1951, Dylan was asked to write a script called *A Poet Looks at Persia*. Nothing came of it, and on October 5th 1951, L.A. Woolard of the Persian Section wrote to Dylan asking for the script "which was commissioned some time ago". At the bottom of Woolard's letter is written "Cancelled. He did not write it."[141] Nothing sinister should be read into Dylan's failure to write; it was just one of many commissions that he did not complete, including one for the BBC on his trip to America in 1950. Dylan had also included an article on Persia in a list of topics that he might write for the *Observer*, but nothing came of this, either.[142]

The outcome of Dylan's visit to Iran has continued to puzzle, and all those who have written about it have assumed that a film was never made. In fact, Callard asserts "No script was ever written" and argues "there was probably no plan to make a film", implying that the absence of a film contributes to the 'proof' that Dylan was working for the intelligence services. Callard's research seems to have gone awry here: a film certainly was made after Dylan's visit to Iran. It was called *Persian Story*[143] and released by Greenpark in 1952, in association with the Film Producers Guild, and distributed by United Artists. The script, however, was by James Cameron, not Dylan. The intriguing tale of *Persian Story* is told in the next section.

Under Green Wood

Greenpark Productions had been established in 1938 by Walter Greenwood (author of *Love on the Dole*, nine further novels and several film scripts) and James Park, an accountant. Early shareholders included Ralph Keene, John Davenport, and the director and wartime film propagandist, Sidney Box, who had employed Dylan at Gainsborough Films in 1948. The company was set up to

Carry on the Business of Producers and Promoters of Electric
Cinematograph Pictures, Picture Theatres, Music Halls, Stage
Plays, Operas, Operettas, Burlesques, Vaudevilles, Ballets,
Pantomimes, Reviews, Concerts, Spectacular Pieces and
Bioscopic Pictures.[144]

After the Second World War, Greenpark specialised in making
company PR films, sometimes focusing on economic development in
the Middle East and in the newly-independent former colonies of the
British Empire. Greenpark was bought in 1979 by the late David
Morphet, and continues to trade today. Between 1938 and 1996, it
made 145 films, the vast majority for British companies and govern-
ment departments like the Central Office of Information.
Greenpark's 1986 brochure lists the famous writers, producers and
composers who had worked for it, including Penelope Mortimer,
John Mortimer, James Cameron, Laurie Lee, H.E. Bates, Spike
Milligan, Mikis Theodorakis and, of course, Dylan Thomas.

Greenpark, who had already made four *Oil Review* magazine pro-
grammes for the AIOC in 1950, had been commissioned by the
AIOC's General Department in London, whose head was A.H.T.
Chisholm. The General Department – its name was later changed to
Public Relations and Information – worked closely with, and gener-
ally supervised, the AIOC's Information Office in Tehran (see
below), from whose headquarters Dylan sent his first letters to Caitlin.
Responsibility in Iran for Dylan's visit lay with Julius Edwards, one of
the Company's senior public relations managers there.[145]

The person in the General Department who took the lead on
commissioning films was Ronald Tritton. Before joining AIOC, he
had worked during the war for the Army Film Unit, and had then
become Director of the Films Division at the British Council and
afterwards at the Central Office of Information. He later became
Assistant Manager of the AIOC General Department and then its
Manager in 1957.

Film was a powerful sales and public relations medium at that
time, and the AIOC had started making its first films as early as the
1920s. It had taken the lead in 1939 in forming the Petroleum Films
Bureau, which by 1950, reports Tritton, was "achieving shows of
films at the average rate of 2,500 a month to all sorts of users."
Tritton was particularly enthusiastic about what he called prestige
films:

This can be Public Relations on the grand scale. This sort of con-
ception – the so-called 'prestige' film – can back up the specific
selling job by making people feel well disposed towards an indus-
try, a company, or a public authority. It was with this thought in
mind that such great companies as ICI, Shell, Richard Thomas
and Baldwins, my Company, and many others decided to use
films. The publicly-owned Railways, the Gas Industry, the
Electricity Authorities, are all great users of films, too, to inform
and mould public opinion." (Tritton, 1950, written when he was
with the AIOC).

Tritton's conception for the Persian project was "a feature-length
film in Technicolor... it was to be a 'biggie' and was intended as a
grateful 'tribute' to the Shah for all his co-operation with AIOC."[146]
To carry this through, Greenpark first commissioned Terry Bishop,
one of Britain's leading young film makers. He dropped out, lured
away to make *You're Only Young Twice* for the new Group 3 pro-
duction company at Beaconsfield. John Eldridge was another of
Greenpark's leading directors, but he, too, was busy with Group 3
making *Brandy for the Parson*. Ralph Keene – "always a reliable
Greenpark standby" – was then brought in as a replacement.

Perhaps it was Keene or even John Davenport who suggested that
Dylan might do the script. Keene and Dylan had already worked
together and they were good friends – Keene's wife, Mary, had been
present on the night of the Majoda shooting. Dylan's first letter to
Caitlin from Iran in January 1951 confirms that he was being paid by
Greenpark, not by the AIOC:

You will be receiving, at the beginning of each week, ten pounds
in notes from Bunny's firm, for five weeks – by which time I shall
be back in England.

According to Ferris, Dylan was paid £250 plus expenses for the
work. This amounts to £4,858 in today's terms, not £9,000 as
Callard mistakenly calculates.[147]

It is not surprising that the AIOC would have approved of Dylan.
He was well-known not just for his poetry and film work but also
through his radio broadcasts: he had made over a hundred between
the end of the war and 1950. It would have been a bonus to the oil
company in making a 'prestige film' to get someone who was both an
accomplished scriptwriter and a well-known broadcaster. The AIOC

'tended to go for the best', and would have disregarded personal factors such as Dylan's drinking habits.[148]

Dylan and Keene flew to Iran on January 8th, together with Martin Curtis and his two assistants, who were to work with the Technicolor camera. The involvement of Technicolor

> was part of the plan to make the whole venture as prestigious as possible. Eastmancolor stock was available at the time and could be used in normal 'silent' cameras such as those generally used for documentaries such as Arriflexes and Newman Sinclairs.

The film crew arrived at a time of growing civil unrest. There were demonstrations in Tehran and the provinces, culminating in a mass rally in mid-January held outside the Masjid Shah mosque in Tehran. Anti-British feelings ran high, and

> the crowd passed a resolution calling for the nationalisation of the oil industry. Seven leading Moslem clerics declared that it was the religious duty of every Iranian Moslem to support the nationalisation movement. Ayatollah Mohammad Taki Khonsari issued a *fatwa* declaring that the Prophet Mohammad condemned a government that gave away the people's inheritance to foreigners and turned its own people into slaves. (Elm, 1994, p.74).

It was not the best time for British people to be in Iran making a film about oil. Keene made 'desperate' phone calls home, concerned about the safety of the crew members. There was considerable worry, too, that the Technicolor camera – "as big as a dog kennel" – might be stolen or destroyed. Keene demanded that the project be called off. Tritton refused; there was too much at stake to abandon filming, and he insisted that Keene shoot something – "anything" – in parts of Iran that were under the control of the AIOC. In consequence, much of the filming was done on AIOC property or from the air.

Keene returned to London after some five weeks, extremely dissatisfied, and "despising" what he had been forced to shoot. He demanded that the film be scrapped, and refused to print much of the footage that had been developed. Again, Tritton insisted that the project continue, and brought in John Trumper, who had previously worked for Greenpark as an editor. Trumper was asked to make a cut of the material but he had no script or any planned structure to work with. Influenced by Cocteau's *Orphée*, Trumper built his version around the black-leathered motor cyclists that had escorted the crew in Iran, and whom Keene, for some reason, had filmed in detail.

Trumper showed Tritton his edit in May, and Tritton "hated" it. This time Joe Mendoza was drafted in to assemble something from Keene's footage. Mendoza had worked for Greenpark before as a director, and sometimes as a supervising editor. He had made the four *Oil Review* programmes for the AIOC in 1950, and was thus

> au fait with the film needs of the AIOC and the 'emotional climate' of that company as expressed by the films they commissioned and the personality of Ronnie Tritton.

The feeling in both Greenpark and the AIOC "was that we couldn't not make a film", but it turned out to be "the most unloved film in the world." Mendoza printed all of Keene's material, which included a good deal of footage of the "glorious sunset" over the oil refinery at Abadan. The idea came

> of making the film as a tribute to the Oil Company who had given so much of their lives and skills to Iran to develop an industry there and brought such prosperity to it.

This was approved by Tritton, and Mendoza was asked to edit the film through to its final stages, which he completed by July. The Mendoza edit was shown to the AIOC in August at a number of 'approval shows'; there were also discussions throughout September (at the very moment that AIOC's British staff were being evicted from Abadan) about the commentary. Dylan had produced

> some sort of script, but Ronnie Tritton did not like it... Dylan was a prestigious choice to write the film but that is not always a guarantee of a good movie.... The whole project was an excellent example of the usual failure to combine 'high art' with the demands and self-image of Industry.

Mendoza suggested that James Cameron, with whom he had previously worked on two other films, be brought in as the script writer. The viewings, discussion, writing and recording of the commentary were done in October, and then Elisabeth Lutyens was recruited to write the music. *Persian Story* was released to the AIOC in January

1952, and went on general release a few months later. The credits show Ralph Keene as the producer and director, and Joe Mendoza as the editor, wholly understating the role he had played in rescuing the entire project.

Persian Story is an example of the AIOC's covert propaganda activities. There is no reference in the film to the AIOC's involvement and sponsorship, so the British public would have been left with the impression that it had seen an independent assessment of the situation in Iran. However, the reviewer in the *Monthly Film Bulletin* was not wholly taken in:

> The makers of Persian Story explain that the film 'was shot in 1951, as the oil dispute was developing, and has been completed in the light of the present situation.' If so, little light has been shed, for the film's content is that of the conventional travelogue – the landscapes of Southern Persia, the oil fields, the refineries, the people. The well-written commentary suffers from the producers' evident reluctance to make a direct statement about the cause of the disputes.... This indecisive approach is to be regretted, for in other respects the film is executed with much skill.[149]

Today, a reviewer might take a tougher line. The film, including Cameron's script, is everything the AIOC could have hoped for in its Trittonian aim to "mould public opinion" and make "people feel well disposed" towards the oil industry. *Persian Story* is a well-produced panegyric on the benefits of oil-borne technology and civilisation, with not a mention, or camera shot, of the poverty, inequality and disease that had so upset Dylan.

Breaking the Camel's Back

Dylan may have lost interest in the film, in much the same way as Ralph Keene had. He may have been preoccupied with his writing; in the months after his return from Iran, he worked on *Under Milk Wood*, completed 'Lament', 'Poem on his Birthday' and 'Do not go gentle into that good night', revised 'In the White Giant's Thigh' and wrote an early version of the 'Prologue'. There was nothing afterwards to match the creativity of this post-Iranian period; Dylan wrote no further poems save the unfinished 'Elegy' to his father and the revisions of the 'Prologue'.

It is possible, too, that Dylan had no financial incentive to complete a script that the AIOC would find satisfactory; after all, he had "spent all the Persian money" by early April.[150] There had also been continuing ill-feeling between Dylan and the oil company – "there was no-one more ill-suited to each other than Dylan Thomas and the AIOC." His conflicts with the company about the content of the film had started in Iran, not when he returned to London. Olive Suratgar told Colin Edwards that Dylan expressed

> ...tremendous disappointment about the difficulties they'd been experiencing in connection with the film... they were not happily received by the authorities... (the oil company people)... I don't know what the oil company expected of him... they could be very awkward... people wanted to show only the new... probably the oil company people wanted to exhibit what they had done... and I should imagine that Thomas and Co. wished to show the romantic side of the country... which would be the charm for any poet. Probably the Persians themselves would wish to show their modern progress, not necessarily oil company progress. I would imagine they [Thomas and Co.] must have met with difficulties on all sides...they seemed rather discouraged, they didn't seem to have done what they wanted to do.

It is reasonable to assume that Tritton had disliked Dylan's script both because of the attention it drew to poverty in Iran, and Dylan's concern with the lives of ordinary people – "the romantic side of the country". This interest in the people and places of Iran is evident in several pages of notes that Dylan made about his visit. They are written in a way that suggest they were notes towards a film script. They contain only one reference to poverty, a comment on drinking water that Dylan had also made in his second letter to Caitlin from Tehran.[151]

It is also likely that Dylan would have been reluctant to write corporate propaganda. Certainly, on his return from Iran, he had been under no illusion about what the purpose of the visit had been:

> The Anglo-Iranian Oil Company sent me out to write a filmscript to show how beautiful Persia is and how little as a mouse and gentle is the influence there of that Company: my job was to help to pour water on troubled oil. I got out just before martial law – a friend of marshall plan's – and perhaps, disguised, will be sent back to write a script to show, now, suddenly, how beastly Persia

is and how grandly irreplaceable is that thundering Company.[152]

There is no evidence that the dark hand of the intelligence services lay behind the rejection of Dylan's script. Tritton simply didn't like it, and it was not the first time that a script by Dylan had been turned down. In 1942, the British Council had rejected the script he had written for *Wales – Green Mountain, Black Mountain*.[153]

We also have to consider whether the AIOC began to have doubts about Dylan after hearing his contribution to the radio documentary *Report to the People – Persian Oil*, broadcast on the Home Service on April 17th 1951. The programme had been discussed in advance with the Foreign Office, which had recommended against it. Indeed, on April 4th, it had called "a conference on public information policy" to "discuss with the media how news and programmes on Iran should be handled."[154] The conclusion of the conference was that the media should stress the AIOC's latest offers to settle the dispute, as well as "the enormous benefits which it [the AIOC] had brought to Persia."

The Foreign Office maintained its view that *Persian Oil* should be abandoned but if the BBC could not be persuaded to stop the programme then

> it should confine itself to the performance and achievements of
> the Company in Persia, and it should not include any of the following subjects: the case for nationalisation... the strategic importance of Middle East oil and the part which the AIOC may play
> in a future war... Russian interest in Middle East oil... Soviet-United Kingdom/United States rivalry in the Middle East.[155]

Not only was the Foreign Office highly doubtful about the programme, but both the Treasury (the majority shareholder in the AIOC) and the propaganda Information Policy Department advised strongly against it.[156] There was much discussion within the Foreign Office and between it and Chisholm of the AIOC, who was encouraged to take up the matter with the BBC. Chisholm met with Dennis Bardens, the BBC editor in charge. Bardens reassured him that the programme

> would consist of a history of Persian oil development up-to-date,
> ending with a brief statement of the attitude of either side to the
> nationalisation dispute.[157]

On this basis, Chisholm agreed "to assist... to the fullest extent", and he provided the names of two ex-employees, and one employee, that the BBC could approach. A few days later, he informed the Foreign Office "that he believed the script would be harmless."[158]

The broadcast, parts of which were live, went ahead on the Home Service, written by Aidan Philip and Reggie Smith, and also produced by Smith. Philip had worked for the AIOC before the war, and had been an "oil and intelligence attaché in Teheran and Baghdad 1942/44."[159] Besides Dylan and John Davenport, the contributors included Robin Zaehner, Christopher Sykes, Ann Lambton and Edward Hodgkin. Zaehner was an Oxford lecturer, Foreign Office adviser on Persia and MI6 agent. During the war Sykes had been in GCHQ Cairo, the Near East Arab Broadcasting Station run by the Foreign Office, and the SOE. In peacetime he was a Special Correspondent for the *Daily Mail* in Persia (most certainly an intelligence cover) and Deputy Controller of the BBC Third Programme. Ann Lambton was a Reader, and later a Professor, in Persian Studies at the School of Oriental and African Studies, London. She had been a Press Attaché in the Embassy in Tehran during the war, and was a key adviser to the Foreign Office in dealing with Muhammad Mossadeq. It was Lambton who had first suggested to the Foreign Office that Zaehner lead a covert operation in Iran.[160] Hodgkin, who had been in the British Embassy in Baghdad 1943-45, was Director of the Near East Arab Broadcasting Station, Palestine 1945-47, and a journalist on *The Spectator* since 1948.[161] Other contributors were David Mitchell, an economic historian, E. Lawson Lomax, an ex-AIOC oilman and A.H. Hamzavi, Press Counsellor at the Persian Embassy in London.

Dylan said nothing in the broadcast, for which he received ten guineas, that was critical of the AIOC but what he did say mostly "concerned poverty and starvation" and "the lives of the few very rich who lived on the Persian poor."[162] The last lines of Dylan's brief contribution were so striking that the Foreign Office summary of the programme quoted them in full:

> Engineers curse their dehydrated ale in the income-classed clubs.
> The rich are rich. Oil's oily. The poor are waiting.[163]

The Foreign Office received no complaints about the programme "from Persian circles" but the AIOC, who felt its achievements had been completely overlooked, "considered that the broadcast was disastrous in many ways...." A note from E.A. Berthoud, assistant under-secretary at the Foreign Office and a former AIOC employee, sent two days after the broadcast said simply:

> Two fairly senior AIOC people on my train this morning told me that the BBC Brains Trust on Persia... was quite disastrous.... I was told that the general impression was that the Persians had an unanswerable case.[165]

Thus, from the AIOC's point of view, a great deal came to rest on the Greenpark film to counter the damaging effects of the radio broadcast and to present the AIOC in the best possible light, with particular emphasis on its social services, and its role as a "welfare corporation" in a welfareless state.[166] It is reasonable in these circumstances to ask if the content of Dylan's contribution, together with his disagreements with the AIOC in Iran about the film, may have led the oil company to require Greenpark to find another writer to do the script for *Persian Story*. At the very least, the AIOC would have been more than happy not to insist that Dylan should fulfil his contractual obligations.

There seems to have been no further collaboration between Dylan and Keene after their Iranian adventure. Keene went off to Ceylon to run the Government Film Unit, taking with him journalist Lester James Peries to write the scripts. Dylan turned his attention to America and *Under Milk Wood*. His last words on Iran were:

> No, Persia wasn't all depressing. Beautiful Isfahan & Shiraz. Wicked, pompous, oily British. Nervous, cunning, corrupt and delightful Persian bloody bastards. Opium no good. Persian vodka, made of beetroot, like stimulating sockjuice, very enjoyable. Beer full of glycerine and pips. Women veiled, or unveiled ugly, or beautiful and entirely inaccessible, or hungry. The lovely camels who sit on their necks and smile. I shan't go there again.[167]

Greenpark continued to work with the AIOC: it made a further fourteen *Oil Review* magazines in 1951 and 1952, and a film called *Tanker Story* in 1953. Thereafter, it made another thirteen films when the AIOC had become BP. For Greenpark at least, *Persian Story* had a happy ending.

I Spy with My Oily Eye...

Dylan's host in Iran, the AIOC's Information Office, was no ordinary public relations department; it was the company's espionage, intelligence and propaganda unit, responsible for 'non-business' activities, as the AIOC coyly put it. It was more effective, and better resourced, than either MI6's and the CIA's activities in Iran, and its intelligence usually more comprehensive and reliable. Sir William Fraser, AIOC's chairman, once told officials from the US State Department:

> The trouble with you is... that you are operating on the basis of wrong information.

The AIOC policy in 1949 and 1950 was to make as few concessions as possible to the Iran government, and to win the hearts and minds of the Iranian and British populations with an aggressive propaganda strategy through the Iranian media and the BBC home and overseas services.

When the new regime in Iran raided the AIOC Information Office in 1951, they found documents which showed that it had interfered in every aspect of Iran's economic and political life. Staff at the Information Office had written speeches for politicians opposed to the nationalisation of the oil companies, placed articles in newspapers, and had even recruited Bahram Shahrokh, the Director of Iran's Radio and Propaganda Department. The espionage activities of the Information Office were like those of a nation state. For example, in July 1950, it had sent a report to London providing extensive personal details on members of the Oil Committee of the Iranian National Assembly, indicating who could be embarrassed, blackmailed and bribed.

Not surprisingly, the *Sheipuré-Mardé-Emriz* called the Information Office "a branch of British Intelligence and a hive of corruption and spying." The Information Office was certainly buzzing with spies but it was by no means a branch of MI6. On the contrary, the Americans were increasingly worried, perhaps unfairly, that the Foreign Office "was in awe" of the AIOC and "in its in bondage." People like Monty Woodhouse (see below) who joined MI6 to work on Iranian issues needed the expertise and knowledge of the Information Office. Such was the extent of the co-operation between MI6 and the Information Office that the AIOC's most confidential papers were taken for protection to the British Embassy when the company was raided. The British Foreign Office allowed the AIOC to send messages in code from the Embassy and from *HMS Mauritius* in the Persian Gulf. An AIOC staff member from the Information Office was sent to the Embassy cipher room specifically to dispatch and receive messages.

A description of the co-operation between the Information Office, MI6 and the BBC is contained in Mostafa Elm's illuminating book (1994), from which the above quotations have been drawn. The film that Dylan and Keene had been sent to make was a small part of AIOC's extensive propaganda strategy in both the UK and Iran. In June 1951, just two months after Dylan's radio broadcast on Iran, the AIOC was in discussions with the Foreign Office and the BBC Persian Service to broadcast fictitious letters "purporting to come from British residents in Persia" to praise the good works of the AIOC. The BBC declined on the basis that people in Iran would see through the ruse. On another occasion, Geoffrey Furlonge, Head of the Eastern Department in the Foreign Office, wrote to the British Ambassador in Tehran:

> we meet the organisers of the Persian Service of the BBC every fortnight when we attempt to indicate the line which that Service might follow... [the BBC] were very glad to have an indication from you of what was likely to be most effective and will arrange their programme accordingly. (Elm, 1994, p.225)

Elm provides more information in his book on the co-operation of the BBC, and he concludes that the use of the BBC, the manipulation of the Iranian press and the activities of MI6 agents Monty Woodhouse and Robin Zaehner were a major contribution towards the success of the coup in 1953 that overturned Mossadeq.

The AIOC and the BBC also worked very closely with the Information Research Department (IRD) at the Foreign Office. The IRD had been set up in 1948 by the Labour Government

> to check the inroads of Communism by taking the offensive against it and to give the lead to our friends abroad and help them in their anti-Communist struggle. (quoted in Lashmar and Oliver, 1998, p.27).

The IRD was funded through the Secret Intelligence Services

Budget, and ran a covert propaganda war across the world. It worked closely with MI6 – with whom it shared many personnel – and was headed by Ralph Murray, previously in the BBC and the Political Warfare Executive. The real driving force within the IRD was ex-*Daily Mirror* journalist Leslie Sheridan, who had been in SOE and MI6, and was married to MI6 agent Adelaide Maturin. The mission of IRD was to influence the media, and particularly the output of news from the BBC and Reuters. Lashmar and Oliver describe how some journalists "moved effortlessly" between the IRD, MI6 and national papers, including the *Guardian, Economist, Telegraph* and *Times*, whose leader-writers came heavily to rely on IRD materials.

The IRD developed a world-wide network of media organisations and publishing companies through which it covertly carried out its anti-Communist crusade. It also commissioned work from writers, including George Orwell, Harold Laski, Leonard Schapiro, Richard Crossman, Stephen Spender and Arthur Koestler. Fay Weldon joined the IRD in 1952 and worked on the Polish desk. The IRD worked closely with the Congress for Cultural Freedom, which was directed and financed by the CIA from 1950 to 1967 to carry out anti-communist propaganda through prestige journals, book publishing, music events and art exhibitions. The most well-known of its journals was *Encounter*, edited by Stephen Spender. Saunders has given a full account of the CIA's "cultural warfare" programme and indicates some of those who had become involved with the Congress for Cultural Freedom (1999). She describes a spaghetti dinner party attended by some of the people associated with the Congress. The guests included Stephen Spender, Saul Bellow, Hannah Arendt, Daniel Bell and Pearl Kazin, who had married Bell in 1960.

Lashmar and Oliver's book reviews the political and military events in which the IRD played a significant part. One of their conclusions is that the IRD worked closely with MI6 to plot against the Mossadeq regime. The details of IRD activity in relation to Iran are still secret, but it certainly would have included co-operation with the AIOC Information Office, and the commissioning of propaganda films and articles, as well as the influence of the British and Iranian media.

Night's Black Agents

One of the common responses to Callard's article about 'Dylan the Spy' was to call the whole thing improbable because Dylan was too unlikely a figure to have worked in intelligence. This is an understandable response but misguided simply because in the 1940s and 1950s, MI6 and MI5 recruited the most unlikely and eccentric of characters. We need only to think of the cross-dressing alcoholic Brian Howard ("an outrageous, delicious, homosexual sauce-box"), or the excessive drinkers like Burgess and Maclean, the opium-smoking Robin Zaehner, the cartoonist Osbert Lancaster and the senior MI5 officer – who I shall discuss later – who came to the office with his pockets full of insects, snakes and lizards. Dylan would have fitted in rather nicely.

Likewise, Paul Ferris is too hasty in his view that "If a spook had so much as looked at him, Thomas would have hurried to turn it into one of his gothic anecdotes for saloon-bar consumption."[168] Dylan was on friendly and familiar terms with a good many 'spooks'. During the 1930s and 1940s, MI5 and MI6 had recruited men and women were who writers and journalists, as Cavendish (1990) and Andrew (1987) have made clear. Indeed, the head of counter-subversion in MI5, Maxwell Knight, published thrillers whilst he was at MI5. He was a member of the literary Paternoster Club which was chaired by Dennis Wheatley, his closest friend. The intelligence services also worked with the publishers Hamish Hamilton and Fredric Warburg, and the film director Alexander Korda. Malcolm Muggeridge, an MI6 go-between, had recruited Korda in 1952 to channel IRD money to *Encounter* magazine (Saunders, 1999).

Dylan moved in literary circles that overlapped with political and intelligence personnel. He knew, or came into convivial contact with, a good number of writers who were working, or had done so, in the espionage agencies, including Norman Cameron (Political Intelligence Department of the Foreign Office and the Political Warfare Executive), Graham Greene (SIS – Secret Intelligence Service), Alec Waugh (MI5), Katherine Raine (SOE and MI6), and Antonia White (SOE and MI6). Dylan was on close terms with White, and through her (and through Sir Samuel Hoare – see below), he met Silas Glossop. He, like William Killick, had been a mining engineer in Africa and his wife, Sheila Felton, was in the SOE. There was also a group of thriller writers: Selwyn Jepson (Military Intelligence and SOE) who had also written film scripts, John Dickson Carr (MI5), John Bingham (MI5), and Bill Younger (MI5), "the knuckle-duster poet", who dedicated his 1944 collection – *The Dreaming Falcon* – to Maxwell Knight. After the war, Younger, who was Dennis Wheatley's stepson, wrote detective stories under the name of William Mole.

Then there were the writers David Footman (MI6), George Hill (SIS and SOE), Christopher Sykes (SOE), Phillip Brocklehurst (MI5), Derek Tangye (MI5) and Desmond Vesey (MI5). Rosamond Lehmann was never on the payroll but she was extremely close to senior people in MI5 and MI6, and was one of those who attempted to warn both agencies about Guy Burgess. Sir Samuel Hoare was another acquaintance. Hoare had been in SIS and held senior Cabinet posts in the 1930s. But he led a double life: he was an active member of the Oakley Street set of writers and poets that included Dylan, David Gascoyne and George Barker. His closest friend was Silas Glossop.

Constantine FitzGibbon, Dylan's friend and biographer, worked for SIS at Bletchley Park during the war, under the command of F.W. Winterbotham, Chief of the Air Department in SIS from 1930 to 1945. FitzGibbon was involved in some of the most highly classified sectors of both British and American intelligence, including membership of the Ultra operation set up to decipher the German Enigma machine. Both FitzGibbon (1976) and Winterbotham (1974) have written about their experiences. Vernon and Gwen Watkins were also stationed at Bletchley, as was Daniel Jones. The Watkinses worked on decoding low-level (i.e. not needing decoding within twenty-four hours) German air traffic. Jones was in the Italian-Rumanian section, and then in the Japanese Army section, having taught himself Japanese.[169]

Dylan also had intelligence friends in the worlds of art, film and music. He was close to composer Humphrey Searle, whom he had first met at John Davenport's house in 1941. Searle had been an instructor in the SOE, and had been involved in preparing the SOE Vicarage Party, including William Killick, for its work in Germany. Searle remained friends with Dylan to the end. They collaborated in January 1953 when Searle set Edith Sitwell's *The Shadow of Cain* to music. Dylan did the speaking parts, and at the party afterwards he "danced wildly like a faun, and stuffed sausage rolls down the ladies cleavages" (Searle, 1985).

Dylan had also met composer Lennox Berkeley at Davenport's house. One of Berkeley's librettists was Paul Dehn, who was a Major in the SOE, and an instructor in its 'finishing school' near Beaulieu (and had taught Searle). Dehn, who had been a film critic and columnist on the *Sunday Referee* before the war, was to draw on his time in intelligence to write the screenplays for spy films such as *Goldfinger* and *The Spy who Came in from the Cold.* He was also a poet, and a collection – *The Day's Alarm* – was published in 1949.

The connections between the literary and intelligence worlds often included gay relationships or friends. Dylan was a patron of the Arse and Battledress club in Wardour Street. Cardiganshire man Evan Yardley, who was a CIA radio operative in China and Korea, met Dylan in the club in the early 1950s. Evan was with his boyfriend Ritchie, and Dylan with the radical lesbian journalist, Nancy Spain.[170] Dylan frequently drank with double-agent Guy Burgess (SOE and MI5) and Brian Howard (MI5). On one occasion, the three of them were in the Gargoyle Club. Dylan licked the leg-paint (stockings were in short supply) from the legs of Mrs Marie-Jacqueline Lancaster (War Office) and then knocked Burgess out for not standing for the National Anthem.[171] Dylan had met Donald Maclean as early as 1941.[172]

Tom Driberg (MI5) drank at the Gargoyle, and in his autobiography he describes a session there with Dylan and Brian Howard. The Gargoyle was a favourite with the writer-spies; it was owned by David Tennant, brother of Lord Glenconner, who was Director of Missions at SOE and then Head of Mission in Cairo when Killick arrived there in 1943. Dylan and Tennant were friends; Dylan stayed often at the family home, East Knoyle in Wiltshire, and Tennant supported him financially – the last known time was in July 1949.

Alec Waugh was a writer-spy who also had interests in petrol and Iran. Like Dylan, Waugh was a member of the Savage Club, and Dylan refers to him in his cryptic, if not encrypted, letter from the Club on the eve of his trip to Iran.[173] Waugh was generally uncharitable about Dylan but this does not necessarily exclude him from our considerations. At the start of the war, he was a Staff Captain in the Petroleum Warfare Department, part of the Ministry of Mines. Much of Waugh's work was with the film section of the department and he worked closely with the Shell Oil Company's Film Unit. In 1942, he joined a branch of MI5 (not MI6), and became responsible for operations in Iran and Iraq.

Dylan's work at Strand Films for the British Ministry of Information would have ensured that he was known to those in intelligence who had been in and around the Political Warfare Executive. And Dylan would certainly have been known to MI6. His visit to

Italy in 1947, and his contact with left-wing intellectuals and Elba communists would have been noted. Likewise his visit to Prague in 1949, preceded by dinner at the home[174] of Czech cultural attaché Aloys Skoumal. And then there were his extensive drinking sessions in Prague with Vitezslav Nezval, head of the Ministry of Information (Bill Read, 1964, p133). Nezval was a poet and novelist but, like Dylan, had been forced by need into hack work: he helped write the film *Ecstasy*, starring Hedy Lamarr, and reputed in the 1930s to be "the most whispered-about film in the world."

Understanding this complex set of relationships is necessary to evaluating the story about Dylan spying in Iran. Dylan was close to the world of spooks throughout and after the war whenever he happened to be in London. It would have been very easy for MI6 or the IRD to ask an old friend to approach him about going to Iran. It may not have happened in this way, but the network of friendships was certainly there to make it happen.

The Daisy Chain

Any credible attempt to show that Dylan worked for intelligence must reveal the chain – in effect, the people – that may (and I stress 'may') have connected him *both* to the intelligence services and to Iran. Alastair Graham and Goronwy Rees emerge as significant links in that chain, because they can be connected both to the Middle East and to MI5 and MI6. These links are not evidence of Dylan's work for intelligence but they suggest how such involvement on his part could have come about.

The first link, through Alastair Graham, starts with Sir Percy Loraine, to whose wife Graham was related. In the early 1920s, Loraine was Britain's Minister in Tehran. He was instrumental in arranging loans from Britain to Iran and in negotiating the oil concessions for the AIOC. He worked closely with his State Department counterpart, Cornelius van Engert. Loraine was later posted to Greece, Egypt and Turkey, and then to Italy as Ambassador in 1940. Throughout the war, he was an adviser to the Political Warfare Executive. He stayed in touch with other Iranian experts, including Harold Nicolson.

Alastair Graham had travelled extensively in the Middle East before going up to Oxford. In February 1926, he became personal assistant to Loraine in Athens and then, on September 2nd. 1929, his

64. Alastair Graham, centre, at the launching of the St Albans lifeboat, Newquay, June 1949

honorary attaché in Cairo. Graham's nominal post was to organise Loraine's entertaining, hardly taxing work and one that provided excellent opportunities for networking through the Middle East. There may have been another side to the relationship: according to Sinclair (1993), Loraine was vigorously bi-sexual, and he and Graham (who was living with Leonard Bower, an attaché at the Embassy) may have been lovers. It may have been Loraine who had taken his distant nephew, the painter Francis Bacon, to Berlin in 1927 and seduced him.[175]

Graham continued to work and travel in the region until he left the diplomatic service in December 1933. In his *Sunday Telegraph* articles, Fallowell describes Graham in this period as a "shadowy figure... [his] life enters a fog of obscurity and strangeness." He certainly continued to travel in the Middle East, including a journey through the Empty Quarter. Graham was an accomplished linguist, speaking Arabic (though poorly), classical and modern Greek, German and French (modern and medieval).[176] He could have been extremely useful in gathering intelligence (though we cannot be sure that he did), and was well connected to politicians and ruling families in a number of countries, including King Farouk of Egypt and Mussolini's daughter, Edda.

Graham cultivated a number of contacts within the broader intelligence community. During the war he was a liaison officer with the American navy and a lieutenant in the Royal Observer Corps. Graham's house parties in the Wern, Newquay, were invariably gay, and included people from the Foreign Office and armed forces. Comments from local people in Newquay seemed suggestive of Graham's links to intelligence: he intensely disliked being photographed (there are hardly any post-Waugh photos); he had been "on sorties behind enemy lines"; he had "something to do with Military Intelligence during the war"; he had been summoned back to London during the Suez crisis to provide advice; and he had played a significant part in encouraging Newquay man Neville Thomas into the Foreign Office and intelligence work. Thomas was killed by a sniper in Beruit in the 1980s.

None of this added up to much until I had a letter from Griff Jenkins Junior telling me that Graham had been heard referring to a frequent guest at the Wern, a senior person in the Navy, as 'the Dirty Knight'. There were several knighted admirals in intelligence but I wondered if the reference was to Maxwell Knight of MI5, who in the First World War had briefly been in the Royal Navy, and in the Ministry of Shipping during the 1920s. Then Rachel Willans phoned with another piece of important information: when her father, William Killick, decided later in life to tell his daughters about the shooting at Majoda, he described Graham's role in walking him home to Ffynnonfeddyg. Graham, he said, was the basis for John le Carré's 'Smiley'. This seemed unlikely, but it was more than possible that Killick was alluding to Graham's friendship with Maxwell Knight, who is generally recognised as the model for Ian Fleming's 'M'.

Knight's record at MI5 was not particularly distinguished, and he must be held responsible for the early failure to catch the Soviet spy Melita Norwood, who was not unmasked until 1999. Still, Knight was a colourful character. He played the clarinet, liked jazz and often featured on the drums at the Hammersmith Palais. He was mad on animals and wildlife: he kept dogs, insects, snakes, salamanders, bush babies and parrots. He always had something alive in his pockets, even at the office. Knight presented nature programmes on the BBC. Like his friend Dennis Wheatley, he had a voracious appetite for the occult.

I sent Griff Jenkins Junior a list of senior MI5 and MI6 officers, asking if he had heard mention of any of them in the context of

Alastair Graham and the Wern. By now I was convinced that Graham must have known Maxwell Knight, though the evidence was circumstantial. Both men were gay, and interested in fishing, books and music: I could visualise house parties at the Wern with Graham on the oboe and Knight on clarinet. Graham may also have been interested in the occult or pandered to Knight's obsession: Graham had converted the music hall at the Wern into a chapel and painted it green. Fallowell has noted that it was not used for religious purposes because Graham was "a very lapsed" Catholic, according to Lottie Evans, his housekeeper. Furthermore, the young Griff Jenkins, exploring the Wern whilst his father sat downstairs drinking with Graham, had found a human skull in a cupboard in the Library.

While I waited for Griff's response, I did some research on Graham's lover, Lord Tredegar. It seemed likely that he would have known Maxwell Knight. They shared the same passion for animals, especially snakes and parrots, and Tredegar kept a large menagerie at his home, Tredegar Park, outside Newport in South Wales. Like Knight, he carried animals about his person, and would attend his garden parties with his parrot 'Blue Boy' on his shoulder. Tredegar also shared Knight's interest in the occult, and the necromancer Aleister Crowley ('The Beast') and Dennis Wheatley were guests at Tredegar Park. It wasn't hard to imagine Knight leaving London for a long weekend in Wales: a call first with Tredegar, and then just a few miles to the Knight family home at Tythegston Court, Glamorgan, to visit his uncle Robert.[177] Duty done, it would be a couple of hours motoring to Newquay and the warmth and hospitality of the Wern, with the prospect of a few day's fishing for salmon on the Aeron. Not to mention the nostalgia: Knight had been a teenage pupil, as had Dennis Wheatley, at the Incorporated Nautical Training College based on *HMS Worcester*, anchored off Greenhithe near Tilbury. The boys from the Nautical School evacuated to Newquay would have brought back fond memories.

Griff Jenkins' reply came by e-mail on February 20th 1999: "I don't know date(s) when Maxwell Knight visited the Wern, but Percy[178] told me about him. So it is fact."

So there it was. Alastair Graham was connected to both Iran and MI5. As Griff Jenkins put it:

> It is quite obvious that Alastair Graham was in a major network with high ranking military and civil servants, and the gay status

must have been a major influence with these people. Graham must have led a double life....[179]

But what about Graham and MI6? I have already noted in Chapter 4 that Graham was on good terms with Lt. Col. David Talbot Rice, who had given evidence at William Killick's trial. Talbot Rice had been educated at Eton and Christ Church, Oxford. His friendship with both Evelyn Waugh and Graham started at Oxford, where Talbot Rice was a member of the Hypocrites' Club. In 1934, he became Professor of the History of Fine Art at Edinburgh. He was an expert on Byzantine archaeology and art. He had led many expeditions, and had travelled extensively, in the Middle East, particularly Iran. He had organised the Persian Exhibition in London in 1931. He joined SOE during the war and was in the Directorate of Finance and Administration, with responsibility for the Balkans and Middle East, including Greece.

Talbot Rice provides a link via the SOE to Christopher 'Monty' Woodhouse, who was an MI6 agent in Iran. Woodhouse was second-in-command of the SOE operation in wartime Greece, of which William Killick was a distinguished member. Woodhouse had testified to Killick's courage and dedication behind enemy lines at Killick's trial in Lampeter in 1945. Talbot Rice also knew Woodhouse as a fellow classicist, not just as an SOE officer.

Woodhouse, son of the 3rd Baron Terrington, was educated at Winchester and New College, Oxford, gaining a Double First in Greats. Woodhouse was in the Foreign Office from 1945-46 and from 1950-55, where he worked mainly on Greek and Iranian matters. He joined MI6 in July 1950, and immediately began gathering information on the growing political crisis in Iran. He has written[180] that his main concern as an MI6 officer was the possibility of Soviet expansion in Iran. He admits, however, that he was out of date both "on Communist methods" and affairs in Iran. He would certainly have called upon Goronwy Rees and David Footman who worked in the Political Section of MI6, whose major concern was the world-wide "spread of communism."[181] He would also have received help from BBC experts on Iran and from the AIOC Information Office. There were people in the AIOC at this time who had worked for the intelligence services during the war: the BP historian and Persian scholar Laurence Lockhart, for example. He had been with the AIOC before the Second World War and was in intelligence in Iran and Aden during it.[182]

Woodhouse eventually arrived in Iran in August 1951 and worked in partnership with MI6 agent Robin Zaehner (later Professor of Eastern Religions at Oxford) and CIA agent Richard Cottam (later Professor of Political Science at the University of Pittsburgh) to plot against the Mossadeq government.

Like Alastair Graham, 'Monty' Woodhouse moved in the overlapping circles of aristocracy, political and military intelligence, academia and literature. After his return from Tehran, he was assigned to the IRD in the Foreign Office, and was closely involved with his CIA counterparts in setting up *Encounter*, and in appointing Spender as its first editor. Woodhouse was later to become President of the Classics Association and Chairman of the Council of the Royal Society of Literature. In the post-war period, he would certainly have known of Dylan Thomas through Thomas' work and reputation, through the Killick shooting incident and Talbot Rice and possibly, too, through Harold Nicolson. He might also have heard of Dylan through Guy Burgess, whom Woodhouse had known since 1938.[183] I have no evidence that Woodhouse knew Alastair Graham, though it is a possibility through the mutual friendship with Talbot Rice and the common interest in matters Greek. Graham had certainly spent a lot of time in Greece and Crete, and had seriously considered buying a house in Cyprus.[184]

Another source of information about Dylan may have been Louis MacNeice. Dylan and MacNeice saw a good deal of each other in the late 1940s, both at the BBC and socially, usually in St. John's Wood with Goronwy Rees, who lived a few doors away from MacNeice. When MacNeice was in Athens as Director of the British Institute, one of his first guests in the spring of 1950 was Monty Woodhouse.[185] They were both Classicists with Double Firsts from Oxford, but we do not know how well they knew each other.

Woodhouse seemed the ideal person to confirm whether or not Dylan had worked for intelligence in Iran or on any other assignment. He had been frank in his autobiography about his work for MI6 in Iran, and had been helpful to Frances Stonor Saunders in describing his role in the IRD in setting up *Encounter* magazine. I wrote to Woodhouse, briefly outlining what I knew, and asked if he had any further information on Dylan and the intelligence services. He replied: "I am sorry that I cannot help. I have never met Dylan Thomas, either in Iran or anywhere else."[186] Such a response settles nothing.

Another friendship that 'linked' Dylan both to MI6 and the Foreign Office was that with Goronwy Rees, a native of Cardiganshire. Rees, who had succeeded Geoffrey Faber as Estates Bursar at All Souls, Oxford, was an author, academic and MI6 agent, and was also on the closest terms with Guy Burgess. From 1948 to the late summer of 1950, Burgess was in the Eastern Department at the Foreign Office. We have already noted his friendship with Dylan (Green, 1977, p.384).

According to FitzGibbon, Rees had known Dylan since the 1930s. Their friendship was interrupted by the 1939-45 war but was renewed soon afterwards. Rees' daughter has written that

> ...my father's drinking days with Dylan took place when we lived in St. John's Wood at the end of the 1940s. There was a pub called The George, where a lot of BBC people hung out – Louis MacNeice, Reggie Smith etc. – and a nearby drinking club called The ML.[187]

Jenny Rees makes clear in her book that the gatherings that took place at the family house in St. John's Wood with Dylan also included MI6 officers and "BBC cronies".[188] Goronwy Rees, who was in MI6 until the early 1950s, also met with Dylan at the Gargoyle Club, where again they mixed with BBC people and staff from the intelligence services. Rees and Dylan had many things in common, including David Higham, who acted as literary agent to both of them. John Harris has noted

> how temperamentally similar Rees and Thomas were; how the discipline and order they brought to their writing evaded them in their personal lives. And Goronwy saw something of himself in Dylan: the two of them, products of a Welsh cultural environment undergoing fundamental change, were faced by an English society that appeared altogether more stable and powerful. Both of them, Rees suggested, tried to take that society by storm and in part succeeded, though at considerable personal cost. Both became classic outsiders, in England and Wales (no bad position for a writer, of course).[189]

Goronwy Rees knew about Dylan's financial problems, and was always prepared to help, not least with accommodation. Jenny Rees told me:

As a little girl... I remember Dylan and Caitlin coming to the house; they were very, very badly off at the time and were really dependent on subs. from friends. Indeed, my mother used to say that D. and C. virtually camped at our house for a while....[190]

MI6 officer and thriller writer, David Footman, was also another frequent visitor to the house, so frequent that "he almost became part of the family."[191] Footman was MI6's leading Soviet expert but he also knew a good deal about the Middle East. He had been in the Levant Consular Service in Egypt and Yugoslavia between 1919 and 1929, and then in business in Vienna and the Balkans between until 1934, before re-joining the Foreign Office and MI6 the following year. He left in 1953.

Robin Zaehner was a colleague of Goronwy Rees in MI6. Zaehner, a lecturer in Persian at Christ Church, Oxford, had worked in Iran against the Germans during the Second World War. Afterwards, he advised the Foreign Office on Iranian matters and joined MI6, and, as we've already noted, worked in Tehran with Monty Woodhouse. Rees and Zaehner became good friends and Zaehner spent a good deal of time in the new family home in Highgate.[192]

Old Nick

Very little of significance could happen in Britsh foreign policy in relation to Iran without the involvement of Harold Nicolson. He had been born in Tehran in 1886, the son of a British Minister, and had spent much of his childhood there. After he entered the diplomatic service, he was soon appointed Counsellor to the Legation in Tehran in 1925. He continued to advise on Iranian and Middle Eastern affairs after he left the Foreign Office, and his diaries record meetings and eatings in the Iranian Embassy in London, and with Foreign Office ministers and officials. Throughout 1939-1945, Nicolson advised the Foreign Office, especially Anthony Eden, on Iran. Indeed, Mostafa Elm records that Nicolson was called upon to advise the Foreign Office in September 1941 on the succession to the Peacock Throne (1994, p.41). His views were heavily relied upon in the post-war period (his diaries record his exasperation with Foreign Minister Ernie Bevin). Nicolson's advice was crucial in the crisis with Mohammad Mossadeq's government. After Mossadeq's overthrow,

Nicolson's contribution was acknowledged by way of an invitation to "a dinner of reconciliation", hosted by Anthony Eden, for the Iranian Ambassador in London in April 1954; and in luncheon at Buckingham Palace in February 1955 with the Queen, and the Shah of Iran.

Nicolson was a former agent and often had parliamentary responsibilities that involved work with the intelligence services. His contacts with these services were so good that he was often used as a conduit for people to gain access to MI5 and MI6 – Penrose *et. al.* (1986, p.363) give an example. He knew several of the key players dealing with Iran in the late 1940s and early 1950s and who appear in the two chains that 'link' Dylan to MI5 and MI6. For example, Nicolson knew Monty Woodhouse, who was at the Foreign Office and in MI6 when Nicolson was one of the principal sounding boards about Iran. Woodhouse's wife was Lady Davina, daughter of the 2nd Earl of Lytton. Lytton was a powerful political figure and a good friend of Nicolson. Woodhouse was likely to have been a member of the Classical Association, when Nicolson was its President in 1950-51.

Nicolson also knew Sir Percy Loraine. They had been friends from the time they were both in the Middle East. The friendship continued and when Loraine returned to Britain from Italy, Nicolson was, as he mentions in his diary, one of those who tried in 1942 to find a parliamentary seat for Loraine. It's not surprising, either, that Nicolson was on good terms with Guy Burgess and also knew Goronwy Rees and Robin Zaehner.

We should note, too, that Nicolson knew Dylan. He also realised that Dylan was desperately in need of money, as we can see from Dylan's letters of the autumn and winter of 1950.[193] Indeed, Nicolson had become acquainted with Dylan's penury as early as 1941, when Dylan called upon him looking for help with securing a job at the BBC (Nicolson had been a Governor). All he got from Nicolson was a pound note, and the following entry in Nicolson's diary for September 12th of that year: "He does not look as if he had been cradled into poetry by wrong. He looks as if he will be washed out of poetry by whisky."

Poetic Licence or Licence to Kill?

Dylan's visit to Iran with Ralph Keene was one element of a wider propaganda and political strategy developed by the General

Department and the Information Office of the AIOC. Its planning most certainly involved discussions with the IRD and MI6, both of which would have been helpful to the AIOC in securing co-operation from the BBC for future radio broadcasts. This does not mean that Dylan or Keene were 'spies' or even gatherers of low-level intelligence material. There is no evidence yet that they even knew of the wider strategy of which they were a small part, though Dylan certainly did realise that they had been sent to put a fine gloss on the AIOC's activities. His letters suggest that when he got to Iran he found the extremes of wealth and the prevalence of poverty and disease so overwhelming that he was unable to carry out the work that the AIOC had commissioned. That there were difficulties with the company is confirmed by Olive Suratgar's interview with Colin Edwards.

Dylan knew people such as Goronwy Rees and Guy Burgess who would have been privy to the AIOC's propaganda campaign and the work of the IRD. Dylan was also on good terms with many others who were, or had been, officers in MI5 and MI6. He was also 'connected' to Iran and the intelligence services by people such as Alastair Graham and Monty Woodhouse. None of this 'proves' Dylan was in the pay of the intelligence services but it should warn us to be open-minded until the release of the IRD and MI6 files for the period. There may be material in them that makes Callard's canard sit up and quack.

A Pub Poem

(untitled)

Sooner than you can water milk or cry Amen
Darkness comes, psalming over Cards again;
Some lights go on; some men go out; some men slip in;
Some girls lie down, calling the beer-brown bulls to sin
And boom among their fishy fields; some elders stand
With thermoses and telescopes and spy the sand
Where farmers plough by night and sailors rock and rise,
Tattooed with texts, between the Atlantic thighs
Of Mrs Rosser Tea and little Nell the Knock:
One pulls out Pam in Paris from his money sock;
One from the mothy darkness of his black back house
Drinks vinegar and paraffin and blinds a mouse;
One reads his cheque book in the dark and eats fish-heads;
One creeps into the Cross Inn and fouls the beds;
One in the rubbered hedges rolls with a bald Liz
Who's old enough to be his mother (and she is);
Customers in the snugbar by the gobgreen logs
Tell other customers what they do with dogs;
The chemist is performing an unnatural act
In the organ loft; and the lavatory is packed.

Dylan Thomas, Newquay 1943, in *Dylan Thomas: The Poems* edited by
Daniel Jones, 1991.

7. The Plot

Under Milk Wood comes out of Laugharne, New Quay and
Swansea; no man can tell where its influence will end.
(Harold Hobson, 1956).

Under Milk Wood is a powerful work of imagination, but it draws
on Dylan's experience of a number of places, not just those men-
tioned by Hobson, but probably Llanstephan, St. Clears, Ferryside
and Lampeter as well. But of all these, the place most associated with
the play is, of course, Laugharne. In this chapter, I will explore
whether or not this is well-founded.

Laugharne has certainly taken the lead in promoting its associa-
tion with Under Milk Wood, not least through the Visitors' Centre at
the Boat House and the re-naming of pubs and cafes. Both the
county council and local people have been enterprising in branding
Laugharne as Dylan's home and the origin of Llareggub. In
Newquay, little has been done to promote Dylan's association with
the town. There is a Dylan restaurant in the Black Lion and a tree
with a plaque outside Majoda – though the planting ceremony was
boycotted by some, including a local dignitary who protested that his
family was still owed money by Dylan. The Newquay Museum con-
tains little that tells the visitor anything about Dylan's time in the
town. Sadly, Newquay's attitude to Dylan has largely been one of
indifference, tinged with some hostility.

There has been a tendency to exaggerate the importance of
Laugharne in Under Milk Wood, partly because we've come to a
point where it seems that, in the popular mind, Dylan only ever lived
in Laugharne. The myth is perpetuated even by those who know
Dylan's life and works well. For example, Leslie Norris has written
in his introduction to Collected Stories that, in the late thirties, Dylan
and Caitlin "had moved into a small house in Laugharne, the little
Carmarthenshire town which was to be his home for much of the rest
of his life." Daniel Jones made a similar error in his Preface to the
1954 edition of Under Milk Wood, writing that "Before the war he
[Dylan] lived for many years in Laugharne...."

Dylan's first residence in 1938 was for a mere six months, and then another ten months in 1939. In 1940 and 1941, he was at Laugharne only for brief and intermittent visits. From August 1941, Dylan lived everywhere but Laugharne until, in May 1949, he moved there for the third time, and it was his home until his death in 1953. But it was hardly 'quality time': his marriage was in serious trouble, and he was pursued by those in Laugharne to whom he owed money, and by the income tax and national insurance authorities. The period was clouded by his parents' illnesses, his father's death and the range of "little disasters" (as he called them) explored in Chapter 5 (and shown in the Chronology). Indeed, Dylan's letters indicate that he, and particularly Caitlin, were tiring of Laugharne as early as the spring of 1951.

Dylan himself claimed on two occasions[194] that the setting for *Under Milk Wood* was Laugharne. It is doubtful that we should take this seriously, not least because both letters were seeking money. The last in particular, in October 1951 to Princess Caetani, was a blatant attempt to secure £100 (almost £2,000 in today's terms) for the unfinished script. Laugharne is brought in to make the project look more complete than it really was.

Neither is Caitlin's "first-hand testimony" contained in her book with Tremlett (who lives in Laugharne) "unequivocal", as Davies and Maud have put it (1995, xv). The kind of material that Caitlin says Dylan picked up in Laugharne – the characters, gossip, feuds, affairs, eccentricities etc. – had been available to him at Newquay, both through his own visits to the town and his friendship in London with Newquay and Cardiganshire people. We noted at the end of the Introduction that Dylan was assiduous in making notes whilst he was in Cardiganshire and particularly in Newquay. Olive Jones told Colin Edwards that

> Dylan was one of us, one of everybody....that's where he got his material from...he was a great student of humanity... I think I can recognise quite a few [Newquay people in *Under Milk Wood*]....

Likewise, Thomas Herbert had no doubts that Dylan's daily walk from Majoda provided him with rich material:

> Whenever he walked from Cnwc y Lili [Majoda] to the shops in Newquay, he would spend time chattering with the locals, and, I

believe, partly adopted them as his characters. After a while, after shopping and gossiping all over the Quay, he would land up in one of the pubs, and that's where he'd be until closing time.[195]

This 'village' experience would be reproduced in the pub as Dylan gathered local characters around him. As Jack Patrick put it: "He was so interesting that he had one little corner of my house where we used to gather... it seemed to develop into a little Welsh village...."

The influence of Newquay on *Under Milk Wood* has been greatly under-estimated, perhaps because people think Dylan was there only for the nine months of his Majoda residence. Hilary Laurie's book (1999) provides an example when she writes of Newquay that Dylan "was not to spend enough time there to get to know the people really well." I hope that Chapters 2 and 3 will set things right: Dylan's association with Newquay and Cardiganshire began sometime in the 1930s and continued at least until 1945. This chapter will show that Newquay was not an extra or supplementary source as Davies and Maud have suggested (1995); it was central to the development of *Under Milk Wood*, and it was Laugharne which had the minor role in providing the characters and topographical detail that Dylan drew upon.

Roman à Quay

Writers and critics, not to mention the general reader, have generally taken the claims for Laugharne at face value, and have not subjected the text, or the two towns, to careful appraisal. There have been some notable exceptions. FitzGibbon (1965) has observed "...in some ways the village [Llareggub] resembles New Quay more closely [than Laugharne], and many of the characters derive from that seaside village in Cardiganshire where he lived at the end of the war." Cleverdon (1969) has written that "The topography of the town of Llareggub... is based not so much on Laugharne, which lies on the mouth of an estuary, but rather on New Quay...". And, as we noted in Chapter 2, Ackerman has pointed out the powerful influence of Llanina in the play, though he is one of those to have fallen most under the sway of Laugharne's false pretences.

Both FitzGibbon and Cleverdon have indicated that some of the main ideas for *Under Milk Wood* were beginning to emerge by late 1944 in Newquay. FitzGibbon goes further and says that Dylan had started to write *Under Milk Wood* in Newquay. FitzGibbon's wife, Theodora, has also written that Dylan had told her in 1944 that he was writing a radio play "peopled with what he called a 'good cross-section of Welsh characters'. He was going to call the village Buggerall..." (1982, p.156).

It was at Majoda that Dylan proposed a book called *Twelve Hours in the Streets*, though at this time he was still thinking of a day in the life of an English street.[196] The ideas were not taken forward in any substantial way for some time, though they appeared in proposals for work called *The Town that was Mad* (with Captain Cat). There is, however, a clear line of continuity: Dylan's January letter from Majoda describes *Twelve Hours in the Streets* as being an "imaginative... cross-section" of the life of English streets from twelve noon to twelve midnight. By July 1953, his letter to David Higham describes *Under Milk Wood* as an "evocative description" of a Welsh town from midnight to midnight.

We should note, too, how *Under Milk Wood* is prefigured in 'Sooner than you can water milk', a 1943 pub poem about Newquay. The poem contains several of the ideas that later appeared in *Under Milk Wood* – the prying deacons, the spying telescopes, the fish-heads (Lord Cut-Glass is Llareggub's "fish-head nibbler") and the watered-down milk. The poem itself can be found in the 1991 edition of Dylan's poems edited by Daniel Jones, with a helpful note on its drunken, Newquay origins. It is a bawdy and humorous roll call of a cast of seaside characters that were to be properly developed in *Quite Early One Morning* and *Under Milk Wood*.

We also find elements of *Under Milk Wood* in another work from 1943. Cherry Owen's fish-frail of bottles appears in the February broadcast, *Reminiscences of Childhood*. This story also anticipates Utah Watkins of Salt Lake Farm, when Dylan writes about Cwmdonkin Park and "the far-off race of the Mormons, a people who every night rode on nightmares through my bedroom."

Quite Early One Morning, Dylan's 1944 radio talk about Newquay, is universally recognised as the 'seed' of *Under Milk Wood*. Both works are concerned with the passage of time in a small town; both deal with the dreams of the waking inhabitants, and the routines of their daily lives. In both, we see inside the hearts and houses of the characters. But much of the detail is also carried across: some of the shops in *Quite Early One Morning* (Manchester House; the cobbler's), as well as the ships (*Kidwelly*), the chapels (Bethesda), and the characters (Mrs Ogmore-Pritchard) later appeared in *Under Milk Wood*. Some of the names (e.g. Phoebe) in *Quite Early One Morning* are the real names of Newquay people that were changed when they appeared in *Under Milk Wood*.

Key words and phrases in *Quite Early One Morning* re-appear in *Under Milk Wood* (Dai Adam; done-by-hand watercolours; bombazine black). Others are re-worked: in *Quite Early One Morning*, the words "Thou Shalt Not" are stitched on a bosom, whereas in *Under Milk Wood* they appear on a wall (p.3). The capstans of *Quite Early One Morning* look "like small men in tubular trousers" but by the time of *Under Milk Wood* the milk churns at Coronation Corner are "like short silver police-men" (p38). Davies and Maud (1995) give other examples, and they conclude that *Quite Early One Morning* "was a veritable store-house of phrases, rhythms and details later resurrected or modified in *Under Milk Wood*."

Further elements of *Under Milk Wood* are found in Dylan's letter poem from Newquay to Tommy Earp in September 1944, and in his letter to Margaret Taylor of August 29th, 1946. These are identified and discussed below. Taken together, *Quite Early One Morning*, 'Sooner than you can water milk' and the Earp and Taylor letters indicate how firmly *Under Milk Wood* was being established in the people and places of wartime Newquay.

Davies and Maud (1995) have indicated that the other important milestones in the development of *Under Milk Wood* were the radio scripts *The Londoner, Margate – Past and Present, How to Begin a Story, Holiday Memory* and *The Crumbs of One Man's Year*, all broadcast in 1946. They are closely connected in time to Dylan's stay at Majoda, and anticipate some of the material and ideas of *Under Milk Wood*. Indeed, in his review of *Holiday Memory* in November 1946, Edward Sackville-West wondered "why this remarkable poet has never attempted a poetic drama for broadcasting."[197]

In April 1947, Dylan and family went to Italy for some four months. His letters confirm that he intended to write what he called a "radio play", but both the oppressive heat and his work on 'In Country Sleep' meant that he made little progress with it.[198] In June, his pre-recorded radio feature, *Return Journey*, was broadcast. Buoyed by its success, Dylan wrote in July to his parents: "I want very much to write a full-length – hour to hour & a half – broadcast play; & hope to do it, in South Leigh [Oxford], this autumn."[199] Dylan's intent was now clear, as are its Newquay roots. The early development of *Under Milk Wood* was within the gravitational pull of Cardiganshire, as was 'In Country Sleep' that had been inspired by Gelli and the Aeron Valley. It seems that while Dylan was in exile in Oxford and Italy from early 1946 to May 1949, his muse was hunting the lanes of Cardiganshire. This is hardly surprising since it had been in Newquay that Dylan had last experienced a sustained period of creativity as a poet. He also had to hand his Newquay notebooks.

From South Leigh to Tenby

Dylan was as good as his word. His money-seeking letter from South Leigh of March 6th 1948 to John Ormond indicates that he was working on what was to become *Under Milk Wood*: "A radio play I am writing has Laugharne, though not by name, as its setting." Work continued on the script at South Leigh and the play resonates strongly through Dylan's October letter to Margaret Taylor. FitzGibbon notes (p.304) that Dylan read a "first version" of the play to a group of poets in Prague in March 1949, before his move to Laugharne in May. It is not clear from Colin Edwards' interview with Jirina Haukova, Dylan's guide in Prague and FitzGibbon's source, whether Dylan read extracts from the play or merely gave an extended description.

Dylan worked on the script through the rest of 1949, apparently to the neglect of other writing, as he complained in a letter to John Davenport in October. Whilst the play was taking shape, both Newquay and Cardiganshire continued to be in Dylan's mind: Llanina and the Aeron Valley were mentioned in his 1949 broadcast *Living in Wales*, as is "Mrs Evans the Pop", who was, I shall suggest later, Mrs Mary Evans of the Emporium in Newquay. Such recall is hardly surprising since Newquay in particular was, as Davies and Maud have put it, "one of those characterful islands [Dylan's] soul always needed to return to." (1995, p.xxix).

Dylan's move to Laugharne in 1949 came after almost ten years absence from the town, apart from odd visits. After his initial happiness, most evident in the often-quoted letter of May 11th to Margaret Taylor, life in Laugharne became more difficult and uncertain, and the task of writing no easier. 1950 was particularly demanding: Dylan's father was seriously ill in January, and in February Dylan went to America for three months. A good deal of energy was expended in preparing and recovering from the trip, not least because

Caitlin had found out about Pearl Kazin, who had arrived in London in September 1950. For most of this autumn, Dylan was in London, often ill and without proper accommodation.

We must then be cautious in assessing Laugharne's impact on the first half of the play, which he sent to Douglas Cleverdon in October 1950, and, with a few alterations, to *Botteghe Oscure* a year later. It was, as Davies and Maud have confirmed, much as we know that part of the script today.[200] It is of little consequence that over the next three years, when Dylan was trying to finish the play, he lived in Laugharne. Almost all the people, places and topography of Llareggub make their appearance in the first part of the play.

On Friday October 2nd 1953, Dylan gave a reading at the Tenby and District Arts Club. Garlick has given an extended description of the event, and written a poem about it.[201] Dylan arrived late, and the audience ("...retired army officers and wives in hats...were generously represented...one had the feeling that they had come to watch a native make a fool of himself...") were listening to a Brahms piano recital, which the organisers had arranged in case Dylan failed to turn up. The audience was hostile at first but Dylan read the whole of *Under Milk Wood* and they were soon won over. The radio play that was written in Oxfordshire and Carmarthenshire, and was largely inspired by Cardiganshire, seems to have had its first complete British reading in Pembrokeshire, and the reporter from the *Tenby Observer* was duly impressed:

> The Salad Bowl was full to capacity and expectation was high when Mr Dylan Thomas rose to speak.... His 'dream-drama' gives twenty four hours in the lives, sleeping and awake, of the inhabitants of the village of Milk Wood, opening in the 'bible-black' night as they lie in their beds. This strange drama... shows unmistakably the fire and power of genius. It is at once rich and arresting, as mercilessly satirical as Swift's satires, as uproariously amusing and broad as Rabelais. Inimitably and, as it were, with a careless exuberance and vitality, the poet brings before our eyes a crowd of men and women.... If they have mean little souls, lewd and sensual motives and unappetising habits, the foul body of the infected world is held up to ridicule unsparingly in a torrent of language virile and ruthless, in balanced lines of intricate poem, rich in onomatopoeia and alliteration. 'With wanton heed and giddy cunning' Mr Dylan Thomas's rich and vibrant voice made members aware of all this.... Perhaps at some future date the

Tenby Arts Club may have the joy of hearing the same voice in his poems of moving beauty and vision."[202]

Just Cockles and Dabs

It is well to remember that *Under Milk Wood* is "rooted in particularity and locality". There is a "literal base to the imaginative truth" (Ackerman, 1998). Dylan had a considerable intellect and a powerful imagination but his work was based in the realities of everyday life. In this respect, he was at one with the tailors and drapers that he so ridiculed: he was highly dependent on the quality of the material that came to him, either through his own observations or the stories and gossip of his local friends.

Let's start with the obvious. *Under Milk Wood* is about a small Welsh seaside town: the "Welshness of the majority of its characters and situations" stands out, as T. James Jones has rightly noted (1971). Why then would Dylan model Llareggub on Laugharne? Laugharne is in Wales but it is not Welsh. It has always been an English-speaking and English-cultured enclave within Welsh Carmarthenshire. The bardic Rev Eli Jenkins, dreaming of druids and his eisteddfodau, would not have felt at home in Laugharne, for eisteddfodau were not an important part of its life. Newquay, on the other hand, had a flourishing culture of eisteddfodau and concerts, including the impromptu summer ones on the pier given by the holidaying South Wales workers. The place of worship in Llareggub is a chapel called Bethesda, and the text of *Under Milk Wood* has many references to preachers, parchs and chapels. The snooping chapel elders first appeared in Dylan's Newquay pub poem, then again in the Newquay poem sent to Tommy Earp, re-appearing once more in the form of the grim, reproving Newquay chapels of *Quite Early One Morning*. The chapels in Newquay were thriving concerns. Sunday observance was very strict, to the extent that many families took their Sunday meals to the bakers on Saturday evening to be cooked there overnight. Laugharne, on the other hand, was a church-going town. The chapels had always been a minor element of its life, as Cleverdon noted on a visit to the town:

> It was a wonderful experience staying [in Laugharne] with Dylan – the village is in Wales, but on the Pembrokeshire border; and instead of having one pub and seven chapels, it had one derelict chapel and about twenty pubs... (1954)

Cleverdon's recall is not without some exaggeration but the Englishness of Laugharne, and the insignificance and decline of its chapels, are described by Min Lewis in her 1967 book, *Laugharne and Dylan Thomas*.

It is strange that, in the forty-five years since *Under Milk Wood* was first published, few attempts have been made to identify those residents of Laugharne upon whom the characters of *Under Milk Wood* are supposed to be based. Min Lewis has tried but her account is often partisan and confused. Nevertheless, she identifies Rosie Probert as a woman of that name who had once lived in Horsepool Road, Laugharne. Lewis suggests that Beynon the Butcher was Carl Eynon who ran both a butcher's shop in St. Clears, and a pub next door called the Butchers' Arms where Dylan used to drink and scrounge cawl from Mrs Eynon. Min Lewis' papers in the National Library of Wales contain interesting information on Dylan and Laugharne, and the range of people there with whom he was friendly.

It is also curious that none of Laugharne's well-known features appear in *Under Milk Wood*. If Llareggub is rooted in Laugharne, as Ackerman for one claims, then we should expect some reference or allusion to Laugharne's distinctive and historic characteristics. Yet we find nothing about the Town Corporation, the tradition of walking the bounds, the Portreeve, a walled town, the jail in the Town Hall, or the ferry to Llanybri and its deaf and dumb ferryman, Booda. Apart from the cockles and dab fish, there's very little evidence from *Under Milk Wood* that it is rooted deeply in the "particularity and locality" of Laugharne.

What's in a Sketch?

One factor that tells us that Llareggub is Newquay is Dylan's own sketch of Llareggub. It's a sketch of Newquay seen from Majoda. The sea is on the right of the town. Go to Laugharne, look across the estuary from the Boat House to Sir John's Hill, and the sea is on your left. In the sketch, the houses of Coronation Street march across the flank of the hill. This is what they do at Newquay whereas at Laugharne there are no houses at all on Sir John's Hill. In *Welsh Dylan*, Ackerman says that Laugharne's streets descend to the mud-flats and estuary at the foot of Sir John's Hill (1998, p.128), so that the town is literally below ('Under') Milk Wood. Nothing could be further from the truth. The bulk of Laugharne is nowhere near Sir

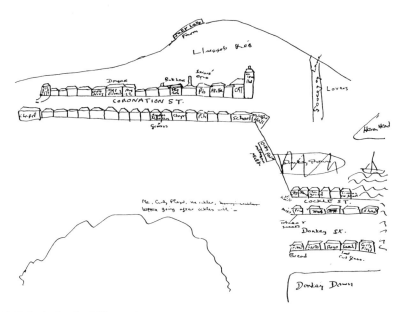

65. Dylan's sketch of Llareggub

John's Hill but is almost opposite on its own little hill. Most of the town cannot even be seen from Dylan's writing shed.

In the sketch, Goosegog Lane goes across the hill, as does the coastal footpath in Newquay from Lewis Terrace across the cliff to the old coastguard hut. This was the path that Dylan probably took in *Quite Early One Morning* (p.19) with the town behind and below him. However, this path was not the actual inspiration for Goosegog Lane. This was Brongwyn Lane, which is discussed below.

Then we have to consider the shape of the hill in Dylan's sketch. It would be wrong to think that Dylan randomly chose the shape because, as Ackerman has noted, Dylan's imagination was rooted in "topographical precision". The shape of Llareggub Hill in the sketch is the shape of the hill on which Newquay stands. It is high and steep-sided. Sir John's Hill, on the other hand, is low and flat, slug-like even, quite unlike the hill that Dylan drew. In the sketch, he placed Heron Head at the foot of the cliff. This is as it is at Newquay: the large rock Carreg Walltog sits at the base of Newquay Head.

Dylan first positioned Donkey Down in the middle of his sketch and then crossed it out. This crossed-out Down is approximately where Newquay's Downs are to be seen looking from Majoda, and I will return to them shortly.

We should note that, on a map of Laugharne, Ackerman erroneously sites Salt House Farm at the top of Sir John's Hill, blindly copying Dylan's sketch. (1994, p.290). Davies and Maud have made the same mistake, writing that "the real Sir John's Hill is topped by Salt House Farm" (1995, p.65). Salt House Farm is at the foot of the hill, on its far side. There is a farm near the top – Sir John Hill's Farm – but it cannot be seen from the Boat House or from Laugharne.

Right up his Street

Dylan's concern with the life of streets fed into the development of *Under Milk Wood*. We have already noted his proposal for a book about London streets called *Twelve Hours in the Streets* which was conceived at Newquay. This interest continued: Dylan formulated ideas for a new play called *Two Streets* which he discussed with Phillip Burton a few days before he left for America in 1953. This was to be a play about two families in neighbouring streets in a small industrial town in South Wales. Other writers were also interested in streets, including Dylan's fellow club member at the Savage, Louis Golding, who wrote *Magnolia Street*.

Dylan was not interested in just any old street. His experience was of *terraces* and the communities they produce. As early as 1933/34, he told Bill Trick that he wanted to write a sketch "centred on a row of terrace houses in a Welsh seaside town" (Read, 1964, p160). A 'terrace' is not simply a row of joined-up houses. It's a row of houses built along the face of a slope, or built on the flat as one block in the same style. It is this last type that Dylan was to encounter in London, but in Wales it was the hillside terrace that was the residential form common to the hills of Swansea, the coastal towns of North and West Wales, and the slate and coal mining areas which Dylan wrote about in *Green Mountain, Black Mountain* in 1942.[203]

Dylan was brought up in "the terraced row" of Cwmdonkin Drive, as Daniel Jones described it in his book on Dylan, with Cwmdonkin Terrace not a stone's throw away. By the time he had made his comment to Bert Trick, Dylan had also seen many other examples of the Welsh hill terrace. In 1929, when he was 15, he went to stay with his cousin Doris Fullylove in Abergavenny. Her husband,

34207   THE THREE TERRACES, NEW QUAY.

66.

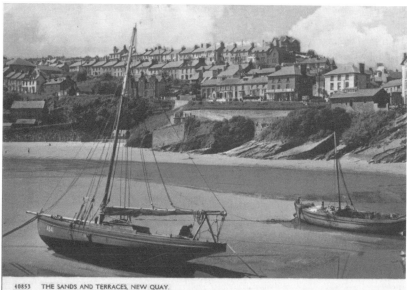

40853   THE SANDS AND TERRACES, NEW QUAY.
67.

Randolph, was a dentist there. At the end of his visit, they took Dylan home via Brecon, Sennybridge and the Cray Reservoir, then returning to Swansea via Craig-y-Nos, and the terraced towns of the Swansea Valley.[204]

From an early age, Dylan had sat on the bus from Swansea to

Blaen Cwm, and he gives one uncharitable description of the mining towns and their terraces in his letter to Hansford Johnson of early October 1933. It's often forgotten that the The Little Theatre was a touring company, and it provided the teenage Dylan with other opportunities to travel through industrial Wales. Dylan's involvement with the Little Theatre has been understated by his biographers; there is more information in Colin Edwards' unpublished biography (1968). Dylan went with the Theatre to Trecynon (Aberdare), Gwaun-cae-Gurwen and Llandybie, and probably to Pembrey, Gorseinon and Kidwelly as well. The bus journey to Llandybie would have taken him through some of the coal mining villages of the lower Gwendraeth Valley, and his performance there in *Upstream* earned him a mention in the *Western Mail*.[205] Some of Dylan's journeys to the Welsh valleys are referred to in his letters to Pamela Hansford Johnson of November and December 1933.

Newquay was one of the most popular seaside resorts for the South Wales miners. I suppose it was a bit of a home-from-home. It is a fine, even uplifting, example of a terraced, hill-side settlement, and this is reflected in both the steepness of its streets, and in some of their names: High Terrace, Marine Terrace, Picton Terrace, Lewis Terrace and Glanmor Terrace, on which the Black Lion stands. Newquay was proud of its terraces and they were often prominent in postcards of the town.

We can see from Dylan's sketch that, like Newquay, Llareggub is also terraced. Laugharne, on the other hand, is not. In Dylan's time, Laugharne was essentially a piece of coastal, albeit Georgian, ribbon development, bearing little resemblance in its English quaintness to the kind of seaside town that Dylan told Bert Trick he wanted to write about.

Lost in the Woods?

People rightly search *Under Milk Wood* for material about Laugharne and Newquay. Ackerman, for example, suggests in *Welsh Dylan* that the wood on page one of *Under Milk Wood* that comes down to the sea is the wood on Sir John's Hill. It is something we have to be careful about for we need to understand how Sir John's Hill looked in the early 1950s. Contemporary maps of Laugharne (in the National Library of Wales) show Sir John's Hill as mostly open farmland, with just a thin strip of trees around the shore line. The definitive 1951 metric map indicates trees confined to the shore. A large-scale colour photograph of the hill taken in 1967 shows that it was not wooded (National Library, J.R. Jones papers, A/1991/116, Box 40). The photograph accompanied an article by Alan Road (1967).

Nevertheless, we can still say that the view today of Sir John's Hill from the Boat House is very misleading, as is the photograph on page 105 of Ackerman's *Welsh Dylan.* Both give the impression of a wood coming continuously and thickly down from the top of the hill to the shore, thus lending credence to the view that this is the wood of *Under Milk Wood.* But this bears some qualifications. There is no seamless continuity in the 'woodland'. Between the thin shoreline strip (not much more than twenty metres at its widest) and the trees at the top of the hill are fields. On the sea side, these have been colonised by fern and scrub, giving the false impression in the photograph, and even in a hasty, or loving, glance that *wants* this to be Llareggub Hill, of continuous trees. To the right, there are still fields of grazing cows but they are completely hidden from view, both from the Boat House and in Ackerman's photograph, and you will find them only if you walk up there off the path. The trees beyond these fields that are at the top of Sir John's Hill, as well as those that make up the hedgerows between the fields, are mostly very young i.e. the last twenty years, comprising hawthorn, blackthorn, ashes and sycamores, and would not have been there in Dylan's days. In his time, Sir John's Hill was considerably more naked than it now is. In

68. Newquay, 1933, from above Brongwyn Lane

the poem 'Over Sir John's hill', Dylan refers only to elms, hedges and bushes, hardly suggestive of thick woodland, which is why, perhaps, the hawks were hunting there.

It is as likely that Dylan was thinking of the woods that dominate Newquay. They come down the hill above Francis Street, and then fall from Stryd Bethel and Brongwyn Lane to the cliffs. You need only to drive into Newquay, or stand in the field next to Majoda, to see how thickly the trees descend from the hills around the town to the shore line. This was how they were in Dylan's time and before, as contemporary photographs reveal, as local people will tell you, and as Dylan himself noted in *The Crumbs of One Man's Year*, broadcast in December 1946. In this story, he describes his journey from Majoda past "the flayed and flailing cliff-top trees", weaving his way

> towards the toppling town and the black, loud Lion where the cat, who purred like a fire, looked out of two cinders at the gently swilling retired sea-captains in the snug-as-a-bug back bar

After all, Newquay was built on Penwig Hill. "Wig" is one of the Welsh words (gwig before the mutation) for wood. It is thus Newquay, not Laugharne, that is literally on, below and under the wood, "nestling", as one contented tourist wrote in the *Welsh Gazette* on July 18th 1935, "between green and wooded hills." We should note, too, that the woods extended on the other side of Majoda, around Llanina and Cei Bach, as described by Howard de Walden's daughter, Rosemary Seymour:

> The woods round the house (Llanina) seemed so old and haunted and the garden had a very old mulberry tree grafted onto a vine by Cistercian Monks.[206]

Lovers, Rabbits and Gooseberries

In *Welsh Dylan*, Ackerman takes another clue from *Under Milk Wood* (p.1) where Dylan indicates that Milk Wood has rabbits and is used by courting couples. Do the rabbits and courters suggest Newquay or Laugharne? Ackerman points to a lane in the wood on Sir John's Hill that may have been used by courting couples and so, he suggests, it must be Llareggub's Goosegog Lane. But what was this lane like in the 1950s? It has only in the last few years become part of the

Carmarthen Bay coastal footpath, opened up by a group of French students camped out in Pendine. And would couples have really sweated up Sir John's Hill? Would they have wanted to walk into the bangs and flashes of Pendine's bombing range that Dylan so deeply complained about, rather than go to the quieter, warmer and much-closer-to-home snogging grounds around, for example, the Boat House? Warmer? Yes, for in the evening the sun shone on the Boat House side of Laugharne, whereas Sir John's Hill was in the chilly shade.

I suggest that Goosegog Lane was Brongwyn Lane in Newquay, one of Dylan's routes into the town, which started just the other side of Ffynnonfeddyg. It was used by courting couples,[207] and it is still a quiet spot, though most of the fields and trees have now been lost to the sea. The First Voice refers to the hedges of Goosegog Lane (p.47). Thick hedges ran almost the whole length of the sea side of Brongwyn Lane, marking the boundary of the fields of Maesgwyn Farm. Undoubtedly, Goosegog Lane is a reference to gooseberry bushes under which babies are said to be found, but, typically, it is also a play on the white breast (Brongwyn) of the goose, providing further confirmation that Brongwyn Lane was Goosegog Lane. Dylan first refers to gooseberries in his letter/poem to Tommy Earp of September 21st 1944. The poem is about Newquay.

Finally, we should note that not a minute's walk from Brongwyn Lane was Glanmor Rees' cobbler's shop, Arnant, on Stryd Bethel (and two more bootmakers in George Street, even closer to Brongwyn Lane). This is important in identifying Brongwyn Lane as Goosegog Lane because it is Jack Black the cobbler who chases the courting couples in Llareggub. He pursues them "*down* the grass-green gooseberried double bed of the wood" (p.7, my emphasis), a detail that corresponds with the topography of Newquay where the town stands above the woods around Brongwyn Lane. In Laugharne,

69.

Jack Black would have been chasing *up* the double bed of the wood. But why does Dylan pick on a cobbler to chase courting couples? Perhaps this is something to do with saving souls, yet another word play.

And what of the rabbits? Dylan's own words are conclusive: the place of courters and rabbits is above Traethgwyn, between Majoda and Newquay. The whole area was infested by rabbits – see Dylan's letter to Vernon Watkins of November 22nd. 1944 and that to an unknown woman of May 21st 1945. The infestation continues to the present day.

Searching for More Clues

If we accept that Dylan was topographically precise, then we can find many other clues throughout *Under Milk Wood* which suggest that Llareggub is more Newquay than Laugharne. For examplee, the First Voice tells us on page 23 that the spring sun is rising above Llareggub's green hill. This is exactly what it does at Newquay, but in Laugharne it rises over the estuary. On page 81, the First Voice describes Llareggub as a "hill of windows." This is how Newquay looked from Majoda, but there were no such windowed hills to be

70. Newquay: the "hill of windows"

206

seen in Laugharne. The houses on the tiny hill on which the top part of the town stands cannot be seen, even from the foreshore. The larger hill behind the Corporation Arms Hotel had no houses on it in Dylan's day, save a handful around its base, and a new council estate being built on its top in the early 1950s.

On page 23 of *Under Milk Wood*, the Voice of a Guide-Book (and note that the first *Guide to Newquay* appeared in 1895) describes Llareggub. The main street (Coronation Street) consists, it says, of "humble, two-storied houses." Laugharne's main street, King Street-Market Street, consists largely of handsome, three-storied houses, together with a town hall, hotel, mansion and castle. Even its two-storied houses are Georgian, and rather grand. No, it is Newquay's main streets that are mostly small, two-storied houses, as befitting a respectable chapel-going township, and this is particularly so on Stryd Bethel. Incidentally, Ackerman in *Welsh Dylan* seriously misrepresents the wording of the Guide-Book. He writes (p.131) that the Guide-Book talks of "the small pink-washed two-storey houses that crowd the lower sea-end of the town, while the upper part of Laugharne's main street boasts Georgian houses....". The Guide-Book says no such thing; Ackerman appears to be re-writing *Under Milk Wood* in order to make the wording fit Laugharne.

Note, too, that Dylan would not have used such a prosaic word

71. A Guide to Newquay, 1948

as "two-storied" without good reason. He was, in fact, indulging in yet another word play: the houses are two-storied because they appeared in both *Quite Early One Morning* and in *Under Milk Wood*. This was a double entendre that Dylan had used in a letter of August 25th 1953, at the time he was making final revisions to *Under Milk Wood*. It is a further pointer that the houses of Llareggub are those of Newquay.

There are yet more small details in the text of *Under Milk Wood* which are true to Newquay. For example, there are references to geese (p.16), a goosefield (p.8) and an orchard (p.22). These were rooted in Dylan's daily routine in Newquay, and the people he knew. When he walked to the Black Lion via Pilot Lane, he would pass Mrs Huw Davies' orchard, with its many geese, well-fed and plump on mackerel heads. Mrs Davies was the mother of Cadwell and Tydur, who ran the taxi service that Dylan used. The reference (p.22) to an old man playing a harmonium in the orchard may come from the American harmonium that was in the vestry of Tabernacle chapel, opposite the Memorial Hall. It was played by Sara Letitia Davies. She later married Dai 'Chicago' Williams, who had once driven prohibition-busting beer trucks for Al Capone. (Double-agent Guy Burgess, whom Dylan knew well, had a similar harmonium in his flat in Clifford Chambers – see Fisher, 1977 p.54. He also had a frigate in a bottle, which may have come from Dai Fred, who had made one for Margaret Taylor).

Another example of the rootedness of Dylan's imagination is the reference in *Under Milk Wood* to buttermilk and whippets (p.5). This is no fanciful phrase but draws on the fact that Jack Patrick kept whippets and greyhounds, and made buttermilk at the Black Lion dairy. Alastair Graham also kept greyhounds, as well as goats, from whose milk he made cheese.

The bones of the sailors of *Under Milk Wood* (pp.4, 5) may just be from Dylan's imagination. But bones were also part of Dylan's daily walk around Newquay. When he called on Norman Evans at London House, or was on his way to the Dolau, Dylan would walk past Traeth-y-Dolau. This beach was usually strewn with animal bones and it is not hard to imagine that Dylan might muse that these were the washed up bones of the drowned sailors of Cardigan Bay. The bones were actually there because the local butchers would dump them in the sea at the end of Rock Street and tidal action would eventually bring them round to Traeth-y-Dolau.

Newquay and Llareggub have much in common. Llareggub is a seafaring village, and so, too, was Newquay. Its prosperity from the eighteenth century onwards was based on shipbuilding and trading operations across the world, and then fishing. The Rev. Eli Jenkins' White Book of Llareggub refers to the shipping and industry of the town, phrases that were wholly appropriate to Newquay but certainly not to Laugharne. There is a harbour in Llareggub, as there is in Newquay. There is no harbour in Laugharne, save a small basin in the mudflats that little boats could come into on high tide. It is so insignificant that it is not shown on even large scale maps of the area.

The many parakeets, parrots and pollys in *Under Milk Wood* point to Newquay, not Laugharne, which was not a seafaring town. It was more a small fishing and cockling village whose little boats seldom went further than Bristol, and were mostly confined to the river Tâf and the estuary. Newquay's sailors, on the other hand, went across the world and the sailors of Llareggub reflect this; Captain Cat had been to San Francisco (p.69), had slept with a mulatto, and knew a little French (p.48). His drowned companions had been to Nantucket (p.3), and brought home coconuts, shawls and parrots for their wives (p.5). It is these long-drowned, ocean-going mariners of Newquay and Llanina – "iron men in wooden ships" – that open *Under Milk Wood*, not the cockle gatherers of the Tâf estuary.

One for the Birds

Dylan's move to Laugharne in 1949 gave a further push to the developing pastoralism of his poetry. This was discussed in Chapter 4 in terms of the large increase in the number of references in Dylan's later poems to wildlife, and especially to birds. As one might expect, the Laugharne poems[208] contain many references to birds of the estuary and its marshland – heron, crane, curlew and wild geese, in particular. There are more references to these birds in the eight Laugharne poems than in all of Dylan's previous poems together. If *Under Milk Wood* is steeped in the particularity of Laugharne, then we would expect this to be reflected, as it is in the Laugharne poems, in the kinds of bird referred to in the text. This is not the case. When the drowned sailors ask what it's like up above (p.5) they don't ask about herons or curlews or godwits, but about linnets, parrots, robins and sparrows. There is, in fact, only one reference to an estuary or marshland bird in the whole of *Under Milk Wood*.[209]

The birds of Llareggub are overwhelmingly the gulls of Newquay, domestic geese and ducks, land birds such as the lark and cuckoo and the parrots brought home by its ocean-going sailors.

Found on the Cliffs

The Peeping Tom, and voyeurism more generally, is a theme in three of Dylan's 'Newquay works', namely, 'Sooner than you can water milk', the 1944 letter/poem to Tommy Earp, and *Under Milk Wood*. In the first, the chapel "elders stand/With thermoses and telescopes and spy the sand...." In the poem to Earp, the snooping, sniffing 'parchs' take part in the romp in the lecherous caves. Jack Black in *Under Milk Wood* takes participant observation even further when he chases the courting couples through the wood. Telescopes and crystal balls appear in the text as devices for 'spying'. There's also good, old-fashioned peeping when, for example, Mrs Organ Morgan catches Polly Garter and Waldo 'nesting' in the wood. And Mrs Ogmore-Pritchard's first husband wanders round the town looking through keyholes at women undressing.

This interest in voyeurism comes from Dylan's own Newquay experience. The man who brought electricity to the town in the 1920s, went round at night armed with a twenty-five foot ladder looking for faulty bulbs in the street lights. It was soon noticed that he only ever checked lights that were "conveniently located next to some lady's boudoir." More significantly, there was a tradesman who built himself a nest on the cliff, overlooking the beach:

> Ladies [on the beach] would turn in towards the cliff to change/dry, exposing their wares to the cliff-top watcher, armed with binocs. and engaged in erotic conversation with himself.... He was discovered due to curiosity of a local plumber who noticed his travels regularly. The plumber followed one day and observed at a safe distance! (Anon)

What's in a Name?

A survey of some of the names of Llareggub as they appear in *Under Milk Wood* is instructive. Note, for later discussion, the number of appearances of Stryd Bethel (or Margaret Street, as it is also known), a narrow, street at the top of the town that leads you gently into the other parts of Newquay's hugger-mugger, terraced community. (The page numbers refer to the 1961 edition.)

Town clock p.1. Taken together with Dylan's sketch, this is certainly the clock tower on the Town Hall at Laugharne.

Welfare Hall p.1. There is a Memorial Hall in Newquay, about a hundred yards from the Commercial where Dylan drank. Captain Cat's words on pages 43-44 suggest the close proximity of the Welfare Hall to the Sailors Arms. (There is also a Memorial Hall in Laugharne, at the edge of the town).

Coronation Street p.2. This could simply be a topical reference to the coronation of Elizabeth II. There is certainly no such street in either Laugharne or Newquay, though Laugharne has a King Street and Newquay a Queen Street. However, the Coronation Gardens are to be found in Newquay, on the right of the street going down from the Black Lion, and they would have been in the forefront of Dylan's view looking towards the harbour from the pub. The cherry trees of Coronation Street come from the main street of Laugharne, and Min Lewis (1967) describes their prominence in the town. Dylan also refers to them in his letter to Margaret Taylor in October 1948.

Cockle Row p.2. Laugharne has cockles but Newquay has the rows – Farmer's Row, Mason Row and Mariner's Row. Dylan had previously written about cockles at Newquay – in his letter to Tommy Earp of September 21st 1944.

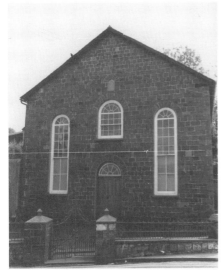

72. Bethel Chapel, Newquay

211

Bethesda p.2. Probably Bethel chapel in Newquay on Stryd Bethel. I've already noted that Dylan used the word 'Bethel' in a letter to Hansford Johnson in October 1934, and in his 1947 poem 'In Country Sleep'. In the 1940s, Mr John's bakery (called The Cake Shop) was on one side of Bethel and, on the other, Mr Rees the shoeshop and repairer. In Dylan's letter to Tommy Earp of September 1944, it is Mr Jones the Cake (Mr John becoming Mr Jones) who is the black "Bethel-worm" spying on courting couples. In *Under Milk Wood*, however, Dylan switches to the other side of Bethel chapel, and the scourge of the snoggers in Goosegog Lane becomes Jack Black, the cobbler.

Sailors Arms p.2. This is the Sailor's Home Arms, which stood on the corner of Stryd Bethel and Glanmor Terrace. It was re-named the Commercial, and was one of Dylan's favourite pubs in Newquay. It is now called the Seahorse. There is a photograph inside which shows the pub in its days as the Sailor's Home Arms, and another of its time as the Commercial, taken in 1968. Dylan is even true to the small topographical details of Newquay: on page 50, the sailors walk *uphill* from the harbour to the Sailors Arms. No doubt, there are bits of the Black Lion in Llareggub's Sailors Arms; for example, the stopped clock of the Sailors Arms (p.36) is probably the stopped clock of the Black Lion, mentioned in Dylan's letter to Margaret Taylor of August 29th 1946.

Donkey Street p.2. Some see this as just a fanciful name but it is rooted in the history of Newquay. Donkeys were used to draw carts through the town and were often found roaming the streets. Passmore's history of Newquay indicates (1992, p.114) that even as late as 1947 Maisie the donkey was still rambling around Newquay. She was owned by Jack Patrick of the Black Lion. Many of the donkeys were kept in the stables behind the Commercial and on the site of the present amusement arcade near the Black Lion. Dylan refers to the braying of donkeys in a letter from Majoda of May 21st 1945.

Maesgwyn p.6. This was a smallholding on the cliffs above Traethgwyn, between Majoda and Newquay. According to Passmore, it was still inhabited in the 1940s before the sea took the farm and fields away. Ieuan Williams, a retired carpenter in Newquay, remembers children playing cowboys and indians in the abandoned farmhouse after the war. Maesgwyn is marked on the map on page 44 of Passmore's history of Newquay.

Dowlais p.6. This is not a gratuitous reference to the town near

73. The Sailor's Home Arms, 1901

74. Last days at Maesgwyn

Merthyr. From the 1880s onwards, Newquay was a favourite holiday resort for the miners and metal workers from South Wales, who came in their busloads. I myself remember the miners from Cory colliery in Pontarddulais leaving for the Cardigan coast. As Passmore describes, the visitors gave impromptu concerts on the pier so that the tenors of Dowlais (and from other places, of course) were often heard singing in the summer months at Newquay. *The New Quay Chronicle* noted that the visitors sang with tenor voices, as opposed to the local men who sang with bass voices "due to the sea air having a tendency to make the voice harsher and deeper."[210]

The quarry p.10. Frondolau Quarry, at the end of Rock Street, provided the stone for the construction of the pier and many of Newquay's houses. There was also Neuadd Quarry where lead was mined, and we noted in Chapter 3 that its manager, Evan Joshua, was one of Dylan's drinking companions.

Bay View p.14. This is where Mrs Ogmore-Pritchard lived. There is a house of this name at the top of the town in Laugharne, as it is in Llareggub. There is also a Bay View in Newquay but it is at the bottom of the town, in Rock Street. There is more on Bay View in the next section.

River Dewi p17. The well in Newquay that was the first source of water for the town was the Dewi (see Lewis, 1988, p.35). The River Dewi flows into the sea outside Newquay at Cwmtydu. There is a river in Stryd Bethel, flowing between Bethel and the Costcutters shop. It is now in a culvert but Ceredigion Council confirm it was an open river in 1944-45 that went underground at Stryd Bethel. It was called the Alun.

Rose Cottage p.19. Jacques de Schoolmeister, the garage owner in Laugharne, lived in Rose Cottage. There is also a Rose Cottage outside Newquay, at Gilfachreda, just a few minutes drive from Majoda on the way to Alastair Graham's house, Plas y Wern. It may be that Dylan derived the name from two houses in the town: Rose Villa which is in Gomer Crescent opposite the Black Lion, and Rose Hill which is between the Black Lion and the Commercial, on the other side of the road.

Salt Lake Farm p.19. Undoubtedly based on Salt House Farm on the other side of Sir John's Hill in Laugharne. There are, however, some in Newquay who point to the Salthouse that used to be near the pier in Newquay as the basis for Salt House Farm. The 1951 metric map of Laugharne does *appear* to support the anti-Laugharne camp: it shows that the farmhouse in question was called South Hill Cottages. But the farm had changed its name some time before but the map makers did not catch up until the 1975 Pathfinder edition. The Register of Electors shows clearly that Salt House Farm was there in 1951, and occupied by a William and Mary Davies.

Donkey Down p.25. As described above, Dylan based this on the Downs in Newquay. It is an area of steep grass land that stretches from the Craft Shop (behind the lifeboat station) to the Black Lion. It was used for grazing donkeys. The Downs are marked on the map of Newquay in Passmore's history.

Goosegog Lane p25. I have already suggested that this was Brongwyn Lane in Newquay.

Heron Head p.25. This is a perplexing name. Herons belong to Laugharne not Newquay, though the Aeron Valley is full of them. But the choice of "Head" also shows that Dylan was thinking of a place that had *cliffs* as, for example, in Beachy Head. This seems confirmed by the Rev Eli Jenkins who compares Heron Head with Carreg Cennen, a huge limestone crag near Llandeilo. Newquay has cliffs but Laugharne does not. Heron Head is probably Carreg Walltog beneath Newquay Head. Carreg Walltog means Hairy Rock or Hair Rock. It's so called because it's crowned with earth and grass and from the sea looks like a man's head. But why does Dylan call it Heron Head? In a typical Dylan word play, Hair Rock becomes Hair-on-Head.

Manchester House p.37. This was on Stryd Bethel, Newquay. It was a draper and milliner's shop owned by D.E. Thomas. Manchester House in Llareggub was also a drapers. Cardiganshire people have long been associated with drapers shops, and Dylan refers to them again in another Newquay poem.[211] There is, of course, a Manchester House in Laugharne but in Dylan's time (and for long before) it was a general store selling anything from cheese to paraffin. It closed in 1995. The drapers shop was next door, Gwalia House, where Mr William Watts lived. Min Lewis confirms that Watts actually did wear a boater, just like Mog Edwards (p.37) and she quotes his daughter, Gwen: "Dada always wore a straw hat, a butterfly collar and a bow tie" (1967). This is as good an example as any of the way Dylan interwove Newquay and Laugharne.

Ty-pant p.38. Parc-y-pant is a large house a few hundred yards up from Majoda; but it most likely derives from Ty-nant, Doctor James' home and surgery, whose garden is on Stryd Bethel, next to Manchester House. 'Pant' means valley so Ty-pant means Valley House. But 'pant', as Thomas Herbert the vet might have pointed out, also means 'dent', so Ty-pant can also refer to Dylan's publishers, the House of Dent.

The school p.38. There is a small primary school just off the corner of Francis Street and Stryd Bethel.

The fair day p.66. Newquay was famous for its fairs. There were three a year in the nineteenth century. Dylan's letter to Vernon Watkins of November 15th. 1944 also mentions a visit to the farmers' fair in Cardigan.

There are other names in *Under Milk Wood* – Bottom Cottage, Sunday Meadow, Handel Villa – that seem to have no associations with either Laugharne or Newquay.

What's in a Face?

Some of the key characters in *Under Milk Wood* seem to have their origins in Newquay. Let's start with Captain Cat. Where did the name come from? It's likely Dylan took the name from a retired sea captain in Newquay, Captain Charles Patrick (1870-1949), who lived in Rose Hill, the house already mentioned as being almost opposite the Black Lion. He was a well-known figure in the town, not least because of his parrot and his involvement with the annual regatta. He was a tall, distinguished white-haired man, a master mariner who had worked for Shell for most of his life. He was known locally as Captain Pat, and was always to be seen each morning pottering around outside his house wearing his Captain's cap. It was usual in Newquay to call the various Patricks 'Pat', as in Jack Pat of the Black Lion, a name that Dylan used.

75. Captain Charles Patrick, seated, 1940

216

It is also of interest that Catrin Davies, the landlady of the Blue Bell pub in Newquay, was known as Auntie Cat. The Blue Bell was a dingy, spartan pub near the harbour. It was favoured by the boys from the boats, who hosed themselves down on the flag floor when they needed to sober up. Dylan enjoyed their company, the smokey wood fire, Auntie Cat's fish broth and, best of all, her point-blank refusal to serve affected or ingratiating customers. Howard Evans, a bus driver for Western Welsh who later ran the post office at Cross Inn, encountered Dylan and the young Richard Burton in the Blue Bell in early summer 1945. Burton was on holiday in the town, and "was well known here even at that time."[212]

There was no shortage of seafarers in Newquay's streets and pubs to provide material for Captain Cat. There were also the sea-going experiences of Dylan's own friends such as Dewi Ianthe, Dai Fred and even Alastair Graham, who had been on a boat at the relief of Dunkirk. There were, too, Jack Patrick's stories of his only adventure at sea: on one of his visits to London, he drank so much that when he woke up he found himself on a freighter bound for the West Indies.

But there is general agreement amongst Newquay's older residents that Captain Cat is based largely on Tom Polly (Tom Davies), the retired master mariner who was a regular drinker with Dylan in the Black Lion. Captain Cat sat in his home, Schooner House, listening to the comings and goings of Llareggub. Tom Polly was well known for standing outside his home, Gomer House in Gomer Crescent, opposite the Black Lion, watching the world of Newquay go by. It might be thought that Dylan chose the name 'Schooner' randomly and that it bears no relationship to 'Gomer'. Not so. 'Gomer' was the name of the insurance company set up in Newquay in the nineteenth century to insure the schooners, smacks and brigs of the town. Dylan knew all about metonymy.

It's also possible that Tom Polly's wartime work as a censor reading letters going to and from Ireland helped form Dylan's image of Captain Cat, as someone who was privy to the everyday lives and secrets of the people of Llareggub. We might also consider that Tom Polly's role as censor played a part in Dylan's thinking about the letter-opening activities of Willy Nilly, the postman. It's likely that Willy Nilly is a composite of three of Newquay's postal workers, Jack Lloyd, Will Evans and Lil Dolau (also an Evans). It is reasonable to suppose that Will and Lil inspired the name 'Willy Nilly'. Jack Lloyd, who we've noted was a good friend of Dylan's, was also Newquay's Town Crier. Willy Nilly's penchant for spreading the town's news from one house to another is a strong reflection of Lloyd's role as Crier. Dylan's note on the worksheets of *Under Milk Wood* at Texas confirms that he was drawing on Lloyd:

> Nobody minds him [Willy Nilly] opening the letters and acting as [a] kind of town-crier. How else would they know the news? (quoted in Davies and Maud, 1995, p.xxxvi).

The minister of Bethel during the 1940s was the Rev. W.O. Jenkins. He lived in Goytre on Stryd Bethel, one house down from the corner with Francis Street, opposite Manchester House. Perhaps he provided the name for the Rev Eli Jenkins of Llareggub. The eccentricities of the Rev Eli Jenkins, dipping his pen in cocoa, are those of Vera Killick, living a life on cocoa.[213]

The behaviour and character of Cherry Owen appear to be based on William Killick, who would have fitted smoothly into the imbrication of nautical fact and fantasy in Dylan's mind as *Under Milk Wood* was being written: a Killick is a small anchor. It is also naval slang for a leading seaman. When Dylan describes Cherry Owen returning home with a fish-frail of flagons (p.33), he's drawing upon William Killick's habit of pushing a pram full of bottles home from the pub. Cherry Owen's drunken rowdiness is exactly that of Killick's described in Amanda Williams' first interview (see Appendix 1). Dancing wasn't natural, Killick had once told Caitlin, and that was a line that Dylan gave to Cherry Owen (p.82). "My father," Rachel Willans told me, "hated dancing."

But the name 'Cherry' undoubtedly came from Walter Cherry who lived in Clarita House (re-named Brooklands for most of the war) on Stryd Bethel and ran the Western Welsh buses in Newquay. The schoolchildren called him Cherry Blossom. He was Chairman of the Town Council, a magistrate, church warden, bookmaker and a regular at the Black Lion where he was an unstoppable conversationalist, "a bumbling bumble bee in Berkshire brogue". His son-in-law, Dan Jones, was usually referred to as Cherry Jones or Dan Cherry.

Evans the Death in *Under Milk Wood* (p.8) may have been Carsey Evans, another Black Lion regular, who was an assistant in the 1940's to Griffy Arthur Rees, one of Newquay's joiners who made coffins for the Methodists. The woman on whom Polly Garter was based is

76. Dai Fred in his younger days

well-known in Newquay amongst the older generation, but her chil-
dren and grandchildren are still upset if her name is mentioned.
"Polly" was a common Newquay nickname because of the number
of mariners who brought back parrots to the town. Nogood Boyo
first appears in Dylan's Newquay poem to Tommy Earp of
September 21st 1944. Gomer Owen, who once kissed Bessie
Bighead, probably owes his first name to Gomer House – and Gomer
wasn't an uncommon first name in Newquay. And what of store
owner Organ Morgan? One of Newquay's well-known organists in
the 1940s was shoe-shop proprietor and cobbler, Dafi Dafis (David
Oswald Davies) of Church Street. Did he inspire the assonance of
Organ Morgan?

We noted in Chapter 3 that Dai Fred of the *Alpha* was one of
Dylan's drinking friends, and the person who bottled a ship for
Margaret Taylor on her visit to Newquay in 1946. It's reasonable to
suppose that Dai Fred was the basis for Tom-Fred the donkeyman,
on page four of *Under Milk Wood*. Dai Fred did not keep donkeys,
but he was the donkeyman on board the *Alpha*, in charge of the don-
key engine and also responsible for making sure that things were in
working order.

And Dai Fred was famous in Newquay for the dildoes that he carved and so 'donkeyman' is also a sexual allusion. The carvings were usually made from wood, and sometimes he

> covered them with mole skin to give an ethnic distinction. I don't think there was much of a market for dildoes in Newquay... I think they were conversation pieces, and perhaps this explains Tom-Fred's comment in *Under Milk Wood* about him being a talking bone. (Anon.)

It's likely that Dylan drew partly on Thomas Herbert the vet for Mister Waldo, herbalist, cat doctor and quack (p.8 of *Under Milk Wood*). In the early days of his practice in the 1940s, Herbert was, according to his assistant David Birch, keen on using herbal and natural medicines. He built up the pet side of the practice at this time, particularly cats and dog, and began patenting devices for castrating tom-cats. It was not uncommon for Herbert to treat farmworkers, often stitching up their wounds after accidents. And, like Mister Waldo, the young Thomas Herbert was very active in sowing his wild oats.

Min Lewis' identification of Carl Eynon, butcher in St. Clears, as the basis for Butcher Beynon has been confirmed by Road (1967). But Dylan may also have drawn a little on Thomas Jones (Butcher OK), who walked to the Black Lion with Dylan most evenings and was a good friend. There were several colourful butchers in Newquay during the war, including Hell Fire Jones of Church Street, a loud and abrasive character who drank in the Commercial.

I've already suggested that Jack Black the cobbler was based, at least in part, upon Glanmor Rees in Stryd Bethel, brother of Myra Evans, Newquay historian and, as we saw in Chapter 3, Dylan's portraitist. But there is a wider aspect to this. Newquay was well-known for its cobblers and bootmakers: there were seven of them in Newquay during the war, a large number for such a small town. They served the wider region, including the supply of clogs to farmers and boots to fishermen. There are various references to clogs and seaboots in *Under Milk Wood* (e.g. pp.21, 24). The name Jack Black probably came from a cobbler in the Uplands of Swansea who had a shop there during Dylan's childhood (Hardy, 1995).

The name Dai Bread would have been common enough in Wales amongst bakers and delivery men. But in Chapter 3, I suggested that it may have come from Dai Hughes the Bread who ran the bakery and the Commercial in Llanon, which Dylan sometimes visited with Thomas Herbert. Mr John's bakery, The Cake Shop, was opposite the Commercial in Newquay and, as I noted in the last section, appeared in Dylan's letter poem to Tommy Earp. Mr Johns was a well-known figure in Newquay:

> John's was a highly certificated life saver, a superb swimmer, and during the regattas he would entertain the crowds with his aquatic stunts, including being tossed overboard in a secured sack (armed with a knife) and after a 'prolonged' under-water interval, reappear.[214]

Dylan may have witnessed these stunts, for John performed them during the war when 'limited edition regattas' were held, confined to swimming competitions and small boat events. Mr John's sack stunt may lie behind Dylan's "man-trapping" fears in his letter to Princess Caetani of September 1953:

> Why do I bind myself always into these imbecile grief-knots, blindfold my eyes with lies, wind my brass music around me, sew myself in a sack, weight it with guilt and pig-iron, then pitch me squealing to sea, so that time and time again, I must wrestle out and unravel in a panic, like a seaslugged windy Houdini, and ooze and eel up wheezily, babbling and blowing black bubbles, from all the claws and bars and breasts of the mantrapping seabed?

There are several further references in the letter to sacks, the 'stuntman's sacking', escapologists in their cages and a 'blind bag'. It seems that, even at the end, Dylan was going back in his mind to Newquay and drawing upon his memories of the town and its people.

As for Miss Myfanwy Price, Dylan's description in *Under Milk Wood* of her shop refers to liquorice, and several sorts of pop – "dandelion and burdock, raspberry and cherryade, pop goes the weasel and the wind" (p.60). Dylan may well have drawn on Mrs Mary Evans' sweet and groceries shop called the Emporium, on the corner of Francis Street, at the start of Stryd Bethel. The shop was just in front of the school, whose headmaster was Eifion Price. Note, too, that Mr Mog Edwards promises to carry off Miss Price to his own Emporium (p.7). Dylan seems to refer to Mrs Mary Evans in the 1949 broadcast *Living in Wales*:

Remember the shop at the corner, Mrs Evans the Pop, full of liquorice, bootlaces, lamp oil, pear-drops, and a smell that was comfier than roses.[215]

Mary Evans was known as 'Mrs Evans Emporium' not as 'Mrs Evans the Pop' but she certainly sold it and the bottles were on display outside her shop. (Dylan's childhood sweetshop in the Uplands was run by a Mrs Ferguson).

There are some names in *Under Milk Wood* where the connection with a Newquay resident is easy to see, for example Tom-Fred and Dai Fred. But there are others where a number of people and circumstances seem to have been woven into a Llareggub character but the process of the weaving is hard to discern. Mrs Ogmore-Pritchard is a case in point. She is a guest house proprietor who lives in Bay View with her two husbands, Mr Ogmore, who was in linoleum, and Mr Pritchard, a bookmaker. There are some in Newquay who believe that Bay View is Belle Vue, which has a magnificent view of the bay. Mrs Warfield-Darling lived in 2, Belle Vue and she and Dylan were on good terms. She, like Mrs Ogmore-Pritchard, had been married twice, to a General called Warfield, and then to a doctor named Darling. We know from the Colin Edwards' tapes that Mrs Warfield-Darling's friendship with Dylan was at its strongest in late 1944 when Dylan wrote *Quite Early One Morning*, in which, of course, Mrs Ogmore-Pritchard first appeared. There is no evidence that Mrs Warfield-Darling inspired the character traits of Mrs Ogmore-Pritchard, nor did she keep a guest house, though the family next door, Mr and Mrs Garfield Harries, did.

It's not hard to imagine Dylan scouring his Newquay notebooks to construct a name that caught the rhythmic hyphenation of Warfield-Darling. He settled on Ogmore-Pritchard, a combination of the names of two well known business people in Newquay. One was Ogmore Davies, in drapery at the top end of Church Street, and the other was Pritchard-Jones, not a bookmaker but a bank manager at Barclays, also in Church Street.[216]

Once we accept that Dylan's imagination was rooted, as Ackerman rightly observes, in real people and places, then we have another pointer to Newquay's influence in *Under Milk Wood*. This is Lord Cut-Glass.What is an aristocrat doing in a Welsh seaside town? Do we find such a person in Dylan's time at Laugharne or at Newquay? At Newquay, there were two blue-bloods who were part of Dylan's world: Howard de Walden and Alastair Graham of Plas y Wern. Lord Cut-Glass was mostly based on Graham. The name 'Lord Cut-Glass' is a development of "thin-vowelled laird", Dylan's previous description of Graham.[217] Fallowell later gave the following account of Graham's accent: "The voice, issuing from slightly pursed lips, was fastidious and well-bred but not at all affected."

The words of the First Voice in *Under Milk Wood* that Lord Cut-Glass "lives in a house and a life at siege" (p.65) refer to Graham's misanthropy and his expulsion from London society over the Tredegar affair. The following line about an unknown enemy looting and savaging downhill (Plas y Wern is in a deep hollow, "hunkered down in a gulley among woods as though trying to hide itself", wrote Fallowell) points to Graham's well-known sensitivity about protecting the privacy of his new life in Wales. Dylan had intended to include something about "The tragedy behind Lord Cut Glass's life" but it remained one of many unused ideas (see Davies and Maud, 1995, p.xxxviii).

Another clue that tells us that Lord Cut-Glass is based on Graham are the references to fish-scraps (pp.32, 65) and to Cut-Glass' fishy kitchen (p.65). Graham was known in Newquay for his fish dishes, his recipe book on different ways of cooking mackerel and his inclination sometimes to serve pickled herring to guests at the parties he threw at his mansion (see next section).

And Lord Cut-Glass' collection of clocks? Graham was obsessed with good time-keeping; his days were set to a strict routine which he rarely left: "people in Newquay set their watches by Graham's battered car leaving for the Dolau Inn, he expected his bathwater drawn at the exact time every morning...."[219] Perhaps, too, Lord Cut-Glass' clocks were Dylan's fanciful way of saying that Graham was 'doing time' in Newquay, a punishment for his gay affairs.

Dylan's portrait of Lord Cut-Glass also incorporates other aspects of Graham's life. Cut-Glass has a dog, as did Graham, who, we've already noted, kept greyhounds. Lord Cut-Glass lived in poverty. Whilst Graham was certainly not impoverished, there was a certain air of self-neglectfulness about him. This was manifest in his run-down car, the empty gin bottles that were often to be found around him and in the complete neglect of Plas y Wern's sixty acres.[220] Graham gave the impression, writes Selina Hastings, Waugh's most recent biographer, "of *fin de race* etiolation, [an] air of decadence and melancholy."

Who's in Bed with Whom?

Inspiration for the lusty liaisons of Llareggub may have come from both Laugharne and Newquay, as well as from Dylan's imagination. But we do know from Thomas Herbert's papers that Newquay during the 1940s was a place to party, despite the disapproving chapel Bethels. Dylan had a number of guides to the town's promiscuous activities. There was Thomas Herbert himself, who led an active sex life as a young bachelor vet, and Alastair Graham who, wrote Herbert, "drifted around his guests catalysing affaires where he could."[221] Meurig Fisherman and Norman London House also knew a great deal about Newquay's intimate affairs, particularly those that revolved around the Penwig Hotel.

Some, but not all, of the sexual adventuring involved the incomers to Newquay, as well as its small artistic community, and it gave rise to gossip that burns the town's parched lips almost as strongly today as it did then. The reading and drinking circle around Dylan was soon being talked about. There was Caitlin swimming naked in the sea, and dancing naked in the Wern. Augustus John chased young girls around the lanes of Newquay on the pretext of wanting to learn the Welsh names of wild flowers. Graham was gay, enough said, and the Killick shooting proved, did it not, that the gossips were right, for why else would he have done it if Dylan hadn't been bedding Vera?

The townspeople may sometimes have put two and two together and made sixty-nine, but there was a good deal of factual basis to the talk. But Graham's house, Plas y Wern, was implicated far more than tiny Majoda. There is no doubt that there were wild parties in Graham's library, and Thomas Herbert wrote a piece describing one. Here's how it begins:

> The revellers drove through the gateway at Wern and tumbled out of the cars and waited whilst Alastair went into the stable to get a light. He emerged carrying a hurricane lamp and led his guests down the rough path to the house. He unlocked the massive oak door. At the end of the entrance hall, the ancient polished oak staircase reflected the weak light of lanterns placed on the banister posts.... The lanterns were of thick plate glass and carried a lighted candle. There was no electricity at the Wern. We trooped warily up the stairs with an occasional clang of bottles to the second landing which was also bathed in the light of lanterns....

Alastair opened the door of the library and we trooped in with much mirth and squeals from the women who were being 'touched up'. More lamps were lit and the large room with its thousands of books was mellow and inviting.... Dewi the carpenter fetched glasses and Meurig the fisherman opened a bottle of rum. Alastair produced jars of herring fillets pickled in brine, and the company settled down to the strange repast.[222]

Soon the rum and herring take effect: Captain John Davies, the artist, uses his walking stick to reveal Lady B.'s "marvellous legs and expensive and glamorous silk French knickers." She tires of him, and decides she would much prefer a handsome young vet to an old war horse. They make off to one of the bedrooms where "we fell on each other... in an all consuming animal lust."

Stories about these goings-on were soon doing the rounds, usually via Meurig Fisherman, who was a regular at the parties. Parts of Newquay were shocked, and Dylan was caught in the disapproving blast. But it is unclear how far Dylan was involved in the hanky-panky. Graham was loathe to invite him to the parties because he drank too much and was boring in such company. When Dylan did manage to gatecrash, he was, according to Thomas Herbert, far more concerned with reciting poems and drinking beer than cavorting in the library and adjacent bedrooms.

The liaisons, however, went wider than Graham's parties, and they are captured in Herbert's papers which he wrote in the late 1980s when the major characters had died. He writes (as an active participant) of the "slack morals" in Newquay, particularly amongst the professional classes: he learns from the woman he is sleeping with that her husband has gone off for the weekend with the cook. Herbert describes the end of one party: "G. phoned H. – his wife's lover – to take the New Quay crowd home." Another time in an unlicensed bar

a fellow took off his shirt revealing the tell-tale scratches made by N. The other seven men took off their shirts and proudly showed similar scratches. P., in whom N. confided a little, told me that N. took money off her next door neighbour, an elderly man with an ailing wife. She gave him the odd kiss and an occasional hand job to keep him on the boil.

These matters were not confined to the party or pub: Herbert tells of W. whose office clerk "surprised him when he was on top of his typist on the desk. W. summarily dismissed him." Then there was T. caught in a house after snow had fallen and there was no way out without leaving his prints.... The schoolmaster and Mrs S.... The pub that was closed down because it was a brothel. "Sex in Newquay?" asked one ex-resident now living in England, who had just given me chapter and verse on the extra-marital liaisons of some of the chapel deacons and organists. "This requires serious addressing since there was such a lot of activity." Dylan's gibes against the snooping, chapel-Bethels may have been cheap, but he knew exactly what was happening in some of the bedrooms and barns of 1940s Newquay: many of the elders, if not the parchs, were indeed snuggling "deep amongst the chapel thighs." The pillars of the community, said one informant, "were more than usually upright."

Herbert's papers, and other confidential information I have received, indicate that there was enough happening in Newquay (and Aberaeron) to provide Dylan with a wealth of material to inspire his description of the lustings and couplings of the people of Llareggub. He could also draw on the stories that appeared in the local newspapers: a gay sex ring in Aberystwyth, for example, and a Mr Bean prosecuted for bigamy.[223] In short, Dylan did not have to rely on his imagination for much. He may have thought that Swansea and London had made him a bohemian, a man of the world; but Newquay was a real eye-opener, perhaps his first personal exposure, and maybe the most lasting, to the sexual shenanigans of a small Welsh town.

Newquay locals may say that Herbert showed Dylan only what the newcomers were up to. Not so. Thomas Herbert's papers reveal that he, young Tommy the vet, had first-hand experience of many warm, Welsh welcomes. Praise the Lord! We are a nation that likes musical beds.

To the Lion and Back

An understanding of how far Dylan rooted Llareggub in the particularity of Newquay can be enhanced by retracing his steps from Majoda to the Black Lion. Many of the names and places in *Under Milk Wood* can be found on his walk to the pub, and they are mostly on Stryd Bethel. Indeed, it is Stryd Bethel itself, rather than Newquay, that is the 'village' on which *Under Milk Wood* is based. In Dylan's time, Stryd Bethel (which is only some sixty yards long) held a draper's, grocer's, chemist, shoe shop/cobbler's, ironmonger's, gents' hairdresser, bakery, chapel, cafe and a small bed and breakfast business. It was Newquay's sea-borne prosperity that enabled the growth of the number and variety of shops on Stryd Bethel and which were present in Llareggub. *Under Milk Wood* is a play that features tradespeople and their customers and that helps to fix Llareggub in Stryd Bethel.

Dylan had three routes from Majoda into Newquay, two of which brought him out at the start of Stryd Bethel. First, along the beach (but only when low tide coincided with opening time), to climb up via the lifeboat station to the Black Lion, with perhaps a diversion to the Blue Bell on the way. Second, the lunch time and dry weather route, though he might also go this way when the nights were long and there was plenty of light. Dylan would leave Majoda and walk for a few minutes across the cliff-top to Ffynnonfeddyg, descend the wooden steps to the beach, hop across the little stream, and climb up the other side into the wooded area around Traethgwyn House. Here he might stop and chat with John Beynon and his sister, Magdalen Annie and further along the cliff with the Lloyd family in their little green chalet. He would then walk up the tree-lined slope of Brongwyn Lane, which in his day was a sturdy footpath, though difficult in wet weather. He would first pass Evelyn Milton in Traethina and then some of the cottages which still remain, such as Brongwyn Cottage and Brisbane House. Half-way between the two, on his right, was Maesgwyn Farm, soon to be washed completely into the sea. Reaching the top of Brongwyn Lane, Dylan would emerge at the start of George Street, with the police station (Handcuff House in Llareggub) on his left and slightly behind him.

It is one of these two routes into Newquay that Dylan describes in his story and radio broadcast, *The Crumbs of One Man's Year*, written towards the end of 1946.

In the evening, however, Dylan would usually walk up the road to Ffynnonfeddyg, calling for Vera Killick if it were her turn to accompany him. Then a brisk five minutes walk to the cross roads at Cnwc-y-Lili, where Butcher OK would sometimes be waiting, having already walked down from his home in Bwlchcefn. Whether with Butcher OK or on his own, Dylan would walk along, or cadge a lift from the school bus,[224] soon passing Tylegwyn (the house rented by Ira and Olive Jones), and then Mrs Warfield-Darling in Belle Vue. He would continue along the main road into Newquay – in those

77. 'Handcuff House', The old police station, Newquay

days it would have been virtually free of traffic – and within twenty minutes or so he would be in George Street.

Whether lunch time or evening, it took no time at all to proceed along the hundred yards or so of George Street. Dylan would first pass the concrete Nissen building housing the fire engine, and opposite, in complete contrast, an old-style, once-thatched but then-sheeted, Newquay cottage occupied by Miss Jones Fach. She rarely ventured outside, except to shop and draw water from the tap on the street. Like Captain Cat, she spent her days in an open window watching the townsfolk go by. The other shops in George Street included two cobblers', a newspaper shop, Mrs Hell Fire Jones' grocery store, Brooks the photographer's and, at the end, Mr Adams' garage. Dylan might pause here to catch his breath, at the corner of Stryd Bethel and Francis Street, listening to the penny-a-kiss voices of Gwennie, Billy, Dicky and Johnnie Cristo (p.56) in the school playground across the road. Just in front of the school, was Mrs Mary Evans' sweet shop, the Emporium (Miss Myfanwy Price in Llareggub), where Dylan might have bought his sweet rations.

From this point, Dylan would choose one of two routes to the Black Lion, depending on whether or not he wanted to go to the Commercial first. To go direct to the Black Lion, he would turn down Pilot Lane, passing the orchard and its geese, and take the back way into the Black Lion through the kitchens. To go to the Commercial, Dylan would set off along Stryd Bethel. He would pass the garden wall of Ty-nant where Dr James lived; Manchester House (run by Mog Edwards in Llareggub); Sheffield House the ironmongers and general store (run by Mrs Organ Morgan in Llareggub); and Compton House, now the Newquay Football Club, where downstairs was a chemist, and upstairs a bed and breakfast run by Mrs Phillips, though for part of the war it also provided dormitory space for the Nautical School.

On the other side of the road, were the homes of Rev. W.O. Jenkins (Rev. Eli Jenkins) and Walter Cherry (Cherry Owen). Next to them were Tim Thomas', and later Mr Herbert's, barber shop in the basement of Maglona (Waldo was Llareggub's barber); Mr Glanmor Rees of Arnant in his cobbler's shop (Jack Black); Bethel (Bethesda) chapel; the river Alun running alongside the chapel (the Dewi in Llareggub) and, next to it, Mr John's bakery (run by Dai Bread in Llareggub). The original two-storey wooden building that housed the bakery was burnt down in a fire and replaced by the present-day Costcutter supermarket.

Next but one down from Compton House was the Commercial (The Sailors Arms). As Dylan stood outside, he could see the Memorial Hall across the road (the Welfare Hall in Llareggub, where Polly Garter scrubbed the steps). After a few pints, Dylan would walk the short distance to the Black Lion, passing first the donkey stables on his right, and on his left, Rose Hill, home of Captain Pat. From the Black Lion he could see Coronation Gardens and hear Maisie the donkey braying not at all angelically on the Downs.

If you took this walk today, you'd find little of what Dylan saw. Some houses and shops have changed their names and function. Manchester House, for example, now sells fishing tackle. But it wouldn't take much wit or imagination to develop and signpost a Dylan Thomas Walk, starting in Llanina, taking in Majoda and then going up through Brongwyn Lane to Stryd Bethel, and down to the Black Lion. Special plaques and information boards could mark out all the shops and other places on the route.

One might say that, in Newquay, Dylan had fully realised the potential of 'the street' as a dramatic force: *Under Milk Wood* is connected both to place-based TV soaps like *Pobl y Cwm*, *Eastenders* and *Coronation Street*, and to neighbourhood anthropological enquiry such as that of the Opies, and Wilmott and Young in the grubby back-doubles of London's East End. Dylan's failed project about a day in the life of the streets of London came to fruition in Stryd Bethel, Newquay.

78. The Newquay Patricks, 1940, at the wedding of Patricia Evans (the youngest sister of Jack Patrick Evans) and John Lloyd, taken outside the Black Lion. Seated far right: Captain Patrick Evans and, next to him, Alice Kate Patrick Evans, mother of the bride and of Jack Patrick. Middle row: Jack Patrick's aunts who gave him the Black Lion: Maria ('Baps') Patrick (3rd from left), Lucilla Patrick (4th from left) and Mary Patrick (4th from right). Top row left: Rev. Eben Davies, Neston Church, Wiltshire, husband of Maria. Jack Patrick and Betty are standing on the right of the middle row. Standing next to the bride is Jack Pat's other sister, Janey Patrick. A brief family history is given in Note 60.

231

Appendix 1. Interviews with Local People

This appendix contains some of the interviews carried out as part of the research for this book. The interviews were tape-recorded, and done in the interviewees' homes. There were also brief interviews with other people that are not reproduced here, though they are referred to in the text.

1. First interview with Amanda Williams, Ciliau Aeron. November 7th 1997

We used to live in Gelli with my grandmother and grandfather and the front part of the house was rented out to the Phillips from Swansea, and their two girls Vera and Evelyn, who were great friends of Dylan Thomas, especially Vera.

Dylan came up and stayed in Gelli for a while with his wife Caitlin. I was about six or seven at the time. They were in the mansion with Vera and Captain Killick, in the front part. Captain Killick was in the army, and he used to come home on leave. Vera wasn't a writer, she used to design, art and things like that. There was plenty of room for them in Gelli. Vera Killick knew Dylan from school in Swansea.

Dylan used to write sitting underneath the big tree there, and when my grandmother was going up, he was shouting "You going milking, Mrs Davies?" "Yes," she used to say. And then he would go in the house and get this big tumbler and he used to go up to the cow shed. "This is a treat," he used to say. He loved it, with a big froth in the tumbler and there he was drinking the milk, and he'd say "Give me half a cup again, then." He did like his cup of milk. He used to have it when he was a boy with his uncle and auntie down in Llanstephan. Well, he was talking a lot to my grandmother.

Then they used to go, him and Captain Killick, every day to the pub in Talsarn and in the afternoon he used to write if he hadn't too much drink. Thomas Herbert the vet was another drinking partner. Dylan liked his drink but he was alright with it but Captain Killick had a temper... he was quite cussing at times. You could hear a bit of commotion going around there. He could go a bit aggressive at times, you see, when he had a drink, he used to shout and shout. I don't think he hit anybody... he was just very noisy and that after he'd had a few pints.

Dylan used to hear my grandfather telling me to go over the shop and get some tobacco, and he would ask me to bring him some fags. And every time he would ask us to go, he would give me sixpence. But if I asked him if he wanted something from the shop, you wouldn't get anything. So being a Cardi we wouldn't ask him but wait for him to ask. And we'd say we weren't going but we would if he wanted us to and then he would give us sixpence. In those days that was a lot of money.

There was races in Talsarn every year, and Caitlin used to go over then to John Jenkins Pentrefelin and she had a pony there and was racing... she was a very keen horse rider, very, very keen and she went pregnant of course but she did ride the pony in the last races when she was pregnant and my grandmother was very cross with her. My grandmother said she *shouldn't* have done it. And Caitlin said, "Well there you are, Mrs Davies, I've done it now." And she asked my grandmother: "How do you spell the river Aeron?" And my grandmother would tell her. "Oh, if it's going to be a boy. I'll be calling him Aeron."

"What if it's a girl," asked my grandmother.

"Oh what can I call her Mrs Davies?"

"Well, call her Aeronma, or Aeronwy or one of those names."

So that's how Aeronwy came, of course.

There was a ghost in Gelli. And my grandmother asked Dylan one day: "Have you seen the old girl that's walking around here?" And he said: "You know, I have heard something but I was a bit drunk that night." Everyone who used to stay in the mansion used to come over the next day and ask my grandmother if there was anything funny about the place, especially evacuees and those...

No, he didn't help on the farm but when we were haymaking and things, he used to walk around, writing a lot. Caitlin and he used to walk quite a bit, especially down to Talsarn to the Red Lion, and then they would come back and have their lunch and then you'd see him on his stool writing, facing our entrance, we couldn't miss him, when we were little kids coming back from school, he was always underneath the tree writing. And he was always telling us about his life down on the farm with his uncle and auntie.

Oh, he was a nice man. We thought a lot of him, you know. He wasn't so well known then, you see. I never saw him drunk. He used to like his pint and chatting with the locals. Dylan was very, very nice, peaceful, very quiet, and he used to talk a lot to my grandmother, because my grandmother had good English, she used to work in London... they used to get on fine together. He was a nice man, and I hear a lot of stories about him, and they go under my skin, to tell you the truth, they used to say he was drunk, but we never saw him like that. I read a story not long ago that he didn't die of drink. It was diabetic. As a matter of fact, my eldest boy, he's Richard Dylan. We thought Dylan was a gentleman, and his wife. It does upset me now what some say about him... we were kids and in the old times you didn't get much sweets and things like that but he was kind, very kind, fair play

79. Margaret Phillips in Lampeter, on her way to Gelli.

to him. He was gentle and kind, definitely, and he had time to talk to you, he didn't ever ignore you.

But he used to come and shout at some of the boys for baiting the goat, old Griselda, I think he had a fondness for animals because he used to come up to the cowshed and he used to talk about the cows with my grandmother.

I've been thinking about it, the name of the fields and things like that, but, no, there's nothing with llaeth [milk] there. I don't know if it's anything to do with Dylan having the milk. That's the only thing I can think of. But him and my grandmother were very close. My grandmother had been to London as a young girl, she could speak English fluently and she was a person who communicated.... Dylan loved that milk from my grandmother.

2. Second interview with Amanda Williams, July 10th 1998.

It was the Revd Felix Davies who owned Gelli and he lived in the vicarage in Llanddewi Brefi. He owned the place when my grandparents, Thomas and Mary Davies, were there as tenants. They finished 1952 and they'd been there about 48 years, I should think. Farming the land, yes. Was it 75 acres? I'm not quite sure. Yes, I think it was about that. And the fields are all the same now as it was then. My grandfather was born in the neighbouring smallholding, so he knew about Gelli from an early age.

Gelli had two parts. The Plas at the front was only two up and two down

80. Evelyn Milton (née Phillips) with baby Jane, 1943

but the rooms were big, as you know. We lived in the back, it used to be the farmhouse then. When we lived there Gelli was done as two sections. There was a door leading from the Plas bit to the Gegin Goch, as it was called – that used to be the servants' quarters, and it was locked when we were there and there was furniture over the door; nobody could have seen it. And the same in the bedroom upstairs. We had the Gegin Goch and the kitchen, and then there was a scullery in the back. We used to call it *yr eil*, but that's an old name, the Welsh name for a scullery, you know. And it had flags, the stone flags there, and it had one tap, a cold water tap. We didn't have the hot or cold or nothing then.

Dylan and the Killicks lived in the front part, in the Plas, as we called it. Well, I don't know why it was called the Plas. It was a bit posher, with the big windows and things. As you went upstairs in the Plas, now then, Dylan and Caitlin were in the bedroom on your left as you went up and with the window facing out towards our house, looking over the farm yard. Dylan used to sit a lot at the little window there, watching the goings on in the yard. The room had the old wooden type beds, you see, and she had wardrobes and things there. Very nice furniture, mind, because they brought the furniture down with them from Swansea, you know, from the blitz in Swansea, Mrs Phillips did. And then there was a double bed there and a single bed. And then in the other room for Vera she had two double beds, with the wardrobes and things....

Downstairs there was a sitting room, where they lived mostly. The three of them used to sit together in there, and Captain Killick when he was home. They had lots of chairs, armchairs, with a nice log fire, and they had a large table there where Vera used to do a lot of her sewing. As you go in, then, there was a little butler's table, as they called it... yes, it was very nice. On the other side was the drawing room or library they used to call it, and Eddie Evans did all the carpentry there, and he did all these bookshelves, right round the library and they had, oh, books galore there. And they had a table then by the window, with these glass cabinets and things and settees. It was kept for best but Dylan used to go in there sometimes for peace and quiet.

The stables were across the yard at the back of the Ty Pair, we used to call that house – that used to be the outdoor servants' quarters when the farm was all in one, and it had an upstairs to it where there were two bedrooms and then the stables were underneath. There was an old 'pair' there, I don't know what you call it in English, 'pair' we used to call it. That's still there, it's like a big oven, and you put the fire underneath it for doing the potatoes and things for the cattle. Then there was an open fire on the ground, where they used to boil the water, and there was an oven where they used to make the bread and things. I think they're all there still. And then at the back of the Ty Pair there was these stables, and my grandparents used it, the top, to keep potatoes, and the breath from the horses would keep them frost free.

It was a place to keep four horses in the stable. And as you went in through the stable, cemented to the wall as you opened the door there was a statue there; it was a military man. And the old legend used to say that he was there to guard the horses, that used to take these gentry in their cart and floats or what-you-call-them. But it's gone now, you see. Somebody must have taken it – they've ripped it off the wall. Somebody's seen it when Gelli was empty, 'cause it was empty for quite a while.

As for the ghost, my grandfather always used to go out to the cowshed about nine o'clock every evening to see that the cows and things were all right overnight and used to come back and used to say "Oh, she's there tonight again!" She was sitting in the little window of Dylan's bedroom. Vera and her mother were there one night and Mrs Phillips was doing the washing-up in the scullery and she felt a hand on her shoulder and she thought it was Vera and she looked round and there was nobody there and she said "What do you want, then, Vera?" And Vera said: "I haven't moved from here." "Oh, said Mrs Phillips, "she's been here again tonight." Everybody knew about it you see, Dylan as well. Everybody staying at Gelli has heard or been disturbed by the ghost.

And another time, there was a lady – Gelli was empty now, and there was a rose in the front door – I don't think it's there now – a very pretty pink rose. It was at the side of the pillars and there was a lady, Miss Lewis, she said "Oh, I'd love a piece of that rose" and she went over there one evening and she was cutting off the rose and a voice came from inside "That's mine, leave that alone" and she had a hell of a fright, you know, she ran and she left everything as it was. And people were telling her "You imagined it." "No," she said. "I heard a voice inside and there was nobody there." The house was empty then.

The evacuee teacher, she was Muriel Corkish from Liverpool, and her sister, they came down there, and they stayed in Gelli for a while, but they never slept all night there because oh, the ghost was pushing them out of bed and everything, you know. It was there, and pulling the clothes off them and, you know, they didn't sleep there at all tidy.

It didn't come if there were children in the house.

My uncle when he was courting he was coming in late. In the Gegin Goch we had an old fashioned dresser with jugs on it, and when he was coming home the next morning he would say "Oh, she was there last night again, she was moving the jugs, taking them off and putting them on again, you could hear her doing it." She was looking she was for the money, there's money been hidden, because when her mother was expecting, her father had put his heart on having a son but it turned out to be a girl. He was ever so disappointed, that's what the story is, that he hid the money that he had put away for the baby boy he was wanting and that she's coming back to look for the money that she thinks is hers by right.

When my grandmother saw the ghost it was all in brown. She had a long brown skirt and a brown coat that they used to ride in years ago, and her hair was very dark and with a parting in the middle and with these two earphones each side, and that's the one that everybody else has always seen. And my grandmother one day, she was in the WI in Trefilan, and one of the girls told her "D'you know what was going on in the Welsh Club in London?" "No." "We were talking about the ghost in Gelli." And she said "Don't be silly! There isn't such a thing. I've been there forty-odd years and there's nothing there. I haven't seen a thing." She didn't believe it. She thought it was rubbish, but my grandfather, he definitely knew it was there.

And then my grandmother came home that night. Well, she went to bed and then there was no light, candles we had, so she lit the candle and she went to use the chamber-pot and then she went back, blew the candle out and she was laying there awake in bed and all of a sudden she saw a light coming in through the door and she could see this wardrobe and the dressing table and this lady came in. And she said she couldn't move her hand nor foot or couldn't say a word. My grandfather was in bed with her, but he was sleeping, and then this lady came towards her and she looked down at her and smiled, and she thought, you know, till the end that she was there to tell her "Well, I am here. You don't believe it, but I'm come to show

237

myself so that you know I am here."

Well, I haven't seen her myself, but when I was older I was locked out coming home late. I came in through the Cegin Goch where the ghost was supposed to be. So I came in through the window and as I was walking across from the window to the door I could feel cold going down my back. I was nearly too weak and too stiff to open the door to go in. And I've heard her very often as if she was sawing wood.

The house used to be surrounded with trees and rhododendrons but they've cut them down now. It's spoilt it really.

3. First interview with Jenkin Emrys Davies, Felinfach. March 25 1998

I was born up in a little place by Temple Bar here, Cwm-ysgawen. I was working on the farms, started at 14 years of age. We got married in 1945, that makes us 52 years together. We've been here in this place 21 years. First place we went to was in Silian, then we moved to Abermeurig in 1954 and was there 15 years, and from there to the Red Lion in Talsarn. We kept the Red Lion for six years before coming here.

Dylan Thomas only occasionally was coming to Gelli. The thing I remember vividly was the people living in Gelli, Mr Killick and Mrs Killick. They used to come down to the Red Lion with a pram to get their quota of beers and that. A pram full of them and then back to Gelli, almost a mile up the road and up hill all the way.

Local people liked Dylan. He was a very nice man, I met him several times, in other company, of course. Funny part about it, he wasn't drinking much in the pub, they were only fetching the quota and bringing it home to Gelli. He was very humorous, he was very good for socialising with people, everybody was talking to him. He wasn't famous then, of course. We were pretty young in them days, you see, we weren't drinking much, only on the sly in the night, but we saw them and the Killicks coming down. And the old lady in the Red Lion, old Miss Evans, if there was somebody like that around, it was 'Hush, hush', you know. We had to be quiet then, you see. She liked him very much, she would, wouldn't she, taking a pram full of beers everyday?

I remember Caitlin well. She got on well with the ladies here. She was a very nice lady, and it struck us at the time that she was Irish, you never saw any strangers much in Talsarn, you see. There was horse racing in Talsarn in them days, local trotting and that, and Dylan's wife, Caitlin, she used to ride a pony for John Jenkins, Pentrefelin, a nice, little, fast pony, Princess Marina. I remember at the time she was pregnant and everybody was worried about her. Caitlin was mad about horses, mad. I remember her well, I can see her riding now, and she was well gone, very pregnant, how can she ride, the women said, look at her, she's nearly going.... I can see her now, quite plainly.

These Killicks, now, the ones that were staying there with them, we looked up to them, they were English people from London.... in them days you did cap to people. Big bugs, we used to call them. Mr Killick's wife, she married during the time she was in Gelli. Lil, do you remember old Shanco, Ty Mawr? He fancied her for a bit. He was old, of course, retired police or something he was, but he fancied her very much, but this Killick came along, he came from somewhere and they got married. Mrs Killick was a lovely blond, very attractive girl. Oh, Mrs Killick was very, very attractive. Mr Killick, he had fair hair, with a longish face, rather lanky, not a big robust bloke, rather tall and lanky. He was only coming occasionally to Gelli, just the weekends and like, pushing the pram home full of bottles. My brother-in-law who worked in Gelli used to say Killick had a heck of a temper, mun, a heck of a temper.

We had someone like you once in the Red Lion, doing something about Dylan Thomas. I couldn't get on with him at all, he was asking some questions, but I couldn't dare answer him, you know. All kinds of silly questions, well, I didn't know Dylan Thomas' private life. He was snooping, asking too much, going too far. I suppose he wanted me to tell him the dirty stories but I didn't know them, you see. There's a lot of people, they call Dylan Thomas just bosh, you know, some people do, but they don't see *his* side of things. Oh, he was a great man.

There was no gossip about Dylan that I know of, apart from the drinking, I don't know whether he was a womaniser or anything, I never heard anything like that. It was only years after that came the big drinking. No doubt he was a very brainy man, you get them people, don't you, they just go over the top a bit, that's why I'm nearly mad, I think!

What do *you* think of Dylan Thomas' poems? He wasn't the proper, original Welsh poet, was he? Do you remember old John Jenkins, Penbryn Mawr? Dylan wasn't a poet like him, was he? He had sentences, but there wasn't any rhyme or anything. But with the old Welsh poets, every two lines they rhyme, don't they, but not Dylan Thomas. I noticed that.

Dylan had a funny feature, you know. Once you saw him, if only a glimpse, you'd always remember him. I don't call him ugly or anything but he had a peculiar feature. Have you noticed that? He had a peculiar look about him.

They were lovely people, him and the Killicks, lovely people. We only met them in the sports or horse racing and events like that. What they did with their own lives, I don't know. They must have been drinking pretty heavy from the loads that were going up. We all could notice that. And that was a terrible thing in them days, you see. Lucky my Mam didn't see that, Mrs Killick and them in the pub, you weren't supposed to be in the pub, mun, it wasn't the ordinary, everyday thing, going into pubs. We had a lady up in Temple Bar here drinking, my Mam was calling her Old Sow, that's how it was in them days. There was my dad out for his drink Christmas Eve, two pints, that all he had through the year. If he went more often, everyone would call him a bloody boozer. The women were all disgusted with Caitlin and Mrs Killick being in the pub. All the women in Talsarn had one eye out of the door watching them going in the Red Lion. That's how it was in them days. It wasn't our way of living. What was wrong with it? Nothing was wrong with it. Now they take the kids and everything to the pubs.

What would *you* call Dylan, then? A bit of a rebel or proper gentleman? The things he writes about, he must have a unique mind, very individual wasn't he, you take that *Under Milk Wood* or whatever it was, out of this world, mun. I'm not twp, but I could never bring myself to write things like that. I'd write a little rhyme about somebody. He must have a terrible mind on him, terrible... unique, mun, well, he saw something well above me, anyway. I don't know the right words to describe him, really.

4. Second interview with Jenkin Emrys Davies, July 2nd. 1998

The Red Lion is exactly the same as now from the outside but the inside there's a tremendous change.

You went in through the front door with the old stone slab floor, and there was a little bar facing you, a round little bar, so you could serve from the Lounge, from the front passage, and from the Bar. Of course, that's all gone now. The old lady Miss Evans used to go in, she was on a huge step, you'd think she was a six foot tall woman but she was only about five feet or less, and there she was serving from there. She had an old bottle cork opener, and I've still got that machine in the shed outside here now. She puts the bottle there and turns the handle and pop, out it came. She had one brother there then, Johnnie he was called. They had a smallholding as well you see, they were milking four or five cows besides the beer selling. And they were brewing their own beer, in the back kitchen, the old boiler and everything was there when we came. You ordered your beer, and he brought the beer in from the back kitchen in a jug, enamel jug, two or three pints at a time. Then he stopped the home brewing and he used to take the old horse and cart down to the station in Felinfach, there were casks coming from Aberystwyth Brewery. They also had Ansells beer, from where, I don't know.

You went in the Bar, there was an old settle along one wall, a table in the middle, and another little table behind the door with a settle again, big huge open fire, you could take a horse and cart in it. There was an old dresser there, must have been a hundred years old. The man who came there a few years after Johnnie he was offered £2,000 just for the top of the dresser. I've got two parts of the dresser here now. They had an oval mirror on the mantelpiece, a hanging mirror, Ind Coope and Allsopp Beers, beautiful thing. Old Johnnie always had a goldfinch in the cage in the window.

It was very, very homely, there was about seven or eight real local people, not many young boys or anything. If you went in there as a crowd of us sometimes, then we were only about nineteen or twenty years of age, there was heck to play if you had more than one drink. Old Miss Evans soon told you it was time you went. And no singing, they didn't like a lot of noise. Oh, it was a lovely place then.

Up the top of the village was a petrol pump, Stanley Jones and Reggie Jones. They had a bicycle shop, selling boots and doing a bit of mechanical work and that. I bought a Raleigh bicycle there, four pounds nineteen pence and three-farthings. Took me about three years to pay for it. You couldn't have it any other way. I was only earning then about seven shillings a week. The wife bought a bicycle off him, a Hopper, a ladies' bike. You didn't have to pay down for anything, call when you like with half-a-crown now and again. They were selling watches at half-a-crown each, you couldn't pay for that at once even. You could ask old Stanley Jones for practically anything you wanted, he had it somewhere in the building.

Then across the road, there was a grocery shop. That was old Llew Evans. Deaf as a door nail. He was selling everything in the grocery line, everything to do with the household. We used to go in there, it was dark as anything, only small windows, you walked up from the doorway to the shop, it was slanting downwards to the road. That was stone slabs again, and the old doors had a wooden latch with a hole to put your finger through.

Then further down there was the post office, Ellen Jones, was there, stamps and yeast, though she didn't sell sweets or anything. Across the road was a big water pump, and then old Ty Job as we called it. We were playing billiards and darts and things in there. Job used to work in Llanllyr, in the gardens. It was his house, but they made it just like a little village hall, and we were going there for meetings with the Home Guard during the war, meeting there every Sunday morning, marching up and down the road in our uniforms with a gun each with no ammunition! Oh, Ty Job was very popular, whist drives and everything there. Job lived in the kitchen and the parlour, we had tilley lamps to play billiards and that. They took it down after the war and the council houses came in the end.

Further down then was a blacksmith, that was a very popular meeting place for people. I remember we had practice in the Home Guard, teach us the way to put an incendiary bomb out. And what we did then was to put them in the shoeing shed and put a match to them and then try and put them out. There was a lot of fun about it! They were shoeing seven or eight horses a day in them days and banding the cart wheels and that. A busy time.

Across the road, there was a house there, Cae Bont we used to call it. And every now and again there was terrible floods in Talsarn, before they cleared the river Aeron. And in Cae Bont, the bed was floating in the parlour, 1936 it was. Terrible floods. A foot deep in the Red Lion. The old lubricating machine with old Stanley Jones, we saw it going down the road standing up in the floods. Nobody saw it ever again, and the chickens from Ty Mawr were floating down the river. There was a hole in front of Stanley Jones shop, you could put three cars in it, where the flood water ditched the road up.

D'you know one thing, I never saw Dylan in a car, nor Killick because they were always walking down with a pram to get their beer consignment. No, no taxi, only Dan Evans with a bus service to Lampeter. I remember him having his first car, Austin Seven, the old square type, £100, and everybody was amazed, how could he afford a car, there were dozens of people going down there to have a look at it. Dan Evans used to catch rabbits and sell them, four pence each, catch three of them and you were a wealthy man. You could afford a packet of Woodbine! And a pint. Good ychan!

5. Interview with Jacqui Lyne, second wife of the late Thomas Glyn Herbert, friend of Dylan Thomas. August 30th 1998

Thomas Glyn first met Dylan when Dylan was staying in Talgarreg in 1942. I don't know where Dylan was staying but there was talk of a cottage in the village somewhere. That's where Thomas Glyn met Caitlin for the first time, after the pub in Talgarreg. Thomas and Dylan went back from the pub and poor Caitlin was in bed and that was where he was introduced to her and she was made to get up and go and make tea for them. They met quite by accident in the pub; he knew Dylan was in the area, Thomas' mother was quite excited about the fact, which is strange because he wasn't really that famous then. I don't know how she knew about him.

As a vet, Thomas Glyn had a petrol allowance, and he'd go on his rounds and collect Dylan and drive him about a lot, especially to the Black Lion at Newquay. Thomas would also go to Gelli, Talsarn, and he and Dylan would be drinking in the Red Lion. His relationship with Dylan continued off and on over the years, they met whenever Dylan was in the area. Poetry and literature were my husband's great thing which is where the association with Alastair Graham came in. That's what the three of them spent most of the time doing, discussing books and drinking in the Black Lion in Newquay.

Dewi Evans (Dewi Ianthe) was at Majoda that evening. No, not 'the shooting', but 'the evening' as they always referred to it. He would never actually talk about it. There was a sort of reunion one night with Thomas, and Dewi and Islwyn Jones (who was married to the opera singer, Dame Gwyneth Jones) and it was briefly discussed then. They all seemed to stay pretty quiet about it, in this very strange way they would all close ranks, it was a very private thing and no-one else's business. Nobody would talk about it. Alastair escorted Killick out of Majoda? I didn't know that but he was the kind of man with the authority to do it.

Alastair was one of the Scottish Grahams... he was in the diplomatic service, in Greece and Cairo, I think, before the Second World War. He was at some stage thrown out of London society. I think the other person involved – his lover – was the second Viscount Tredegar. The place where they used to meet was Rosa Lewis' hotel, the Cavendish. And that affair was the reason he got thrown out and came to live in Wales. I don't think he had any gay relationships in Wales. He was very respected in Newquay, no one has a bad word for him. And they were all very protective of him. When *Brideshead* was hitting the headlines in 1981, I think, newspaper people kept coming down like mad to interview him and he didn't want that and no-one in Newquay would talk about him.

I think he missed London society, he found himself in Newquay with very few people who had his interests. I always used to feel very sorry for Alastair. The newspaper reporters descended on him after the scandal in London. The first time I met him I disliked him intensely. I thought he was arrogant and he used to pretend to be German. Later on, I got to like him and he was actually quite kind.

Yes, he was rather reclusive. Later on, it got to the stage where he wouldn't come to a dinner party or anything. He had the shakes, I don't know whether it was early Parkinson's or maybe alcohol but he didn't like to be seen eating with people. But he would be quite happy to sit and talk to you. He lived on his own in the Wern, but he had Lottie his housekeeper. She was very loyal to him. It was while he was at the Wern that people like Dylan and Augustus John would go there. They stayed there occasionally, because Alastair always complained about little Aeronwy wetting the beds. Alastair refused to have electricity in the house so it was all oil lamps. And Caitlin used to dance on the kitchen table! Augustus John at that stage was painting the portraits of the girls who were in Llanina and Dylan was certainly there at that time, visiting Alastair.

Alastair died about 1988. He was a Catholic.... He wasn't well off but he wasn't impoverished. In his early days it was his mother who was funding him. I suppose he had a pension from his diplomatic days, and a state pension. He certainly had enough to keep Lottie on. He ate and drank reasonably well, he had good wines, and always beautiful books, never paperbacks, just beautifully bound books. Alastair loved books. Yes, I'm sure he funded Dylan, he certainly used to fund Waugh.

Under Milk Wood is based much more on Newquay than Laugharne. Thomas my husband used to tell who the characters were in Newquay. The postmistress in *Under Milk Wood* steaming the envelopes open to read the letters – I actually met her in Newquay. Thomas used to lecture on Dylan and *Under Milk Wood*, and the people in Newquay. I've got some of his papers somewhere but they're mostly in Welsh.

6. *Interview with Gwilym Jones, Head Gardener, Ty Glyn Mansion. November 5th 1997*

Faber came to Tyglyn Aeron when I was nineteen years old. They didn't mix from the start. He brought his own staff down, three girls and a nanny. No-one from the village was working much in the house. He even stopped us taking water from the well, which we had always done for generations.

The first thing he did was get a new Head Gardener, to make sure no-one ever came near the place, he was an ex-policeman, a Mr Oaten, he was a very savage man from South Wales. That was why Faber employed him, I suppose. Well, first of all, the under-gardener, Jack Davies from Cilcennin, came to see me. 'Do you know that Oaten's trapping your chickens?' They were trespassing, flying from my field to his.

It was a shocking thing, to catch poultry in gin traps like that. It was a bad start with Faber.... I didn't meet him at all, but we passed each other, or when he was in the shop, there'd be a little queue there perhaps, and he would come in and he would push the people out of the way: 'I wish to be served' and everyone gave way to him. I believe the people wanted to know Faber better because they knew the gentry, very well, all the gentry when they came to the shop they would speak to the customers but not Faber.

They were disappointed. You couldn't get near him. He was above you, you were only really a peasant. I would touch my cap to him when we passed, but he wouldn't take any notice. He wasn't from this world. Once, the young boys from the village were on the square, and Faber was having trouble with the car, and he asked us to push the car up to Tyglyn Aeron. There were about ten of us, I think. We pushed the car up, and it was a hard going, about a mile up the hill, it was a Humber, a big one, with an open top. And we pushed it up, and in our minds we thought we'd have a reward between us, but he just told us to go, and went into the house. Of course, he was not very popular after that.

We didn't see Eliot on the road. Most of the people would come down to the bridge, that was the place we would meet very often, but we never saw Eliot. Faber didn't mix, you see...If he had been more sociable, he might have learnt more. He seemed to hate the Welsh, he wanted to be shut in, he didn't do anything with local people. In Faber, Eliot had a man who was exactly like him, I wonder how they got on. I suppose Eliot wasn't a mixer either, and that's why we didn't see him about the village. You wouldn't know much about people like that, you couldn't come to know him. He kept himself to himself, there were plenty of grounds in Tyglyn Aeron.

Dylan Thomas came down to Talsarn, he was *too* sociable. I think he was drinking very heavy there... he mixed a lot with the Welsh people, he was not afraid. I think he would go to the pub and carry half a dozen bottles home... and he would have plenty of help to carry them home.... He was a very big scholar, Dylan, and he was known more than Eliot, wasn't he?

Oh yes, it was a treat to live with some of them, the gentry, they came to know you, they made an effort, but not Faber. We would have been very pleased to know him better. He must have lost the best of the Welsh for not mixing. It was his loss.

Appendix. 2
Birds, Fish and Animals in the Poems of Dylan Thomas

These data were obtained by counting the number of times different kinds of wild and domestic creatures appeared in Dylan Thomas' poems. The tables provide one way to examine the development of the pastoral theme in his post-war poetry. They also indicate how the number of references both to predators and birds increased in the poems written after the Majoda shooting in March 1945. Note that the increase in the total number of references (132), as well as that in birds (66) and predators (47), was yielded by a smaller number of poems (11).

The data are presented as an aid to analysis, and should be cautiously used within the context of the themes and meanings of particular poems or collections.

Table 1. An analysis of the number of references to animals, birds, fish etc. in *Collected Poems*. Notes of Explanation.

	18 Poems	25 Poems	Map of Love	Deaths and Entrances	Post-shooting Poems
Total Poems	18	25	16	23	11
Fish/Sea Creatures	5	6	3	11	12
Birds of Prey	0	3	1	7	14
Water Birds	0	5	1	9	30
Other Birds	4	4	3	18	22
Total Birds	**4**	**12**	**5**	**34**	**66**
Farm Animals	4	14	7	17	26
Wild Animals	3	3	4	7	6
Worms, Maggots	13	7	0	0	0
Insects	3	2	2	1	1
Reptiles	2	8	1	5	2
Cats & Dogs	1	2	0	4	3
Rats & Mice	0	1	0	0	3
Fox	1	0	2	0	9
Slugs & Snails	0	6	1	0	0
Hares & Rabbits	0	0	0	0	2
Other	0	1	0	0	2
Total References	**36**	**62**	**25**	**79**	**132**

Appendix 2. Birds, Fish and Animals in the Poems of Dylan Thomas

1. The analysis was carried out on *Collected Poems 1934-1953*, ed. Walford Davies and Ralph Maud, (Dent, 1997).
2. 'Post-Shooting Poems' comprise those written after the Majoda shooting incident on March 6th 1945. They are: 'In my craft or sullen art', 'Fern Hill', 'In Country Sleep', 'Over Sir John's hill', 'Poem on his Birthday', 'Do not go gentle into that good night', 'Lament', 'In the White Giant's Thigh', 'In Country Heaven', 'Elegy' and 'Prologue'.
3. *Deaths and Entrances* excludes 'In my craft or sullen art' and 'Fern Hill'.
4. 'Total Birds' is the total of the three preceding columns and is not included in the total figure of references.
5. 'Farm Animals' comprises horses, sheep, cows, pigs, goats, donkeys, bulls and chickens.
6. 'Others' comprises squirrel (2), mole.
7. 'Water Birds' comprises sea and fresh water birds.
8. 'Wild Animals' comprises ape, monkey, wild pig, lion, tiger, lynx, duck-billed platypus, deer, kangaroo, hyena, wolf, reindeer, otter, tortoise, baboon and bear.

Table 2. The number of references to predators in *Collected Poems*, and as a percentage of the total number of references to animals, birds, fish etc. Predators comprises: reptiles (16), birds of prey (25), bear, foxes (12), lions

	18 Poems	25 Poems	Map of Love	Deaths and Entrances	Post-shooting Poems
Total Poems	18	25	16	23	11
Total References	36	62	25	79	132
Predators	7	15	8	21	47
% Predators	19	24	32	27	36

and tigers (5 in total), lynx, hyena, wolves (2), ravens, rooks and crows (12 in total), heron (13), otters, seals (2), cranes (2), pelican, albatross; shear-water; cormorant. Gulls are not included because not all gulls are predators. The stalking, preying, shrouded heron is a particularly strong symbol of death in 'Over Sir John's hill' and 'Poem on his Birthday'. The increase in predators would be even more marked in the post-shooting poems if we included curlews, which have a predatory presence, for example, in 'Poem on his Birthday'. It is a basic-level analysis but I hope it encourages other people to look more precisely at the significance of individual creatures in particular poems, and then to aggregate the results. For example, I have treated all references to ravens as references to a predator. But there may be some poems where Dylan refers to ravens in a neutral or benign way; conversely, there may be references to non-predators which are sinister or are meant to convey evil. Aggregating on a creature-by-creature basis may produce a more satisfying picture.

Table 3. An analysis of the number of references to animals, birds, fish etc. in *Under Milk Wood.*

1. 'Other' comprises: mole (3), ferret, shrew, weasel (2) and bat.

Fish/Sea Creatures	23	Insects	6
Birds of Prey	3	Reptiles	2
Water Birds	9	Cats & Dogs	23
Other Birds	18	Rats & Mice	7
Total Birds	30	Fox	3
Farm Animals	55	Slugs & Snails	5
Wild Animals	6	Hares & Rabbits	2
Worms, Maggots	1	Other	8
		Total of References	171

Predators in *Under Milk Wood.*

The number of predators mentioned in *Under Milk Wood* is 12, only 7% of the total number of references. Of these 12, the only bird of prey is the owl; there are no hawks, ravens or rooks.

Appendix 3. William Killick: Some Biographical Notes

William Richard John Killick. Born Java, November 30th 1916, to William Myrtle Killick, a tea trader, of Herefordshire, and Gladys Harriet, née Lindsey. Educated in the UK, first at Preparatory School, Trearddur House, Anglesey, then Harrow School (1930-34). The Harrow School Register notes that Killick was in the Gymnastics VIII from 1932-34. One of his subjects was Ancient Greek.

1934-39	Worked in gold mining in southern Africa.
September 1939	Returned to UK
October 1939	Enlisted in the Royal Engineers (R.E.)
January-May 1940	Served with the B.E.F. in France
June 1940	Commissioned and posted to Gibraltar (180 Tunnel Company, R.E.)
March 1941	Attached to Joint Interrogation Centre, Gibraltar, exfiltrating Belgiums, Poles etc. from North Africa.
April-Oct 1942	In hospital in the UK
November 1942	Posted to 2nd Parachute Sqn., R.E. (broke leg in training.)
January 1943	Posted to Special Operations Executive, SOE (62 Commando, cover for Small Scale Raiding Party, which carried out cross-channel raids, in two of which he participated.)
May 1943	3 months training on miniature submarines (Welman Course)
July 1943	SOE Course, Arsaig House, Inverness
Aug-Sept 1943	In Cairo – further training in demolitions etc. with Force 133
20 Oct 1943	Flown into Greece and worked in Macedonia as Sapper Officer with the Allied Military Mission to the Greek guerrillas.
Nov 12 1944	Ceased active service in the field
Nov 20 1944	Joined office staff of Force 133 in Salonika
Dec 4 1944	Flown to Cairo
Feb 1945	Returned to Newquay pending redeployment.
6 March 1945	Shooting incident at Majoda.
May 1945	Training as a prospective member of the 'Vicarage Party', a reconnaissance team to investigate German POW camps

21 June 1945	Trial at Lampeter Assizes.
23 July 1945	Signed off from SOE. Posted to R.E. Depot.

Source: SOE Adviser

On leaving the army in 1947, William Killick joined T. Phillipson and Co., a firm of civil engineering contractors in Long Melford, Suffolk.

Appendix 4. 'The Ffosyrheligs'

There can be no doubting the significance within the family of Margaret Phillips of the 'Ffosyrheligs', Newquay and Cardiganshire. But surprisingly little reliable information has survived about Margaret Phillips' birth and parentage. The main sources of information available to me were a family tree given to Jane Gibson by a distant relative, and the recollections in old age of Jane's mother, Evelyn Milton, and aunt Vera Killick. Jane herself has memories from childhood of visiting places and relatives around Newquay. I was able to carry out a little research on the matter, using the 1881 and 1891 census returns, and through conversations with a number of local people.

Margaret Maria Phillips

Birth: In or near Llanarth, Cardiganshire. Vera Killick told Jane Gibson that the date was 1881. But she also said that Margaret Maria had been married in 1909 at the age of seventeen, making her birth date 1892. Margaret's death certificate gives her age as sixty-one, making the birth in 1888. This last is probably the most likely. No birth certificate has been found.
Mother: Known only as 'Maggie'.
Father: Vera Killick said she never knew his name. The family tree given to Jane Gibson says it was a William Jones. It has been usual to refer to the father as "a wild young man". Nothing else is known about him except that he came from a farm near Newquay called Ffôs Helyg.
Siblings: Margaret Maria had a sister called Ellen. Another sister called Anna is shown on Jane Gibson's family tree but this cannot be confirmed.

Ffôs Helyg Farm

The farm in question is Ffôs Helyg-isaf, near Synod Inn, Newquay. At the time of Margaret Maria's birth, it was lived in by Hannah and John Jones, and their seven children: James (17 in 1891), Henry (19 in 1891), Ben, Samuel, Harris, Elizabeth, Mary (Marie) and Ellen. (1881 and 1891 census returns). This corresponds with the names on the family tree held by Jane Gibson, though William, Margaret Maria's putative father, is not shown in the census, presumably because he was not living on the farm at that time. The farm was burnt down during the war and nothing remains of it today. Its location is SN 402 531 on OS Map 146. It was on the A486 road from Synod Inn to Newcastle Emlyn, some four miles from Newquay. There were four Ffôs Helyg farms clustered at this point – Ffôs Helyg-isaf, Ffôs Helyg-ganol, Ffôs Helyg-fach, and Ffôs Helyg-uchaf. Only the last remains, and can be seen on the OS map today. All four farms can be found on the 1964 OS map 1:10,560, Sheet SN 45 SW.

The 1891 census reference is Fiche 604 Aberayron, Llandisilio Fiche 2+, page 8.

The great-grandchildren and grandchildren of the seven Ffôs Helyg children have a varied list of interests and occupations, including a sculptor, painter, teachers, scientist, electrician, doctor and an Air Marshall – Sir Lawrence Jones.

Hannah and John Jones' daughter Ellen (referred to in the text as 'Auntie Ellen'), lived in Allen View, Cross Inn, outside Newquay, and kept the post office there, which Jane Gibson remembers visiting as a young child. Her husband was Evan Evans, who was the postman, as well as a cobbler. Their neighbour was David Thomas, tailor and outfitter, whose workshop is now in Museum of Welsh Life, Cardiff. Dylan used to drink with Jack Patrick in the Cross Inn pub, and it is mentioned in his poem 'Sooner than you can water milk'.

Appendix 5. Sources of Information

This book has been written with the help of interviews and correspondence with a great number of people, most of whom are referred to in the Acknowledgements. I have also consulted archival material at the National Library of Wales, and made use of maps, street directories, registers of electors and a good many local histories. Where possible, I have tried to find at least one other source to confirm information received from people who were drawing on their memories of people and events in the past. Sometimes, but not always, written material was available to confirm information given.

Descriptions of the people and shops of Stryd Bethel and George Street in the 1940's were provided principally, but not only, by Eleanor Lister, Sue Passmore, Griff Jenkins Junior, Ieuan Williams and John Evans.

Material on the Majoda shooting and the trial of William Killick was obtained from a number of newspaper reports, information provided by Killick's family and local people and by the SOE Adviser at the Foreign Office. William Killick's own account of his service in Greece can be obtained from the Public Record Office, Kew, quoting file HS 5/701.

The material for Chapter 6, The Spying, comes from the Public Record Office; the BP Amoco Group Archive; the BP Amoco Video Library; the BBC Archive; the British Film Institute; Greenpark Productions; Joe Mendoza; Griff Jenkins Junior; Rachel Willans; Evan Yardley; Hugh Wilford, Michael Williams; Laura Beresford, Keeper at Tredegar Park; Fallowell's articles on Alastair Graham; Hastings' biography of Evelyn Waugh; West's account of the SOE; Waterfield's biography of Percy Loraine; *Who's Who* and *Burkes Peerage*; the van Engert papers at Georgetown University (available on the Internet) which confirm Loraine's pre-war involvement in the affairs of the Anglo-Iranian Oil Company; Woodhouse's biography; Mostafa Elm's book; the Colin Edwards tapes; Bill Read's book; Saunders' book on the CIA; and the web sites *Evan Frederic Morgan* (www.data-wales.co.uk/morgane.htm); *The Price of Oil, The Price of Life* (http://member.aol.com/kfishe/rushdie.html); *Character Assassination* (iran-e-azad.org/english/special/chap12.html); *A 'great venture': overthrowing the government of Iran* (www.knowledge.co.uk/lobster/articles/130iran.htm). This last is an abridged version of Mark Curtis' book (1995). Information has also been gleaned from the various accounts of British espionage listed in the References, particularly Masters, (1984), Lashmar and Oliver, (1998) and *A Who's Who of the British Secret State* (1989).

I have drawn throughout the book on four collections of material:

The private papers of Thomas Glyn Herbert held by his widow Jacqui Lyne (referred to in the book as the 'Jacqui Lyne Papers'). These contain some twelve papers and two video tapes with references to Dylan Thomas and to life in Newquay.

The papers that Thomas Herbert deposited in the National Library of Wales. Only one item is relevant to Dylan Thomas.

The papers of Min Lewis in the National Library which, when used with her book (see References), give some helpful information on Laugharne and Dylan Thomas.

The audio tapes of Colin Edwards' interviews in the 1960s with Dylan Thomas' friends and family, including interviews in America, Italy and Iran. The tapes are in the Sound and Moving Image Collection at the National Library. They are a valuable, but much neglected, resource. Edwards' unfinished biography, *Dylan Remembered*, is in the Manuscripts department of the National Library. It contains detailed information on Dylan's life between 1914 and 1934. I am presently working with the National Library to transcribe and publish the Edwards interviews. Edwards' biography draws on the work of an American psychoanalyst called B.W. Murphy. I have also placed in the National Library a copy of an extended paper written by Murphy, *Creation and Destruction: Notes on Dylan Thomas*. This examines Dylan's creativity and output within the context of oral fixation, castration anxieties and superego anomalies.

Unless otherwise stated, quotations from, or information attributed to, Evelyn Milton, Jeff Milton, Olive Jones, Edward Evans, Jack Patrick, Mrs Warfield-Darling, Charles Fisher, Olive Suratgar, A.H.S. Shaffari and Ethel Ross are taken from the Colin Edwards tapes.

Information on the Bryn-y-Mor Girls has come from the Colin Edwards tapes, and from discussions with, and material provided by, Rachel Willans and Charlotte Bacon, daughters of Vera and William Killick, and Jane Gibson, daughter of Evelyn and Jeff Milton. Further information came from Robin Sheldon, who lodged with Vera and William Killick in the 1960s.

I have not referenced every piece of information from local people; if I had done so, the narrative would have become tedious. I am willing to discuss any detailed points of reference and verification with researchers. Please contact me through the publisher.

References

I have drawn upon and sometimes quoted from the following books and articles, and I am grateful for the help, and often the inspiration, they provided.

By Dylan Thomas

Under Milk Wood by Dylan Thomas (Dent, 1961). *Dan Y Wenallt* gan Dylan Thomas, translated by T. James Jones (Gomer, 1992). *Under Milk Wood: A Play for Voices* edited by W. Davies and R. Maud (Dent, 1995). *Quite Early One Morning* by Dylan Thomas (Dent, 1987). *Portrait of the Artist as a Young Dog* by Dylan Thomas (Dent, 1964). *The Crumbs of One Man's Year* by Dylan Thomas in *Collected Stories* edited by W. Davies (Dent, 1993). *Dylan Thomas: Collected Poems 1934-1953* edited by W. Davies and R. Maud (Dent, 1997). *Dylan Thomas* edited by W. Davies (Everyman, 1997a). *Dylan Thomas: The Poems* edited by D. Jones (Dent, 1991). *Dylan Thomas: The Collected Letters* edited by P. Ferris (Dent, 1985). *Dylan Thomas Notebook Poems 1930-34* edited by R. Maud (Dent, 1989). *Dylan Thomas: The Filmscripts* edited by J. Ackerman (Dent, 1995). *Dylan Thomas: The Broadcasts* edited by R. Maud (Dent, 1991). *Dylan Thomas: Letters to Vernon Watkins* edited by V. Watkins (Dent and Faber, 1957).

About Dylan Thomas

Books

A Dylan Thomas Companion by J. Ackerman (Macmillan, 1994). *Welsh Dylan* by J. Ackerman (Seren, 1998). *Dylan Thomas in America* by J. M. Brinnin (Arlington Books, 1988). *The Growth of Milk Wood* by D. Cleverdon (Dent, 1969). *Dylan Thomas's Places* by J.A. Davies (Christopher Davies, 1987). *A Reference Companion to Dylan Thomas* by J.A. Davies (Greenwood Press, 1998). *Dylan Thomas* by W. Davies (OUP, 1986). *Dylan Remembered* by C. Edwards (unfinished biography, 1968, National Library of Wales). *Dylan Thomas* by P. Ferris (Hodder and Stoughton, 1977 and Dent, 1999). *Caitlin: The Life of Caitlin Thomas* by P. Ferris (Hutchinson, 1993). *The Life of Dylan Thomas* by C. FitzGibbon (Little, Brown, 1965). *The Last Days of Dylan Thomas* by R. Gittins (Macdonald, 1986). *Dylan Thomas: The Code of Night* by D. Holbrook (Athlone Press, 1972). *My Friend Dylan Thomas* by D. Jones (Dent, 1977). *Dylan Thomas's Wales* by H. Laurie (Weidenfeld and Nicholson, 1999). *Laugharne and Dylan Thomas* by M. Lewis (Dobson, 1967). *The Death of Dylan Thomas* by J. Nashold and G. Tremlett (Mainstream Publishing, 1997). *The Days of Dylan Thomas* by B. Read (Weidenfield, 1964). *Caitlin: Life with Dylan Thomas* by C. Thomas with G. Tremlett (Secker and Warburg, 1986). *Double Drink Story: My Life with Dylan Thomas* by C. Thomas (Virago, 1998). *Dylan Thomas in Swansea* by K. Thompson (Ph.D., University of Wales, 1965). *Dylan Thomas: Word and Image* by J. Towns (Swansea, 1995). *Dylan Thomas: In the Mercy of his Means* by G. Tremlett (Constable, 1993). *Portrait of a Friend* by G. Watkins (Gomer Press, 1983).

Articles

'Under Milk Wood' by D. Cleverdon in the *Journal of Design and Fine Art* no. 13, 1954, Royal College of Art. 'Dylan Thomas and Broadcasting' by D. Cleverdon, *Poetry Wales*, Autumn 1973, vol. 9, no. 2. 'Dylan's Vintage Town' by M. Lewis (unpublished paper in the Min Lewis Papers, National Library of Wales, paper 3). 'Dylan at Gelli', by L. Ebenezer, *Cambrian News* (24/2/1967). 'Local interviews on the occasion of the 25th anniversary of Dylan Thomas' death', by L. Ebenezer, *Y Cymro*, (7/11/1978). 'Dylan Thomas and Film' by G. Goodlad, *New Welsh Review*, Summer 1990, vol. 3, no. 1. 'At 'Dame' school with Dylan' by J.A. Hardy, *New Welsh Review*, Spring 1995, no. 28. 'Big Daddy Meets the Nogood Boyo's by J. Harris, *Poetry Wales*, vol. 18, no. 4 1983. A Review of *Under Milk Wood* by Harold Hobson, the *Sunday Times*, 23/9/1956. 'A Bilingual Llareggub' by T. James Jones, *Planet* 8, October/November, 1971. 'Delinquent Free Spirit or Astute Operator?' by R. Jones, *Planet* 16, Spring 1992, vol. 4, no. 4. 'Creation and Destruction: Notes on Dylan Thomas' by B.W. Murphy (undated, National Library of Wales). 'Dylan and the Scissormen' by C. Page in *Anglo-Welsh Review*, Summer 1974, vol. 23, no. 52. 'The Ghost of *Under Milk Wood*' by A. Road, *Observer Colour Magazine*, 1/10/1967, reprinted in *Newspaper Dragon* by A. Road (Christopher Davies, 1977). 'Dylan and the Stormy Petrel' by N. Sandys, *Western Mail*, 7/1/1961. 'The Face on the Slate: a Memoir of Dylan Thomas' by G. Williams, *Planet* 20, Autumn, 1973.

Touching on Dylan Thomas

'Sixty Glorious Years: The Story of the Swansea Little Theatre up to 1984' by A. Davies, *Transactions of the Honourable Society of Cymmrodorion*, 1996. *Two Flamboyant Fathers* by N. Devas (Collins, 1966). 'Gwilym Marles: Dylan Thomas's illustrious forebear' by John Edwards, *New Welsh Review*, No. 47, 1999. 'Flyte of Fancy' by D. Fallowell, *Sunday Telegraph*, (17/6/1990). 'Bohemia Revisited' by D. Fallowell, *Sunday Telegraph*,

References

(24/6/1990). 'Dylan Thomas and Others' by R. Garlick, *Planet*, February/March 1995. 'Dylan Thomas at Tenby' by R. Garlick in *Raymond Garlick Collected Poems 1946-86* (Gomer, 1987). *With Love* by T. FitzGibbon (Century Publishing, 1982). *Idris Davies of Rhymney* by I. Jenkins (Gomer, 1986). 'Some Letters of Idris Davies' by G. Jones, *Poetry Wales*, vol. 16, no. 4, 1981. 'A. Edward Richards: writer from mid Wales' by D.A. Matthews, *New Welsh Review* Autumn 1994, no. 26. *Where Silver Salmon Leap* by T. Macdonald (Gomer, 1976). *Memoirs of the Forties* by J. Maclaren Ross (Penguin, 1984). *Francis Bacon* by M. Peppiatt (Weidenfeld, 1996). *War like a Wasp* by A. Sinclair (Hamish Hamilton, 1989). *Francis Bacon* by A. Sinclair (Sinclair-Stevenson, 1993). *The Writings of Anna Wickham* edited by R.D. Smith (Virago, 1984). *Madly in All Directions* by Wynford Vaughan-Thomas (Longman, 1967). *Pages from My Life* by Margherita de Walden (Sidgewick and Jackson, 1965).

About Newquay and Aberaeron

'Shipbuilding at New Quay, Cardiganshire, 1779-1878' by S. Campell-Jones, in *Ceredigion*, vii, 1974/75. *Farmers and Figureheads: the Port of Newquay and its Hinterland* by S. Campbell-Passmore (Dyfed C.C., 1992). *New Quay and the Great War 1914-1919* by S. Campbell-Passmore (Undated). *One Village's War: New Quay 1939-1945* by S. Campbell-Passmore (1995). *Atgofion Ceinewydd* gan M. Evans (Cymdeithas Llyfrau Ceredigion Gyf. 1961). *Herbert Y Fet* gan T.G. Herbert (Gomer, 1989). *Newquay and Llanarth* by W.J. Lewis (1988). *The Lampeter, Aberayron and New Quay Light Railway* by M.R.C. Price, (Oakwood Press, 1995). *The Growth of an Isolated Rural Settlement into a Tourist Resort – New Quay, Dyfed* by M. Tinkler, (Dissertation, College of St. Mark and St. John, April 1983).

Spies and all that

Secret Service by C. Andrew (Sceptre, 1987). *The History of the British Petroleum Company: Vol 2: The Anglo-Iranian Years 1928-1954* by J.H. Bamberg (Cambridge University Press, 1994). 'Dylan Thomas in Iran' by D. Callard in *New Welsh Review*, December 1998. *Inside Intelligence* by A. Cavendish (Collins, 1990). *Antonia White: Diaries 1926-1957* edited by S. Chitty (Virago, 1993). *A Greek Experience 1943-1948* by N. Clive (Russell, 1985). *Sir Samuel Hoare* by J.A. Cross (Mackay, 1977). *The Ambiguities of Power: British Foreign Policy since 1945* by M. Curtis (Zed Press, 1995). *Ruling Passions* by T. Driberg (Quartet, 1978). *Oil, Power and Principle* by Mostafa Elm (Syracuse University Press, 1994). *Burgess and Maclean* by J. Fisher (Hale, 1977). *Secret Intelligence in the 20th Century* by C. FitzGibbon

Dylan Thomas: A Farm, Two Mansions and a Bungalow

(Granada, 1976). *Children of the Sun* by M. Green (Constable, 1977). *Brian Howard: Portrait of a Failure* by M-J. Lancaster (Blond, 1968). *Britain's Secret Propaganda War 1948-1977* by P. Lashmar and J. Oliver (Sutton, 1998). 'A Who's Who of the British Secret State', a special issue of *Lobster*, published Hull, May 1989. *Ian Fleming* by A. Lycett (Weidenfeld, 1990). *The Man who was M: The Life of Maxwell Knight* by A. Masters (Blackwell, 1984). *Philby: the Spy who Betrayed a Generation* by B. Page et. al. (Deutsch, 1977). *Conspiracy of Silence: The Secret Life of Anthony Blunt* by B. Penrose and S. Freeman (Grafton, 1986). *Looking for Mr Nobody* by J. Rees (Weidenfeld, 1994). *Countercoup: The Struggle for the Control of Iran* by K. Roosevelt (McGraw-Hill, 1979). *Quadrille with a Raven* by H. Searle (1985, on http://www.edu.coventry.ac.uk/music/searle/lesley.htm). *Who Paid the Piper? The CIA and the Cultural Cold War* by F. Stonor Saunders (Granta, 1999). *Professional Diplomat: Sir Percy Loraine* by G. Waterfield (John Murray, 1973). *The Best Wine Last* by A. Waugh (W.H. Allen, 1978). *Secret War: the Story of the SOE* by N. West (Hodder and Stoughton, 1992). *The Time has Come* by D. Wheatley (Arrow, 1981). *The Ultra Secret* by F.W. Winterbotham (Weidenfeld and Nicolson, 1974). *Something Ventured* by C.M. Woodhouse (Granada, 1982). *Five O'Clock Shadows* by E. Yardley (The Book Guild, 1988).

The Great and the Good

T.S. Eliot by P. Ackroyd (Sphere, 1985). *The Letters of Evelyn Waugh* edited by M. Amory (Penguin, 1980). *The Diaries of Evelyn Waugh* edited by M. Davie (Penguin, 1984). *Evelyn Waugh: A Biography* by S. Hastings (Minerva, 1995). *Michael Ayrton* by J. Hopkins (Deutsch, 1994). *Q: The Biography of Desmond Llewelyn* by S. Hernu (SB Publications, 1999). *Dewi Emrys* gan E. Phillips (Gomer, 1971). *Compton Mackenzie: A Life* by A. Linklater (Chatto and Windus, 1987). *Harold Nicolson: Diaries and Letters* edited by N. Nicolson (Collins, 1966). *The Scholar Gypsy* by A. Sampson (John Murray, 1997). *Louis MacNeice* by J. Stallworthy (Faber, 1996). *New York Jew* by A. Kazin (Secker and Warburg, 1978).

From the Savage Club

Old Herbaceous by R. Arkell (Harcourt-Brace, 1951) – see also his gardening verses on the Internet. *Trees in Britain* by L.J.F. Brimble (Macmillan, 1946). *Magnolia Street* by L. Golding (Hutchinson, 195?).

And the others

Madocks and the Wonder of Wales by E. Beazley (Faber, 1967). 'Notes on

References

Welsh Music and Welsh Drama' by T.E. Ellis (Lord Howard de Walden), *Transactions of the Honourable Society of Cymmrodorion*, 1920-21. *Voices from a Burning Boat* by Stevie Krayer (University of Salzburg, 1997). *Oil on Troubled Waters: the Gulbenkian Foundation and Social Welfare* by D.N. Thomas (Directory of Social Change, 1996). 'An Indirect Aid to Sales' by R. Tritton, *Imagery*, September 1950. *Diawl y Wenallt* gan M. Williams (Y Lolfa, 1990).

Use has been made of material from the *Cambrian News, The Guardian, Carmarthen Journal, News of the World, Sunday Telegraph, Sunday Times, Y Cymro, Western Mail, Evening Post, Tenby Observer and County News* and *Welsh Gazette*.

Notes

Introduction
1. Now in the possession of Dr. T.E. Faber.
2. *Sunday Times*, 15/11/1953.
3. See Appendix 5 for information on the Colin Edwards interviews.

Chapter 1. The Farm
4. Undated letter from Vera Killick (née Phillips) to her niece Jane Gibson (née Milton).
5. *ibid.*
6. *ibid.*
7. *South Wales Evening Post*, 3/7/1948 and from a list of exhibitors provided by the Killick family.
8. Harry Leyshon, Colin Edwards tapes.
9. Colin Edwards tapes.
10. Information from Evelyn Milton (née Phillips), Colin Edwards tapes.
11. Colin Edwards tapes.
12. Hanging on display in the Dylan Thomas Theatre, Swansea.
13. Colin Edwards tapes.
14. Letters to the author, 4/7/1999 and 9/7/1999, and *Woman's Weekly*, undated.
15. Undated letter from Vera Killick to Jane Gibson.
16. Indeed, Vera's portrait was done by Swansea artist Kenneth Hancock.
17. Theatre programmes supplied by the Killick family.
18. Vera was offended mostly by Caitlin's shawl which had circular stripes of green and white. It had been crocheted by Margaret Phillips.

Chapter 2. Two Mansions
19. Undated letter to Jane Gibson
20. Ethel Ross, 1981, in the exhibition in the Dylan Thomas Theatre, Swansea.
21. I am grateful to Dillwyn Miles and Jeff Towns for this information. The album and poem are in the National Library of Wales: NLW MS 12043B. The poem is also in the *Notebook Poems* with the title 'The Shepherd to his Lass' (Maud 1989). The farm is on OS Map 145 at SN124 473. It was occupied by Lawrence and Margaret James, Mary James and Margaret Davies (Register of Electors).
22. Miles also took Dewi Emrys to the Sailors Safety in 1949. This was at the end of a day's pilgrimage by Emrys and other members of the

Fforddolion Ceredigion to Pwllderi, a cove on the north Pembrokeshire coast. Emrys "stood over the cliffs, his eagle face looking out to sea as the wind tossed his hair, and recited the poem 'Pwllderi' in a memorable fashion." The Fforddolion Ceredigion was a society of literati of the county set up in 1948, at Emrys' instigation, at the Brynhoffnant Inn.

23. Dillwyn Miles, who knew Dylan and is now President of the Pembrokeshire Historical Society, believes that the party first visited the Duke of Edinburgh pub at Newgale, where Caitlin bathed, and then St. David's, before going on to the Sailors Safety. Brinnin (1988) does not name the Sailors Safety as the pub but the visit was confirmed by Monté Manson for Dillwyn Miles. Mrs Manson remembered the visit because "they were pretty drunk and difficult." Billy Williams, who was the party's driver, remembered a "tasty" lobster dinner (see Min Lewis, 1967).

24. In an article by Davenport, National Library of Wales, MS 14934E. Davenport also visited in June/July 1939 – see a letter to Vernon Watkins in that month in *Collected Letters*. Davenport was Kingsley Amis' uncle – see MS 14934E for some of their vigorous correspondence about Dylan. Davenport's house in Wiltshire provided a refuge during some of the war for writers, artists and composers. One visitor was Dylan's "great old friend" Jim Thornton, whom Dylan then introduced to Vernon Watkins (*Collected Letters*, 8/8/1940). James Cholmondeley Thornton had left Cambridge with a First in English. He worked for Dent and other publishers as a reader and reviewer, before joining the BBC in 1936. He served in the Royal Engineers during the latter part of the war before re-joining the BBC in 1946. He was Director of the Calouste Gulbenkian Foundation from 1961 to 1969. The Foundation provided grants to University College, Swansea, in 1966-67 and 1968-69 to employ Vernon Watkins as a Poet-in-Residence. I have written a history of the social welfare programme of the Gulbenkian Foundation, including the period that Thornton was there (Thomas, 1996).

25. *Western Mail*, 7/1/1961. See also J. Harris (1983).

26. He sent a telegram to Emily Holmes Coleman on that date from Machynlleth (Ferris 1999, p.144).

27. *Collected Letters*, 1/9/1938.

28. Gaenor Amory, de Walden's daughter, letter to the author, 20/7/1998.

29. Letter to the author, 5/8/1998.

30. Letter to the author, 21/11/1997.

31. A note from Rosemary Seymour, 9/5/1999.

32. Letter from Gaenor Amory, 9/12/1997.

33. Letter to the author, 21/11/1997.

34. Conversation with Tatiana Mallinson, 23/1/1998.

35. Letter from Davenport to Vernon Watkins, inviting him to give a reading at Repton, where Davenport had taken up a teaching post. (National Library of Wales 21818E 314 Miscellaneous Letters).

36. *Collected Letters*, 28/8/1942
37. Vera and William were not actually married at this time.
38. Interview with the author. Harry Leyshon, a friend of Dylan's parents, told Colin Edwards that Dylan's uncle, the Rev. David Rees of Paraclete Chapel, had stimulated Dylan's interest in plants: "David Rees... was really a student of the fauna and flora of Gower and Dylan used to go down every Saturday and go for rambles with David Rees and I think David had a great influence on his knowledge of flowers and plants all through the district...and he [Dylan] took an interest right through his life in it."
39. *Collected Letters*, 19/12/1950.
40. Dai Isaac Morgan, interview with the author.
41. Jenkin Emrys Davies, interview with the author.
42. Interview with the author.
43. Herbert was in his final year at vetinerary college and doing his "seeing practice" in the area. He was to become good friends with Dylan – see Chapter 3.
44. Letter to the author, 10/9/1998.
45. 2/2/1945
46. *Collected Letters*, p518n.
47. Bruce Cardwell, conversation with the author.
48. Royal College of Art, *Journal of Design and Fine Art,* issue 13, 1954, p36. The painting was used to illustrate an article by Douglas Cleverdon about *Under Milk Wood.*
49. Grid Reference SN 519 652 OS Map135. The farm has been called Wernllaeth since the 1890s. It was previously Wernllaith, meaning damp alder grove. It's of interest that there was a farm called Wernllath just up the road from Dylan's parents' house in Bishopston, Swansea.
50. *The Dictionary of the Welsh Language* says that llaethliw = llaeth + lliw. Llaeth, of course, is milk. Lliw means colour, appearance or aspect. The farm has been called Llaethliw (Milk Aspect) since the nineteenth century but in the eighteenth century it was called Llaithliw, probably meaning "Damp Aspect Farm." The far less common meaning of lliw is 'basis or foundation of a story'.
51. It is possible that Dylan knew, e.g. from Richard Hughes, the other house called Tan yr Allt that had strong poetic and historical associations. This was the home of William Madocks in north Wales near Tremadoc. Shelley stayed there for a while and wrote part of *Queen Mab.* Hughes lived in the area, at Parc and Mor Edrin, as did Clough Williams-Ellis, and Robert Graves at Erinfa, just outside Harlech. I am grateful to Lowri Hughes for this information.
52. 7/11/1978
53. Jacqui Lyne Papers.
54. SN 520 575 OS Map 146.

Chapter 3. The Bungalow

55. Conversation, 12/5/1999.
56. Griff Jenkins Junior, 3/5/1999, who is Wendy Flenard's cousin.
57. Conversation, 5/11/1997.
58. 'Sooner than you can water milk'. The quotations are from Vaughan Thomas (1967, p.121) who, says Daniel Jones (1991), was with Dylan when he wrote the poem. Jones has dated the poem to September 1943, presumably after discussion with Vaughan Thomas who discovered the poem in 1977. However, when Vaughan Thomas wrote to Paul Ferris in 1984 he said that Dylan had given him the poem in the Chelsea pub circa September 1943. There was no mention of Vaughan Thomas being present when it had been written. The poem later formed the basis of a letter, not in the first edition of *Collected Letters*, to Tommy Earp dated May 28th 1945. It is in the collection at Ohio State Universities Libraries (Paul Ferris).
59. Griff Jenkins Junior.
60. The Black Lion had been in the Patrick family since at least the middle of the nineteenth century. It was run then by John Patrick and Helen Guy, who were married in 1861. They had sixteen children, of whom ten survived birth and childhood ailments. Their eldest daughter was Alice Kate Patrick. She married William Evans in 1898. They had three children: Jack, Patricia and Janey Evans. When old John Patrick died, the hotel passed to his two unmarried daughters, Lucilla and Mary, and his unmarried son, Llewelyn. Another daughter, Maria ('Baps'), had run away from home at the age of 40 to marry Eben Davies, the vicar of Neston Church in Wiltshire. Eventually, Lucilla and Mary gave the Black Lion to their nephew Jack, who was always known as Jack Patrick or JP. Jack Patrick married Betty in the mid 1920s but there were no children. His sister Janey did not marry. Patricia, his other sister, married John Lloyd (who is not the same person as Jack Lloyd the postman) in 1940. There were two children, David Charles Patrick Lloyd who died in New Zealand in 1977, and Ann Brodie, who lives in California.

Jack Patrick also ran the Pier Hotel, at the bottom of Newquay, though its day-to-day management was in the hands of a friend called Nora Rachelle. The Pier has since been incorporated into the Blue Bell.
61. Griff Jenkins Junior.
62. A letter of 1944 in the Augustus John collection at the National Library of Wales indicates that John first met Graham in 1944, even though they had both been friends with Viscount Tredegar for many years.
63. *Western Mail*, 3/12/1929.
64. Conversation with Michael Williams, 16/4/1999.
65. Griff Jenkins Junior.
66. Jacqui Lyne Papers. One programme was *Cefn Gwlad* in 1986.
67. June 1955, in Herbert's papers in the National Library of Wales, Aberystwyth.

68. Elizabeth Ruby Beaufoy Milton (no relation of Evelyn Milton). Cochran, who knew Augustus John, also auditioned Caitlin and John's daughter, Vivien (Ferris, 1993, p42).

69. See the *Weekend Mail*, June 24th-26th, 1954, for the story and photographs of Meurig and Harrison.

70. *Collected Letters*, 29/8/1946.

71. Ffynnonfeddyg means 'The Doctor's Well', a word play that Dylan would have relished.

72. Letter to the author from Griff Jenkins Junior, 15/11/1998.

73. *Y Cymro*, 7/11/1978.

74. September 1944. John was painting the portrait of Alicia Gower Jones in Aberaeron. (National Library of Wales 21818E 314 Miscellaneous Letters).

75. There is more on the Nautical School in the *Cambrian News*, 11/2/1999.

76. *Welsh Gazette*, 9/11/1944.

77. *Collected Letters*, 28/4/1945.

78. *Collected Letters*, 30/8/1944.

79. *Collected Letters*, 28/10/1944.

80. Theodora FitzGibbon's description (1982, p179).

81. *Collected Letters*, 28/10/1944.

82. *Evening Times and Echo*. The date is not known but the article is pasted in the front of Evans' *My People* (Melrose, 1919), copy XPR7535 V12 in the National Library of Wales.

83. *Collected Letters*, 8/2/1945.

84. *Y Cymro*, 7/11/1978.

85. *Collected Letters*, 3/1/1945.

86. Harris (1983).

87. Information from Bill Davies, who was a pall bearer at the funeral of Oliver Sandys, Evans' wife.

88. Jacqui Lyne Papers.

89. *Collected Letters*, 24/6/1945

90. *Collected Letters*, 30/7/1945.

91. *Y Cymro*, 7/11/1978

92. *ibid.*

93. *ibid.*

94. Conversation with Jacqui Lyne, 16/4/1999.

95. Jacqui Lyne Papers.

96. The engagement was broken off just after the war and Tessa married the Rt. Hon. Peter Thomas QC, MP in 1947.

97. Both Evan Davies and Ernest Mann are shown as resident at the Central in the 1945 Register of Electors.

98. Conversations with Davies and Jones, 7/12/1998.

99. Conversation with the author, 18/7/1999.

100. Letter to the author, 21/12/1998.

101. There is nothing in Dylan's engagement book for 1952, in the Texas collection, which indicates how he travelled. His departure from Aberystwyth for London via Shrewsbury would certainly have been by train (*Collected Letters*, 21/11/1952).

Chapter 4. The Shooting
102. This account is taken from Killick's own description on file in the Public Record Office, Kew.
103. Paul Ferris notebook.
104. Colin Edwards tapes.
105. Paul Ferris notebook.
106. *Y Cymro*, 7/11/1978.
107. Conversation with the author, 24/3/99.
108. The SOE Adviser.
109. *Y Cymro*, 7/11/1978.
110. See *Who was Who*, vol. 5, 1951-1960. Mr Justice Singleton had been educated at Pembroke College, Oxford, and his clubs included Brooks and the Athenæum.
111. *Collected Letters*, 24/6/1945.
112. Colin Edwards. This comment was not made as part of the interview with Evans but is recorded in Edwards' notebook "Interviewees A-Z, on later years, after Wales" dated April 1st 1964. The notebook is in the Manuscripts Department of the National Library of Wales. It should be clearly stated that William Killick was acquitted on all charges on the clear direction of the judge on the basis of lack of evidence.
113. Conversation with former Aberaeron resident, Chris Sewell, 1/4/1999.
114. Mrs Warfield-Darling, Colin Edwards tapes.
115. SOE Adviser.
116. Richard Jones seems to take a certain pleasure in 'outing' William Killick in the Spring issue of *Planet*, 1992.
117. 15/2/1957. Killick's brief correspondence with Vernon Watkins is on display at the Dylan Thomas Centre, Swansea.
118. Letter from Robin Sheldon to Charlotte Bacon, 30/5/1999. Sheldon had lodged with the Killicks in the 1960s.
119. *Collected Letters*, 28/3/1945.
120. Paul Ferris notebook.
121. Rachel Willans.
122. There are five letters in *Collected Letters*. The new edition will include a sixth to Tommy Earp.

Chapter 5. The Murder
123. The letter of February 16th 1953 is given in full in Jenkins, 1986, p235. It is not in the first edition of *Collected Letters*.

124. *Collected Letters*, 22/6/1953.
125. Williams, 1973, p52.
126. This account of events outside Laugharne was put together by reading the front page of the *Western Mail* from January to October 1953; it is indicative of what Dylan would have picked up had he simply glanced at the headlines or skimmed the major stories of the day. Dylan did read the *Western Mail*, though how frequently and carefully we do not know. See *Collected Letters*, 15/2/1953 and its Index.
127. See Devas (1966).

Chapter 6. The Spying
128. *Collected Letters*, ?/1/1951.
129. *Collected Letters*, 16/1/1951.
130. British Council records. McAlpine stayed with the Council until his retirement in 1975. He was Deputy and then Acting Representative in Japan, and Representative in Burma, Norway and Ceylon. He was awarded the OBE in 1964.
131. Public Record Office, Kew, BW49/10 British Council papers.
132. *NAFT*, the AIOC in-house magazine, February 1951, BP Amoco Archive.
133. Pearl was a senior publishing executive. Her brother was Alfred Kazin, one of America's foremost literary critics. His visits to London in 1945 (where he met, amongst others, T.S. Eliot) and to Cambridge at the beginning of the 1950s are described in *New York Jew* (1978). As with Edmund Wilson and Lionel Trilling, Alfred Kazin's views could be the making or breaking of a writer's reputation in America.
134. *Collected Letters*, 16/1/1951
135. 24/3/1952. Public Record Office FO 371/98593.
136. There is a succinct article in the *Spectator* of June 20th 1947 on the widespread poverty and disease in Iran. The following week's issue noted that the annual profits of the AIOC had increased to £9,624,938.
137. Dylan had once been mistaken for a German spy, or so he claimed in a letter to John Davenport in January 1941. He was in good company. In 1797, locals in the village of Kilve, Somerset, thought that Coleridge and Wordsworth were French spies and a Home Office special agent was sent to investigate.
138. Michael Gasson, Group Archivist, BP Amoco plc. The three films are *Cattle Carters* (1962), *North Slope Alaska* (1964) and *Shadow of Progress* (1970).
139. BP Amoco Archive.
140. BBC Written Archive Centre, R19/1025.
141. *ibid.*
142. Contained in a black notebook in the Jeff Towns/Dylans Bookstore

Collection, which Towns acquired as part of Liz Reitell's papers.

143. Available on VHS from the BP Amoco Video Library in London.

144. Greenpark brochure, 1986.

145. A.H.S. Shaffari, Colin Edwards tapes.

146. Unattributed quotes in this and the next section come from a correspondent who wishes to be anonymous.

147. The usual way to make this calculation is to multiply the amount – £250 – by today's average Retail Price Index (165.2 in April 1999) and divide it by the average RPI in the year in which the amount was paid (8.5 in December 1950). This yields the figure of £4,858.

148. Michael Gasson, *op.cit.*

149. Vol 19. no. 224, September 1952 p132.

150. *Collected Letters*, 12/4/1951.

151. Black notebook in the Jeff Towns/Dylans Bookstore Collection.

152. *Collected Letters*, 25/3/1951.

153. Public Record Office, INF 6/483 and BW 2/33 British Council papers.

154. Memo from A.H.T. Chisholm to the AIOC Chairman, May 11th 1951, BP Amoco Archive BP 43859.

155. D.A. Logan, Foreign Office, 6/4/1951. Public Record Office FO 953/1152.

156. *ibid.*

157. Chisholm, *op.cit.*

158. D.A. Logan, Foreign Office, 24/4/1951. Public Record Office FO 953/1152.

159. BBC Written Archive Centre, R19/1025.

160. Public Record Office, FO 371/91548. Letter from E. Berthoud to R. Bowker.

161. The list of contributors is in the Public Record Office, FO 953/1152. The biographical information was obtained from *A Who's Who of the British Secret State* (1989), the *Balliol College Register 1930-1980*, and Mostafa Elm's book (1994).

162. Foreign Office summary of the programme, Public Record Office, FO 953/1152.

163. The full text of Dylan's contribution is in Maud, 1991.

164. D.A. Logan *op. cit.*

165. E.A. Berthoud to R. Bowker, 19/4/1951, Public Record Office, FO 953/1152. Berthoud worked for the AIOC from 1926 to 1939.

166. Foreign Office summary of the broadcast, Public Record Office, FO 953/1152.

167. *Collected Letters*, 12/4/1951.

168. *The Guardian*, 1/1/1999.

169. Letter from Gwen Watkins, 24/8/1999 and see p.103 of her *Portrait of a Friend.*

170. Conversation, Evan Yardley, 6/1/1999.

171. See Masters (1984) and Green (1977).

172. See Theodora FitzGibbon (1982).

173. *Collected Letters*, 19/12/1950.

174. 32, Chatsworth Road, Willesden, London.

175. Sinclair deduces that it was Loraine who went with Bacon but it is not wholly certain. Peppiatt in his later biography of Bacon (1996) thought it too speculative to mention Loraine.

176. Conversation with Michael Williams.

177. The Knight family still live at Tythegston Court. In 1999, they sold a 1770 Johann Zoffany portrait of the Knight family for £1.1m. at Sotheby's. (*Western Mail*, June 9th.)

178. Percy Evans, Griff Jenkins' uncle, and County Dental Officer for Cardiganshire in the 1940s.

179. Letter to the author, 22/2/1999

180. 1982, pp.104-107

181. Rees, 1994, p.147.

182. *The Times*, an obituary, May 9th 1975.

183. Woodhouse, 1982, p.94.

184. Michael Williams.

185. Stallworthy, 1996, p.385.

186. 19/7/1999.

187. Letter to the author, 10/3/1999. Cleverdon (1973) has also mentioned the ML Club.

188. Rees, 1994, p153

189. Letter to the author, 20/3/1999.

190. Letter to the author, Jenny Rees 10/3/1999.

191. Rees, 1994, p.147.

192. Jenny Rees, 1994, p224.

193. *Collected Letters*, 7/12/1950

Chapter 7. The Plot
194. *Collected Letters*, 6/3/1948 and ?/10/1951.

195. Jacqui Lyne Papers.

196. *Collected Letters*, 3/1/1945.

197. *New Statesman*, November 2nd. The review described Dylan as a "verbal steeplejack" reaching "the dizziest heights of romantic eloquence... this was radio at its purest."

198. The radio play is mentioned in his letters of May 24th and 29th and June 5th.

199. Dylan received letters in Italy about the broadcast from Mrs Ferguson of the sweetshop and Mrs Hole of the school in Mirador Crescent. See *Collected Letters*, 11/7/1947. Margaret Taylor also sent him the good review

in the *Spectator* of June 20th. The *New Statesman* of July 5th. referred to the "poet's astonishing eloquence... this is the best way to write for the medium."
200. Davies and Maud, 1995, p.xviii. The thirty nine pages sent to Cleverdon correspond to the first forty two pages of the 1954 edition, to the end of Captain Cat's lines "...oh the cost of soapflakes!" Dylan's undated letter to Cleverdon from the Savage Club enclosing the handwritten script must have been sent in October because a note in the BBC Archives indicates that Cleverdon returned the typed script on November 3rd 1950.
201. The article was in *Planet*, February/March 1995, and the poem, 'Dylan Thomas in Tenby', can be found in *Raymond Garlick Collected Poems*. Dylan had previously read at the Tenby and District Arts Club in November 1949; an account is given in the *Tenby Observer and County News*, 24/11/1949. Dylan read Pound, Auden, Yeats, Alun Lewis and W.H. Davies but his introduction was "itself a poem... a brilliant profusion of character drawing, colour and wit, describing or suggesting all the motives and reactions which impelled him to leave England and the many vivid recollections of childhood and youth which drew him back to his native land." Caitlin and the children, and sometimes Dylan, came to Tenby in the late 1940s and early 1950s, and stayed in Little Rock House. This was owned by Geraldine Lawrence, a wealthy and stylish amateur artist, who encouraged writers and artists to stay. These included Laurie Lee (see his 1951 poem 'Pembroke Evening') and Nicolette Devas (Caitlin's sister) and her husband Anthony Devas, the painter. (Information from John Beynon, Tenby Museum and Art Gallery).
202. 9/10/1953, page 2.
203. This film can be viewed by appointment at the Sound and Moving Image Collection, National Library of Wales, Aberystwyth and the British Film Archive, London. There is a helpful discussion of Dylan's films about Wales in Goodlad (1990) and Ackerman (1995).
204. Colin Edwards tapes, interviews with the Fullyloves.
205. 23/11/1933.
206. Letter to the author, 21/11/1997.
207. Including Griff Jenkins Junior. Letter to the author, 28/11/1998.
208. 'Over Sir John's hill', 'Poem on his Birthday', 'Do not go gentle into that good night', 'Lament', 'In the White Giant's Thigh', 'In Country Heaven', 'Elegy' and 'Prologue'.
209. Curlew, on page 44. A sanderling is also mentioned but this bird is found in great numbers around Newquay's beaches.
210. August 8th. 1902. Quoted in Tinkler (1983).
211. *Collected Letters*, ?/10/1944.
212. Conversation with the author, 12/7/1999. Burton has told of drinking with Dylan in 1944 (Ferris, 1977 p130n). Burton acted with Dylan in 1946 in a radio version of David Jones' *In Parenthesis*, and made his film debut in the *Last Days of Dolwyn* in 1948.

213. *Collected Letters*, 15/11/1944.
214. Letter from Griff Jenkins Junior; also Ieuan Williams.
215. I wonder if Dylan meant "liquorice bootlaces" for this was the name given at that time to the long strings of liquorice on sale in sweet shops.
216. Letters from Wynford Harries and Griff Jenkins Junior.
217. *Collected Letters*, 29/8/1946.
218. *Sunday Telegraph*, 17/6/1990.
219. Conversation, Dr Dulyn Thomas, who bought Plas y Wern from Graham in 1958.
220. Dr Dulyn Thomas.
221. Jacqui Lyne Papers.
222. *ibid.*
223. *Welsh Gazette*, 30/11/1944 and *Cambrian News*, 12/1/1945.
224. Audrey Richards remembers that the bus was always willing to pick up Dylan. This would have been around five o'clock in the evening.

Acknowledgements

My greatest thanks to Stevie Krayer for her love, encouragement, and insight. Her poem 'No Ghosts at Gelli' was specially written for this book; there are other poems about the Aeron Valley and Cardigan Bay in her first collection, *Voices from a Burning Boat*.

The production of a book is a team effort: I am grateful to Stevie Krayer for help with proof-reading, to Mick Felton, Simon Hicks and Lisa Jones at Seren, and to Maureen Webley for the index.

My gratitude to those I interviewed about Dylan Thomas' time in Talsarn: Amanda Williams, Jenkin Emrys Davies, Dai Isaac Morgan, Bob Gwastod, and Delme and Maggie Vaughan. I am particularly grateful to Amanda Williams for her continuing patience with my questions about Plas Gelli.

Gwilym Jones talked to me about Geoffrey Faber and T.S. Eliot. Gwilym died in October 1998. His voice and humour live on, not only in the recordings about Faber and Eliot, but also in his tapes about the Ty Glyn walled garden in Ciliau Aeron. They consist of Gwilym's descriptions of the garden, in which he worked for more than twenty years. The tapes, and Gwilym's drawings, are being used to restore the garden, with the help of a grant from the National Lottery Charities Board.

Vera and William Killick's daughters, Rachel Willans and Charlotte Bacon, and Evelyn and Jeff Milton's daughter, Jane Gibson, were marvellously open and sharing with their memories of their parents' friendship with Dylan and Caitlin. I am grateful for the information they provided, as well as their support and trust.

Jacqui Lyne provided unfettered access to Thomas Herbert's papers, helped in understanding Dylan's friendship with Herbert, and was always willing to explore new leads on Dylan's friendship with both Herbert and Alastair Graham.

Griff Jenkins was a patient, hardworking and reliable source of information on Newquay, and always enthusiastic. I am very grateful for all the help he has given. This book would have been much less useful without his contribution.

Ann Brodie provided a good deal of information on Jack Patrick Evans of the Black Lion, as well as a history of the Newquay Patricks.

I am especially grateful to Duncan Stuart CMG, the SOE Adviser, for the care and patience with which he responded to my requests for information about William Killick's war record. Dr T. E. Faber generously shared with me his memories of Tyglyn Aeron in the 1930s, as well as details from the

Visitors' Book and his father's personal diary. Paul Ferris was equally gener-
ous in allowing me to have some unpublished material about the Killicks from
his notebooks, and with his general advice and support. Ferris' biography of
Dylan and the *Collected Letters* were constant points of reference. Professor
Walford Davies, too, was always helpful with his advice and comments.
Likewise, Jeff Towns never failed to share information or suggest new leads.

Others gave freely of their time to talk, or write about, about Newquay,
Aberaeron and Llanon, including Eleanor Lister, Ieuan Williams, Sue
Passmore, Megan Uncles, Margaret Evans, Phyllis Cosmo-Jones, Audrey
Richards, Jill and George Holeyman, Beryl Rees, George Legg, Wynford
Harries, Dr. Roger Seal, Michael Williams, Dr. Dulyn Thomas, Douglas
Ward, Diane and Brian Nicholls, Tom and Cathy Hunter of the Black Lion,
John Evans of the Harbourmaster's Hotel, Aberaeron (formerly of the
Seahorse, Newquay), Margaret Jones, Wendy Flenard, Gwyneth Jones,
Cadwell Davies, Gina Potter, Catherine and Micky Davies, David Birch,
Rowland James, Hayden Evans, John Lewis y Glo, Dai Edwards, Ron
Matthews, Rhiannon Davies, Chris Sewell, Huw and Dilys Lewis, Hywel
Raw-Rees, Eunice Thomas and Peter Chetcuti. Some informants wished to
remain anonymous.

Information about Plas Llanina was provided by Rosemary Seymour,
Gaenor Amory, Tatiana Mallinson, Betty Davis, James Maurice, and V.B.
Keen, Property Manager at Chirk Castle. Help with the story of Ffôs Helyg
farm came from Jane Gibson, Nen Jones, Gwyneth Thomas and Howard
Evans.

My thanks, too, to the following for help on a range of topics: Lowri
Hughes, Charles Burroughs, Joe Mendoza, Paul Henderson, Paul Curno,
Richard Mills, Peter Duff, Gethin Evans, Robin Ramsay, Joan Hardy,
Gwerfyl Hughes-Jones, Gus and Rene Krayer, Dillwyn Miles, Robin
Sheldon, Alun Evans, Bill Davies, Frances Stonor Saunders, Hugh Wilford,
Mostafa Elm, Evan Yardley, John Harris, Jenny Rees, Aeron Thomas, Gwen
Watkins, Raymond Garlick, George Tremlett, Andrew Sinclair, Dr. James
Davies, Richard Clogg, John le Carré, Rupert Allason, Euros Lewis and
Joyce Jenkins at Theatr Felinfach, Alwenna Williams, John and Jean Jones,
Wendy Symonds Jones, Rosemary Thorpe, Dr Helen Herbert, Dr. Hugh
Herbert, Kevin Williams, Lyn Ebenezer, Mary Edwards, Norma
MacManaway and Clem Thomas, famous for being the only Laugharne
man of his generation who didn't know Dylan Thomas.

I am indebted to Donald Evans and Eluned Phillips for information on
Dewi Emrys of Talgarreg. The Bardic chair that Emrys won in Bridgend in
1948 had been presented to the Eisteddfod by my great-great uncle, Thomas
Edwards of Llanedi and Vancouver, who had emigrated to Canada in the
1890s.

I have benefited from the help of the National Library of Wales – thanks

Acknowledgements

in particular to the marvellous staff on the desks of the Reading Room, the Map Room and in Manuscripts, and to Huw Owen, Iestyn Hughes, Paul Johnson and Leith Haarhoff. I am grateful to the National Library of Wales, and to Mary Edwards, for permission to quote from the Colin Edwards tapes.

I was greatly helped by the Aberaeron and Aberystwyth branches of Ceredigion Libraries; Michael Freeman at Ceredigion Museum; John Beynon of the Tenby Museum and Art Gallery; volunteer staff at Newquay Museum; Helen Palmer at the Ceredigion Archives Office; David Webb, Senior Librarian at News International Newspapers; and Peter Bursey, Librarian at the Foreign and Commonwealth Office, London.

Michael Gasson, Group Archivist, BP Amoco plc, did much to help me access material in the BP archives, which are held in the University of Warwick, Coventry. I am very grateful for his unflagging interest and advice. Thanks, too, to Gôsta Johansson, BP Amoco Video Library; Leonore Morphet of Greenpark Productions; and Simon Brown of the British Film Institute.

I received help from staff at the BBC Archives in Caversham, the British Council and the Public Records Office at Kew. Thanks also to my son, Daniel Thomas, who carried out the research at Kew into the archives of the British Council and matters relating to the Foreign Office and the Anglo-Iranian Oil Company.

My gratitude, too, to Tara Wenger at the Harry Ransom Humanities Research Center, The University of Texas at Austin; Robert Bertholf and Michael Basinski of the State University of New York at Buffalo; and Geoffrey D. Smith and Sara Brooks, Rare Books and Manuscripts, Ohio State University.

Material on Gelli and Llanina was provided by Richard Suggett of the Royal Commission on the Ancient and Historical Monuments of Wales and by Rosemary Jones of the National Monuments Record of Wales.

Others who have helped are Wyn Williams, Greg Evans and Nigel Thomas, of the Royal Mail sorting offices at Lampeter, Llandyssul and Aberystwyth; Bleddyn Jones, Mrs E.D. Roderick and Wyn Jones of Ceredigion Council; and the staff at the Boat House, Laugharne, the Dylan Thomas Theatre, and the Dylan Thomas Centre, particularly David Woolley, Jo Furber and Hugh 'Shorts'.

I am grateful to the Trustees of the estate of the late Dylan Thomas and to David Higham Associates for permission to use extracts from *Under Milk Wood*, *Collected Poems*, *The Poems* and *Collected Letters*, all published by J.M. Dent, as well as the map of Llareggub and the holograph from the Gelli notebook. I acknowledge Crown copyright of William Killick's account of his service in Greece.

Finally, my gratitude to the Arts Council of Wales for the award of a Writer's Bursary in 1998.

Photographs

My thanks to Bruce Cardwell for his excellent photographs that are used throughout this book. The photographs, all taken on one day in May 1999, are numbers 13, 15, 17, 18, 19, 20, 21, 24, 25, 27, 28, 29, 30, 50, 53, 55, 56, 70, 72, 77.

Contemporary photographs came from the Dr. T E. Faber, Betty Davis, Jacqui Lyne, Nen Jones, Ann Brodie, Gina Potter, Beryl Rees, Margaret Evans, Dr Roger Seal, Karen James, Rachel Willans, Charlotte Bacon, Jane Gibson, Griff Jenkins, Megan Uncles, Peter and Judy Hegarty of the Seahorse Inn, Newquay, and Sara and Langley Forrest of the Sailors Safety, Pwllgwaelod. Thanks, too, to Simon Raw-Rees, Cherry Davidson, Jo and Peter Smith, May and Daniel Davies, Stan and Eleri Thomas and Tim Quirk and Adriaan Stoop of the Tyglyn Aeron Hotel, Ciliau Aeron.

The National Library of Wales gave permission for the use of photographs from its Newquay collections, and from that of Colin Edwards. Thanks to the National Library and Ron Davies for permission to use his photograph of the milking wood. Postcards came from the Ceredigion Museum.

The front cover photograph, taken from the BP Amoco Archive, is reproduced with the kind permission of BP Amoco plc. The Archive also provided the photograph of the 1950 Eisteddfod Chair being made in Abadan. Thanks, too, to Ben Shephard for allowing reproduction of Rupert Shephard's photograph of Booda carrying Dylan across the estuary at Laugharne.

The photograph of Lord and Lady Howard de Walden was first published in *Pages from My Life* by Margherita Howard de Walden (Sidgwick & Jackson, 1965).

Illustrations

I am grateful to Jacky Piqué for her drawing of Majoda and for the sketch map of the Aeron Valley. BP Amoco plc gave permission to use the BP advertisement that appeared in the 1950 programme of the National Eisteddfod of Wales, to whom thanks are also given. I am grateful to *Y Cymro* for permission to reproduce part of a page containing a portrait of Dylan drawn by Myra Evans, whose estate we were unable to find. Thanks to Professor Christopher Frayling of the Royal College of Art for permission to reproduce Roy Morgan's painting of Llareggub. We acknowledge Roy Morgan's copyright but we were unable to trace him.

Index

Hancock, Kenneth 36
Hardy, Joan 33
Harries, Mr and Mrs John 150, 151
Harries, Ronald, hanging for murder 151
Harrison, Rex 91
Haukova, Jirina 195
Hawkins, Desmond 41
Hell Fire Jones 220, 228
Hendre Farm, St Dogmaels 42
Herbert, Mr 229
Herbert, Thomas 23, 53, 62, 76-7, 80, 84-5, 87, 103-4, 108-9, 111, 191-2, 224-6
    as inspiration for 'Mister Waldo' 220
Higham, David 185, 193
Hill, George 177
Hoare, Sir Samuel 176, 177
Hodgkin, Edward 171
Holbrooke 46
Hole, Mrs 33
Howard, Brian 176, 178
Hughes the Bread, Llanon 110
Hughes, Richard 46
'hyleg', Thomas' use 41

intelligence services 87
    Alastair Graham's connections 181-3
    Dylan Thomas' connections 159, 175-9, 184-88
    eccentric agents 176
    Iran agents and operations 162, 171, 186-7
    MI6 173-4, 175, 183-6
    Special Operations Executive and Killick trial 123-4
Iran
    anti-British demonstrations 166
    Mossadeq government overthrow 17, 143, 144, 159, 174, 184, 186
    Nicolson and British policy 186-7
    oil company film 163, 165-8
    radio documentary 170-2

St David's Society 157
    Thomas' visit 17, 25, 154-9, 163, 166, 187-8
Italy holiday 17, 156, 161, 179, 194
'In Country Sleep' poem 65-6, 194

Jac Pentrefelin 77
Jack the Post, Newquay 92, 217-18
James, Bonnie 42
James, Dr 229
James, Evan Joshua 92, 214
James, Gwen 30
James, Gwyn 91
Janes, Fred 42
Jenkins, Capper 87
Jenkins, Griff Junior 98, 123, 181-2
Jenkins, Griff Senior 84, 89, 90, 95-6, 120, 122, 123, 131
Jenkins, Rev W.O. 218, 229
Jepson, Selwyn 176
John, Augustus 15, 42, 47, 80, 84, 86, 89, 92, 96, 102, 106, 224
Johns, Mr. 221, 229
Johnson, Pamela Hansford 27, 79, 202, 212
Jones, Daniel 102, 153, 177
Jones, Dafydd (Isfoel) 109
Jones, Glyn 43
Jones, Gwilym 23
    reminiscences 244-5
Jones, Gwyn 108, 111, 135
Jones, Ira (Taffy) 92, 101, 227
Jones, John Eric 143
Jones, John Oswald 83, 84
Jones, Margaret 111
Jones, Miss 228
Jones, Olive 38, 96, 98, 100-1, 108, 191, 227
Jones, Ron 147, 150
Jones, Thomas (Butcher OK) see Thomas OK
Jones, William 27
Joshua, Evan *see* James, Evan Joshua